MANAGED

VIP SERIES

KRISTEN CALLIHAN

MANAGED

It started off as a battle of wits. Me: the ordinary girl with a big mouth against Him: the sexy bastard with a big...*ego*.

I thought I'd hit the jackpot when I was upgraded to first class on my flight to London.

That is until HE sat next to me. Gabriel Scott: handsome as sin, cold as ice. Nothing and no one gets to him. Ever. He's a legend in his own right, the manager of the biggest rock band in the world, and an arrogant ass who looks down his nose at me.

I thought I'd give him hell for one, long flight. I didn't expect to like him. I didn't expect to want him. But the biggest surprise? He wants me too. Only in a way I didn't see coming.

If I accept his proposal, I leave myself open to falling for the one man I can't manage. But I'm tempted to say yes. Because the real man beneath those perfect suits and that cool façade just might be the best thing that's ever happened to me. And I just might be the only one who can melt the ice around his heart.

Let the battle begin...

ABOUT THE AUTHOR

Kristen Callihan is an author because there is nothing else she'd rather be. She is a RITA award winner, and winner of two RT Reviewer's Choice awards. Her novels have garnered starred reviews from Publisher's Weekly and the Library Journal, as well as making the USA Today bestseller list. Her debut book FIRELIGHT received RT Magazine's Seal of Excellence, was named a best book of the year by Library Journal, best book of Spring 2012 by Publisher's Weekly, and was named the best romance book of 2012 by ALA RUSA.

You can sign up for Kristen's new release at

 @Kris10Callihan

 KristenCallihan

www.kristencallihan.com

ALSO BY
KRISTEN CALLIHAN

AUTHOR NOTE

A long time ago, I fell in love with a young man, and his favorite band in the whole world was Soda Stereo, a Spanish rock band from Argentina. Many of you probably have never heard of them, but they used to sell out 100,000 plus stadiums, sold over seventeen million albums, and even had an MTV Unplugged session—which I highly recommend looking up.

I've only seen my—now husband—cry on a few occasions. The day he learned Gustavo Cerati, Soda Stereo's lead singer, had died was one of them. That is the power that music can wield—that musicians can feel like friends, someone who expresses your pain, joy, love, or hate with their sound. I always think about this when I write these novels. And how wonderful it would be to play even some small part in bringing music to the world.

Love is what you do in life—

GABRIEL SCOTT

*Love is **who** you do in life—*

SOPHIE DARLING

SOPHIE
1

YOU KNOW those people who Lady Luck always seems to be kissing on the cheek? The one who gets a promotion just for showing up to work? Who wins that awesome raffle prize? The person who finds a hundred-dollar bill on the ground? Yeah, that's not me. And it's probably not most of us. Lady Luck is a selective bitch.

But today? Lady Luck has finally turned her gaze upon me. And I want to bow down in gratitude. Because today, I've been upgraded to first class for my flight to London. Maybe it's due to overbooking, and who knows why they picked me, but they did. First fucking class, baby. I'm so giddy, I practically dance to my seat.

And, oh, what a beautiful seat it is, all plush cream leather and burled wood paneling—though I'm guessing it's fake wood for safety reasons. Not that it matters. It's a little self-contained pod, complete with a cubby for my bag and shoes, a bar, an actual reading lamp, and a widescreen TV.

I sink into the seat with a sigh. It's a window seat, sectioned off from my neighbor by a frosted glass panel I can lower with the touch of a button. Or the two seats can become one cozy cabin by closing the glossy panel that sections off the aisle. It reminds me of an old-fashioned luxury train compartment.

I'm one of the first people on board, so I give in to temptation and rifle through all the goodies they've left me: mints, fuzzy socks, sleep mask, and—*ooh*—a little bag of skin care products. Next I play around with my seat, raising and lowering my privacy screen—that is until it makes an ominous-sounding *click*. The screen freezes an inch above the divider and refuses to rise again.

Cringing, I snatch my hand away and busy myself with removing my shoes and flipping through the first class menu. It's long, and everything looks delicious. Oh man, how am I supposed to go back to the cattle-roundup, meat-or-chicken-in-a-tin hell that is economy class after this?

I'm debating whether to get a preflight champagne cocktail or glass of white wine when I hear the man's voice. It's deep, crisply British, and very annoyed.

"What is that woman doing in my seat?"

My neck tenses, but I don't look up. I'm assuming he means me. His voice is coming from somewhere over my head, and there are only male passengers in here aside from me.

And he is wrong, wrong, wrong. I'm in *my* seat. I checked twice, pinched myself, checked again, and then finally sat down. I know I'm where I'm supposed to be—just not how I got away with it. Hey, I was as surprised as anyone when I went to the ticket counter, only to be informed I was in first class. No way am I going back to coach now.

My fingers grip the menu as I make a pretense of flipping through it. I'm really eavesdropping at this point. The flight attendant's response is too low to hear, but his isn't.

"I expressly purchased two seats on this flight. Two. For the simple purpose that I would not be seated next to anyone else."

Well, that's...decadent? Whacked? I struggle not to make a face. Who does that? Is it really so awful to sit next to someone? Has this guy *seen* economy? We can count each other's nose hairs back there. Here, my chair is so wide, I'm a good foot away from his stupid seat.

"I'm so sorry, sir," the flight attendant answers in a near purr, which is weird. She should be annoyed. Maybe it's all part of the kiss-the-first-class-passengers'-asses-because-they-paid-a-shit-ton-to-be-here program. "The flight is overbooked, and all seats are spoken for."

"Which is why I purchased two seats," he snaps.

She murmurs something soothing again. I can't hear because two men walking past me to get to their seats are talking about stock options. They pass, and I hear Mr. Snooty again.

"This is unacceptable."

A movement to my right, and I nearly jump. I see the red suit coat of the flight attendant as she bends close, her arm at the man's screen button. Heat invades my cheeks, even as she starts to explain, "There's a screen for privacy..."

She stops because the screen isn't rising.

I burrow my nose in the menu.

"It doesn't bloody work?" This from Snooty.

The rest goes just about as well as you'd expect. He rants, she placates, I hide between page one and two of the menu.

"Perhaps I can persuade someone to exchange seats?" the helpful flight attendant offers.

Yes, please. Fob him off on someone else.

"What difference does it make?" Snooty snaps. "The point was to have an empty seat next to mine."

I'd love to suggest he wait for the next flight and save us all a headache, but that's not in the cards. The standoff ends with the jerk plopping into his seat with an exasperated huff. He must be big, because I feel the whoosh of air as he does it.

The heat of his glare is tangible just before he turns away.

Fucker.

Slapping my menu down, I decide, *Fuck it; I'm having some fun with this.* What can they do? They're loading the plane; my seat is secure.

I find a stick of gum in my purse and pop it in my mouth. A few chews and I have some superior gum-smacking going on. Only then do I turn his way.

And freeze mid-chew, momentarily stunned by the sight sitting next to me. Because, good God, no one has the right to be this hot and this much of a jerk. This guy is one-hundred-percent the most gorgeous man I've ever seen. And it's strange because his features aren't perfect or gentle. No, they're bold and strong—a jaw sharp enough to cut steel, firm chin, high cheekbones, and a bold nose that's almost too big but fits his face perfectly.

I'd expected a whey-faced, graying aristocrat, but he's tanned, his coal back hair falling over his brow. Sculpted, pouty lips are compressed in irritation as he scowls down at the magazine in his hand.

But he just as clearly feels my stare—the fact that I'm gaping like a speared fish probably doesn't help—and he turns to glare. I'm hit with the full force of all that masculine beauty.

His eyes are aqua blue. His thick, dark brows draw together, a storm brewing on his face. He's about to blast me. The thought hits along with another: I'd better make this good.

"Jesus," I blurt out, lifting my hand as if to shield my eyes. "It's like looking into the sun."

"What?" he snaps, those laser-bright eyes narrowing.

Oh, this will be fun.

"Just stop, will you?" I squint at him. "You're too hot. It's too much to take." This is true, though I'd never have the guts to say so in normal circumstances.

"Are you quite well?" he intones, as if he thinks the opposite.

"No, you've nearly rendered me blind." I flap a hand. "Do you have an off switch? Maybe put it on low?"

His nostrils flare, his skin going a shade darker. "Lovely. I'm stuck next to a mad woman."

"Don't tell me you're unaware of the dazzling effect you have on the world." I give him a look of wide-eyed wonder. At least I hope that's what I'm doing.

He flinches when I grasp the divider between us and lean in a bit. Hell, he smells good—like expensive cologne and fine wool. "You probably have women dropping at your feet like flies."

"At least dropped flies are silent," he mutters, furiously flipping through his magazine. "Madam, do me the favor of refraining from speaking to me for the remainder of the flight."

"Are you a duke? You talk like a duke."

His head jerks as if he wants to look my way, but he manages to keep his gaze forward, his lips compressed so tightly they're turning white at the edges. A travesty.

"Oh, or maybe a prince. I know!" I snap my fingers. "Prince Charming!"

A blast of air escapes him, as if he's caught between a laugh and outrage but really wants to go with outrage. Then he stills. And I feel a moment's trepidation, because he's obviously realized I'm making fun of him. I hadn't noticed how well-built this guy is until now.

He's probably over six feet, his legs long and strong, encased in charcoal slacks.

Jesus, he's wearing a sweater vest: dove gray and hugging his trim torso. He should look like an utter dork in it, but no... It only highlights the strength in his arms, those muscles stretching the limits of his white button-down shirt. Unfair.

His shoulders are so broad they make the massive first class seats look small. But he's long and lean. I'm guessing the muscle definition under those fine and proper clothes is drool-worthy too, damn it all.

I take it all in, including the way his big hands clench. Not that I think he'll use his strength against me. His behavior screams pompous prick, but he doesn't seem like a bully. He never truly raised his voice with the flight attendant.

Even so, my heart beats harder as he slowly turns to face me. An evil smile twists his lush mouth.

Don't look at it. He'll suck you into a vortex of hot, and there will be no return.

"You found me out," he confides in a low voice that's warm butter over toast. "Prince Charming, at your service. Do forgive me for being short with you, madam, but I am on a mission of the utmost import." He leans closer, his gaze darting around before returning to me. "I'm looking for my bride, you see. Alas, you are not wearing a glass slipper, so you cannot be her."

We both glance at my bare feet and the red Chucks lying on the floor. He shakes his head. "You'll understand that I need to keep my focus on the search."

He flashes a wide—albeit fake—smile, revealing a dimple on one cheek, and I'm breathless. Double damn it.

"Wow." I give a dreamy sigh. "It's even worse when you smile. You really should come with a warning, sunshine."

His smile drops like a hot potato, and he opens his mouth to retort, but the flight attendant is suddenly by his side.

"Mr. Scott, would you like a preflight beverage? Champagne? Pellegrino, perhaps?"

I'm half surprised she didn't offer herself. But the implication is there in the way she leans over him, her hand resting on the seat near his shoulder, her back arched enough to thrust out her breasts. I can't blame the woman. Dude is potent.

He barely glances her way. "No, thank you."

"Are you sure? Maybe a coffee? Tea?"

One brow rises in that haughty way only a Brit can truly pull off. "Nothing for me."

"Champagne sounds great," I say.

But the flight attendant never takes her eyes from her prey. "I really do apologize for the mix-up, Mr. Scott. I've alerted my superiors, and they shall do everything in their power to accommodate you."

"Moot at this point, but thank you." He's already picking up his magazine, the cover showcasing a sleek sports car. Typical.

"Well, then, if there's anything you need..."

"I don't know about him," I cut in, "but I'd love a—hey! Hello?" I wave a hand as she saunters away, an extra sway to her hips. "Bueller?"

I can feel him smirking and give him a look. "This is your fault, you know."

"My fault?" His brows lift, but he doesn't look away from his magazine. "How on Earth did you come to that conclusion?"

"Your freaky good looks made her blind to all but you, sunshine."

His expression is blank, though his lips twitch. "If only I could strike women speechless."

I can't help it, I have to grin at that. "Oh, I bet you'd find that marvelous; all of us helpless women just smiling and nodding. Though I'm afraid it would never work on me."

"Of course not," he deadpans. "I'm stuck next to the one afflicted with an apparently incurable case of verbal diarrhea."

"Says the man who is socially constipated."

He stills again, his eyes widening. And then a strangled snort breaks free, escalating into a choked laugh. "Christ." He pinches the bridge of his nose as he struggles to contain himself. "I'm doomed."

I smile, wanting to laugh too, but holding it in. "There, there." I pat his forearm. "It will all be over in about seven hours."

He groans, his head lifting. The amusement in his eyes is genuine, and a lot more deadly because of it. "I won't survive it—"

The plane gives a little shudder as it begins to pull out from the gate. And Mr. Sunshine blanches, turning a lovely shade of green before fading into gray. A terrified flyer. But one who clearly would rather the plane actually crash than admit this.

Great. He'll probably be hyperventilating before we level out.

Maybe it's because my mom is terrified to fly as well, or maybe because I'd like to think Mr. Sunshine's horrible behavior is fear-based and not because he's a massive dickweasel, but I decide to help him. And, of course, have a little more fun while I'm doing it.

GABRIEL

I'M IN HELL. It's a familiar place: a long, narrow tube with wobbly wings. A death trap with five hundred seats, stale air, and droning engines. I've been here frequently. Only this time, the Devil herself is my seat partner.

I've been in the entertainment industry long enough to know that the Devil always appears in an attractive package. Better to lure in unsuspecting sods. This particular devil looks as though she's stepped out of the 1950s—platinum blond hair swirling around her cherubic face; big, pansy brown eyes; red, red lips; and an hourglass figure I'm trying my best to ignore.

It isn't easy ignoring those tits. Every time she talks, those plush mounds seem to bounce as if they have a mind of their own. Given that this strange, gobby girl never shuts up, I'm in danger of being mesmerized by a fantastic rack of what are surely double-Ds.

God, and she keeps on chattering. Like some nightmare Jabberwocky intent on driving me insane.

"Look, you—" More bouncing tits, red mouth pursing... "I know your game, and it isn't going to work on me."

I pull my gaze up. "What?"

"Don't you *whhhat* me with that proper British accent and think I'll fall for it." A thin finger waggles in front of my nose. "I don't care how sexy your voice is, it won't work."

I will not smile at that. Not a chance. "I have no idea to what you're referring, but if I were you, I'd seek medical intervention as soon as we land."

"Pfft. You're pulling this terrified-to-fly act in the hopes that I'll take pity on you."

An ugly feeling crawls up my gut, and I fist my hands so I won't shout—not that I can get a word in edgewise. She's still at it, spewing nonsense.

"You think if you sit there, looking petrified and tense, I'll offer a blowjob to distract you from it all."

My humiliation comes to a screeching halt upon hearing the word *blowjob*. "What?"

"Well, it's not going to happen."

Ignore the cock. Ignore him. He's an idiot. Focus on the problem at hand. "You are deranged. Completely deranged."

"And you are a handsome but crafty bastard. Unfortunately for you, good looks aren't enough. I won't do it."

I lean in close as I dare. "Look, even if I wanted your mouth anywhere near me, why on Earth would I ask for a blowjob here?" I wave my hand toward the aisle. "When the entire cabin can see. Who does that?"

"Not me," she shoots back with a disgusted look. "But nice slip of the tongue. You've obviously been thinking logistics."

Must not throttle headcase. Gritting my teeth hard enough to hurt, I light into her. "Madam, if this death trap of a conveyance were hurtling toward the Earth in a fiery ball of doom, and your mouth on my cock was the last bit of sex I'd ever have the chance to receive, I'd take off my seatbelt and throw myself toward death."

She blinks, those pansy eyes large and owlish and not a bit put out. "That's a lot of words, sunshine. But I think you're lying. You want it bad."

My mouth works like a fish, gaping and struggling for air. I cannot think of a single thing to utter, which is a rarity. I might not converse with most people, but I'm fully capable of a set down when the action calls.

Over our heads, a little chime sounds. I glance at it and notice that the fasten seatbelt sign has been turned off. We're level and steady now.

By the time I turn my attention back to the she-devil, she has her nose in a magazine, happily flipping through the pages, a tiny, smug smile twitching at the corners of her lips.

It hits me like a fist to the gut: she has been, yet again, fucking with me. She distracted me from takeoff. So effectively, I hadn't even felt the plane lift. Now I'm stuck between grudging admiration, uncomfortable gratitude, and a burning need for revenge.

Revenge is the louder voice in my head, and I bite the inside of my cheek to keep from grinning. Leaning forward, I crowd her space, ignoring the scent of lemon tart that floats around her.

She tenses right up, her head jerking back, her body bolting straight. I love it.

"All right," I murmur low in her ear, as she shivers and wiggles to get away. "You caught me. I do want oral satisfaction. Badly. Be a dear and take the edge off for me?"

She gasps, velvety skin going pale. "Are you kidding me?"

"We already went over this." I reach beneath my seatbelt to undo my actual belt. "I'm in need, and it has to be you."

"Whoa, wait a minute, buddy." Her hand presses against my chest and quickly flinches back, as if the contact burns.

Oddly, it was rather warm, and I still feel the imprint of her hand through the layers of my clothes. I ignore that too and give her an exaggerated brow wiggle. "Don't worry. I've a plan. Just pretend you have a headache and need to rest your head in my lap. I'll put a blanket over you to block the light. They won't even question your moans that way."

I get my belt undone, as if I'm going to whip out my cock. "Better yet, I'll close our seating compartment doors, and we'll have complete privacy. You can really work me over then."

A strangled sound leaves her. "You...nasty...I don't believe this..."

"Oh, come on, love. Give us a suck, eh? Just a little teasing lick of the tip?"

Shite. I shouldn't have said that. My cock perks up, liking that idea immensely. Her parted lips are red and soft and full... *Get it together, you git.*

I grin with all teeth, leaning close, even as she flushes bright red. "A little tug and bob. I'm so tense, it'll only take five or ten minutes max."

A choking sound dies in her throat, and I make a pained whimper. "Put me out of my misery, tarty girl."

That does it. Her brows lift high. "Tart? Tart?!?" She bunts her nose against mine, her eyes dark slits of fury. "Suck you off? You pompous, arrogant—"

"Those words basically mean the same thing, sweets."

"Dick-faced..." She trails off, rearing back a little, her gaze darting over my face. And then she smiles. It's full-out and pleased, and I find myself a little light-headed with the speed at which she can change emotions. "Oh, well played, sunshine," she drawls, grinning. "Well played. Caught on to my act, did you?"

I can't meet her eyes or she'll be on to me. This woman might be the most obnoxious person I've met on a plane, but she's clearly intelligent. "Was that an act?"

A scoff pushes through her lips. "You should buy me a drink now as thanks."

"The drinks are free in first class, chatty girl."

"It's the principle."

I'd get her an entire bottle of the champagne she wants if it would get her to stop talking, but alcohol usually loosens the tongue. I shudder at the thought of her talking even more.

At that moment, the flight attendant who's been eyeing me as though I'm steak sways over, a glass of champagne balanced on a silver tray. She smiles wide for me. "Mr. Scott. Your champagne."

"Oh, for fuck's sake," my chatty neighbor mutters under her breath.

Keeping a bland expression, whatever the circumstance, is rote for me at this point in my life. But it's an odd struggle right now. Something about my tormentor brings out the five year old in me, and I want to tug her hair in the manner of a schoolyard brat. But I don't. I accept the drink the flight attendant sets down before me.

"Thank you," I tell her as I pass the glass on to Chatty Girl. "However, my seatmate requested this, not me."

The flight attendant blanches. "Oh. I'm...I'm so sorry," she says to the woman next to me—and I really ought to get her name, or perhaps not. Further conversation isn't a good idea; she might be entertaining, but she's still unhinged. I don't like unpredictable elements.

"I didn't realize. I thought..." The attendant trails off at an obvious loss.

"It's all right." My seatmate leans in, crowding my space as she gives the flight attendant an understanding smile, and I'm assaulted with another whiff of sweet lemons and warm woman. "Sunshine here got me so flustered, I nearly pulled out my credit card and offered to pay him for sex."

I choke on my own spit. "Bloody hell."

The flight attendant flushes magenta. "Yes. Er. Can I get you anything else?"

A parachute.

"Nothing more for me," the crazy bird to my left says, happily taking a sip of champagne.

"A club soda on ice," I say. At this point, I want to ask for a whole bottle of gin. But alcohol makes my jitters worse on a plane. *Just breathe, relax, get through this flight from hell.*

I get a sympathetic look from the flight attendant. At my side comes another happy hum. I'm waiting for the next volley of outrageousness but am oddly disappointed to discover my neighbor bringing out her phone and headphones. So she plans to plug in and tune out. Brilliant. Just what I needed. I'm thankful for it.

I pick up my magazine, stare at a picture of a red Lambo Centario. I own the same model in graphite. I flip the page. Hard.

More girlish humming ensues, just loud enough to sound over the drone of the engines. Lovely, a singalong. The bloody woman has infected me with a bizarre case of immaturity, because I'm tempted to needle her, point out that she's off key, if only to hear how she'll respond. A weird sort of anticipation fills me at the idea. Except I recognize the song.

Disappointment, and the way it washes over me, is something of a shock. I hadn't expected it. Not this strong. Because she's listening to Kill John, and obviously loving it. I love Kill John too. They're the biggest band in the world right now, and they're part of me, tied up in the very fiber of my being by way of blood, sweat, and tears.

Because I manage the band. Killian, Jax, Whip, and Rye are my boys. I will do anything for them. But one thing I will never do is interact with their fans. Ever.

I learned that lesson early on. Fans, no matter who they are, lose their shit when they know I manage Kill John. I refuse to be their gateway.

Another off-key lyric comes from Chatty Girl's lips. She's bobbing her head, her eyes closed, a look of bliss on her face. I turn away. No, not disappointed. Relieved.

I keep telling myself this as my soda arrives and I drink it down with more enthusiasm than normal. I. Am. Relieved.

SOPHIE
2

I HAVE SAFELY WITHDRAWN from my sexy seat partner. I had to do it. I'd been having too much fun pestering him, and I know the signs. I'd soon start crushing on the prickly man; he's too hot and too stern to resist. You'd think stern wouldn't be a turn-on, but somehow the idea of him setting me over his knee...

Yeah. So I did the smart thing and pulled on my headphones. Now I'm listening to music while flipping through *Vogue.*

He's done the same, reading his car mag before tossing it aside in favor of his laptop. It's torture not peeking at his screen. What does a guy like this do for a living? Maybe he really is a duke; I swear he fits the bill. Or maybe a billionaire? But I suppose both those types of men would have their own plane.

I lose track of time imagining Sunshine lording over some English manor, or flying clumsy virgins in his personal helicopter, when a cart rolls over to provide us with cocktails —apparently drunk is the preferred way for rich people to fly —and hors d'oeuvres. And though Mr. Happy apparently doesn't want any of it, I whip off my headphones, ready to dig in.

"Oh, yes please," I say.

Beside me, Sunshine snorts under his breath.

I ignore him. I love food. Love. It. And this stuff actually looks good. The flight attendant hands me a silver tray topped with a variety of cheeses, mixed nuts, tiny little melon balls with prosciutto, and roasted tomato compote on toasts. Awesome.

"You're missing out," I tell him when we're alone again. "This stuff is pretty good." I pop a melon ball in my mouth and hold back a moan. I officially hate first class. It has ruined me for all future flying. Poor suckers in the back.

"You'll be sorry later," he tells me, not looking up from his work, "when your stomach is full and this tin tube starts jumping about from the inevitable turbulence." He barely suppresses a shudder.

"And it's always during dinner." I take a bite of creamy white cheese. "You ever notice that?"

"Not particularly."

"Maybe they time turbulence for coach service." I frown. "Wouldn't be surprised."

He makes a noncommittal sound.

A bowlful of laughs, this one.

"It wouldn't kill you to relax, you know."

With a sigh, he closes his laptop and tucks it away. "What makes you think I never relax?" Those killer blue eyes of his pin me with a look. *Jesus*, it really is hard staring directly at him. My breath swoops down into my belly, and my thighs clench. *Normal reaction to hotness. That is all.*

Still, it sucks that my voice sounds all sorts of breathy when I answer. "I'm guessing those pinched lines between your brows aren't from laughing."

Said lines deepen in a scowl.

I can't stop from smiling. "Don't worry, despite your crabby demeanor, you actually look kind of young."

He shakes his head once as if trying to clear it. "Was there a compliment somewhere in that spew?"

"Someone as hot as you doesn't need any more compliments. How old are you, anyway?" I'm pushing it, but it's so fun to tease him, I can't help myself.

"That's rather personal. You don't see me asking you how —"

"I'm twenty-five," I say happily.

His lips quirk, and I know he's trying to keep hold of his cool façade. But the capitulation in his eyes is warm. "I'm twenty-nine."

"Twenty-nine going on ninety."

"You're deliberately trying to provoke me, aren't you?"

"Maybe you answer my original question. Do you ever relax, sunshine?"

"What will it take to get you to refrain from calling me that?"

His voice is too delicious—husky yet crisp, deep yet easy. I want to find a phone book and ask him to recite it. I push away the thought. "You'll have to give me your name. And I notice you didn't answer the question."

His frown grows. It's kind of cute. Though he'd probably snarl if I told him as much. The frown gives way to obvious hesitation, as if he's at war with himself.

"Look..." I shrug, eating another melon ball. "If you don't want to tell me, that's cool. Lots of people are weirdly paranoid."

"I am not paranoid."

Sucker.

"Sure. I get it. I might be an international hacker of renowned skill, just waiting to tap into your private business. All I need is a name to get started."

"I was going with escapee of some sort," he says before drinking up the dregs of his glass and scowling down at it.

"Just call her and get your cocktail on," I suggest.

Instead, he reaches for one of the complimentary water bottles we have in our little personal bars. A decisive twist of the wrist, and he's guzzling down water like he's just crawled out of the desert. I absolutely do not watch. Much. That throat. How does a throat become that sexy? He must take pills or something.

I stuff a roasted tomato compote toast in my mouth and chew with vigor.

"Gabriel."

His sudden answer has me looking back at him. He's facing straight ahead as though he hasn't spoken, but at my stare, he turns. "My name. It's Gabriel Scott."

I've never seen someone so uncomfortable with giving his name in my life. Maybe he is a spy. I'm only half kidding.

"Gabriel," I repeat, not missing the way he sort of shudders when I do. I don't know if he's uncomfortable or something else, but I feel as though I've been let in on a dark secret.

The champagne must be getting to me. I push it aside and reach for my own water bottle.

"I'm Sophie," I tell him, unable to make full eye contact for some reason. "Sophie Darling."

He blinks, and that tight, strong body moves a fraction closer before halting as if he's become of aware of his action. "Darling?"

I've lost track of the men who've tried to make my name sound like a come on. He doesn't do that. In fact, his tone is downright skeptical, but somehow it sounds like an endearment just the same. No, not an endearment. It's not sweet, the way he says it. He makes it sound illicit, as if my own name is caressing my skin with heavy hands.

Shit on a toothpick. I cannot be crushing on this dude. He's a dick. A hot dick, but still. Even if I could overlook that, he'll be gone and out of my life as soon as we land. I imagine sprinting will be involved. Dignified sprinting, of course.

"That's me," I tell him with false levity. "Sophie Darling."

Another noise rumbles in his throat. This one sounds like, "God help me."

I could be interpreting that incorrectly, though.

"Well, Ms. Darling," he says, going back to the crisp, stern voice I imagine he uses to tear wayward underlings a new one, "to answer your previous question, you are correct; I do not, in general, relax."

"Wow, you went right ahead and admitted you're a stick in the mud."

"Stick in the mud makes absolutely no sense. Who comes up with these ridiculous idioms?" He steals a tomato toast from my plate. "And I think you can do better."

I watch as he pops the toast in his mouth and munches away. The corners of his eyes crinkle. It's so slight, I doubt many people would notice. It feels like a full-fledged, smug-ass grin right now.

"You want me to insult you?" I manage.

"At least be a little more creative when you do." He pulls his laptop back out, dismissing me. "Give me something I haven't already heard."

Something about this guy activates my lizard brain in the worst way, because I find myself leaning forward to murmur in his ear. "I'm thinking you're the poster boy for Rough Roger. And one day, that hand of yours isn't gonna cut it."

His head jerks up as if I've goosed him. I hear the small intake of breath, and refuse to be turned on. Even if his heady scent is wafting over me. The leather armrest creaks under my elbow as I retreat.

He gives me a sidelong glare. "Rough Roger?"

"You've got internet working. Look it up, sunshine."

It's my turn to smile smugly and bury my nose in my magazine.

The drone of the engines fills the silence between us, and I hear the distinct click of his keyboard, followed by a strangled sound in his throat.

My grin grows. I know he's read the definition of a guy who jerks off so much and so desperately, he's rubbed his cock raw. Unfortunately, that image is far too sexually disturbing for my comfort.

From beside me, his voice is low and tight and slightly husky. "Well played, Ms. Darling."

BEFORE BEDTIME, we're politely encouraged to visit the first class lounge—yes, they have a motherfucking lounge on the plane. I mean, I knew about plane bars...the way a person knows about unicorns and Smurfs. But to experience it? Holy hell.

I take the spiral stairs up to the top of the 747 to sit at a bar and have watered-down cocktails with my cabin mates. Even Sunshine comes along, though he stays at the fringe and orders a glass of ice water.

"They're prepping the cabin," an older man in a slightly rumpled suit tells me as we sip our drinks.

"For what?" I toss a sugared pecan in my mouth and take another sip of my Cosmopolitan. If you're going to sit around in a bar-lounge at thirty-five thousand feet, you might as well go full-on *Sex and the City*.

He leans closer, his gaze sliding just south of my neck for a brief second. "The beds."

"Oh, right." I perk up. "I'm going to enjoy that."

"The comfort and privacy can't be beat," he says with a nod before edging even closer. "You know, I have a single seat cabin. But it's big enough for two."

For a second I just stare back. "Are you actually propositioning me in an airplane bar?"

He shrugs. "Heard your seat mate raise a fuss. Sounds like

a real prick. Thought you'd prefer better company."

I'm about to apologize for jumping to conclusions when he raises a brow and leers. "But if you'd rather view it as a proposition, I'm not going to object."

"I prefer my original seat partner," I deadpan.

He snorts. "Shocker."

I'm about to ask him *what the hell*, when a muscled shoulder edges between us. I know that arm, that scent: expensive, haughty man. Gabriel stares down his nose at the guy. It's impressive, the amount of disdain and dismissal he packs into a look.

"Actually," he says, "I'm more of an asshole than a prick." He flashes a tight smile that's really a baring of teeth, but his bored tone never changes. "Which means I'm rather an expert in dealing with bothersome little shits."

I nearly choke on my drink.

Mr. Suit tries to hold Gabriel's stare but fails. He slinks off with a muttered, "Asshole."

"I thought we'd already established as much," Gabriel says to me.

"So proud of your asshole ways." I give him a nudge on the shoulder. "And yet here you are, saving me from lechers."

"Hardly," he mutters into his glass. "I was defending my own honor. And it was rather boring, at that. I thought he'd put up more of a fight."

"Why?" I'm compelled to ask, though really I'm just surprised he's talking to me when this is our one chance to escape to neutral corners.

He takes a sip of his water before answering. "He's the CEO of a Fortune 500 company and has a reputation for being a relentless badger." His lips curl in a sneer. "More like a weasel, if you ask me."

I stare at him. "How do you know this?"

He finally turns his gaze to me, and I'm hit anew with

those brilliant blues. "I just read an article about him in *Forbes*."

A small, helpless laugh leaves me. I'm so not in Kansas any more. "Well," I say, "maybe you'll find someone to properly cross dicks with later."

It's his turn to sputter on his drink, though he recovers nicely. With precise movements, he sets his glass down and crisply tugs each of his cuffs back into place. "I'm fairly certain I've all I can handle with you at the moment."

"Aw, a compliment."

He looks down at me and slowly blinks, the dark sweep of his lashes nearly touching his cheek. Then he shocks me into stillness when he leans in close enough that his lips brush the curve of my ear. "Yes, chatty girl, it was."

I'm still reeling from the low rumble of his voice—it tickles down my spine and flares along my thighs—when he moves away. "Do not drink too much or you'll have a headache," he advises before walking off, heading back downstairs.

I hate to admit, he takes all the excitement of being in the bar with him. Now it's just a novelty situation that's grown stale. I slide my half-finished drink away and hop off the barstool.

Downstairs, the seats in the little cabins have indeed been converted to beds. I hold in a squeal of joy. It's an actual bed, with full-sized pillows and a brilliant white duvet trimmed in scarlet. A single red rose has been placed on each pillow. I swear, I'm about to hop up and down, but I catch a glimpse of Mr. Happy, who is standing at the threshold of our seating cabin, hands on his trim hips, brows knitted so tightly they almost touch.

"What's wrong," I ask him. "No hospital corners?"

He gives me a sidelong glare before turning his attention back to the beds. "I asked for my seat not to be converted. And the flight attendant is obviously operating under an extreme misconception."

Glancing back, I finally notice what he's talking about. I'd been so happy about the existence of a bed, I hadn't realized that our two seats have been converted into one smooth double bed. There's even a tray with an ice bucket of champagne on it.

A laugh escapes me before I can hold it in. "Honeymoon special?"

"You find this amusing?" His nostrils flare in annoyance, though he's not looking at me, just mentally destroying the bed with his laser gaze.

"Honestly? Yeah, I do." I kick off my shoes and crawl over the bed. It's firm to the point of being stiff, and there's a small ridge down the middle. But I'm not about to complain. Sitting cross legged on my side, I look up at his looming figure—he still hasn't fully entered the compartment. "Come on. You have to admit it's a little bit funny."

"I'll admit nothing," he bites out, but then his shoulders lower and he steps into the compartment, turning to slide the doors shut with a definitive click. "And to think that woman was flirting with me."

He sounds so disgusted, I have to laugh again. "I'm not following."

He sits on his side of the bed and toes off his shoes, scowl still fully in place. "The flight attendant clearly assumes we're together now, and yet just a moment ago she…" He trails off with a faint flush, which is kind of cute, almost as if he's embarrassed. And yet.

"She hit on you in the hall?" My ire rises swift and hot—not jealousy. It's the principle of the thing.

He grunts, glances at the bed, wrinkles his nose in distaste, and turns his back to it once more.

"That little hussy," I say, glaring at the door.

At that he looks over his broad shoulder at me. A glint

enters his eyes. "Jealous, Ms. Darling?"

"Hey, you pointed out how messed up it was!"

"Insulting it was," he corrects. "She assumes I'm the sort to double-dip my wick. And obviously so shady, I'd do it in full sight of my current paramour."

"Are you sure you're not a duke?"

I can almost see him roll his eyes, though he's facing the other way. "I'm going to ring her."

"No, you're not." I get up on my knees.

He half turns, bringing one thick thigh up onto the bed. His expression is perplexed. "Why wouldn't I?"

"Because this bed is the coolest thing yet about this flight, and I don't want it taken down."

The corner of his mouth lifts slightly. "They'll set up a single bed for you."

Yeah, and that sneaky flight attendant will smirk the whole time. "If you ask her to take it down, you're opening the door for more advances."

His eyes narrow.

"Unless, of course, you want that," I say lightly. Nope. Not even a little jealous.

"She's not my type," he says with a sniff.

"You actually have a type?" It comes out before I can stop it.

"Yes," he drawls. "Quiet, dignified, and discreet."

"Lie."

He turns all the way to face me. "I beg your pardon?"

I burrow under the covers. They're just the right weight and softness. Nice. "Pardon yourself. You said that to put me in my place. But I'm not biting."

"You're imagining things," he grumbles as he sits back and, with clear reluctance, brings his legs onto the bed. "And annoying."

"You just can't manage me. That's what annoys you."

I pull out the cute little sleep mask provided in my kit and slip it on with a happy sigh. I'll just ignore him for the rest of the trip. No problem. Silence rings out, and the drone of the engines comes back full force.

His gruff voice breaks our stalemate. "Are you going to drink any of this champagne?"

"No. I've been nagged into refraining from drinking too much, remember?"

A soft huff sounds. Then the bed dips as he leans close and picks up the tray. A clink and another bed dip and everything settles.

"I've never met a person I couldn't manage," comes his tight reply a few seconds later.

Not bothering to take the mask off, I extend a hand his way. "Sophie Elizabeth Darling."

A set of teeth catch the edge of my hand and nip me. I'm so shocked I yelp, snatching my hand back. Lurching up, I whip off my mask to find him staring back at me with a bland look.

"Did you just *bite* me?" It comes out in an indignant squeak. Not that it hurt. He only nipped me, and playfully at that. Still. Really?

"That sounds like a rather juvenile thing to do," he says, resting his head on his pillow.

"It was a rhetorical question," I snap. "You bit me!"

His lips quirk as if he's trying very hard not to laugh. "Best not to stick your hand in my face then."

I gape at him for a full beat. "And you call me insane."

His blue gaze meets mine. "Do you mind? I'm trying to get some rest."

"I don't like you," I mutter, sliding my mask on.

"Lie," he points out, mimicking my earlier tone. "You've told me repeatedly now that you find me blindingly attractive."

"That doesn't mean I like you. Besides, your brand of

pretty is like a weapon. You reel victims in with it, just like a vampire does. I wouldn't be surprised if you sparkle in the sun."

"I cannot believe I'm arguing with a woman who references *Twilight*."

"The fact that you know I'm referencing *Twilight* betrays you as a secret Edward-loving fanboy."

His snort is loud and scathing. "Team Jacob all the way."

I can't help it, my eyes fly open, and I lift a corner of my mask to glare at him. "That's it. We can never be friends."

He gives me wounded look that's entirely manufactured. "Words hurt, chatty girl."

Muttering about asshat Brits, I turn my back to him and ignore his badly concealed snicker. And I'm a traitor to myself because I want to laugh with him. Only I fear the moment I do, he'll slam up those walls again and make me feel ridiculous.

Gabriel Scott might not know how to manage me, but I sure as shit am clueless when it comes to him too.

With that in mind, I concentrate on my breathing and the gentle hum of the plane around me, and soon drift off.

SOPHIE
3

I THINK it's the "fasten seat belts" chime that wakes me up. I'm too disoriented at first to even figure out where I am, other than it's loud and vibrating. And too dark. Then I remember my sleep mask. I pull it off and blink a few times to wake up.

The plane is shaking like an irate fist in the air, which isn't doing my stomach any favors. The fact that I'm lying down makes it feel even stranger, almost as if I might soon achieve weightlessness.

But I heard a chime, didn't I? Only, where are the seat belts on this bed? I grope around and come in contact with something hard. A thigh. I remember Gabriel, aka extremely bad flyer. One glance his way, and I know it's bad. He's lying rigid as a plank, fists at his side, his expression so blank, you'd think he was dead. Except he's panting, and a fine sweat covers his skin.

I don't blame him this round. The turbulence is awful. The plane rattles so hard, my butt is in danger of leaving the bed.

"Sunshine," I whisper.

He doesn't acknowledge me. I'm pretty sure his jaw is locked shut.

Edging closer, I tentatively touch his shoulder and find his body trembling. "Hey," I say in a soothing voice. "It's okay."

The cabin drops a few feet to mock that statement, and he

closes his eyes, turning his head away from me. He's gone utterly pale, his breath coming faster. "Go. Away."

"I can't." I move closer. "Look, I know you don't want me to witness this. But I'm here. Let me help you."

He sucks in a breath through his clenched teeth. "Distracting me with blowjob jokes won't work right now."

"I know." I'm actually worried about him. He appears to be on the verge of an outright panic attack. "Here's what we're going to do." I push back the covers and crawl toward him.

He snaps out of his terror, his eyes going wide. "What are you doing?"

"Cuddling," I tell him.

If anything he grows more alarmed, and I'm sure he'd back away if he was capable of moving. "What? No."

"Yes." I settle down at his side. God, he's cold. I sit up. He gives a sigh of apparent relief, but I merely pull my end of the covers over his legs before lying back down.

He squirms, making a half-hearted attempt to move away, but he's already at the edge, and there's nowhere for him to go. "This is highly irregular…"

"Yep. But we're doing it." In normal situations, I wouldn't dare force this on a person. But he's already focused on me instead of the turbulence, which is a step in the right direction. I rest my cheek against his biceps. The muscle is rock hard and quivering.

He clears his throat. "I don't—"

"You're one breath away from totally losing your shit. Accept the torment that is physical comfort."

His arms twitch as if he's trying not to lift them but really wants to. And then he gives up the fight and raises an arm, making room for me to come closer. *Victory.* I lay my head on his shoulder, wrapping my body against his side.

The contact feels good. Too good. Because, holy hell, touching him—really touching him—sends a jolt of warm pleasure through me. All the sensitive nerve endings in my body seem to perk up and pay attention. Which is wrong in this situation; I'm here to help the poor man, not get off on him.

I have no idea what he's thinking. For a second he holds me. Or, rather, he holds on to me like a lifeline. Tremors rack his body, but it's clear he's fighting it.

"Shhh," I murmur, stroking his chest. It's a nice chest, broad and densely packed with muscle beneath the proper clothes. His heart thuds against my palm, and I feel him take a deep breath. "Just think of me as your friendly neighborhood cuddler."

He's quiet again before another question bursts from him. "Are you telling me you'd do this for anyone?"

I snuggle down. "No. That you're insanely hot is a huge factor. I get to cop a feel under the guise of civic duty."

"Oh, for fuck's sake."

A smile pulls at my lips. "Can it with the outrage. I know for a fact that most people would rather snuggle up to a hot dude. If it makes me shallow for admitting that, so be it."

He grunts even as his hand slips to the top of my arm. Long fingers stroke once before stilling. "Your honesty is astounding."

"I know. Now hush, I have feels to cop." I run my hand just a little down his firm pec, loving the way his abs suck in with his hitched breath. I'm teasing him, but damn, he's nicely built. I force myself to stop. Only when I do, he tenses, and the tremors return. I realize my petting actually does soothe him.

I consider this a green light. Sinking into his hold, I stroke his chest and hum under my breath. He slowly eases, his body turning more toward mine, and my breasts press into the side of his ribs. The plane continues to jump and shake, and it's a battle to keep him calm. Every inch of ground I gain, stupid turbulence pulls it back from me.

"I think we should name our kids by number," I tell him.

His muscles clench and shift under my cheek. I can almost hear him internally debating how to respond.

"Dare I ask why?" he says finally.

"Because we'll have so many, numbers seem easier. We can do like the king in *Stardust*. Una, Secundus, Septimus…"

"That seems inordinately cruel. Think of the shit they'll receive in grammar school."

"They'll be too tough to be bullied. And I see you're warming to the idea."

I grin when he grunts. It's not a *no*—more like a *you're crazy*. I can work with that.

"I hate this," he says.

"Snuggling?" But I know what he means.

His laugh is wry and brief. "Weakness."

"Everyone is afraid of something."

"What are you afraid of?" he lobs back, sounding dubious.

Never being good enough. Being used up and tossed aside. I swallow hard. "Tidal waves. I have nightmares about being swept away. I blame all those disaster movies."

"Somehow I suspect you'd be the sort who would survive."

I smile at that.

A gust of warmth along at the top of my hair makes me realize he's pressed his lips to my head and is breathing me in. "What color is your natural hair?" he asks, almost idly.

"That's an awfully forward question, Mr. Scott." Turbulence aside, our little cabin is quite cozy with the cream-colored finishings and the lights dimmed.

"Supposedly I'm fathering at least seven of your children. A fair enough question to ask."

The plane makes a particularly nasty thump, and he sucks in a sharp breath. I nuzzle closer, my nose filling with the scent of his cologne and, underneath it, the sweat of fear.

Closing my eyes, I spread my hand out, pressing my palm against his abdomen where his muscles quiver. "I'm a blonde."

"I see that," he deadpans.

"Natural blond, I mean. I went a few dozen shades lighter this time. Last week I had blue hair." I smile a little, imagining how he would have reacted to that.

"I'm not surprised in the least."

"Mmm..." The tip of my finger toys with a wrinkle on his sweater vest, which is cashmere—and I still resent the fact that he looks so good in it. The hem has ridden up, exposing his shirt beneath. My fingers drift to one of the buttons.

As soon as my finger rests against the little circle, the air seems to grow thicker. My body seems heavier, somehow, as if intent has made it laden and hot.

Because I feel the firm abs beneath his shirt, and I now know a way in. What gets me even hotter? I realize he knows this as well. We both seem to hold our breath.

I pluck the button open.

It's as if I've plucked a chord instead. Tension vibrates between us so strong, I can nearly hear it. Gabriel stiffens, his abs clenching, his fingers halting their exploration of my hair.

What the hell are you doing, Sophie? Stop now. My fingers don't seem to get the message. They slip through the open space in his shirt to find the hot, smooth skin beneath.

Oh, hell. Because he *is* hot, his skin firm and tight, and I want more of it. My fingers barely move. As if, by being sly, he won't notice that I'm feeling him up. Nice dream.

I clear my throat, searching for my voice. It comes out rusty. "Red hair is always fun. So many shades to work with."

Yes, talk and you won't come off as such a creepster perv. Brilliant idea.

I can't seem to shut up. "Bright red. Auburn. Strawberry red." *Great, you sound like the Bubba Gump of hair coloring.*

He grunts, his body stiff, unyielding, but he doesn't protest my roaming fingers. Doesn't say a damn word. Which speaks volumes, really. Because this guy is not the type to remain silent if he doesn't want to.

A band of heat clenches low around my belly at the realization that he's letting me explore.

Gently, I stroke the small patch of skin I can reach. The tip of my finger glides over smooth skin to find rough hair.

Jesus on a motorcycle, he has a happy trail.

The urge to follow that trail down is so strong, I nearly moan. I clench my teeth, take a breath. "I've also had purple hair. Green doesn't do anything for me, though."

Without my permission, my fingers slink downward to the where the next button is secured, waiting for me to open it. His whole body stills, as if he's just willed himself not to move. But when I start to free that small button, he expels a breath and his hand comes down on top of mine.

It is warm, firm, and clearly states, *no more.*

And nothing is more effective at snapping me out of this madness. Because, really, what the hell am I doing? I don't even like this guy. Well, I kind of do. Which just blows. *Dead end* might as well be stamped on Gabriel Scott's forehead.

The plane has started to rattle hard again. Gabriel shudders, our awkward pause forgotten, and clings to me once more, his breathing erratic.

Comfort. Don't grope. Just comfort.

That I can do. I think.

GABRIEL

OH, how the mighty have fallen. If anyone had photographic evidence of my current predicament, my reputation as a fearsome bastard would be dead in the water. I can almost hear the snickering now—the great, implacable Scottie wrapped around a woman as though she was his woobie.

Killian would never let me hear the end of it. I don't even want to imagine the shit I'd get from Brenna.

In some ways, plummeting to my death would be preferable.

That was a stupid thing to think. Terror arcs through my body, making my insides swoop and my limbs tingle. And I find myself clinging just a bit more tightly to the strange, softly rounded woman at my side. Perhaps this truly is a nightmare; nothing seems real or makes much sense.

I do not engage in continued conversations with strangers, especially ungovernable, chatty, irreverent women. And I most certainly do not cuddle. I cannot remember the last time I held a woman. The sensation is so foreign, yet pleasurable.

My entire body seems to be straining for greater contact, my skin sensitive and hot beneath my clothes. I want them off with a fierce agitation. I want to feel skin on skin, the warmth and plush give of her flesh.

I will not think about the fact that she snuck her fingers beneath my shirt to stroke my abdomen. The phantom of her touch still burns like a brand on my skin.

The second she played with the buttons of my shirt, I went intensely and painfully hard. I very nearly let her find that out. And if she had? I'd have begged her to give it a squeeze, a friendly stroke and tug. I'd probably have promised her anything if she'd only continue to touch me.

Alarming to say the least. I haven't a clue what this woman will say or do from one moment to the next. For a man whose life revolves around exerting control over all things, this flicker of attraction is unwanted and unsettling.

Yet for all that, it's preferable to the well of mindless fear I'd been in before Sophie Darling latched onto me like a limpet.

I take the opportunity of our close proximity to really observe her. At first I thought her pleasant to look at, but nothing remarkable. I was mistaken.

Her profile, clear against the gray of my vest, is a study of graceful curves, gentle swoops, and delicate lines—not merely pleasant but sweetly pretty. However, it is her skin that captures my attention.

I've been with women of all skin colors—from deep rose brown to the palest milk white—and that never factored beyond being a basic framework of the woman's overall beauty. In short, skin as a singularly attractive feature never entered my mind.

But Sophie Darling's skin is a thing of beauty. Because it's luminous, extremely smooth, and fine, not a blemish in sight. Its buttery golden hue reminds me of shortbread biscuits. Then again, everything about Sophie reminds me of some sort of sweet treat: tempting but ultimately bad for one's health.

Doesn't matter. The longer I look at her skin, the more I want to touch it just to see if it's as satiny as it appears. I think of Marilyn Monroe—the way she looked on screen, flawless and glowing. But that beauty came from makeup and good lighting. I'm close enough to tell Sophie isn't wearing foundation or powder.

Without my permission, my hand drifts up her arm, and I trace the curve of her shoulder, heading toward her bare skin. She holds very still, as if she's tracking the progress. I am too, my heart pounding against my ribs. I can almost hear the beat shouting, *stop, stop, stop.* But I don't.

Just one touch. That's all. I'll satisfy my curiosity and move on.

The tip of my finger skims the edge of her collarbone. And I close my eyes, fighting a groan. More delicate than satin. Softer than velvet. Smooth, warm. I suck in a deep breath and slowly release it. My hand falls to the safety of the bed.

It's too quiet, and this damn plane is still shaking.

Keep talking. About anything.

I have no capacity for small talk. Which means I'm in deep shit.

"Why are you going to London?" I blurt out. "On holiday?"

Frankly I'm surprised a woman like Sophie is traveling alone. She seems the type who needs companionship, someone with whom to share her experiences. The idea of her roaming London on her own doesn't sit well with me, which is ridiculous. She's a grown woman.

As if to punctuate that thought, she makes a noise of wry humor. "Actually, I'm traveling on business."

"Really?" Surprise laces my voice, unfortunately.

And she snorts. "Yes, the fluffy-headed woman with big tits has a brain."

Christ, don't mention your tits. It's hard enough ignoring them against my ribs. "What does breast size have to do with brains?"

Her cheek slides over my shirt, and I know she's looking up at me. "You actually sound affronted."

I peer down my nose at her, taking in her wide brown eyes and red lips. "I am. You implied that I'm sexist. I am not. Though I do agree with the fluffy bit. I cannot picture you serious about anything."

Her pert nose wrinkles as she frowns, and the pointy tip of her finger pokes my ribs. I just manage not to yelp. God help me if she realizes I'm ticklish.

"Funny," she says, resting her head on my shoulder once more.

Bloody hell, that feels far too good.

Her voice drifts up, distracting me. "But I guess I earned that one."

She's earned my gratitude and saved my arse from utter humiliation yet again. I sigh and allow my hand to settle on the crown of her head. There's no excuse for making her feel less than. "Tell me about your job."

We're pressed so close, I can feel her body tense up.

"Ah, well, there's not much to tell."

When I don't say anything, but merely look down at her, waiting, her round cheeks flush, and she clears her throat. "I'm interviewing for a position."

"And you're squirming around like a fish on a hook right now because?"

Her nose wrinkles again. I have the mad urge to kiss the tip. Likely it'd shock the hell out her, and turnabout is fair play. But I hold on to my dignity. Because she starts to babble.

"Well, I don't really know what the position is. I mean, I have some idea, but if you want details, I have nothing really to offer—"

"Do you mean to tell me you're traveling to another country to interview for an unknown position?" My voice has raised a few octaves. This girl. I have no words. "Do you even know with whom you are meeting? Tell me you didn't spend all your money on a first class ticket without knowing exactly why you were going."

"Hey." She pokes me. "Don't go all duke on me again." A sigh escapes her as she sags into me. "No, I don't know who I'm meeting. I have a name and a few references from mutual people we've worked with. And no, I didn't spend all my money—"

"Well, that's a—"

"They're paying my way."

"Sodding hell."

Her head lifts, white blond strands pooling on my grey vest. "What? Why is that so bad?"

"I assume you've heard the phrase 'the more you know'? If someone offers to pay for your international flight for the sole reason of interviewing, it would behoove you to know exactly why they're willing to pay for the opportunity and what exactly is expected of you."

"Oh, I know why they offered to pay."

"I shudder to hear it."

Another poke, this one too close to my ticklish spot. I twitch.

"Because I'm the best at what I do," she says.

"And what is it that you do?" *Please don't say stripper.*

All right, perhaps I am sexist.

Pride infuses her tone with steel. "Social media marketing and lifestyle photography."

"Ah, yes. That I can see."

Her eyes narrow. "You were totally thinking paid escort, weren't you?"

"Nothing of the sort."

It's rather impressive how a woman who has the sweet face of a kewpie doll manages to glare with such effectiveness. I have to bite back the urge to confess all. I raise a brow and give her a counter look.

Her eyes narrow further. I swear, it's like *High Noon* on a plane.

"Social media is an essential component of most businesses today," she tells me.

"Ms. Darling, untwist your knickers. I am in complete agreement with you." In truth, the band could use a few lessons in improving their social media presence, and I've been after Brenna to make that happen for months.

It's not that they lack a following, but when Jax attempted suicide, the band withdrew from the spotlight, leaving their fans, and the industry, to fill in the blanks and make the wrong assumptions—something that bothers me on a personal level. Kill John is so much more than what the world thinks of them.

Sophie is still looking at me with a dubious expression, as

if she's often received criticism for her choice of profession. That someone would try to stamp out the hopes and dreams of this vivacious and intuitive woman is a crime.

I make an effort to soften my tone. "Perhaps you ought to start at the beginning."

"Not if you're going to lecture," she says with a sniff.

"I promise nothing." I give a lock of her hair a small tug. "Talk, chatty girl. It's all we have in this hell tube."

She purses her lips. Her fire-engine red lipstick has faded, leaving only a faint stain. She looks softer for it, vulnerable in a strange way. A small scar cuts through the outer corner of her top lip. The faded silvery line is diabolical in its placement, a tiny taunt: *suckle right here, mate.* My fingers curl into a fist to keep from reaching out and touching. *Get a grip on yourself, Scott.*

"All right," she says, snuggling back down with the efficiency of a cat. I close my eyes and concentrate on the sound of her voice. "For the past year, I've been working as a social media liaison, helping people write creative content for Twitter, Instagram, Facebook, Snapchat, and so on."

"You teach them how to be witty."

"That sounded dangerously close to a compliment."

"It was."

The sound of her light laugher goes straight to my gut. "Two in one night? Oh, the shock. I may never recover."

I give her hair another tug. The strands slide cool and soft around my fingers. "Go on."

"Yes, I teach them how to highlight their personalities and gain new followers. I got lucky landing my last client." She tells me the name of the rising television star Brenna and I had drinks with in New York a month ago. The smallness of the world can be a strange thing.

Sophie's long lashes shadow her cheeks as she focuses on some distant spot. "Anyway, with him, I upped my game, taking photos as well. It's funny—they were totally staged, arty, that kind of thing, but his followers love them and believe they're candids."

"We see what we want to see," I murmur.

"Yes, and we build sandcastle dreams around celebrities. All we need is a window into their lives to start."

"Which is what you're providing."

She nods, her cheek rubbing my chest. "So anyway, I got an email from my client, saying his acquaintance wanted to interview me for a big job in Europe. He put us in contact, and I was asked to come to London, all expenses paid. I'm guessing it's someone pretty famous; I was told they'd give me details in person in order to protect the client's privacy.

"The whole first class thing was a happy surprise. I got to the ticket counter, and they told me I'd been moved to first class."

"Did the airline specifically say you were bumped?"

She frowns in confusion. "I was expecting coach. I mean, who sends an interviewee first class?"

"Depends on the interviewer. Perhaps your ticket was always for first class," I point out. "Though I still don't understand why they gave you my extra seat."

"Still crabby about that?"

"It was never personal," I tell her quietly. Regardless of what people believe about me, I don't go out of my way to be a bastard.

The press of her palm against my abdomen grows heavy. "I get it," she says. "You didn't want any witnesses."

Perceptive girl.

She smiles a little. "For the record, though. I'm glad I'm here."

I am too.

When I don't say anything, she gives me a nudge. "Admit it. I made it better."

"No other flight I've been on can compare," I tell her truthfully. "Security precautions aside, surely this company gave you a name."

"Yes, I have a name." She gives me a bright smile as if this is supposed to ease my trepidation. "I'm to meet Mr. Brian Jameson at the— Why are you turning green? Shit, are you going to be sick?"

I might very well be. I almost laugh, full-out unhinged, oh-fuck-it-all laughing. I'm not even surprised it's "Brian" she's interviewing with. It almost feels inevitable, the cherry on top of this strange encounter with this chatty girl.

At my side, Sophie comes up on her elbow, and the nimbus of her moonlight hair seems to glow around her concerned face—though really it's cheap airplane lighting and my overactive imagination. She's just a girl with bleached hair and a talent for small talk.

Lie. She's more than that. She's untouchable.

"Sunshine, you're freaking me out."

"Sorry," I say, retreating. "I'm simply adjusting to the fact that I've been tucked up with a potential employee."

SOPHIE  4

IT'S FAIRLY STUNNING how quickly and effectively finding out you're wrapped around a man who works with your potential boss will kill the mood. Not that I'd expected anything from the stuffy but oh-so-hot Gabriel Scott. I was under no illusions that we wouldn't part ways as soon as the plane landed.

And, really, that would be for the best. I have sworn off hookups, as I've concluded they're bad for my mental health. I've dealt with too many dick biscuits to continue with casual sex. Even if I hadn't, Gabriel isn't exactly offering. I've never met a more standoffish, prickly man.

I'd wonder if he's simply arrogant—a perfectly formed man who doesn't deign to mix with average women like me. But it's fairly clear he's this way with everyone.

So, yes, leaving this beautiful being behind at the tarmac has always been part of the plan. Maybe that's why I've felt so free to be utterly myself with him. What does it matter if he finds me lacking when we're nothing more than strangers forced to endure each other's company for one night of travel?

But now everything is upside down and sideways. I will be seeing him in England. He works with Brian Jameson, which he informs me is actually a false name for Brenna James, who runs the PR department for his organization.

Why Brenna James needed to give me a fake name is beyond me, but definitely piques my interest.

Gabriel spares no time extracting himself from my hold and putting as much space between us as possible. The turbulence has died, so there isn't an excuse to linger anyway. We spend the rest of the flight in awkward silence.

Right before we arrive in London, I try to get him to talk about the job, about Brenna. But he refuses, telling me he'll let her explain everything.

The only good thing to come out of my nagging is that he's too busy bickering with me to notice the landing.

"I'll have my driver drop you at your hotel," he says as we make our way out of the gate and into Heathrow's terminal.

Since it's late at night, and I'm in a foreign country, I'm not inclined to argue. In fact, I'm grateful and more than a little shocked by his offer. "Thank you. That's very nice of you."

He gives me a look as if I'm being ridiculous, but nods in acknowledgment. "I assume you have luggage?"

"Of course," I tell him, looking around at the closed-up shops that line the way. "Don't you? Or I guess you live in London."

"My main residence is in New York now. But I keep a wardrobe here in my London home."

Pondering a life where I jet around the world and have wardrobes and homes waiting for me, I almost miss the escalator to baggage claim. Graceful as ever.

Gabriel, however, walks exactly as I'd expected him to: like a man accustomed to people getting out of his way. His stride is smooth, brisk, and confident.

Here on terra firma, I can appreciate the full effect he has on others. People actually *do* edge out of his path. It's fascinating—they simply part like the proverbial Red Sea and gape at him as he passes.

While Gabriel's masculine beauty is truly breathtaking, the

force of him is earthier, almost brutal. Most charismatic people make you want to be a part of their inner circle, make you feel special. With Gabriel the message is much different: here is a man with whom you do not fuck.

He doesn't talk to me while we walk but focuses his attention on his phone. Apparently he has a million and one emails to answer. His texting-while-walking skills are impressive, though I guess it helps when you don't have to worry about running into anyone.

We halt at the baggage carousel.

"Do you see your bags?" he asks, nose deep in his phone.

Along with my carry-on, which holds my camera and equipment—there was no way I was losing sight of my babies—I have two large suitcases. I usually pack lighter, but "Brian" had suggested I pack for an extended stay should I get the job.

"Not yet."

"Color?"

"Red."

The corner of his mouth lifts. "Not surprising."

"Let me guess," I ask as he taps away at his phone. "Had you the need for luggage, it would be as black as your immortal soul."

He tucks his phone in his pocket and gives me a level look. Amusement lightens his expression. "As it happens, my luggage is dark brown alligator leather."

"I don't know why I bother teasing you," I mutter.

Again that hint of a smile flirts with the edges of his lips. "You are persistent. I'll give you that."

I spot my bags, but before I can grab them, he has a porter attending to us and we're off again. It's ten at night, which is unsettling since we've already spent an entire night on the plane. Taxies are thin, and the majority of people are being greeted by loved ones.

Travel loneliness claws at my belly. I hate landing in new

places at night. It always feels as if I might be left behind and end up sleeping on an airport bench.

Not so tonight. And another swell of gratitude fills me when Gabriel guides me to the black Rolls Royce Phantom waiting at the curb, the driver already opening the door.

Gabriel gestures for me to enter. But then frowns. "You're not going to bounce on the seats and cry *who-eee*, are you?"

I glare at him. "I'm not completely uncouth, you know."

Okay, I might have done so had he not mentioned it.

"I've been in a plane with you for seven hours," he reminds me as he follows me into the car.

I have to grit my teeth, because, *who-fucking-eee!*, the car is fine. I want to rub my cheeks against the butter soft leather and play with the array of buttons so badly my fingers twitch.

Gabriel eyes me for a long moment as the driver shuts the door with a soft thud. "Go on," he says in a cajoling voice. "Give it a little bounce. You know you're dying for it."

With his heavy-lidded stare and deep rumbling tone, he makes this sound illicit. I cross my legs, and his eyes track the movement. His lids lower just a bit more, and a shimmer of unwanted heat licks under my shirt.

"I'm good," I tell him with false lightness.

He grunts in response. The car pulls away from the curb, all smoothness and power, and I sit back in my plush seat with a sigh. Whatever happens from here on out, I'll have this small moment of complete comfort.

We sit in silence as the car heads toward London. I can't look out the windows without being disoriented; it's just wrong to be driving on the left side of the road. I keep expecting to crash into an oncoming car.

Gabriel is already back on his phone. This time he's talking to someone named Jules, peppering him or her with questions —is his house ready, have certain contracts arrived, and so on. The cool-yet-even tone of his voice soothes me in the cozy quiet of the car.

I lean my head back and let my eyes close—until I hear his last line of questioning: Is the hotel room ready and sufficiently prepared for Ms. Darling?

Hearing him discuss my lodging arrangement drives home the fact that I'm truly interviewing for his company. And I can't decide if I'm disappointed or excited. Perhaps a bit of both.

"You're not going to try to talk Ms. James out of hiring me, are you?" I ask when he hangs up with Jules.

"Because we spent time together on the plane, you mean?" His brow lifts as his lips flatten. "I'd be a right prat if I did."

"Your words, not mine."

"Are you saying you think I'm a prat?" He appears so honestly offended, even a bit hurt, that I instantly feel tiny and petty.

"No, no. I'm sorry. I don't know what the hell I'm saying." I wave a hand because I can't stay still. "I'm flustered. It's not every day you antagonize your prospective employer for hours on end."

A small smile creeps up along the outer corners of his eyes. "Yes, well, technically I'm not your employer. Brenna and I are partners of a sort. But I'll take note of your remorse."

"Remorse implies I did something *wrong*. This is more awkward embarrassment."

The smile moves to his mouth, pulling at it. But he won't let it unfurl. I wonder if I'll ever see this man smile with ease. I wonder how long I'll even know him. My chances of landing a job in a business that he's a part of feels slim. I'm not the button-down type.

"You're still not going to tell me what you do?" I ask.

"You could Google my name or Brenna's at any time." He gestures toward my handbag with a tilt of his arrogant, stubborn chin. "So go on then. Pull out your phone and check."

Oh, I'm tempted. So very tempted. But it feels like cheating somehow. "Maybe I want you to trust me enough to tell me."

A soft scoffing noise escapes him. "It isn't a matter of trust. I hardly consider this a secret since you're going to find out soon enough. It is a matter of respecting Brenna's somewhat overzealous but apparently adamant desire to keep you uninformed until the time of the interview."

I flop back against the leather seat with a huff. "You're right. I'll respect her wishes too. But this just means I'll have to use my imagination."

"No doubt you'll have me pegged as an international spy by the time we arrive," he deadpans, though amusement glints in his eyes.

"Hey, I only thought that once."

The corner of his lip twitches, and then his phone chimes. He glances down at it before tapping out a message.

"Is that Brenna?"

"Chatty and nosey." He doesn't look up from his phone. "A winning combination."

"You love it," I counter with false bravado. Nerves are starting to make me jumpy. And I'm seriously considering poking him right now just to get an answer—something I think he knows because he glances my way, and that stern expression of his returns.

"Yes, that was Brenna. I informed her I had the package on board and ready for delivery."

"Har."

He turns toward me in his seat, leaning against the corner, his big body sprawled like some Armani ad come to life. All that harsh male beauty focuses on me; it's like being under stage lights—exposing, blinding, hot.

I try not to squirm. I wonder if I'll ever be able to look at him without being rendered breathless and mushy-brained.

Thankfully, our stare-off is broken when the car pulls up before a small hotel with an unassuming front. The door is Victorian style with glossy green paint, cut-glass windows, and a simple black awning to protect visitors from rainfall. It looks clean and cute but not like a place I imagine Gabriel Scott, with his perfectly tailored clothes and crisp mannerisms, would stay. There isn't even a doorman. Gabriel is definitely the doorman-needing type.

Even so, we're here. I smooth my hands down my plain black yoga pants. Christ, I should have dressed up for the plane ride. I can't even remember what interview outfit I brought. Will it work? Will Brenna be waiting for us now that Gabriel's alerted her? I thought I had until tomorrow morning before I'd meet her.

"Sophie," Gabriel says, his deep voice even and low. "You're fretting over nothing."

"I'm not fretting."

One eyebrow lifts, challenging me.

I pluck at the edge of my shirt. "Okay, maybe a little worrying is occurring."

"You'll fit in fine. Perfectly, actually." He frowns as if this bothers him.

Or maybe he's placating me. "If she's at all like you—"

"She's not." He straightens and adjusts his cuffs. It's a tick. But I don't know what he has to be nervous about. "None of them are like me. You'll love them."

I want to ask who "they" are. But I don't like the implication he's made about himself. "I like you fine," I tell him.

"Well, good." He knocks on the window. The driver opens the door, clearly having been waiting for Gabriel's signal. "If all goes well, you'll be seeing a lot more of me."

He does not make it sound like a reward.

LAST NIGHT, after Gabriel made certain I'd been properly checked in—he refused to leave me at the curb and was affronted that I'd assumed he would—I was so tired, I stumbled into my room and crawled under the covers.

I didn't sleep a wink, which was annoying, but it was dark, and the sounds of traffic coming through the massive, old windows reminded me of home, so I was content just to lie there.

Now, in the light of day, I'm dressed in my favorite '60s-style teal sheath dress with three-quarter-length sleeves. Black buttons run down one thigh and a flirty little black ruffle dances along the hem. I'm wearing black kitten heels and my hair is in a chignon.

I could have gone for something more conservative, but that would be a lie. I'm not conservative and never will be. And really, if Brenna James hires me to run her social media campaign and be a photographer, I'll be in my jeans more than anything else.

I dither in front of the mirror for as long as I dare, then make my way down to the lounge. The hotel is an old, Victorian, four-story townhouse. The staircase is narrow with worn wood risers that creak under my feet. There's a tiny claustrophobic elevator that I used last night when the porter brought my bags up.

I'm on the fourth floor, and the lounge is on the second. It's done up like a classic gentleman's club with various leather arm chairs set around small wooden tables. Emerald silk wallpaper meets white wainscoting, and subdued conversation rises from small groups having their breakfast.

I'm supposed to meet Brenna in an hour. And though I'm not hungry, I manage to order coffee after asking the waitress to decipher the menu. Apparently, I need a flat white, since

I'm not in the mood for a frothy cappuccino.

"Why does it say no pictures at the bottom of the menu?" I ask the waitress as she sets down my coffee.

"This is a private club," she says in a thickly Eastern European accent, "for entertainment professionals. The members want to feel comfortable eating without the threat of someone taking their picture."

I glance around with wide eyes and spot a woman who I swear is an up-and-coming singer. She's eating with a man; they're snuggled up and laughing quietly. I can't see his face, but there's something familiar about the way he holds himself. Or I just might be spinning castles now.

"A club? Really?"

"Mostly music, stage, and screen," the waitress tells me blandly. "And some footballers, I think."

After that, I can't concentrate. I drink my creamy coffee and hear snatches of conversation around me: a documentary producer lamenting his inability to find a proper narrator, a record exec mentioning heading to the studio to work on a new album, a television reporter whining to his agent about his contract.

I have to wonder (again) who it is I'm interviewing to work with. An actor? Is Gabriel an agent too? I could see him doing that with ease. Or maybe he works for a movie studio.

I'm so engrossed in shameless eavesdropping and speculating about Gabriel that I don't notice the stylish woman until she's at my table, pulling out a free chair.

"Hey," she says. "I'm Brenna. Or Brian." She laughs. "Scottie told me the jig was up with my secret identity."

Brenna James is tall, thin, and severely pretty with honey-red hair pulled back in a sleek ponytail. She's dressed in a gorgeous copper-colored suit and sky-high turquoise heels.

"God, that's a cute dress." She plops down in the chair opposite me. "Is it wrong to want to hire you based on that dress alone?"

"I wouldn't complain," I say, shaking her hand. "But feel free to ask me more questions if you must."

"I know we're supposed to meet in thirty minutes, but I saw you sitting here and thought it'd be rude not to come over." She gives me a wide smile that makes her appear impish. "Forgive me for intruding?"

"It's no problem at all." I signal the waitress before asking Brenna, "You said Scottie. Do you mean Gabriel?"

Her mouth falls open as if I've slapped her. "Um...yes. Gabriel Scott. Everyone calls him Scottie."

"Oh, I didn't realize."

She leans in, her eyes wide and curious. "He, ah, gave you his first name?"

Is it some kind of dire secret? I'm veering back toward them being international spies. And I'm only half-joking. "Well, getting him to give me his name was like pulling teeth, but yes."

This seems to placate her because she relaxes in her seat and, after ordering a pot of coffee, black, surveys me with a discerning eye.

"Would you like to view my portfolio?" I ask, handing over the thick leather case I brought along with me.

But she waves me off. "No need. I viewed your work before asking you here."

"Of course." Heat flushes my cheeks. "Sorry, I'm a bit nervous."

She touches my hand. "Don't be. You survived the trip sitting next to Scottie. That's the biggest trial by fire."

I eye her warily. "Did you put me in that seat? I thought I'd been bumped, but now I'm not so sure."

The waitress arrives with her coffee, and Brenna is quick to pour herself a cup.

"Of course I did." She takes a sip and sighs with

appreciation before turning her sharp gaze on me. "As an enticement to working for us. Not so you'd have to deal with him. I'm not cruel."

"I didn't realize it would be a cruelty."

"Well, most people wouldn't, until he opens his mouth and eviscerates a poor soul with a few words."

I have to smile at that. "I don't know if he even has to speak. That glare of his would probably do the trick."

"But you survived," she says again, staring at me as if I'm a rare bird.

A weird sort of protectiveness rises up in me. Not that Gabriel needs it, but I can't stop myself from defending him. "I had fun."

Her red brow wings up at that. "Fun?"

There's so much skepticism in her voice, she's practically choking on it.

"It was a lovely flight," I assure. "Thank you for putting me in first class. I'll never forget it."

She clears her throat. "Yes, well, that's...good. I'm glad. Ah, anyway, I figured Scottie would have that divider panel up before his fine ass hit the leather."

I don't mention the broken panel.

Brenna glances at her phone. "The guys are ready. Shall we head to the interview now?"

Nerves flutter to life in my belly. "Guys? There's a group interviewing me?"

"More or less." She gives me a small smile. "You'll see. Come on. We have a private room set up."

"Okay." My legs are suddenly wobbly as I stand. "Is Gabriel going to be there as well?"

A small part of me doesn't want him to witness this. I don't know if I'll be able to concentrate under his laser gaze. But the needier, base part of me wants to see him again. He's familiar. And oddly, I feel confident when he's around.

Brenna halts a step. "Yes, *Gabriel* will be there." We walk a few paces before she glances at me from under her lashes. "Though, maybe call him Scottie from now on."

"Why?" I don't get the nickname or why someone like Gabriel would allow it. *Scottie* doesn't fit him at all. Scottie is a dude who yells, "We need more time, Captain!" Not an impeccably dressed man who looks like a male model and speaks like an ornery duke.

Brenna's heels click on the floor as she guides us to a back room. "It's what everyone in the business calls him. Honestly, I haven't I've heard anyone refer to him as Gabriel for years."

I'm glad I didn't tell her I also called him Sunshine. She'd probably up and die on me. Or maybe I'd lose the job. I decide not to talk about Gabriel aka Scottie any more than necessary from now on.

We enter a room, and a group of men turn our way en masse. My first thought is that maybe Gabriel and Brenna run a modeling agency, because they're all gorgeous in their own way. But then I really look at them, and horror hits me with a cold slap. I know these guys. I know them well.

Kill John. The biggest rock band in the world. My eyes flit over them. Their expressions range from welcoming to mildly curious to sexually interested. Rye Peterson, the bassist, massively muscled and boyishly handsome, gives me an open grin. Whip Dexter, the drummer, nods politely. Jax Blackwood, the infamous guitarist and sometime singer is the curious one, though he doesn't seem upset.

I shy away from his green gaze, feeling ill and unsteady on my feet.

Then there's Killian James. Dark hair, dark eyes, dark expression. He stood as we entered, his head cocking as if trying to place me.

My heart starts to pound. *Fuck.* I need to get out of here.

I take a step back and collide with a body. The scent of

expensive cologne and fine wool hits my nostrils.

"Going the wrong way, chatty girl," Gabriel murmurs in my ear, gently nudging me forward.

But I need to escape.

Killian is still staring at me like a nearly solved puzzle. At his side is a pretty woman with dark blond hair—the woman who was eating breakfast earlier. She's Liberty Bell, I realize with a start. Killian's wife and a singer in her own right. I should have recognized her sooner. I should have realized that good things do not, in fact, happen to me.

I glance at Gabriel. He's wearing his neutral façade, but there's a small glimmer of encouragement in his eyes. I don't want to look away from him. He'll be gone soon enough, and it hurts. Too much for such a short acquaintance.

Brenna is introducing me. She takes the portfolio from my nerveless fingers and hands it to the guys. "Sophie used to be a photojournalist—"

Killian makes a strangled sound before exploding. "Oh, fuck no! Now I recognize her. Are you kidding me with this shit?" He takes a step in my direction, anger infusing his cheeks with red. "You have some nerve coming here, lady."

I hold my ground, even though my pride is imploding. I don't know any other way.

But Gabriel puts himself between us. "Calm yourself," he snaps at Killian. "Ms. Darling did not come here to be harassed."

"Oh, that's fucking rich," Killian says with a sneer. His eyes are not kind. "Isn't that a pap's job?"

The other guys look confused.

"Kills, man," Rye says. "Ease up. Lots of people are photojournalists without being a sleazy paparazzi."

Oh, if only that were true of me.

"No." Killian slashes a hand through the air. "She's not just a pap. She's the one who took those pics of Jax. Weren't you, honey? Think I didn't see you there, with your fucking camera? Shoving it in my face when he was fucking dying on me?"

Gabriel's head snaps up. "What?"

"You heard me. It was her. She was the one who sold those pictures of Jax."

"Impossible," Gabriel spits out. "Martin Shear sold those pictures. I ought to know; I spent the better part of a year having our lawyers go after that tosspot."

He lifts a hand as if to say he rests his case. I can't decide if he's trying to rationalize my actions or if he's just that logical. I'm afraid it's the latter. His cold demeanor hasn't thawed. And he's waiting for an answer, his brow quirked in that arrogant, impatient way.

I take a shallow breath. "Martin was my boyfriend at the time."

Gabriel's head rears back as if I've slapped him. The look on his face, the utter disappointment mixed with growing disgust—I'm ruined in his eyes. I can see that clearly. I don't blame him. I'm disgusted too. It's amazing how low a person craving love can sink when she thinks she's found it.

If the ground could swallow me up now, I'd be grateful. But it wouldn't change the thick, gritty sludge of regret that fills my insides every time I think about that night, about taking those pictures of Jax Blackwood, unconscious and covered in vomit. I can still hear Killian shout his name as security rushed in. I'd been so blind then, only focused on my next paycheck, egged on by Martin to never think of the subject as human but as potential dollar signs.

I'd been the ugliest, darkest version of myself. So confused and lost. And now that past is staring me in the face.

"Martin was—is—a dickbag," I say. "I know this *now*. At the time...well, I don't really have a good excuse. I met him at a low point, and he had a strange sort of charisma. He made his job sound fun: easy money, providing a service for fans."

Several annoyed scoffs sound in the room.

"They were the lies I let myself believe," I admit. "I wanted to quit, but I hadn't found anything else to do. And then that night happened. When I got home, I told Martin where I'd been. He was…" I clear my throat. "He was over-the-moon happy, said those pictures would have me set financially for at least a year."

I can't miss the way the guys flinch, or the way Gabriel ducks his head, grinding his teeth as if he's fighting not to explode. My stomach flips, and my fingers are ice. But I continue.

"God, I wanted that money. I won't lie. I'd had a slow year and was living off ramen. I could have quit with that money, taken the time to find a decent job. But I looked at the shots, and they were awful. Painful."

It hurts even now to remember them.

Clearly it hurts these people too. So much more than it ever hurt me. I want to cry.

"I was hesitant to sell them after that. Martin picked up on it and, when I went to bed, he took them for himself."

"He stole them from you?" Gabriel's voice is flat. He won't look me in the eye.

"Yeah," I whisper. "I wanted to fight it. And then I didn't. Because they were splashed everywhere, and I felt… ashamed."

Gabriel makes a noise as if to say I should be.

Killian isn't so quiet. "She can't be here. This is too fucking much, Brenna."

"I think it would be good for us," Brenna says. "We can all close that final door and move on."

Killian sneers and looks at Brenna as if he can't believe her words.

Somehow I find my voice. "For what it's worth, I didn't

know the interview was for you. I wouldn't have come."

"Oh, sure, that makes it all better. Because we haven't spent more than a year struggling with the shit you put out in the public eye," Killian snaps.

All at once, everyone starts talking, words bleeding together, bombarding me. I wince.

Jax whistles sharply. "Everyone shut the fuck up and sit the fuck down."

I'm guessing he doesn't often shout, because everyone stops and sits immediately, though Killian gives him a disgruntled glare as he drops down on his chair.

Jax looks at me. When I first met him, he had a boyish quality about him, like a sun-kissed, all-American jock, which was funny as it's well-known that he's half English. Nearly, two years later, all that boyishness is gone, replaced by a hard-baked, rugged handsomeness. Life has battered but not beaten him.

"You remember that night," he says. "Before, I mean."

I'm extremely aware of Gabriel's gaze on me, but I answer Jax without looking away. "Yeah."

Jax nods, biting his bottom lip as if he's ashamed. "I figured. I've wanted to find you. To apologize."

"What?" Killian bursts out, nearly jumping back up.

"Shut up," Jax snaps at him, then sighs and runs a hand through his spiky hair. "At least until you hear me out."

"Ah," I clear my throat. "I have to agree with Killian's sentiment here. You have absolutely no reason to apologize to me."

Jax's smile is weary and lopsided as he holds my gaze. I can see the struggle in his eyes. He doesn't exactly want to say whatever he feels he has to.

Gabriel breaks the moment. "Get to the point, Jax." His expression is so fierce, he appears carved from stone. "And start by explaining exactly how you know Ms. Darling."

He doesn't bother with me. It's as if I'm no longer in the room.

Jax shrugs and leans against the wall. "We met in the hotel bar the night of 'The Incident'."

Gabriel glares at Jax's air quotes. A muscle twitches beneath his right eye. "Go. On."

"You offered to buy me a drink," I fill in, because I'm damn tired of being ignored. And I'm not letting Jax do this on his own.

He smiles. "And you warned me that you were there to steal my face."

The heat of Gabriel's stare burns. But I don't acknowledge him.

Whip shakes his head. "You two hooked up. Of course."

Killian scoffs. I don't dare check to see what Gabriel thinks.

"No," Jax says. "We had vodka tonics with lime and a few laughs about ridiculous people who would pay thousands for a juicy shot of someone famous." His soft smile returns. "Sophie didn't mind that I basically said her job was stupid—"

"It is," Killian cuts in.

We ignore him.

"She needed money to pay off school loans and rent, and we agreed there were worse ways to get it."

"There are?" Killian asks, still disgruntled.

I don't blame him. He's the one who found Jax. The band broke up for a year after Jax's suicide attempt. I doubt I would feel very charitable toward anyone who'd put my pain out in the world.

Jax levels him with a look, though. "Of course there are. And you know it." His eyes find me again. "You remember what I told you then?"

Oh, hell. A lump fills my throat, and I swallow convulsively. Gabriel's frowning as if he might soon explode. His gaze pins me to the spot, but he doesn't speak. None of them do. They're waiting for my answer.

My voice is weak and raspy. "You said… You said… Shit…" I look away, my voice breaking.

"Come to my room tonight," Jax says for me, "and I'll give you something big to sell."

"Fucking hell," Rye mutters.

"God damn it, Jax," Killian snaps.

Because they understand. Finally. I do too. But I didn't then.

My vision blurs, and I blink rapidly, taking a deep breath. "I thought you were just messing with me, and then you gave me a room key." A watery laugh escapes me. "And then I thought you wanted to hook up."

The scoff of disdain from Gabriel lands like a spear in my side. I can't look at him now. Maybe not ever again.

"I know you did, honey," Jax says gently. "And now you know; I was counting on you to show up."

"Why?" I whisper. "Why me?"

He shrugs. "I figured, she's a nice girl. Too nice for her shit job. She needs money. And I won't be here so…why not go out with a good deed?"

Killian lurches to his feet, knocking over his chair. He stalks out of the room without another word. Libby soon follows with a muttered, "I'll talk to him."

The ensuing silence is heavy, and I want to hunch inward, run away. But I can't hide from my mistakes. I tried that before. It didn't work.

"I'm so sorry," I rasp. "That night—it was the worst night of my life. Worst thing I've ever done."

Jax shakes his head. "You were doing your job—"

"No!" I grit my teeth. "No, I was selling short my humanity and yours. I should have dropped my camera and helped. I should have done anything other than take those pictures and let them get out."

"We've all done things we regret," Jax says. "I just want you and everyone else to know I don't hold it against you. I'm cool with you working with us now."

God. I don't deserve his calm acceptance.

"Stay." Whip's face is pale, but he leans forward and nods as if coming to a decision. "Jax is right. And you're obviously good at what you do or Brenna wouldn't have brought you here."

"Yeah," Rye puts in. "It will be good for all of us. And for you too. Cathartic, you know?"

Who are these guys? Really. I expected to be egged at this point.

"Look, I'm cool with this." Rye stands. "I hope you join us. Anything that shakes things up can't be bad."

Whip stands as well. "Killian will come around. Jax will talk to him."

They both come shake my hand. "Sorry for the drama," Whip says with a wink. "But it's kind of hard to escape around here."

Jax makes his way over to me as Whip and Rye leave. His warm hand rests on my shoulder. "I'm glad I got to talk to you. I always meant to track you down and apologize. It was shitty to use you that way."

"I'm so glad you made it," I say in a rush. "That you're healthy and here."

His smile is tight but friendly. "Whatever you decide, come hang out with us later tonight. We'll have fun, Soph. Trust me."

He gives me a kiss on the cheek and Brenna a look I can't interpret before leaving.

"This is a mistake," Gabriel says as soon as the door closes.

I flinch, and he meets my eyes. Everything I saw in him before is gone. He's ice now—so solid, so polished, I'm surprised I don't see my reflection in his skin. His voice is strong but monotone, just another day at the office.

"You regret your actions. Jax takes responsibility for his part. None of that matters when it comes to this tour."

"I'm not following you, Scottie," Brenna says. Mostly, she's been quiet, letting everyone talk. But there's steel in her spine now.

He sits back in his chair, setting one ankle on his bent knee. Such cool repose, as if he isn't kicking me to the curb when he promised he wouldn't interfere.

"We've only just reached the point where the band is a fully functioning unit again. They're finally burying old wounds. You bring this element of mistrust into the mix, and you're risking all of that."

"I'm a person, not an element." I shouldn't let him see that I'm upset, but fucking hell, I am. I thought we had at the very least a small glimmer of mutual…I don't know, regard. I held him in his darkest hour, and now I'm a fucking element? "And if the guys are cool with it, why should you protest?"

"Because it is my job to think rationally when they either cannot or will not." He looks at me as though I'm nothing more than a piece furniture in the room. "This is a matter of business, Ms. Darling. Nothing personal."

"Bullshit. Everything is personal. Especially business. You judge a person and decide whether you trust them enough to work with them or not." A shudder of rage and hurt runs through me. "You've made your decision, Mr. Scott. Don't weaken it by pretending it's nothing personal."

God, he doesn't flinch, doesn't blink. Just sits there, facing me head on with those eyes the color of glacial ice.

"I'm sorry, Ms. Darling."

"Yeah," I say. "I bet you are."

If I hadn't been glaring right back at him, I'd have missed the tremor that flickers along the corner of his mouth. With languid grace, he rises and buttons his suit jacket. Giving me a short nod, he leaves the room without a backward glance.

"Shit," Brenna says when he's gone. "That went well."

I stare at the door. "I'm sorry for wasting your—"

"You're hired, Sophie."

My head whips around, and I'm pretty sure my mouth falls open.

Brenna gives me a long, hard look. "This is the chance of a lifetime. You know it. I know it. Don't you dare puss out because of a little adversity. Trust me, I speak from experience when I say you'll regret it."

I could answer a dozen different ways, from angry to self-pitying. Outside this jewel box of a room, the famous and powerful are having coffee and plotting their lives. I'm in London, being offered the chance to tour Europe with one of my favorite bands. It will be awkward, and facing Gabriel again will definitely be its own brand of torture.

Life in New York would be easier. Familiar.

Not personal, my ass.

"Fuck it," I say. "I'm in."

GABRIEL
5

IT TAKES me two minutes and thirty-six seconds to exit the conference room, leave the hotel, and walk to the end of the block. I know because I count each second. I walk steadily and with purpose.

And if my hand trembles a little, no one fucking sees it because I've tucked it into my pocket. Problem solved.

Lesson one in business: to every problem there is a solution.

Lesson two: never get emotional.

Never get emotional.

The instant I turn the corner, my control starts to crumble. I bobble a step. A red haze falls over my vision. Another step and I'm panting. I spy a newspaper stand and suddenly I'm kicking it.

"Fucking shit!" I give the metal stand a rough slap as well before I begin pacing.

"I had the same reaction, dude."

The sound of Killian's voice stops me cold. He's lounging against a cheese monger's shop and drinking a carryout coffee. "I kicked the shit out the garbage bin there."

Next to the newsstand there's a dented bin. I snort, though I can't truly find the humor in anything. "Of all the garbage bins and newsstands..."

"You're the one who walked to my spot," Killian points out.

I look down the street. "Where's Libby?"

"Giving me time to cool off." Killian laughs without amusement. "I'm not allowed to return to the hotel until I'm ready to apologize to the pap."

"Her name is Sophie." *Don't think of her. Don't fucking do it.* But it's impossible to blot out what I've said to her. Rage flows through me again. I grind my teeth and count to ten. Slowly.

Lesson three: Act on behalf of your client, not yourself. I handled the situation like I've always done—decided what was best for the band. Protected them first and foremost, putting aside personal needs.

Bullshit. Everything is personal.

Oh, how I know it now, chatty girl.

It should have been a simple thing, dealing with this issue. I barely know the woman. The lines of risk are clear. She could easily upset the balance we've struggled to restore.

That didn't explain why each word out of my mouth to her felt like fucking acid on my tongue. Or the way the hurt in her eyes had nearly made me physically ill. I'd barely managed to get through that interview from hell without punching a wall.

And then I'd simply left her. Walked away without a backward glance, leaving her feeling like scum, as though she were unworthy of any of us.

"Cockless git," I mutter, fighting the urge to kick something again.

"You have to find a way to forgive Jax." Killian takes a sip of coffee. "That's what Libby told me. I thought I had. But he keeps finding ways to piss me off."

Hands low on my hips, I study the scuff on my shoe. I don't bother correcting Killian's assumption. I'm not angry at Jax for arranging that Sophie arrive on the scene. I understand him. He wanted a testament to what he'd done. Or perhaps he didn't really want to die at all, but for someone to find him before it was too late.

I can't be sure, but I'm not going to rail at him for being human. A sigh escapes me, and I run a hand over my face. I haven't had a proper sleep in weeks, and exhaustion is catching up on me. Around us, Londoners make their way down the street toward the nearby Tube station. It's already overcast and chilly.

A mother pushes her child along in a gray pram, and stops at a bookstore window. There used to be a picture of my mother kneeling beside me in my pram. I was probably two, and even then I had a surly expression. But my mother beamed at me as though I were her world.

I rub a hand across my aching chest.

Jax, Killian, Whip, and Rye gave me friendship when I had none, a family when mine had gone. They gave my life purpose—a job I love and experiences few people on Earth ever have. In return, I vowed that I'd always protect their interests. I've done a shit job the last few years. I can do better. I *must* do better.

I don't want to think about Sophie Darling. But she's infected my brain. The sound of her teasing laugh haunts me. The pained shimmer in her brown eyes as I called her "a mistake" guts me.

She'd been responsible for exposing Jax's most private moment and the lowest point in his life. Countless times I've cursed the bottom-feeding scum who took those photos. To realize it had been Sophie, the woman I let hold me and ease my fears in a way I hadn't allowed since my mum died, is more than disappointing. She'd knocked me on my arse in that interview.

I start to pace, unable to stand still.

Killian watches me, his head swiveling back and forth as he tracks my movements. "You're not going to need us to set up a fight, are you?"

I cut him a glare. "I'm not as bad off as all that."

He holds up a hand. "I was only asking."

When Kill John first started, I paid for my suits by winning underground fights. A bit of an oxymoron, granted, being a brawler in order to dress like a gentleman. As the years went on, I fought when I was so tense only the sweet release found in sex or pummeling the shit out of another person would do. In truth, sex has never cut it for me the way raw pain does.

"I'm fine," I say, waving him off.

"Brenna gonna hire her?" Killian asks me.

"Of course. She put Ms. Darling in first class. Brenna wouldn't have bothered if she wasn't planning to hire the her."

At this, Killian grins. "Bet that pissed you off, having to sit beside someone."

I grunt, unable to tell him the truth. Best fucking flight of my life.

He starts to laugh. "Damn, Brenna is evil."

I think of all the shit Sophie gave me. A smile tugs at my mouth but promptly dies when my brain reminds me that I just broke any hope of her wanting to be near me again.

"Fucking hell." I pin Killian with a glare. "She's hired. We both know this. Regardless of her past, I've seen her portfolio and her social media work. She's good. And the rest of the boys want her along as well."

"Shit." Killian looks off.

"You'll be working closely with her." Something stirs in my chest at the thought of seeing Sophie day in and day out. I push it down deep. "Which means you will treat her with the bloody respect a trained professional deserves."

"Yes, sir." Killian gives me a salute.

I'm already turning back toward the hotel. "We have a FaceTime meeting with a new sponsor at four."

"What sponsor?" he calls back.

"Some guitar pick company," I say over my shoulder.

"Damn it, Scottie, ten years and you still can't remember which picks I prefer? Details, man."

I know which one, but it's just too easy to aggravate Killian. "A sponsor is a sponsor. Don't be late."

Halfway back to the hotel, I text Brenna.

GS: I assume Ms. Darling is staying on?

She answers quick enough: *Yes. No thanks to you. Next time, discuss your concerns about my staff in private.*

I bypass a man with two poodles who sniff at my ankles.

GS: Understood. Where is she now?

Brenna: Why?

My jaw muscles pulse.

GS: I want to welcome her aboard to show no hard feelings.

Brenna: You can text her for that.

I really loathe when Brenna is pissed at me. Life becomes that much harder, and she is an expert at making me work for my transgressions.

GS: Did I happen to mention I'm meeting Ned later tonight?

Ned is a local promoter and a scummy little shit who has a propensity to hit on Brenna. Unfortunately, the man is also in charge of the best venues, and I have to deal with him whenever we tour London. Brenna doesn't.

GS: I was thinking of inviting him out with us instead.

I almost smile, imagining Brenna fuming right now. Little dots appear and then her answer.

Brenna: Asshole. Jules took her out to lunch at that gastropub down the street.

GS: A little early for lunch, isn't it?

Brenna: Seriously? Translation: she took her to have a much needed drink on account of you and Killian acting like dicks.

Ah, guilt. I had become unacquainted with the emotion over the past decade. Experiencing it now, I cannot say I enjoy the sensation. At all. Tucking my phone in my pocket, I pivot and head back down the street.

It isn't hard to locate Sophie and Jules in the pub. They're bright spots of color in a sea of old wood paneling. Tucked away at a corner table, the two women have their heads close together, Sophie's white blond hair like moonbeams besides the full flower of Jules's tight fuchsia curls.

Their backs are to me as they nurse pints of Guinness—the breakfast of champions, as Rye often lovingly refers to the rich stout.

"I'm not gonna lie," Jules is saying. "If you're expecting praise or kind words from him, it'll never happen. He's just not that kind of boss."

"He isn't going to be my boss at all," Sophie mutters, taking a long drink. Creamy white foam lingers on the soft curve of her upper lip before she licks it away, and my cock grows heavy.

Hell.

"Don't kid yourself," Jules says. "He's everyone's boss. Even the guys. What Scottie says goes. But don't worry. He's not a tyrant. He's just…"

I can't help but lean in a little, wondering what she'll say. They haven't seen me yet, and I'm not about to make my presence known *now*.

"Exacting," Jules settles on.

Sophie snorts inelegantly. "He's an arrogant assmunch."

Lovely.

"And why the hell does everyone call him Scottie? The name doesn't fit him at all. Beelzebub would be better." Sophie spreads her hands in exasperation, and I struggle not to snort.

Jules laughs into her glass. "Girl, I thought the same thing. According to roadie legend, Killian and Jax came up with the name when they were all starting out. It's some joke about *Star*

Trek."

"I was preparing to study engineering," I say, startling them both.

They whirl in their seats, mouths agape.

"Scotty was the Enterprise's engineer," I continue, rounding the table to take a seat. "Star Trek was on, and Rye pointed out that I shared a last name with Scotty. That was that. Little bastards started calling me Scottie, but with an *-ie* so people would be able to tell us apart."

I give the women a dry look as if the whole business is tiresome, but the dark truth is that I never tried to put a stop to the name. It had cemented my inclusion in their group, and I'd never been a part of one before. It was the first time anyone had thought to give me a nickname that wasn't meant as an insult.

The second time I was given such a nickname was on a plane with the gorgeous, chatty girl who currently sits glaring at me as if I've spit in her beer.

"Sophie. Jules." I give them each a nod.

The freckles scattered across Jules's cheeks start to stand out in sharp relief as her pale brown skin goes ashy gray. "I... ah... That is...I was explaining to Sophie that..."

I put her out of her misery. "It's all right if you want to flee. I won't hold it against you."

Jules jumps up, grabbing the massive green hobo bag she's constantly hauling around.

Sophie sits straight, her brows rising. "Hey! She doesn't have to go anywhere. In fact, you should go." She points her finger at me like a weapon.

"No, no," Jules says, already backing away from the table. "He's right. I totally want to flee."

And she does, nearly creating a breeze in her haste. Sophie sits back with a huff, crossing her arms over her ample chest. "God, it's like you're Darth Vader or something."

I missed you. The unwanted thought doesn't even make sense; it's been less than an hour since I last saw her. But that doesn't change the feeling that I've been granted clemency just by sitting here with her.

"We've already established that I'm the engineer of this production," I say lightly. "And you're mixing space dramas."

Her nose wrinkles, and she looks away, giving me her profile. I use the moment to steal her Guinness and take a sip. It's room temperature, thick and dark and perfect. Truly the breakfast of champions.

"Hey!" she snatches the glass from me. "Get your own."

She makes a point of wiping the rim with a soggy cocktail napkin.

"Do you fear I might have cooties?"

"I'm surprised you even know that word."

"I know quite a few."

I've missed sparring with her most of all. Sophie is…fun. When was the last time I had any fun?

"Which reminds me…" I lean in close. "While I do enjoy anal play with a woman now and then, I have never munched an ass."

Sophie chokes on her beer, sending droplets of it across the battered table, as her cheeks flame scarlet. Trying not to grin in victory, I hand her another napkin.

She glares at me as she dabs her chin. "If you're here to try to talk me into going home, don't bother. I'm staying, and you can't do anything about it." She lifts her chin as if to say, *So there!*

I sit back in my chair. "You were right, you know." When her brow wrinkles, I go on. "Business is personal. I simply hadn't thought of it as such until you put it that way."

Her expression goes darker. I nudge the beer glass out of her reach, and she rolls her eyes, but there's a reluctant smile on her lips. It strikes me that my day is already better just for seeing it. *Weakness.* I don't want any. But some things are stronger.

Honor. Honesty. Need.

"I have hated those pictures and what they represent as much as I hate what happened to Jax," I tell her quietly.

Anger melts off her face, and she stares at me with wide, pained eyes.

"No," I correct. "I hated them *more.* They created a monument to that ugliness. That..." My throat closes, and I have to clear it. "Pain."

"I'm sorry," she whispers. "You'll never know how sorry."

"I believe you. I know what it is to lose yourself in a job. We were all spinning out of control before Jax. There were days I'd wake up and not remember what country we were in. Because everything was a blur of having fun and believing the crap lines people fed us. I understand the lies you tell yourself to get through the day."

"I can't imagine that of you."

"Chatty girl, you spin castles on social media. I spin them for the music business. The suits, the mannerisms, the whole fucking façade is part of the arsenal. Back in that room, you saw it full force." My finger touches a drop of beer. "I reacted out of an old anger."

When she answers, it's soft and hesitant. "Are you sure it's old anger and not fresh?"

I meet her gaze and am hit anew with that strange punch of sensation just beneath my ribs. Pain, resentment, remorse, tenderness, it's all jumbled together, making it difficult to settle on one emotion. I want to tell her I'm sorry for hurting her. I want to send her away so I don't have to experience this discomfort.

She is dangerous because I cannot control her. And she is utterly beautiful, like molten glass that tempts you to touch even though you know you'll be burned.

But for all that, there is one emotion I do not feel. "I am not angry with you."

When she nods, an awkward jerk of her little chin, I reach into my billfold and pull out a few pounds. My fingers are unsteady as I drop the money on the table. "Do the tour," I tell her. "I will not stand in your way but welcome you as a valuable asset to the band."

Then I flee, just as desperately as Jules did minutes before. Because I've just consigned myself to months of hell and temptation.

SOPHIE

WE'RE STAYING in London for a week, so I work with the guys, combing through their social media and making adjustments. In other words, adding myself as admin to all their accounts and acting as them from time to time.

And I take pictures. All the time. It isn't difficult with Kill John as the subject matter. All the guys are exceedingly photogenic. I've often wondered about fame. It's rare to find famous people who aren't photogenic, even if they aren't classically attractive. Why is that? Is it the gloss of fame that makes them more compelling? Or is it something within them that draws the eye and facilitates fame?

Whatever the case, shooting moments with Kill John is a pleasure. Not that it's without a few struggles.

Killian is still fairly pissy with me. He gives me a glare as I take a picture of him laughing with Jax while they work through a chord progression in a studio they've rented for the week. "Do you mind?"

"Nope." I snap another shot. "In fact, if you want to give me a big ol' smile and ham it up, even better."

"Jesus. You're relentless. Go away."

"Kills," Jax says with a sigh. "Just fucking let it go." He turns to me and sticks out his tongue, crossing his green eyes.

I dutifully take the pic.

"Excellent." Lowering my camera, I sit on the studio floor. "Look, none of us can change our pasts. All we have is our present. Like it or not, you two are the band's front men, which means you lead by example. People are dying to see you and Jax together again and happy. They need that reassurance."

"And you think taking a few pictures of us doing whatever is going to make everything better?" Killian asks. His tone isn't snide, but he's clearly dubious.

"You tell me," I counter. "You've been in this business longer than I have. Do you think public image matters?"

For a second he just stares at me. But then he huffs out a laugh and smiles. When he does, it's fairly breathtaking. Killian James is extremely hot. Luckily I'm immune to hot men. Well, most of them.

"All right," Killian says, breaking into my thoughts of uptight managers. "I'm being a dick. It matters, even if I don't like it."

"There. Was that so hard?" I ask.

He leans in, cocking his head as if he's going to tell me a secret. "You know, I'm not actually comfortable being an asshole to women."

"Really?" I say, biting the corner of my lip to keep from smiling. "But you do it so well."

Jax laughs so hard he rocks back, clutching his Telecaster to his stomach. From the corner of my eye, I see Gabriel's head lift and turn our way. He's in an adjoining studio, talking to Whip as he practices his drums.

All the studios are connected by glass walls that surround the production booth. I've been aware of his presence the whole time, but didn't think he was aware of mine. He certainly can't hear us, and yet he's noticed Jax laughing. Then again, it's becoming more and more apparent that Gabriel keeps track of everything and everyone.

Killian laughs as well before nudging my foot with the toe of his boot. "You're a hard woman to remain pissy with, Sophie."

"Remember that when I follow you like a tick on a dog's butt."

He laughs again, a deep rumble of sound. "You sound like Libby."

"Uh-oh," Jax says, picking up his beer. "He just gave you his highest compliment. Watch out, you'll soon be subject to noogies and pranks like the rest of us."

I feign horror, but inside a soft warmth swims through me. I have many friends and acquaintances. Meeting new people has never been my problem; it isn't hard when you're a natural-born talker. But I've never been a part of a close-knit family of friends. Maybe I won't really be accepted by these guys either. Time will tell. But I want to be.

It is an odd thing to discover I'm lonely, despite never truly being alone. But I am. I want someone to know the real me, not the shiny shell I show the world.

I leave Killian and Jax to their practice and move on to Rye, and then Whip. After I'm done with photos, I upload them to my computer and pick out the ones I want to use for today's social media.

Time passes quickly, and then we're off to check out the venue for Tuesday night's opening show. The guys are all restless energy. I swear they must be powered by music, because the more they talk about it, the more they play, the more fueled they seem to be.

Me, on the other hand? I'm still feeling the effects of jet lag —I haven't had a true night's sleep since I got here—and the lack of lunch. When did we skip lunch, anyway? How did I miss that?

My stomach growls in protest, and I try to ignore it because no one appears to be ready to leave. I take a break, sitting on the stage and leaning against a set of unplugged amps. My head hurts, and I'd love to nap. Only napping kind of blows here too. I just can't settle down when I get back to my room.

My stomach growls again, and I swear it's started to eat itself because my insides clench in pain. I fumble with the latch on my camera case and curse under my breath. I'm in hangry territory here. Soon I'll be a snarling mess. And these boys don't seem to fucking care that it's been hours since we last ate—

"Here." A boxed sandwich from Pret A Manger is thrust under my nose. A second later, Gabriel sits next to me on the stage.

I'm caught between snatching the sandwich and admiring the effortless way he moves. *Which is just ridiculous,* I grump silently, sinking my teeth into honey wheat bread. Lusting over the way a man moves. What next? Writing poetry about the scruff along his jaw?

Sadly, I could. I really could.

The first bite of food hits my mouth, and I sigh in relief. "Thank you," I mumble between chews.

"It's nothing." His shoulder lifts with a light shrug as he surveys the stadium.

He's brought me egg salad with arugula. My favorite. I clutch the sandwich in my hands like it's a precious gift before taking another bite. And another. Damn, I was hungry. "It's something."

"Don't talk with your mouth full." He pulls a bottled water, covered in condensation, from a bag and twists the top off before handing it to me. "God forbid you choke on your food and are unable to talk any more."

The water is ice cold, and I feel it going down, spreading through me. Sweet hydration.

"How did you know my favorite sandwich?"

He keeps his gaze distant, but his chin lowers a bit. "It's my business to know everything about my people."

His people. His flock.

"I don't see you handing out food to anyone else."

He finally turns my way. Brilliant blue eyes crinkle at the corners with sardonic humor, the curve of his lip tilting slightly. As always, my breath catches. The crinkles deepen.

"No one gets quite as *hangry* as you do, Darling. It's for the good of all to keep you fed."

I suspect he calls me by my last name as a taunt, but he always says it as though it's a caress. I shake the feeling off with a roll of my shoulders. "I don't even care if you're insulting me. It's true. I was about to eat my own hand."

"We wouldn't want that." His arm barely brushes mine. "We need you to work."

My cell phone rings. "Hold that thought," I say as I answer my phone. "Yellow?"

"'Yellow'? That's how you answer your phone? It's your mother, by the way."

I roll my eyes. "Yes, Mom, I'm familiar with your voice."

"Well, you never know," she replies with an expansive sigh. "It's been so long since you called, you might have forgotten."

Smiling, I set my sandwich down. "Mom, you could make guilt an Olympic sport."

"I try, angel pudding. Now, tell me all about your new job. Are they nice to you? Do you like it?"

This is not the conversation I want to have with Gabriel and his bat-power hearing in close proximity, not to mention his eyes are on me in clear amusement. But I can't exactly say that. "Of course they're nice to me. I wouldn't stay if they weren't."

Not exactly true. I've had some shit jobs with even shittier bosses over the years, but I'm turning over a new leaf: accept nothing but what brings me joy from now on.

"And I love it, Ma. Truly."

"Well, that's good. And those band boys?" Her voice dips. "Are they as sexy as they look on TV?"

I told her what I was doing via text. But I hadn't expected her to know about Kill John. I make a gagging noise into the phone. "Seriously? You're trying to scar me for life, aren't you? You do not need to be asking about sexy rockers."

At my side, Gabriel snorts and takes a bite of my sandwich. I snatch it back, giving him a side glare as my mom keeps talking.

"Please," she drawls. "If I didn't like sex, you'd have never been—"

"La, la, la… Not hearing you!"

Gabriel chuckles, so low only I can hear it. But it does illicit things to me, sending tingles where I don't need them.

"Born!" Mom finishes emphatically.

"Mom."

"Don't whine, Sophie. It's unflattering."

A click sounds, and my father's voice filters in. "My baby girl doesn't whine."

"See? Daddy knows," I put in, grinning. It's an old game I play with them, and I don't care if I'm twenty-five; it feels good to act like a kid. Safe and secure.

Here I am, sitting on a stage, about to go on a European tour with the world's biggest band. But for a few minutes, I can just be Sophie Darling, only daughter of Jack and Margaret Darling.

"You spoil her, Jack," my mother is saying. "I have to counteract the ill effects with doses of hard realism."

I am essentially my mother—only younger and with ever-changing hair color. I have to cut my parents off before they can get going. Their back and forth can go on forever, and I have a hot, nosy, sort-of boss to eat lunch with—something that suddenly fills me with bright anticipation.

"Look, my lunch break is about to end. Let me call you tonight when we stop for the day."

"All right, honey," my dad says. "Just remember, men love women who play hard to get. Extremely hard to get."

I don't need to look over to know Gabriel is rolling his eyes.

"And yet you and Mom started as a one-night stand..."

"Damn it, Margaret. You tell this child too much."

Still laughing, we say our goodbyes, and as soon as I hang up, Gabriel speaks again. "And now your slightly unhinged verbal onslaughts become clear."

"Eavesdropping is rude, you know..."

"I would have had to cover my ears to avoid overhearing that ruckus." His gaze slides over me with clear amusement. "They talk as loudly as you do."

"Shouldn't that be the other way around?"

"Details."

I smile, despite myself, and give his shoulder a nudge with my own. It's like trying to move a brick wall.

Gabriel takes my sandwich again, and because I'm feeling generous, I leave him to it and take the other half instead. He finishes his side in two neat bites, then wipes his mouth with a napkin.

"Your parents are lovely, chatty girl."

Warmth floods my chest. "Thank you. I miss them."

He nods in empathy. "Do you not see them often? You talked before of living off ramen..."

"I love my parents," I cut in. "And I see them when I can. But there's also only so much I can take. They're...slightly suffocating in their attempts to watch out for me."

I lift my phone and scroll through pictures until I find the one I want. It's an older one of me, smiling wide and pained as I sit between my parents on a couch. I hand it to Gabriel.

He studies the picture for a long moment. "You look a bit like both of them."

"Yes." I know this well. I have my mom's dark brown eyes, cheeky smile, and pert nose. I have my dad's bone structure and wavy, dark blond hair. I look down at Mom, her caramel colored hair stick straight. I've always wanted her hair too. "This picture is of me at my college graduation party."

He quirks a brow, waiting for me to explain further.

I shake my head, my lips pursing. "It was a kegger. They were the only parents there."

A short, shocked laugh bursts from him before he swallows it. "That explains your knickers-in-a-twist expression."

"Ha. That expression was me plotting their untimely and slowly torturous deaths."

He makes a noise of amusement.

"They've always been like that—really, really involved. Mom's half Filipino, half Norwegian American. She used to bring me care packages: big trays of lumpia and lox."

"Lumpia?"

"Filipino spring rolls, basically. Which are delicious. Paring them with lox? Not so much." I make a face. "And then there's Dad. This big, goofy, half Scottish American, half Armenian sociology professor. He used to tease me, calling me a UN baby while explaining the intricate paths of my heritage to bored friends." I sigh. "So, they're best taken in small doses."

"You're loved," he says gently. "That's a wonderful thing."

"It is." I look out over the wide stadium, watching the roadies pack up instruments as Kill John breaks for the day. "And that was also the problem. I didn't want them to know I was failing. Or what I did to make a living. I wasn't lying when I said I was ashamed of my work. It's only within this past year that I've gotten back to wanting to see them, you know?"

Slowly he nods, a frown pulling at his mouth.

"I'm proud now," I tell him quietly. "I love that Mom is a closet Kill John fan."

"Shall I send your mom a signed picture of the band?" A gleam lights Gabriel's eye.

"God, do *not* encourage her. Next thing you know, she'll be here, and I'll lose my mind."

"It almost sounds worth it."

"I'll sic her on you," I warn. "You're much prettier than any of the guys. She'll follow you around, plying you with food and pinching your butt when you're not looking."

"She's married," he says, as if that matters.

"And has a weakness for pretty men. Go figure," I deadpan.

He makes a face. "Men aren't pretty."

"There are many types of pretty, sunshine." I count them on my fingers. "Pretty girls, so cute and sweet. Pretty women, who are rarely prostitutes with hearts of gold, despite movie claims. Pretty boys, attractive but basically you just want to pinch their cheeks. And pretty men." I give him a pointed look. "You know, the kind often mistaken for internationally renowned models—"

The rat bastard shoves the sandwich in my mouth. "Be a good chatty girl and eat up."

I take a hard bite and slowly chew, my glare promising dire retribution. But inside, my blood feels like champagne in my veins, bubbling and fizzing with happiness. I'm having fun. Too much, because I don't want it to end.

Perhaps he is too, because his pleased expression grows. He sits with me in companionable silence as I devour the rest

KRISTEN CALLIHAN

my lunch and drink my water. When I'm done, he hands me a napkin and packs up the trash, stuffing it into the bag he brought it in. It's all done so simply, neat and quiet. Nothing that would draw attention to the act. It's as if he's always taken care of me—no big deal, just part of his job.

And yet it's all a lie. Gabriel Scott might know everything about everyone under his management, but to them he's the unapproachable shadow in the corner of the room. He likes it that way. The fact that he's taking care of me spreads warmth through my chest.

Before he can get away, I lean in and press a soft kiss to his cheek. He flinches but looks at me through lowered lids as I ease away. "Thank you for lunch, Gabriel. I feel much better now."

His gaze moves to my mouth, and my lips swell and part as if he's licked them. He draws in a deep breath, letting it out slowly, and the tip of his thumb finds the corner of my lip. The touch sizzles in a tight line straight to my sex. Everything there clenches, hot and sweet.

"You've egg on your face." His voice is a rasp laced with dry humor. He flashes me a quick, evil grin, his thumb lingering before he backs away, hopping neatly off the stage. "Back to work, Darling."

I smile with false levity, though my body has been reduced to a hot, quivering wreck. "Yes, dear."

A couple stagehands lift their heads at hearing me call the great Scottie *dear* and gape at me in horror. Which means I'm the only one who sees Gabriel miss a step. He covers it quickly, but it's enough to keep me grinning for the rest of the day.

GABRIEL
6

THERE IS a game I play with myself: delayed gratification. If there's something I really want, I hold off on having it. My first nice car, I waited for a year, told myself it didn't matter if I had the car or not; my life wouldn't be any better or worse for purchasing it. I indulged only in glancing at pictures of the Aston Martin DB9 now and then to feed my need. I let myself pick a color—slate gray with red brake pads—and then finally, finally, when the year was out, I bought the car. By that time, the thrill had dampened, my need for the car muted. I had conquered my desire.

I've done the same with every nonessential need in my life: cars, houses, a small Singer-Sargent painting I coveted. And it has served me well. When you do not yearn for anything, nothing can let you down. And I know full well this stems from losing my mother at an early age. I do not need to sit on a couch to know I use control to protect myself. And I don't give a flying fuck what it says about me. It works, end of story.

I tell myself this again as I prowl my living room. The house is silent around me. Too silent. I can hear myself think, and who the bloody hell wants to hear himself at one in the morning?

I should go to bed, but I can't sleep. As in literally cannot fall asleep. I've been this way since arriving in London. Awake at night, exhausted come morning. In short: I'm in sleep-deprived hell.

Swearing, I take another turn around my room like some sort of deranged character in an Austen novel. Only I'm alone. I'm in the first house I bought myself. Eight million pounds to secure a private sanctuary in Chelsea. I love every inch of the place, every floorboard and old plaster wall. And yet standing in the middle of a room I paid a decorator to furnish, it feels like a tomb.

I should call one of the guys. Someone must be up; they're all night owls. But I don't want to talk to them. I want someone else entirely.

"Hell." I pull at my collar. The cashmere lays light and warm on my skin, but I feel suffocated all the same.

She'll be up. I know it. I can feel it in my bones.

It's so silent, the sound of my feet striding across the floor echoes. I pick up my phone before I can stop myself. *Don't do it. Nothing good can come of engaging. She is an employee.*

I put the phone down and circle the room three more times before my feet take me right back to the sideboard where it lies. My hand hovers over the damn thing. *Just let it go. She'll read too much into it.*

"Bugger. Bugger. Bugger." I grip the back of my neck where the muscles clench in angry protest.

In my head, I hear her light laugh. I see her face and the way the bridge of her nose wrinkles just a bit when she grins. My gaze drifts around the room, with its comfortable furniture and pictures of me and the guys on the wall. Despite the decorator, I had my say in every design decision made here. This house is a reflection of me at my most personal. What would she say about it? Would she find it cold or welcoming?

And why do I give a bloody damn?

"Because you're finally cracked, mate." And talking to myself as well. Perfect. Just perfect.

SOPHIE

MY ROOM IS SO CUTE, I'm still half-convinced I'm dreaming. Cream, white-paneled walls, earthy sisal rugs, a four-poster spindle bed. There's even a clawfoot Victorian tub opposite the bed. It's too romantic, really. The kind of setup where I'd be bathing in a seductive manner while my man reclined on the bed to watch until he couldn't stand the torture any longer and crawled in to join me. We'd make a mess of the floor, spilling water, laughing while we fucked.

A nice picture.

Only I'm alone in the dark beneath crisp linens, utterly awake and watching the lights of passing cars below trail across the ceiling. I should be sleeping, but jet lag has snuck upon me with a terrible vengeance. I'm so freaking awake, my body hums with the need to get up. Bad idea. Sleep is needed.

I'm concentrating so hard on trying to fall asleep, the ping of my phone startles me. Fumbling, I reach for it on my nightstand. I'm not even sure who I expected to be texting me at 2 am. But I certainly didn't consider *him*.

Sunshine: If you don't sleep now, you're setting yourself up for even worse jet lag.

I immediately bite back a ridiculous grin, as if he'll see me through the phone.

Me: If you're so worried about my sleep, you shouldn't text me in the middle of the night.

He pings back an answer.

Sunshine: Small chance of waking you. I knew you'd be up.

Me: Oh? You psychic?

Sunshine: No. Just awake as well. And remembering your inability to calm down.

Me: False! I can do calm!!!!!

Sunshine: As exhibited by your subtle use of exclamation points.

I laugh in the dark of the room, drawing my knees up to my chest. My heartbeat has accelerated. I'm giddy like a damn schoolgirl. And isn't that a bitch?

He'd stuck me firmly in employee land, then he brought me a sandwich. I'm not even sure he trusts me, and yet here he is, texting me in the middle of the night. Maybe he's lonely. Or maybe he's looking for a hookup. He's nothing like the men I've been with before, so I can't be sure. But I can't pretend I don't enjoy flirting with him, even if it ends up leading nowhere.

Me: Your sarcasm smells of slain interns' blood and the souls of missing record execs.

Sunshine: False. That is what I eat for breakfast. Keep up, Darling.

I laugh, though he can't hear me. I can almost see his expression, always deadpan but with that hint of crinkle at the corners of his eyes and full lips. That infinitesimal twitch of a smile most people clearly miss. The world fascinates Gabriel Scott, but he does a hell of a job pretending it doesn't. That much I know already.

Me: Aw…terms of endearment already?

Sunshine: It's your name.

Me: A convenient excuse.

Sunshine: A legitimate answer

Me: I've never had anyone call me by my last name. Should I call you by yours? Call you Scottie like the others do?

Sunshine: No.

I'm half teasing, because I don't want to call him Scottie. That's not his name to me. That's a stranger's name. But the emphatic force of his reply makes me wonder why he doesn't want me to use it, when everyone in his circle does. My thumb shakes a little as I tap out a reply, adopting a more serious tone, because really, what the hell am I doing flirting with the big boss?

Me: Well, you caught me. I can't sleep for shit. I'll have to live with the consequences.

Little dots form at the bottom of my phone screen. They disappear, then start up again. I wonder what the hell he's trying to write and if he's erasing his text.

I almost send him a message just to prod his ass into whatever it is he's trying to say, when his message finally pops up. And I gape. And gape. My heart stops and then picks up pounding. I'm not seeing things; it's there, clear as day:

Sunshine: Would you like to come over?

What. The. Hell?

I'm clearly stuck in shock mode too long because he texts in a barrage of tense explanations.

Sunshine: For tea.

Sunshine: To help you sleep.

Sunshine: I make good tea.

He makes tea? Gabriel I've-no-time-for-mere-mortals Scott actually makes tea? And drinks it? Shut the front door and call me Mama.

He's still texting.

Sunshine: Hell. Clearly sleep deprived.

Sunshine: Ignore request.

I type fast, putting the poor guy out of his misery.

Me: Where are you?

Me: Your house, I mean. Where is it?

He pauses. I know he's frowning at the phone. Probably has been for some time now. I bite back another smile.

Sunshine: A few blocks away. I could send a car.

Me: No. I'll walk.

Sunshine: You will not. I'll meet you.

My grin actually hurts my cheeks. I'm already out of the bed and scrambling for my jeans.

Me: *Okay. Where?*

Sunshine: *In front of your hotel. Ten minutes.*

"This is crazy. This is crazy," I mutter as I haul on my jeans and root around in my suitcase for a bra and top. I don't bother with the light as if it might kick-start my common sense and I'd text Gabriel back to say forget it. Because what the hell am I doing?

Does he really want to make me tea?

Yes. I know he does. Gabriel says what he means. He'll make me tea. But does he want more? Why invite me over?

"Stop thinking." Talking to myself can't be good. I slip on a loose, cream-colored long-sleeve top and toe into my Chucks.

I'm in the lobby before I realize I forgot to put on makeup or brush my hair.

"Shitballs."

The night concierge glances as me as if I'm off my nut, and I give him a tight smile before hurrying past. There's no time to go back to my room, anyway; I might miss Gabriel. He might chicken out if he has to wait.

I love the weather in London. I don't care if I'm the only one in the world who does. It's crisp and cool, with enough damp to make the ends of my hair frizz. And damn if there isn't an actual layer of fog creeping along the pavement. At two in the morning on a weekday, it's also fairly quiet, the streets abandoned.

My hands itch for my camera. That need grows when Gabriel walks out of the shadows, hands tucked deep in the pockets of his dark slacks. A gray cashmere sweater hugs his broad shoulders and big biceps. This man could sell boats to desert dwellers just by standing there, looking pretty.

He strolls toward me, his chin slightly down, peering at me from under those sweeping brows of his.

I almost swallow my tongue. "Hey, sunshine."

"Chatty girl."

He stops a few feet away, and we stare at each other. My heart is going like a metronome. His gaze flickers over me, then steadies on my face. I don't know what to say. *Take me now,* probably wouldn't be appropriate. Or smart.

His voice is low and aggravated. "I don't know why I'm here."

I should be offended. But since he's basically mirroring my own thoughts, I can't throw stones. I fight a smile instead; he's just so disgruntled.

"You texted, asked me to tea at two in the morning, then offered to pick me up."

His lips firm. "I don't...I don't socialize."

No shit. "Yet here we are."

Something sparks in his eyes. "Apparently so." He doesn't move. Another annoyed grunt tears from his throat. "I can't fucking sleep."

That he reached out to me because of it sends a rush of warmth through my chest. "So, let's go do something."

He obviously doesn't want to like that. His shoulders bunch beneath his sweater. "This isn't about sex."

I laugh. "I hope not. It would be awkward to have to turn you down."

Liar, liar, your knickers are on fire.

His lips twitch. "Sorry. I'm shite at this."

"Stating the obvious, sunshine."

With a snort, he turns his head, but I see the smile flit over his lips before he hides it. Then he nods sharply as if coming to some decision.

"Shall we?" He gestures toward the way he came with a tip of his chin.

We walk together in silence, close enough that our shoulders brush every few steps. I don't mind the silence. It gives me a place to hide my racing thoughts.

"Just around the next corner," he tells me in a low, gruff

voice.

"Are you really going to make me tea?"

"Haven't I said I would?" His gaze clashes with mine. "What's wrong with tea?"

"Nothing. It's just…" I search for the right word. "Grandmotherly."

He laughs at that, a short chuff of sound. "I'm English. Tea is the remedy for all our problems. Had a bad day? Have a cup of tea. Head hurt? Tea. Boss a wanker? Tea."

"Ah," I say with triumph. "So I do have a reason to drink tea."

Gabriel's step stutters, and he peers at me. "Are we agreeing that I am your boss? Or does your head hurt?"

"Don't know. Are you going to agree that you can be a wanker?" I smile so wide and fake my cheeks strain.

"A wanker who brings you lunch and is going to make you tea," he points out mildly before nudging me with his elbow.

I'm about to nudge him back when a sharp crack rents the air. It's so loud that I squeak, nearly jumping out of my shoes. Gabriel's hand touches mine in an abortive move. I don't know if he meant to grab on to me or he just flinched in surprise as well. Our fingers brush as light flashes across the sky. And then it opens up. Rain falls so swiftly and so very cold that I lose my breath.

We stand there, gaping at each other as the deluge swamps us. And then I laugh. Hard. Because what else can I do? Rain falls into my eyes, my mouth. I might drown. I'm sure as shit being drenched.

Gabriel is a statue, utterly gorgeous when wet, his black hair plastered to his head and rainwater sluicing over the sharp planes of his face, shining in the streetlight. He blinks, his long lashes spiky now.

"Of course," he says with a raspy huff of breath.

"You aren't going to blame this on me, are you?" I shout

over the roar of the rain, still laughing.

"Everything from the plane trip on out is because of you, Sophie Darling." He grabs my hand. "Come along, chatty girl, before we drown."

We make a run for it, scampering across the slick pavers that make up the London sidewalk. I'm laughing, breathless. He glances over his shoulder at me. Everything is a blur but his features, which are somehow crystal clear in the moment, and my heart turns over in the cage of my ribs when I see glee in his eyes.

He gives my hand another tug, my fingers warmly wrapped up in his. We turn a corner, and then it all goes south. Gabriel skids, his shoes sliding in the wet. One of his arms windmills, his grip on me flexing. My mouth forms the word *no!* but it comes out in a squawk.

He's going down, all that hard-bodied mass toppling, taking me with him. In my mind, it happens in slow motion. In reality, it's so fast we're both just flailing limbs and falling bodies.

I land on him, and my hip jars against his. He expels a hard *Oof!* before strong arms wrap around me, locking me into place on top of him.

Rain splatters around us, and he blinks up at me.

I pant, trying to get my breath. "Fuck."

My breath deserts me entirely when he flashes a grin, all white teeth and dazzling male beauty. "See?" he murmurs. "Your fault."

"Mine? *You* fell. You and those posh shoes."

"Posh," he scoffs. The world upends as he spins. My shoulders meet the wet pavement, rain gets in my eyes. Then he's over me. I part my thighs without thinking, and his hips move between them. I'm treated to that hard, long body pressing into mine, firm, warm, heavy. Thoughts scatter.

"You distracted me," he says, a heated glint in his eyes.

He's close enough that I feel the soft warmth of his breath, catch a whiff of his skin.

He cants his hips, and for one hot second, his cock is against my sex, grinding a sensitive spot that sends my body into overdrive. Heat sparks, my thighs spread wider, and I gasp. God, he's thick there, and I swear he's more than half-hard. Or maybe it's all in my head, because he's already jumping up in that lithe way of the very fit.

I'm rendered stupid on the ground, my breasts heavy, nipples tight, sex hot.

Gabriel's expression is back to bland, but there's something smug in the way he looks at me. *Fucker.* He extends a hand and hauls me up before I can even think.

"Now stop messing around." Yep, he's definitely smug, and laughing at me. "Tea won't make itself."

He tows me the rest of the way in a daze.

GABRIEL'S TOWNHOUSE IS GORGEOUS. No surprise there; this area of London is beautiful. His is fairly modest in size, compared to the others, and is tucked in along a quiet square, all the houses surrounding a small park with flickering Victorian gas lamps. Again, I yearn for my camera. I could happily spend all hours catching little slices of London.

He pushes past a waist-high iron gate and strides up the front walk. Inside, the floors are mellow, worn hardwood planks that have clearly withstood the passage of centuries, and I'm afraid to drip all over them. He doesn't appear to mind. Maybe because he's dripping all over them too.

After kicking off our shoes, we walk past brilliant white walls, eclectic mixes of framed art works—most of them black and white photos of the guys, backstage and on the road. I expect to find pictures of other famous people Gabriel has undoubtedly met, but there are none. Just his boys and

Brenna. All of it mixed up with images of other cities and sprawling countryside. There's even a small postcard from Brighton framed. I'd linger, but Gabriel hasn't slowed his brisk stride.

We head directly up a narrow set of stairs that creak under our weight. This floor is clearly the main level of the house. I spy a living room, a dining room that has been converted into a library, though it still has a dining table, and another lounge —all of it done in comfortable yet slightly funky furnishings. And then we're going up again.

My heartbeat goes erratic when I realize we're headed to the bedrooms. *Ridiculous.* Of course we are; we're dripping wet and in need of towels. My bare feet slap on the soft wood floors. Gabriel hasn't spoken a word, so I stare at his broad back and firm ass, his clothes clinging and covered in street muck. Doesn't mar the picture in the slightest. I'd title the shot: Dirty when wet.

Snorting softly to myself, I almost miss the fact that hardwood has given way to lush, fawn-colored carpeting. We're in his room.

I pause at the threshold. I can't help it; entering Gabriel's room feels like I've just been granted the way into El Dorado or discovered Atlantis. When he stops and quirks a brow in my direction, I tell him so.

He looks at me askance, as if he isn't quite sure what to make of me. "You have the wildest imagination of anyone I've ever met."

"Imagination. Right. I'd bet good money you're the only one who has ever been in here," I counter. "Tell me I'm wrong."

He offers a sly smile. "Wrong. There were the decorators. And the maid."

"Cheeky." I laugh softly as I take a step inside.

I can believe decorators were here. Instead of white walls,

the room is a dark chocolate brown. Soft, creamy plaid drapes cover the windows, and a massive bulky leather bed dominates the far wall. It screams *rich man cave*. I can easily imagine him in here, seated by the ivory marble fireplace, drinking scotch.

"It's perfect."

"Perfect?" His brow wrinkles as if confused.

"This room." I gesture around. "I couldn't dream of a more perfect room for you if I tried. It is intrinsically you."

His frown grows. "I can't decide if that's a compliment or not."

"Are you fishing for one?"

"No."

"Hmmm…"

He scoffs in annoyance and heads toward another door.

My toes sink into the carpet as I follow. "I love your room, Gabriel."

He grunts in response as we enter a walnut-paneled dressing room. It smells of wood, wool, and spicy cologne. It smells of him. I resist the urge to draw in a deep breath and instead let my gaze trail over the endless rows of suits, glossy leather shoes, and a rainbow of silk ties.

"It's like the man version of a Kardashian closet." I touch the sleeve of a charcoal wool suit.

"I'd like to think I have better taste," he says, opening a drawer. He pulls out two sets of pale gray sweat pants and then two T-shirts. He hands me a pair of sweats and the white shirt, taking the black tee for himself. "You can change here. Feel free to use the shower."

I'm covered in grime, just as he is. My skin is cold and clammy, and a shower sounds like heaven.

He points out the bathroom, just through another doorway. "I'll take the guest bath."

He doesn't wait for me to protest that I should take the

guest bath—I'm the guest, after all—but walks out the door with his fresh clothes in hand.

So I help myself to Gabriel's ultra-modern bathroom, washing in the massive, glass-walled shower and using his fancy shower gel that smell like him. It all feels like a dream. A really weird dream. It might very well be. I can't wrap my head around the fact that I'm here. That he's brought me here.

I dry my hair with one of his thick, fluffy towels and pull on his clothes.

You know those books and movies where the girl wears a guy's pants and they hang on her tiny frame? Yeah, I'm not sure what sort of pixies populate fiction, but not so much for me. Oh, the legs are too long, and I have to roll them. But the pants stretch tight over my ass and thighs to a cringe-worthy degree.

The T-shirt fits better, but basically looks like a sack. Sexy, I am not. I'm also not wearing a bra because mine is soaked and cold. I don't think the fact that my girls are free-swinging does much for the cause. I'm just frumpy with limp, damp hair and no makeup.

I laugh though, because does my appearance even matter? The way Gabriel looks at me never seems to change with my outfits. And he's made it clear this is not about sex.

A flash of us on the street streaks through my mind, his hard body and thick cock pressing into me for one heady moment. That was real. But was it a reaction to me? Or just the fact that he was between a woman's legs?

"You do think too much," I mutter to my reflection and then return to his room.

He isn't there. I absolutely *do not* imagine him showering. I'll have to face him soon enough, and I don't need *that* image in my head when I do.

The room is fairly dark, only a bedside lamp glowing and the flicker of embers dying in the fireplace. The chill of the rain is gone now, and my body is warm and relaxed.

Idly, I wander over to his bed. It's huge and plush. The flax linen duvet is slightly rumpled, as if Gabriel had been lying down on the covers, trying to get comfortable, before getting up. Oddly, I can't imagine him allowing himself to relax enough to actually sleep. Which is ridiculous; even gods have to sleep sometime.

I sit on his bed. It feels like a sin, something naughty. I can't help but smile at the thought of him frowning at me invading his personal domain. I run a palm over the covers, smoothing out the wrinkles. They're soft and cool, giving under my hand. And suddenly, it's far too easy to lower myself onto his bed, let his plump pillows cradle my head. Because everything is just too heavy now: my body, my limbs, my eyelids.

His bed smells of fresh linen. So soft. The rain drums against the roof, the dying fire crackles. My eyes close. I take a deep breath, try to open my eyes again. But I'm so comfortable. Everything is still, calm here. And Gabriel is just down the hall. Whatever he thinks of me, he'll make certain I'm safe, watched over. He's a steady rock.

My legs straighten, moving farther onto the bed. With a sigh, I settle down. I'll just rest my eyes until he returns.

GABRIEL
7

THERE ARE ONLY SO many times you can ask yourself what the fuck are you doing before the question becomes pointless. Being a tenacious bastard, I give up only after the hundredth time. Fuck it. I want Sophie here. Denying it is stupid. The moment she agreed to come over, the hard compression that's a near constant on my breastbone eased. It got lighter still when I saw her standing on that foggy street, her white blond hair frizzing in the damp, the lilting sound of her voice and that unflinching honesty of hers working like a balm.

It damn near lifted entirely when I rolled on top of her and pressed my cock between her legs. Her lips had parted in shock, those soft brown eyes widening. I meant what I said when I told her I wasn't after sex. It would be the height of stupidity to get involved with that woman. But there's a perverse sort of pleasure to be had in shocking Sophie Darling.

I find myself wanting to do it all the time.

For fuck's sake, I'm making tea. For the insane chatty girl I met on a plane. If I haven't fallen off the cliff already, I'm certainly teetering on the edge of it.

I finish up the tea tray and carry it to my bedroom. I should call Sophie down here, have tea in the relative formality of my living room. But I won't lie to myself; I want to keep her in my bedroom, where her scent will linger long after she's gone, and maybe I'll be able to breathe a little easier for a while longer.

Somewhere over the Atlantic, at thirty-five thousand feet, she wrapped herself around me, and my brain decided to equate her scent, the sound of her voice, the feel of her skin, with comfort.

I have no idea how I'm supposed to dissuade myself of this notion, and I am not yet ready to try. So we'll have tea in the sitting area of my room. And then I'll take her back to the hotel, whether I want to or not.

The tea cups rattle slightly as I angle myself to slip into the bedroom. It's too quiet. I expected her chatter as soon as I entered. The reason for the quiet is soon obvious: she's asleep on my bed, her pale hair haloed on my pillow. A proverbial Goldilocks making herself comfortable in an unknown lair.

I set the tray down and move to her side. She sleeps the way a child might, sprawled pell-mell and thoroughly invested in the act. She's clutching one of my pillows to her chest, half on her stomach, her plump arse in the air, legs spread.

"Sophie," I murmur, halfheartedly. I don't really want to wake her. It seems cruel given the smudges under her eyes.

She doesn't move. Doesn't even flinch.

Gingerly, I sit on the side of the bed. In sleep, her expression is somewhat perplexed, and I wonder if she's dreaming. What would this woman's dreams be like? I imagine something Seussian with pink trees, *whohoopers* and *trumtookas*, and I fight a grin.

Outside, the rain keeps tapping on the windows. The soft sounds of Sophie sleeping fill the void. She's a mouth breather, and each breath she exhales stirs a lock of hair hanging over her lip.

With the tip of my finger, I brush the hair away and give waking her one more weak try. "Chatty girl?"

A muffled snort answers me, and her knee draws up as if

she's cold. With a resigned sigh, I tug the duvet out from under her feet and cover her. She immediately snuggles down, her features smoothing.

Reaching for my cup, I stay by her side and drink my tea. She's close enough that the heat of her body warms my skin, and scent of my soap on her tickles my nose. She doesn't smell like me, however. Somehow she's managed to make the scent entirely her own.

She stirs again, and her thigh presses against my back. Through the covers, the contact is warm and solid.

Lethargy steals over me, settling on my shoulders like a heavy hand. I'm so bloody tired at this point, everything hurts. But sitting here with Sophie, the old resistance to sleep starts to crumble. I can barely lift my teacup to my lips.

Setting the cup down, I hunch over and rest my head in my hands. For the first time in days, I want to sleep. I should get up, go to the guest room.

Sophie makes another small snuffle, and the covers rustle as she turns in dramatic fashion. I glance over my shoulder to find she's rolled to the middle of the bed, almost as if she's giving me space to lie down.

A snort escapes me. I'm making excuses. And I don't bloody care. Sweet relief washes over me as I ease into the bed, slipping under the down cover. I don't even try to talk myself out of turning off the bedside light.

At my side, Sophie stirs yet again, turning my way. My body stiffens, my breath going sharp. I have no idea what I'll say. *Sorry, love, didn't see you there in my bed? You're imagining the whole thing; go back to sleep?*

But she doesn't wake. No. She snuggles up to me as if we sleep this way every night. And damn if my body doesn't immediately yield to hers—my arm lifting, so she can rest her head on my shoulder, before settling around her and bringing her closer.

Everything within me relaxes. This. This is what I needed. She is soft and fragrant, warm and welcoming. I know if she woke, she'd just laugh in that light way of hers and tell me to go with it, enjoy the moment. So I do.

I close my eyes and allow myself to sleep.

SOPHIE

THE WALK of shame is ever so much more fun when you're leaving the boss man's house. My hair, because I fell asleep with it half dry, is a rat's nest, and that's being kind. I've no makeup, and my eyes look puffy and wan without camouflage. At least I'm wearing my own clothes. Gabriel left them neatly laundered and folded at the foot of the bed.

Gah, the bed. I woke up in his bed, well rested, comfortably warm, and alone. And yet I know he slept with me. At some point during the night, I turned and found myself wrapped in gloriously strong arms, my cheek pressed against a firm chest. And it felt like heaven. So good that I didn't even question it in my sleepy haze but snuggled in, sighing in contentment when he held me more securely, as if he too reveled in the contact.

But that had been in the dark cover of night, when my brain takes a vacation and the wants of my body hold sway. Now? Now, I'm awake and squinting in the rare London sunlight as I try to sneak into the lobby of my hotel without being seen. It's too early for me to say I've been out and about already, and there's my hair, my stupid hair. No one is going to overlook this cotton candy crown I've got going.

Luckily, the lobby is deserted. Only the concierge is on duty, and she's not paying me any mind. I breathe a sigh of relief as I ride the elevator up. I want to be annoyed at Gabriel for not being there when I woke, but at least he left me breakfast—a boiled egg, a ginger scone, and a pot of tea on a tray, all covered with a warming cloth. The note pinned on it had instructions to eat it all, as breakfast is the most important meal of the day.

Gabriel Scott, mother hen hiding in a ten-thousand-dollar suit.

I'm snorting my amusement when the elevator doors open, and I come face to face with Rye. *Shit.*

His brow quirks as he looks me up and down. "Sophie Darling," he drawls. "Doth my eyes deceive me or are you doing the long walk 'o shame?"

I push past him. "I don't know what you're talking about. I always look this way."

"Ridden hard and put to bed wet?"

My steps halt, and I glare at his smugly grinning face. "That is not something you want to say to a woman who can nut you in two seconds flat."

He winces but doesn't look very contrite. "Brenna's always saying I need to learn better manners."

"You should listen to her."

"Where's the fun in that?" He follows me down the hall as I march to my room. "Anyway, I'm all for you getting some. Touring is exhausting. Have your fun when you can, you know?"

The big lug looks so earnest, I give his meaty arm a pat. "Thanks for the advice."

"So…" He waggles his brows. "Who's the lucky guy? Or was it a girl? Please say girl. That fantasy will keep me satisfied for weeks."

"What fantasy?" Whip's voice comes from behind us, and we both jump.

Jesus, are they all chipper morning people?

"Where the hell did you come from?" Rye asks, clutching

his chest.

"My room." Whip nods to the door we're standing closest to. The *duh* is heavily implied. "And you two are making enough noise out here to raise the dead."

Another door opens, and Brenna's head pokes out. "What the fuck is this? A hall convention?"

"Whip is right," Rye says. "The dead are rising."

Brenna hisses at him, baring her teeth like a vampire.

I take the moment to edge away from them all. My door is so close.

"Where do you think you're going?" Whip's cool blue eyes pin me. "You haven't answered the question."

"What question?" Brenna pipes up.

"What kind of fantasy Rye is having of Sophie," Whip says with an evil smile. The fucker. I now know who the instigator of the group is.

Rye scowls at him as Brenna's happy face falls flat.

Rye gives Whip a not-so-gentle punch on the shoulder. "We were talking about Sophie hooking up with a girl. I doubt I'm the only one who'd find that fantasy hot." His gaze lands on Brenna.

A flush hits her cheeks but she shrugs. "Sophie is definitely fantasy worthy."

Well, okay then.

They all turn to me, and Brenna gives me a kind smile. "But her sex life is none of our business."

"Like that's going to stop us," Whip says with a laugh. He nudges me. "I'm kidding, Soph. Run while you can."

"No way," Rye says. "Dish the dirt. Or we'll make assumptions."

Another door opens down the hall, and Jax glares at them before giving me a level look. "Sophie was out getting me a muffin. But she forgot the cash." He holds up a wad of pounds. "Sorry about that."

I sigh. "Oh, for crying out loud. I don't need you to cover for me, Jax. I have insomnia, okay?" I back up to my room. "I was out walking all night."

"In the rain?" Rye squints at me as if to better see through my lies.

"Yeah." I *finally* reach my door. "In the rain. All night."

Whip looks at Jax. "You were the last person I thought would make a move, man."

Jax frowns. "Why? Sophie's hot." He smiles at me. "And I totally respect you this fine morning, Sophie. Don't ever doubt that." He winks.

I groan, thumping my head against my door. "I'm in a nightmare. A bad nightmare."

"Don't worry about it, Sophie," Rye says. "Everyone makes regrettable sex mistakes."

"Yeah," Jax drawls. "Just ask Rye. He leaves tons of women lamenting theirs."

Rye gives him the finger.

Whip grins my way. "See? No harm admitting it."

"Fine," I snap. "I was with Jax. And the experience was so moving, I just had to run around the block to get it all out of my system!" I let myself into my room and slam the door before they can say anything else.

Jax's voice drifts through the wood. "Anytime you want a repeat, sweetheart, let me know. Me and my moving dick make house calls."

GABRIEL 8

GETTING the band ready to start a tour is like herding wild cats. There is noise, there are squabbles, and no one is where they're supposed to be. I gave up overseeing the details a long time ago. I've underlings to perform that thankless task now. And I pay them well. But it still falls to me to make final checks.

I watch stagehands moving to and fro, carrying crates and laughing along the way. For them, this is the experience of a lifetime—a chance to rub elbows with the band they idolize. I envy their joy. My joy ended around six this morning when I woke up and realized I was yet again, as though my life depended on it, wrapped around the woman I had intended to hate. And it had been a bloody uncomfortable realization.

It was bloody uncomfortable to ease my swollen, aching cock away from the swell of her arse and roll myself out of that warm, fragrant bed when all I really wanted to do was wallow there, ease between soft thighs and push...

"Where are we putting Sophie?" I ask Brenna, who stands next to me as the buses are loaded up.

"Why do you care?" She takes a long sip of her coffee.

I don't know. I've gone over the ledge into madness. I give Brenna a look. "She's a new employee. It shifts the balance. Accommodations will have to be rearranged."

"We have five new employees," Brenna retorts. "You know any of the others' names?" One red brow lifts behind purple cat glasses. "Or job functions?"

Hell. Evasive maneuvers are needed.

"What has your knickers in a twist?" I ask. Before she can answer, Rye strides past. They ignore each other as usual, and Brenna's pert nose rises a touch higher. I repress an eye roll. "You two really ought to fuck and get it over with."

I can almost hear her teeth grinding. Her voice is breezy, though, when she finally speaks. "There is entirely too much fucking going around this nosy little bunch, thank you very much."

"Who?" I can't help asking.

Brenna's gaze slides to mine. "Sophie and Jax, for one."

It's as if she's kicked my legs out from under me. The sensation of falling is so strong, the sudden pain in my chest so sharp, I can clearly picture myself on the ground, two stiletto heels implanted in my chest—one of Brenna's and one of Sophie's.

"What?" The question lashes out like a whip. And Brenna visibly flinches.

Slowly she lowers her cup from her face and takes a step back. "Ah, yeah, you know what? That's just speculation."

"Based on what, exactly?" I grind out.

Brenna looks around as if trying to find an avenue of escape. Not bloody likely.

I take a step into her space. "Talk, you."

"This morning Jax said he'd hooked up with Sophie, and she confirmed it," Brenna blurts out. "Though really, she sounded extremely sarcastic when she called the sex 'moving,' so it might have been a joke…"

Her words drift off, as the ringing in my ears grows stronger. My heart knocks against my ribs so hard, I feel the reverberations in my throat. Jax? She's with Jax? She fucking slept in *my bed* while she fucking fucked fucking Jax?

I turn on my heel, not knowing where the bloody hell I'm going, when my gaze lands on the man in question, who is about to get on his bus.

"John," I bark out loud enough for my voice to echo over the lot.

Hearing me use his real name makes him pause and look over his shoulder. "What?"

Whatever he sees on my face gets him strolling over to me. I grit my teeth.

"What's this about you and Sophie?"

The git gives me a stupid grin. "Oh, yeah, just a bit of fun." He glances at Brenna, who is slowly shaking her head. "Right, Bren?"

I don't let her respond. "Did you not give Killian a lecture about sleeping with employees when Libby came on board?"

He rubs his chin, and I have the urge to punch it.

Jax snaps his fingers. "Right. He clearly listened well."

Fuckwit.

"Good advice which would apply to you as well, would it not?"

Jax nods, still grinning that smug little shitter grin. "It would."

I take a calming breath, which bursts out of my lungs when Jax smiles wide and says, "But don't worry, there wasn't much sleeping involved."

My breathing goes haywire.

"Careful," Brenna whispers in my ear. "Your knickers are getting all twisted."

I wrench my head in her direction, and she pales.

"Ack, joke gone bad, joke gone bad," Brenna wails, flapping her hands. "Run away. Run away."

Jax watches her go, a smile on his lips. "What's with her?... Hey, man." He holds his hands up. "Easy with the crazy eyes.

It's just Sophie."

Wrong thing to say.

"What's just me?" Sophie asks, appearing at my side.

I round on her. "You."

"Me." She points to her chest then to Jax. "Jax. We all speak good now."

Jax chuckles, but when I glare at him, he suddenly becomes invested in scurrying off toward Killian and Libby.

Sophie frowns. "What's that all about?"

"Are you fucking Jax?"

Her eyes go wide and shocked. Guilty? I can't tell. It annoys me further.

A flush rushes over her cheeks. "Are you serious with this?"

Yes. No. I don't fucking know.

"Answer the question, Sophie."

She glances around before grabbing me by the arm. I let her lead me away because I want an answer. She stops in the narrow gap between my coach and the band's.

"Look, you," she hisses, poking my shoulder. "I don't have to tell you a fucking thing about my personal life."

"You cease to have one if you start fucking the band members."

"Members?" she squeaks. "So, what? I'm fucking my way through them now? Is that it?"

The thought is so repellant, bile fills my stomach. My fists clench. "Jax. Let's concentrate on Jax now. Did you sleep with him?"

"I cannot believe you're asking me this," she snaps. "That you're actually snorting like some sort of enraged bull and expecting me to answer."

"I did not snort. I merely asked a question. Which I want an answer to. Now."

The flush rushes down to the tops of her breasts. "Fuck

you, *Scottie*. I don't know who you think you are, but let me tell you, I'm not some empty-headed bimbo you can bark at. I am done with this conversation."

She turns to go, her expression utterly closed off for the first time since I've met her. But I saw the hurt I caused, and the humiliation, before she shut down. The bottom drops out of my gut.

"Sophie." I grab hold of her and spin her around.

Her shoulders meet the side of the bus before I cage her in. She struggles, even as I press close. My cheek touches hers, and she stills. For a long, painful moment we both just breathe, heavy and agitated.

"You're right. I have no say," I whisper into her hair. My lids lower, and I draw in another lungful of her sweet scent. "And I don't think you're a bimbo. I only wanted to... That is..." I choke on a curse. "Not with one of the boys, all right? Not them. Please."

A breath shudders out of her, and I feel it along my neck. My back tenses, my skin prickling. It's all I can do to remain still, not rock into her softness. I know she's wondering why I'm demanding this. I won't be able to tell her she'll rip my guts out if she does, that I won't be able to focus for shite if she's with one of the guys. If she's been with Jax...

A tremor runs through my body as I struggle to hold still.

Her breath hitches again. If she touches me, I might shatter. But she doesn't. She simply sighs. "You're such an ass."

"Established."

"A reactionary ass," she says bitterly. "Who apparently can't be bothered to realize there's no way I could have been with Jax last night when I was with *you*."

My head hits the side of the bus with a thud as my body sags against hers. Relief and embarrassment are a warm, sticky cocktail swimming through my blood. "Shit."

"Yeah, shit," she repeats with soft sarcasm. "He covered

for me when everyone caught me doing the walk of shame back to my room. Though he doesn't know who I was actually with." Her small fist nudges my ribs. "Now get off me before someone sees us and they really start talking."

With a grunt, I push off the bus and take a step back. Her cheeks are flushed a lovely rose, her eyes shining with anger. I feel all of two feet tall. I'm not this man—out of control, possessive, foolish.

I run a hand over my tie. "I spoke out of turn."

She purses her full lips, her narrowed gaze demanding more.

I swallow hard. "I should have asked—"

"No," she snaps. "You should have minded your business."

A flush of heat hits my cheeks. "Ms. Darling, I cannot recant my earlier statement. Getting involved with a member of the tour is a bad decision and one that can affect everyone. Which means it will always be my business."

All true. *And I sound like an utter git. Fuck it all.*

"You're talking like a duke again." She straightens and smoothes a hair back from her face. "Which *means* you're feeling guilty."

"Know me so well already, chatty girl?"

"Yes, I do." She moves to pass me but pauses. "You're not fooling anyone. And when you want to admit you were jealous, I'll be waiting."

With that, she walks away, her round hips swaying. I appreciate the view, even as I'm mentally kicking myself.

"It will be a long wait," I call.

She flips me off without missing a step.

Hell, I do like this girl. Too bloody much.

SOPHIE

MEN CAN SUCK IT. Especially hot, suit-wearing, bossy, jealous, chest-thumping men. And he *was* jealous. Gabriel can deny it all he wants, but that whole freakout had nothing to do with looking out for his "boys."

Maybe it's weak of me to admit I'd find the whole incident a turn on *if* he'd done something physical about his jealousy—thrown me over his shoulder, proclaimed me his before fucking my brains out. Yeah, *that* would have been hot. But no, it was much more, *stay away from my friends, and I'll stay away from you.* Not cool.

And embarrassing, because as quickly as I took him off to finish our discussion in private, I know people saw the start of it. You don't bite the head off your lead guitarist in public and expect people not to talk. Especially when your guitarist runs away as though his life depended on it; thanks very much, Jax, you weenus.

I'm still fuming when Brenna seeks me out. "So sorry about that," she murmurs, walking with me to my room.

"Were you going to assign me a bus?" I ask, zipping up my bag. "Or just throw me under one?"

She winces, her nose wrinkling. "I know, I know. I am a gossiping hag. I was low on caffeine and in a pissy mood." Her gaze travels over me as if looking for battle scars. "I didn't think Scottie would flip his shit like that. He doesn't normally have a bad temper, but he's been a bit off lately."

"Off?" I ask, despite not wanting to talk about The Incident at all.

"Distracted. Snippy." Brenna shakes her head, her ponytail swaying over her shoulders. "He's always fairly deadpan and unflappable, stone cold."

Gabriel leaning into me, his breath on my cheek,

whispering *please* flashes through my mind. That man wasn't cold or unflappable. But I don't want to think about that version of Gabriel. My attraction to him is inconvenient and annoying. I have a job to do—one other photographers would kill for.

But Brenna is still eyeing me with remorse and worry. "I am sorry, Sophie. I didn't mean to set him on you like that. Do you want me to talk to him?"

And poke the bear? I can imagine how that would go. "No, it's fine. We worked it out."

She looks dubious but nods. "Right then. You'll be traveling with the guys."

"Really?" I don't know where I expected to be placed in our traveling caravan, but I hadn't thought right with the band.

"They like to travel in one coach for camaraderie, and your job is to capture that, so it makes the most sense."

"And they're okay with this?"

Brenna grabs one of my bags, and we exit the room, heading down to the waiting cars that will take us to the buses. "Yeah. They're a pretty open bunch, all things considered. And they trust me when I say you won't post without permission."

Translation: Don't fuck that trust up for me.

"I want to thank you again for this opportunity," I tell her. "I won't let you or the guys down."

Brenna smiles. "I know. I'm a good judge of character."

I have to laugh at that. "I am too. I just seem to ignore my common sense when I most need it."

"Shit, if we're talking about our love lives, I know I have you beat. I'm a train wreck with an atomic bomb on the top."

Before we enter the coach, Brenna hands me a small key for later use. We're alone for the moment, and she shows me around. There's not much to see. The front has a lounge space and a galley kitchen-bar to the side. It's dark and sleek, and there are three TVs on different walls.

"The guys store instruments and a few small amps in the bins," she says, pointing to ebony wood cabinets overhead. "And then there are the bunks."

Mid-bus is reserved for bunks that line both walls, leaving a narrow hall. Four beds and then a small master bedroom at the very back, with an even smaller bathroom between them.

"Killian and Libby have the bedroom," Brenna tells me. "You get this top back bunk. It's with the guys." Her sherry-colored eyes narrow with worry. "You're okay with this? Because if you're not, it's fine. I can move you to one of the roadie coaches."

"They all have bunks too, don't they?" I ask.

"Yes, I'm afraid we get cozy during tour travel. Except for Scottie, who has an entire bus to himself."

"I'm not surprised in the least."

"And a word of warning; don't try to visit him there. He snarls if he finds anyone near his private spaces."

He left me alone in his house today. Then keeps me at arm's length in the next breath. I'm beginning to think the man simply doesn't know how to let people into his life. "I'll be fine rooming with the guys."

"You will," Brenna assures me. "They might be pigs now and then. But they're good guys. The best. They'll make you feel comfortable, I promise."

"Who's promising what?" Rye says as he hauls his muscled bulk onto the bus.

"That you'll be nice to Sophie," Brenna says with a stern look.

The big guy has one of those open faces that easily shows his emotions. He reminds me of a puppy, cute and exuberant. "Of course." His smile is wide and framed by dimples. "Welcome aboard, lovely Sophie."

Whip steps up behind him, his blue eyes flashing with impish humor. "Did you tell her about the initiation rites?"

"If it involves anything sexual," I say blandly, "I offer free nuttings with a hundred-percent guarantee to leave a man incapacitated for an hour at minimum."

Whip laughs. "I bet. Naw, you just have to drink a lot and make a fool of yourself at least once." He runs his hand through coal back hair that reaches his collar. Effortlessly cool rocker. "But I promise to take the lead."

Jax crams in behind him and gives him a nudge to move on. "Out of the way, pretty boy."

Killian and Libby follow, and soon we're all crowded in.

Brenna leaves us as the bus gets ready to go. But she's right; they all make me feel comfortable and welcome. If I'm going to be stuffed in a bus with minimal privacy and space, bunking with these guys isn't a bad option at all.

I remind myself of this and refuse to think of Gabriel Scott on his own bus, or how much space he must have to rattle around.

After settling in, I join the guys and Libby in the living area. Libby is putting out a tray of biscuits, but stops to offer me one before I sit.

"Get one now," she tells me in her soft Southern drawl, "because these jackals will devour them in a second."

I take a napkin and a flaky, hot biscuit. "You baked?"

She smiles wryly, and her grey eyes light up. "Made the dough before and froze it. Not much room for anything else."

Killian's hand reaches down between us, and he snatches two. "Best baker ever." He gives Libby a quick kiss on her cheek. "Love you, Elly May."

She rolls her eyes and sets the tray down for the guys. "I'm thinking you're more loving my biscuits right now, lawn bum."

"Never."

They grin at each other, and I take a picture before sitting down. Killian is right; Libby is an excellent baker. And Libby is right; the food is devoured in a blink. I find a seat and simply watch the guys interact. There's something comforting about witnessing old friends enjoy each other's company.

But they don't leave me out. Whip turns his attention to me soon enough. "So, Bren threw you right into the lion's den, eh?"

"You guys seem pretty tame."

He laughs, and I'm struck by the fact that he looks very much like Killian, only blue-eyed instead of dark. "Sadly, we are now."

"You miss being wild?" I ask, taking a picture because he's just too pretty lounging in a black leather armchair, his toned body doing nice things for the vintage Def Leppard concert tee he's wearing.

"Naw," he says. "I'm kind of liking this tamer phase. More productive, at the very least."

"He's just getting old," Rye says, opening a small fridge and pulling out a few bottles of beer.

"You're six months older than I am," Whip points out.

"I age better."

"Like moldy cheese," Whip says.

Rye plops down next to me on the small banquet. "I'm surprised Scottie was cool with you sleeping on this bus."

Killian passes me a beer. "Why wouldn't he be? It's her job to record us."

"It's cute that you described my job with finger quotes," I tell him, rolling my eyes.

He grins with teeth, so fake, and I snap a pic before he can stop. At this he scowls, but it lacks any heat.

"Brat. I'm not saying I like my every move being chronicled—and post that goof one at your peril—but I'm admitting it's a needed aspect of the tour, all right?"

I blink rapidly while clutching my chest. "Can't. Respond. Shock. Too. Great."

Libby laughs. "See? You'll fit in just fine."

"Thanks." I click beer bottles with her.

"Still not getting why Scottie would complain about Sophie on the bus," Killian says. "He was adamant that we treat her with..." His voice turns crisp and clipped, mimicking Gabriel's accent to a tee. "...'the bloody respect a trained professional deserves.'"

He said that? I become a little less ticked at him. Just a little.

Rye gives an expansive sigh. "Because dumbass Jax made it sound like he'd hooked up with her."

Killian's mouth falls open, and he stares at Jax as if he's sprouted horns. "You told Scottie you slept with Sophie?" he all but squeaks, which is impressive given his naturally low voice.

"It was a joke," Jax says from his sprawl across the couch. "Calm down."

Killian shakes his head. "Oh, man. That's nothing to joke about. You're dead."

"Scottie needs to lighten up. And you do too."

"He has every right to kick your ass." Killian wings a bottle cap at Jax. "You violated the first law of the man code, Mr. Dead Man Walking."

Jax frowns. "No way."

"Yeah, you did," Whip adds with a laugh.

Even Rye shakes his head. "You didn't know? Who put you up to even telling Scottie that story?"

Jax sits up straight. "Brenna brought it up to him!"

Rye makes a noise of horror. "That's just mean. Even for Brenna."

"Eh," Jax says, rubbing the back of his head. "I think he was giving her shit for something."

"Clearly the man was playing with fire," Rye deadpans.

"Truth."

"What the hell is the first law of the man code?" I cut in.

Killian takes a sip of his beer before answering. "Never encroach upon your buddy's territory."

"Territory," I parrot. "You make us sound like dogs."

"Soph," Whip says solemnly, "when it comes to guys and sex, we're all dogs."

"True," adds Rye.

"I'm not Gabriel's territory for him to piss over." Not that anyone seems to believe me.

Killian's dark eyes fill with amusement. "You're the only one he lets call him Gabriel."

"Shit," Jax says with a wince. "You're right. I missed that."

"You're blind then." Whip gives Jax's flat belly a slap. "Dude, he saw her first. That's like calling—"

"If you say 'dibs'," Libby cuts in, "I will gag."

Killian laughs and slings an arm around her. "Aw, honey, no gagging without my helping."

At this we all gag.

"But still," Jax says when the guys settle down. "How was I supposed to know? We're talking about Scottie, for fuck's sake."

"What's so strange about that?" I feel compelled to ask.

"He isn't known to...er...partake," Rye says with a shrug.

"Partake?" I look around at the guys.

"Fuck around," Killian supplies. "He's kind of like a monk."

Whip nods. "When was the last time anyone saw him with a woman?"

"Fucking forever ago." Rye shudders as if the thought terrifies him. "If he's getting any, he's doing it on the sly."

Something ugly twists in my stomach. I don't want to think of Gabriel with women. And really don't like the idea of the guys discussing his sex life, or lack of one. Gabriel is a proud man; he'd hate this conversation. "We shouldn't be talking about him this way."

"You're right," Killian says. "No doubt his Scottie Sense is tingling."

"We shouldn't be talking about him," Libby says in a stronger voice, "because it's rude and none of our business."

I knew I liked that woman.

Killian kisses her cheek. "Right you are, Libs." He gives Jax a look filled with warning. "Sleep with one eye open, man."

"He's on another bus," Jax grumbles.

"You look worried," I point out. I admit this gives my inner toddler some satisfaction.

Jax's smile is self-deprecating. "Little known fact, honey, Scottie boy is scrappy as shit. I've seen him make men twice his size cry for their mommas with a well-placed kick-punch combo. Fucking bare knuckle legend—"

Killian clears his throat loudly and gives a slight shake of his head.

But I'm a dog on the hunt now. "Hold on, he's what?"

"A stone cold badass," Rye says. "But you didn't hear it from us. Seriously, he really can kick all our asses so...yeah, no more talking about Scottie, 'kay?"

He's laughing as he says it, but I get the feeling he truly doesn't want Gabriel to find out I know about his fighting. I can respect that. Doesn't stop me from thinking of his hard body and muscles that strain his properly cut shirts. Is that how he developed those? As a fighter? I can't picture him getting into a fight out of anger, but a controlled match? I can see that, and it leaves me feeling oddly morose.

They move on to another topic, but I can't help looking out of the tinted window. There's nothing but darkness and the occasional flicker of headlights. Somewhere behind us, Gabriel is alone on his bus. I know full well he wants it that way, but I hurt for him all the same. Isolated from his friends, and why?

Why does he hide himself away? Does he get lonely?

I hate that fate for him. The urge to be with him instead is so strong, I imagine myself leaping from the window and somehow landing on his bus, straight up Super Girl style. No, Wonder Woman. That way I could tie him down with my lasso when he protests my invasion of his Fortress of Solitude.

I'm in the middle of a Clark Kent/Diana Prince cosplay fantasy when Jax shatters my dream by loudly declaring, "'Son of a Preacher Man' is a song that can never be replicated."

Rye leans back in an armchair and idly plucks on a ukulele he unearthed from somewhere. "Okay, I'll give you that."

"Play that song," Jax says, "and women fucking melt, man."

"Someone save me from hearing any more of Jax's seduction routine." Rye looks around desperately.

"Take notes, son, and learn something," Jax drawls.

"Etta James singing 'At Last'," Killian butts in. "Fucking timeless."

"Beyoncé did a pretty good version," Libby says.

"Pretty good," Killian repeats. "But it didn't top the original. Etta still rules that song."

Whip taps on his knees as if he can't keep still. "Don't let the Bee Hive hear that. They'll sting you bad, bro."

Killian shudders. "You're right. I'm sorry, Bees," he shouts to the air. "Don't slay me! I love Queen Bey!"

"Man, I keep waiting for her to break up with Jay Z. Then I'm all in."

"Dude, your dream is dead in the water," Jax says. "You don't have a chance in hell with her."

"You're gonna eat your words," Whip promises. "Our love is destined. She totally winked at me during that charity concert we all did last month."

"It was windy," Killian says with a snort. "She had dust in

her eyes."

"She had me in her eyes."

Rye shakes his head, and then his blue eyes find me. "What about you, Sophie? Got a song?"

They all turn to me. I'm supposed to play? *Fuck.* I love music, but my knowledge isn't encyclopedic like these guys'. I think for a minute. "'Sabotage'."

"Beastie Boys?" Rye gives me a high five. "Excellent."

"Nobody can replicate the Beastie Boys," Jax agrees, clinking his beer bottle to mine. He's relaxed, his pretty green gaze slumberous. I know the guys worry over him, and I don't blame them, but he appears to be taking things easy now. "Hell, I need to get my blood pumping or I'll fall asleep." He looks at Killian. "You got 'Sabotage' on your phone?"

"You have to ask?" Killian jumps up and plugs his phone into the input set up in the wall. "Hold on to your butts."

The familiar hard bass riff pounds through the speakers, followed by discordant record scratches and an angry scream of defiance. Killian immediately starts dancing around, grabbing Libby to join him. She laughs and bumps hips with him.

Jax catches my eye. "At the risk of having Scottie hand me my balls later..." He holds out his hand.

Jax has the most to resent me for. I should feel guilty even being in the same room with him. But I'm comfortable in his presence. He looks at me as if he knows exactly how shitty my job was back then, exactly how soulless I'd become, and he's sorry for it. It's that more than anything that has me taking his hand.

I dance full out, swinging my head, hopping around like a mad woman—there's no way to appreciate the song but to go wild. And the guys surround me, jumping and thrashing, and likely making the entire bus rock as it hurtles down the highway. We don't care. We're young and free. It's a beautiful thing. And we dance for many more songs.

I almost forget about the man on the other bus. Only when the guys finally crash for the night, when I'm tucked away in my tiny bunk by the bathroom and can't sleep at all, do I stare into the darkness and think of Gabriel.

GABRIEL
9

"EVERYTHING FOR FRANCE is basically set. But Chrissy called about the final T-shirt numbers in Rome. The vendors are expecting high sales and… Scottie? Scottie? Mr. Scott?"

Jules's voice buzzes like a fly in my ear and pulls me from the fog that's taken up residence in my head. I blink, force myself to focus. She peers up at me with a frown.

"Why did you stop speaking?" It's nearly a snap, but I don't like what I see in her expression. The boss cannot afford to be worried over. I am the one in control. At all times.

Jules flinches, and I feel it in my gut. Perfect. I've upset the girl for no valid reason.

"Sorry, sir. I thought…" She grimaces.

"You thought what?" I have to will myself not to lean farther into the soft embrace of my chair. I shouldn't have sat down. It's too tempting to slump, and usually I stand when hearing a progress report. Better to focus.

Jules's freckles stand out like cinnamon flecks over her round cheeks. "I thought you…" She swallows hard. "Well, I thought you weren't listening."

I wasn't. Not with the attention I usually give. My head is fucking pounding like my brain is trying to jackhammer its way out of my skull. The floor is either defective and slanted or I'm imagining things. Given that no one else has commented on it, I'm guessing I'm the one off kilter.

"You were speaking of vendors." I know I heard something about shirts. Hell. I want to rub my face in the nearest pillow. But it won't work. I can't sleep. I cannot fucking sleep. And I've tried. Every fucking night I try. But nothing has worked, save for one night in London. We're in Scotland now.

At this point, it's so bad I'm nearly weeping by three in the morning when, yet again, I'm staring up at the ceiling, unable to shut my brain off.

"Yes, the vendors," Jules says happily. She rattles on again, and I try to keep my eyes open.

It wouldn't even matter if I closed them. My body wouldn't shut down anyway. There's a weight on my chest that makes breathing a chore. *Weakness.* I loathe it. But I'm getting weaker every day, and I don't know what to do.

Brenna would tell me to visit a doctor. The mere thought of doing so sends cold dread down my spine. A violent protest screams in my mind. No doctors. Never. I had my fill of them when I was a lad. And nothing short of death will get me to go back.

Best knock on wood, a nasty voice in my head whispers.

The pain in my head expands outward, down my neck, digging into the tops of my shoulders.

Jules keeps nattering on about contracts and dates.

My jaw throbs.

Breathe. Get through this. Then you can crawl to your room and take a hot shower. The lure of taking a sleeping pill is so strong at this point, my hands fist tight. Jax nearly died swallowing a bottle of those bloody pills, mixed with heroin. When I think about it—and I try very bloody hard *not* to think about it—nausea churns my guts and bile surges upward.

I swallow hard, grab my water bottle. My hand shakes as I lift it to my lips. No way to hide the fact other than drinking fast and setting my arm down as soon as possible. The shakes are getting worse.

"What should I tell him?"

With a jolt, I glance at Jules, who waits expectedly. *Fuck.*

"What do you think you should tell him?" Teaching moment. That works.

She frowns, her brow knitting in confusion.

Or it doesn't.

"You'll need to make these decisions one day, yes?" I prompt. *Arse. You're cocking it up. Get your head back in the game.*

Her mouth opens and shuts before she tentatively speaks. "I...uh...I don't think Jax will be asking me if I want to join him for poker. I thought that was your...uh...guy thing."

Sod it.

"Well, you never know." I clear my throat. "And, really, he should be asking me directly about personal things, which is your answer."

I lever myself out of the chair, ignoring the way the room sways. "You are my assistant, not my bloody personal calendar. Tell Jax as much."

"Right." Likely, she's mentally telling me to go bugger myself.

That sits heavily on me as well. I've never given my work or my crew anything less than one hundred percent. I am ashamed of myself. If only I could get some rest.

"Oh, and I'll have those personnel files sent to you by the end of the day," Jules calls toward my retreating back.

"Very good." I have no earthly idea what she's talking about. A vague memory prods at the corners of my mind, but I'm distracted.

A whiff of lemon tart and warm woman spice drifts through the air. My cock reacts as if it's being tugged. Annoyed at myself, I look up, knowing exactly who I'll find.

At some point, Sophie has gone and had her hair colored.

It's now a pale rose gold, shining like a nimbus around her smiling face. The color sets off the dark warmth of her eyes and the pink in her lips. Hell.

"Hey there, sunshine," she says, perky as ever. Her bouncy tits are barely restrained in some sort of off-the-shoulder black knit top. Which means the only thing holding the fabric up are her breasts. One good tug...

"Eyes up, hon."

Immediately, my chin lifts. She's grinning like the Cheshire Cat.

"Is that appropriate attire?" *Shut up. Just shut up now, you git.*

She apparently feels the same. Her hand lands on one well-rounded hip. "As opposed to what? The tit parade we all see on a nightly basis around here? At least I'm wearing a shirt."

She has a point. Damn it.

"Or maybe I should trade in these jeans for a micro-mini? The guys seem to love those."

Not happening. Her skinny jeans might hug her legs and highlight her arse to an alarming degree, but they, at the very least, provide some coverage.

And what the bloody hell am I doing commenting on her clothing?

"I apologize," I bite out. "I'd hand someone their arse if I heard them say as much to a woman."

Her eyes widen, and she gapes at me.

I count down the number of seconds until I can safely make my escape.

Too late. Sophie goes up on her toes as she lays the back of her hand on my forehead. I want to bat it away, tell her to leave off. But she's closer now, her soft breasts nearly touching my chest, her scent surrounding me. Her fingers are cool, soothing.

"Are you feeling all right?" she asks, clearly mocking.

"Go away," I mutter. A lie. I want to lean down and rest my head on the pillows of her fantastic breasts. Burrow right in and happily die there.

She ignores me anyway. "I mean, I did hear that apology, didn't I? I'm not dreaming?"

"If this were a dream, it'd be a nightmare."

Her berry pink lips part on a smile. "There's the Sunshine I know."

I want to shut her up with my mouth. Take. And take. And take. Lick up her words, drink in her laughter. I can't. I won't.

"I'm not myself today." *Truth*. "I think one of the boys spiked my drink. They'd just love to find out if I truly do walk around with my knickers in a twist."

Her laugh has a husky quality to it. Again I want to take her mouth. Her lips are plush, mobile—always volleying something back at me.

"Don't we all?" Her slim fingers pluck at the waist of my trousers, and my cock stirs. "Come on," she murmurs, a wicked gleam in her eyes. "Give me a peek. I promise, I'll only tell…everyone."

I wonder what she'd do if I pulled her hand against me, let her get a feel of my thickening cock, ordered her to give it a nice squeeze.

Nothing I'd want her to, that's one certainty.

Sophie is a tease. Not in a malicious way, but because it's her nature to make life a joke. I envy that ability to laugh at the world. But I won't mistake her sexual innuendoes for anything more than her enjoyment of getting under my skin.

I button my suit jacket, covering my growing interest. "And ruin the mystery? I think not."

"I'll find out one day," she calls after me as I walk away.

One can only hope. I don't turn around, so she can't see me smile. But as her light laughter drifts off, it occurs to me that I spent a few minutes without thinking about pain or exhaustion. My steps slow as my heart rate kicks up.

Sophie.

The last time I had a proper sleep was with her snoring away in my bed. *My* bed. *She* makes it better.

A thought races through my mind, strong and demanding. I kick it aside because it's rubbish and insane. But desperation makes men do stupid things. And even though I tell myself I absolutely cannot consider what my body is begging me to do, I know I will.

"Fuck me," I mutter. I'll take one more night to talk myself out of it. But I'm a man at the end of his rope. I'll do anything to get back on that boat, even debase myself in the worst way I can imagine.

SOPHIE

THE NEXT MORNING, I'm packing my camera when Gabriel approaches. He's so stiff, his back appears in danger of snapping should a strong breeze blow our way. Which is saying something. I haven't seen him this tense since the plane.

"What's up, sunshine?" I glance at him. "Someone piss in your porridge?"

"Lovely." He watches me for a second, the wrinkle between his brows growing deeper until he's full-out scowling.

"Seriously, you look grumpy even for you. Who pissed you off?" I grin at him. "Do I have to break some skulls?"

He finally huffs out a small laugh, his shoulders easing a fraction. "I can see it now, you nipping at someone's ankle like an angry Pomeranian."

"So you're familiar with my methods."

A low chuckle rumbles in his chest, and he lowers himself to a crouch, handing me my flash. Too soon, his relaxed expression fades back to seriousness. Not that I mind; the man is a freaking work of art when he's stern. So hot, I hold back the urge to fan myself. I busy myself packing.

"I wanted to talk to you," he finally says in a low voice.

The anxious way he looks at me, as if he's dreading what he has to say, sends my heart pounding. God, is he firing me? But he can't. Brenna's my boss. *Try to remain calm.* "Shoot."

His fingers twitch, and he rises with me. "Not here. Are you free now?"

I pause and really look him over. He's nervous. I wouldn't believe it if I wasn't right here in front of him, watching the color work over his tanned skin and his hands fidgeting at his sides. The fact that he wants to talk right now freaks me out even more.

"Sure," I tell him past the lump in my throat. "What's up?"

His lips compress. "I'd rather talk in private. Come to my bus?"

I'm so shocked he wants me alone, I can't even form a joke, only squeak out a small *okay.*

The walk back feels like the Green Mile. I'll set one foot in Gabriel's bus—the bus he'll only let his driver and the occasional maid enter—and an axe will swiftly fall to cut off my head. And it suddenly pisses me off. I've done nothing wrong. Why the private talk?

I grit my teeth and march alongside a quiet Gabriel, who has solicitously taken my camera case in hand. His other hand hovers around the small of my back, not quite touching but close enough that I feel its heat. He's guiding me along.

Probably afraid I'll bolt, I think darkly. But no, I'm going to lay into him something good. I thought we were...well, not friends exactly. I don't know if he'd even let anyone other than Brenna and the guys be his friend anymore. But we were something.

I'm horrified to realize I'm on the verge of tears. It hurts thinking he'll soon dismiss me. *He might not be doing that at all. Maybe you should chill out.*

I glare at the bus as it comes into view, but hold my tongue. Well, I do until he opens the door. I halt, unable to take another step.

"Are you firing me?" *That sounded embarrassingly shrill.*

He halts too, frowning down at me. "What?" A smile lights his eyes. The fucker. "There you go again with your wild imaginings."

"Don't give me that. You're taking me aside for a private chat. What am I to think?"

"That I want to talk privately," he suggests as if I'm batty. "Besides, Brenna's the one who hired you."

"And don't you forget it."

He rolls his eyes and his hand finally touches my back, nudging me forward. "Would you get in here and calm yourself?"

"You're acting weird," I counter, but I step inside. "Wow."

I was expecting black leather and gray walls—standard luxury coach fare. Instead I'm greeted with glossy burled wood paneling, milk glass sconces, and smoke velvet chairs. It's like a 1930s rail car.

"Have a seat." Gabriel gestures to the small living area toward the front. I sink into a Deco style club chair and clutch the arm of it. Next to me is a small table where he has a laptop out and a pile of papers beside it.

He moves to tidy it, but his phone rings. Glancing at it, he grimaces. "One moment. I've been waiting for this call."

Mutely, I nod and watch him walk off toward the back. The low sound of his voice is soothing but not enough to stop me from being twitchy. My eyes roam everywhere. Aside from his work, and two car magazines tucked into a side panel, there's nothing personal in here.

I don't know if it's snooping or plain old nerves that prompts me to pick up one of the papers on the table and read it. But as soon as I do, my eyes glaze over from the boring contract language. And then I see the folder below it. My name pops up like a neon sign. I toss the contract aside and pick up what is obviously a file on me.

Gabriel walks back into the room, and his steps slow as he sees what I'm holding. But he doesn't say a word.

I do. "You have a file on me?"

"Of course. I have files on all our employees." He nods toward the table. "Jules sent the newest hires over for review."

"Why you?"

"Because, as they say in America, the buck stops with me."

I flip through the folder, even though I know most of what will be in there. I filled out the numerous forms, after all.

"Jesus, you have my health report. Did you read it?"

His thick brows knit. "Why wouldn't I?"

"Because it's an invasion of privacy," I offer, snappish. I didn't mind giving Brenna the information, but he's been reading everything, down to my last pap test.

"Sophie, why are you upset? This is standard procedure." He cocks his head as if I'm a peculiar puzzle. "Are you embarrassed that I know you're healthy and have never been convicted of a crime?"

"Excuse me if I feel a twinge violated that you know everything, down to the fact that I use a birth control shot, for fuck's sake." I don't even mention that he now knows my exact height and weight too. Fucking shit.

A snort of annoyance leaves him. "Fine." He walks briskly toward me, and I stiffen, but he turns, opens the laptop, and with a few hard clicks, pulls up a file. "Here," he says, turning the screen my way. "My health report. Or did you think I was exempt?"

"Honestly, I did." I can't help it. I read. So sue me, it's right there in front of me, and he saw mine. I now know he's six foot three, one hundred and eighty-five pounds when last weighed, and in perfect health. "Why do you do this?"

"Insurance, in some instances. And it's a safety precaution. If you're going to work for the biggest band in the world, we're going to know all we can about you." His gaze clashes with mine. "I won't apologize for it, if that's what you want."

"No," I shut the laptop. "I just got a little freaked, okay? Is this why you brought me here? You can see I'm not a criminal, or in debt." *Shut up, Soph. You're babbling like a freak.* "And no cooties to speak of."

Gabriel's lids lower, and the look he gives me is calculating. "No cooties at all," he agrees.

I flush, thinking of how we could fuck hard and fast without fear of any consequences. And just maybe he's thinking the same thing.

Only he abruptly stands and walks to a bar across from the door. "Would you like a drink?"

"No tea?" I'm nervous now that I know this isn't about firing me.

He glances over his shoulder at me. "Would you like some?"

"No." I need something stronger. "Bourbon?"

With a nod of approval, he pours us both a good helping. I don't miss the way his hand trembles just once as he passes me the glass. He gives me a tight smile and takes the seat across from me.

The coach is absolutely silent as we sip our bourbon and watch each other warily. He still hasn't told me anything, and I'm pretty sure I just made a fool of myself. So, yeah.

Gabriel expels a soft sigh and gently sets his glass on a small, chrome table. The click of glass to metal is like a gunshot to my overtaxed nerves.

"I can't sleep," he tells me with a small, self-deprecating shake of his head. I stare at him, unable to respond, and he meets my eyes. "Not a fucking wink."

"I'm sorry," I whisper. I empathize. I can't sleep either. I've become some mental princess and the pea. My bed is too hard, the pillow too soft. I toss and turn, my eyes wide open. I'm either too cold or too hot. It's a freaking nightmare. And I think way too much about a certain grumpy man who currently sits in front of me, looking a bit like sleep-deprived death warmed over.

His smile is brief and weak. "I slept that night." Blue eyes meet mine. "When it rained."

Something hot and strong rushes through my limbs. I slept then too. So well. All warm and snug, wrapped up in strong arms. Sometimes, when I'm really weak, I close my eyes and try to remember the exact feeling of Gabriel's hard body behind mine. Try to recall his exact scent. If I'm lucky, I drift off to sleep thinking of that night.

He thinks of that night too. I might turn into a puddle of mush. I manage to keep still, though.

Gabriel leans forward, bracing his forearms on his bent knees. "I want to hire you."

My mushy feels solidify a bit. That wasn't what I expected. I take a hasty sip of bourbon and lick my dry lips. "I'm… Okay, I'm not following."

A dull flush washes over the high crests of his cheeks. "I want you to sleep with me."

"Uh…what?" I can't form better words.

"Just sleep," he clarifies quickly. "I…bloody hell…I sleep when you're there. I have to sleep." For a second, he looks so weak, the circles under his eyes deeper and bruised. So weary. "You can stay here, travel with me. The compensation will be —"

"Sunshine," I cut in. "Are you seriously trying to pay me to sleep in a bed with you every night?"

And holy hell, if his tense, straining body language is anything to go by, he wants this badly. I'm so shocked I have to take another sip of my drink. God, the idea is tempting. But dangerous. He hasn't said, "Sophie, I want you and can't live another night without you." He's trying to hire me, for fuck's sake.

He sits straight, his jaw clenched. "Look, I know it's ridiculous."

"It is," I agree, heartily.

His expression goes blank. "You're right."

He moves to rise, and I reach out, laying my hand on his stiff forearm. "It is ridiculous because you don't have to pay me for that."

If anything, he looks even more put out. "Yes, I do. This isn't... If I don't pay..." He shakes his head with an exasperated breath. "It isn't right not to pay."

My fingers curl around the hard muscle of his arm. "Do you need this?"

He pulls at his cuff. "The fact that I'm humiliating myself ought to tell you as much."

I give him a watery smile. "All I'm trying to say is, even if you don't consider me a friend, I consider you one. I help my friends. And it wouldn't be right for me to take money from a friend. Besides, you're offering to let me stay here. This is flat-out luxurious compared to being cramped in with five other people."

His expression is so perplexed, my heart hurts for him.

"You'll do it?" he asks.

That's what I just said, wasn't it? I didn't even think it over, just blurted out my answer. I should be thinking this over. How am I supposed to live with this man? I'm attracted to him —total understatement. And he expects me to sleep next to him every night? Torture. And yet so very appealing. I want this. For reasons best ignored. Focus on the now. I've always operated on instinct. It has yet to fail me. And my instincts had me agreeing from the start. I'm not going back on that.

Gabriel sits quietly, fidgeting with his cuffs, though clearly trying not to. The man has the most ferocious scowl, and I've never seen grumpy look so hot. Inappropriate visions of a naughty schoolgirl and the punishing headmaster fill my head. *Down, girl.*

He makes a noise of impatience mixed with self-disgust. "I apologize for putting you in an awkward position. It was badly done. Let me walk you back—"

"Show me the bedroom."

He blinks at me as if I've spoken in a language he can't understand.

I start walking to the back of the bus, kicking off my shoes as I go. He watches me the way someone might track a stray raccoon who's found its way inside. But I notice he stands as well, slowly following.

The bedroom is as gorgeous as the living area. With the glossy, mellow wood paneling, it's cozy and warm. His bed is a king, taking up most of the space. I crawl onto it, sinking into the cream-satin covers.

Gabriel stands at the threshold, his gaze darting from me to the space beside me. I lay on my side, resting my head on my hand. This isn't going to be easy. Stretched out on his bed, with him looking on, this feels like something more.

It feels like seduction. I've never been good at lying to myself, either. I want his weight on me, the solid strength of his muscles shifting and bunching as he moves between my legs. I want that heat, to feel his cock sliding thick and wide into my empty, aching sex.

But he didn't ask for that. And the fact that he needs me for something non-sexual means something to me. I'm not just a pair of tits and ass for him to get off on. He could get that anywhere. We both know it. He needs *me* for this.

I let my head fall to the pillows. "Don't leave me hanging, sunshine."

"It's…" He glances at his watch. "Ten-fifteen in the morning."

"And I'm tired. I need a nap."

I really do. I hadn't realized how very exhausted I am until I said it out loud.

A calculating gleam enters his eyes. My nipples pulse in response. *Damn.*

Slowly, he takes off his jacket, the move pure suit porn. He takes his time, hangs it up, slips off his shoes, and removes his cufflinks. Muscles strain against his fine, white shirt. I watch him with a lazy sort of attention. The intimacy of his action soothes in a strange way, and my lids grow heavy.

He pauses at the edge of the bed. "Every night?" It's a husky rasp, with more yearning than I think he realizes.

Soft warmth blooms in my heart. "Naps too, if you want them."

His gaze is liquid heat. "I want them."

He crawls onto the bed. The wary, hesitant man is gone. Gabriel moves with grace, nearly prowling, hot eyes on me, his body coming flush with mine. I start to pant as he deftly rolls me to face the wall and curls himself around me, pressing my back to his front. He does it all as if he's had this planned in his head for some time, as if he's been thinking in great detail about what he'd do with me once in his bed.

His arm wraps around my middle, snaking up between my breasts before I can even blink. He cups my shoulder, holding me close—*snuggling* me.

I tremor, a swarm of bees bumping around in my belly. This feels too good. My skin is burning, my heart racing. He has to notice. I feel the rapid thud of his heart against my shoulder blades and know he's agitated too.

We struggle with the newness of the situation for a few seconds, and then he sighs, his warm breath stirring my hair, and his hard body eases. It's so peaceful, that sound, that I sink into his hold. We're over the covers, but I'm so warm, so secure, that it doesn't matter.

Gabriel's lips press against the crown of my head. "Every night, chatty girl."

The possession in his voice is absolute. I'm in so much fucking trouble.

GABRIEL 10

"SO, what are we going to tell people?" Sophie's big brown eyes gaze up at me with worry as we make our way to the practice room set up at a local recording studio.

Kill John is going to do a run through of a new song before we set off again, and I want to see if they're up to snuff. Sophie, of course, will be there to take photos.

Having gained two hours of sleep—a bloody miracle, by my count—I'm feeling so relaxed and mellow that I nearly hum one of their tunes. I might very well be losing my mind, but I don't bloody care.

"About what?"

"About me rooming with you." She waves an arm in exasperation.

She's adorable, really. And so fantastically soft and rounded and warm. God, she's warm when she sleeps, her lemon tart scent stronger, earthier somehow. I'm tempted to turn us around and demand more nap time.

I have to force myself to pay attention. "Do you not want them to know?"

"Well," she falters. "I don't know. It's just kind of..." Brown eyes narrow on me. "Do you want them to know you need me to fall asleep?"

"Not particularly."

She stops at the threshold of the room. No one has noticed us yet, so we have a bit of privacy. "They're going to think we're together."

A lovely flush pinks her round cheeks. My finger itches to stroke them.

"And that would be a problem?" I find myself asking.

Her full lips part, then snap shut before she answers. "It's a problem if it's a lie. And, no, I don't like the idea of people I work with gossiping about us."

"I see." With a nod, I turn toward the room. "Oy, listen up. Sophie will be traveling with me on my coach. And it's none of your bloody business why, so I'd better not hear a word about it. Understood?"

At my side, Sophie makes a strangled gurgle that sounds like a drowning chipmunk.

My boys, however, just blink back at me before grinning.

"Well, all right then, Scottie," Rye drawls. "Glad to see you taking initiative in your personal life."

Whip shakes his head. "Fucking knew it."

"You know nothing," Sophie hisses at him.

Jax high-fives Rye. "You owe us each fifty bucks, Killian."

"Shit, and I was so sure he'd hold out longer. Thanks a lot, Scottie." Killian glares at me. The little arse.

"What did I say about speculating?" I warn. "One more word and I'll have you all doing a music video with synchronized dancing faster than you can say Backstreet Boys."

Whip lifts up a hand. "Okay, geesh. Got it. You two are an impenetrable wall that no one shall gaze upon. No need to go all Simon Cowell on us."

I don't have time to see how the others react. Sophie pinches my side.

"Ouch. Do you mind? This is a silk-wool blend. You'll wrinkle it."

"It's about to be shredded." She seethes up at me, eyes shooting sparks. "You just totally threw our business out there."

"I told them not to talk about it."

Her nose wrinkles. "Which means they'll be talking about it even *more.*"

"No, they won't."

"Yes, we will," Rye calls.

I point at him. "Start practicing your Running Man."

"Is anyone else impressed that he knows dance moves?"

Sophie pokes me with her finger to punctuate each word. "This is all your fault."

Brenna takes it upon herself to stroll over. Her smile is wide and smug. "What did I tell you, Scottie-boy? I hire the best people."

Poor Sophie is beet red now. I feel a pinch of regret for putting her in an awkward position. But I know these people. They are my family. Better than family. Teasing aside, they'll do as I ask, if only because I've never asked them for anything personal before.

I would tell Sophie this now, but I think it would embarrass her further. So I settle for meeting her gaze and putting all the tender gratitude I feel into my voice. "Yes, Brenna, you do."

My reward is Sophie's expression going soft and luminous. Something cracks open within my chest. I don't know what it is, but I do know one thing: my chatty girl has no idea what she's gotten herself into. Because I'm not letting go.

SOPHIE

"YOU EXCITED ABOUT TOURING?" Jules asks as we sprawl

on the grass lawn in Edinburgh's West Princes Street Park.

Above us is a rare, cloudless blue sky. If I lift my head, I'll see the dark, craggy face of Castle Rock rising almost straight from the earth and the low-slung, imposing fortress of Edinburgh Castle sitting on top of it.

Last night, Kill John played at the castle's Esplande, which is an open, U-shaped stadium on top of Castle Rock with the castle as a backdrop. I've never experienced a concert like that, the glittering lights of the city below us, the medieval-looking castle creating an air of timelessness as Kill John brought fans to a screaming roar. It lifted goose bumps on my skin.

After taking a few pictures of the guys practicing at a recording studio this morning, I was given the rest of the day off. Since Jules also has free time on her hands, and I was too worked up about the prospect of rooming with Gabriel, I convinced her to escape with me and tour the town until we leave later this evening. And so we are taking full advantage, soaking up the sunlight streaming down on this lovely day.

"Completely," I answer, cracking open one eye to glance at her. "This isn't your first tour, though. Does it still hold any excitement for you?"

"Of course. I live for this." She turns my way. In the sunlight, I see that her eyes aren't simply brown but streaked with green. "It's more than a career; it's a dream come true. And one day, I'll be in charge of my own bands."

"I envy you. I don't have a dream like that."

Jules rolls to her side to face me, her head pillowed on the big, green hobo bag she always carries. "What do you mean?"

As I think about how to explain, a mime dressed in a tuxedo stops on the wide walking path and sets down a portable radio, which starts playing Michael Jackson's "Thriller." I watch him dance and fight a smile. At the far end of the park, by the Ross Fountain, a guy in a kilt plays the bagpipes. Their music blends into a disjointed clash of sounds.

It's wonderfully horrible, and nothing I'd ever have experienced if I hadn't taken a leap and gotten onto a plane with only the smallest bit of information to go on.

"I've never had a set dream job," I tell Jules, watching the mime dance. "Never had an intense ambition. And sometimes I wonder if I'm defective that way."

"You are not defective," Jules says with feeling. "Maybe you just haven't found what you love to do yet."

I shake my head and smile. "No, that's not it. I simply don't really care what I'm doing as long as I get to live life, be happy, and enjoy new things. Making money is great because it helps me travel, puts a roof over my head. But at the end of the day? I'm not ambitious and never will be." I shrug and pull a blade of bright green grass from the dirt. "Even worse? Eventually I want a home and to share it with someone who gets me completely, someone I can't keep my hands off. I want babies, and to decorate my porch on Halloween and Christmas."

Jules frowns. "Why is that bad?"

"Okay, it isn't *bad* per se, but all my peers seem to have this drive to make their mark in the world. And here I am thinking that a simple thing like this—" I sweep my arm toward the looming hill face, which looks like a Victorian painting. "—is something to live for."

Jules scans the scene before us, and a slow smile lights her face. "Well, then, I envy you more. Because I should be living in the moment. Worrying about what could go wrong in the future gives me fucking heartburn." She chuckles, and her fuchsia curls bounce around her face. "And I really need to stop worrying about disappointing Scottie."

"That's easy," I say. "Just remember he's all bark."

God, I love it when he barks, gets me all shivery and hot. Which should tell me I'm completely twisted.

Jules certainly looks as me as though I am. "Girl, I've felt his bite. Trust me, it's real, and it's scary." But then she winces. "Shit, I forgot you're with him now."

"Consorting with the enemy, you mean?" I tease.

"Something like that." She doesn't look as though it really bothers her, however.

I rest my forearm over my forehead. "First off, I'm not with him. We're...well, it's complicated."

"You don't say."

I laugh. "Okay, really complicated. But even if I was with him, I wouldn't take sides or discuss anything we say."

"Shit, I'm sorry," Jules says with a breath. "I didn't mean that, you know. I'm just...well, we're all kind of surprised that you and Scottie are...complicated."

I knew there'd be talk, despite Gabriel's insane notion that if he decreed silence, they'd obey. Deluded man. I'm not surprised by Jules's confusion. Oddly, I don't really care if they all speculate or don't understand. Because the flip side is that tonight I'm going to be sleeping in Gabriel's bed.

A near giddy feeling of anticipation tickles my skin and tightens my belly at the thought of being wrapped up in Gabriel; it's a full-body experience lying with him. He's big enough to make me feel small and delicate. Yet his need for my presence makes me feel strong and worthy.

It will be torture pressing up against that hard body, my lips far too close to his smooth, tight skin that burns slightly hot. I love the way he smells, and the steady cadence of his breathing. These things are already indelibly marked in my memory and upon my skin.

Most of all, I love that I see a side of him no one else does. I want to know this man. I've just told Jules I want to live in the moment, but for the first time in years, I look toward the future with a bit of wistfulness and some fear.

I close my eyes as "Thriller" starts up once more. "I'm not very good at complicated," I tell Jules. "But for Gabriel, I'm willing to try."

"For his sake, I hope you succeed." The affection I hear in her voice has me thinking she likes Gabriel more than she'll admit. "Because that man needs a social life more than anyone I've ever met."

SOPHIE  11

I STALL until the last second to get myself on Gabriel's bus. Dusk has settled over the parking lot where the buses are already idling, a snakelike caravan that holds Kill John's tour. Gabriel's bus is toward the end, a glossy black tube against the orange sky.

His driver, a very nice older gentleman named Daniel, greets me with a nod and a smile. "Made it by the skin of your teeth."

I think he knows I was stalling.

"Thanks for driving us," I tell him at the door. "You need anything? Coffee? Dinner?"

"No, miss. I have a very nice setup in the front. Scottie makes certain of that."

As well he should since he's relying on Daniel to keep us alive and safe while driving all night. I asked Brenna about the drivers. They sleep during the day in whatever hotel we stop at and stay up all night driving when we're on the move again. Most of them have been on multiple tours with the band.

Then again, Gabriel truly does make certain every small detail of the tour is attended to. Earlier today, he had Sara, one of the interns, pack up my things while I was goofing off with Jules and put them away in his bus. You'd think I'd find this invasive, but truthfully, I've been living out of my suitcase, and not having to go through the awkward task of unpacking, asking where I should put this or that while he looks on, is a relief.

Instead, I received a text from Sara telling me where everything is. I thanked her profusely and sent her a Starbucks gift certificate. Her delight in a free frap makes me consider sending Gabriel's entire staff certificates. All of them seem to spin constantly like cogs in the well-oiled Kill John machine, with Gabriel at the helm. And while he isn't cruel, he isn't exactly handing out praise for their efforts, either. It's clear he expects jobs to be done right the first time, and that goes for his as well.

The other buses are closing their doors, everyone tucked in for the trip.

I can stall no longer, and after wishing Daniel a good night, I step up into the relative cool and quiet of the bus and close the door behind me with a definitive thud. The pristine interior is empty, Gabriel nowhere to be seen. I admit, I'm unpleasantly shocked. I'd expected him to be lounging in a chair with his feral grace and vaguely admonishing expression. Is he running late?

I glance around as the bus lurches forward. Bracing my legs, I wait until I'm accustomed to the gentle rocking. I'm about to call out, or maybe buzz Daniel to warn him that he's left his boss behind, when Gabriel's deep voice comes from the bedroom.

"About bloody time. Were you trying to miss the bus, Darling?"

Relief swamps me so strongly I have to sag against the kitchenette countertop. "I like to be fashionably late," I call back.

"Just remember," he retorts, still talking from the depths of the bedroom, "the caravan waits for no one."

"It waited for me just now." I stroll toward the bedroom

but come to an abrupt halt at the threshold. For a second, I can only gape at the sight that greets me. It's so shocking, I turn around to check whether there are cameras rolling and I'm being punked.

"Why are you looking about like that?" Gabriel drawls, not taking his eyes from the TV.

"Just checking to make sure I hadn't wandered into an alternate reality."

"Amusing as always, Darling."

Who could blame me for being suspicious? Gabriel Scott is out of his suit and wearing a soft, gray long-sleeve thermal and black sweats. This is shocking enough—but at least I've seen it before. The fact that he's lounging in his bed, while eating some sort of dessert out of a bowl, is what has me flabbergasted.

"You're staring," he says dryly as he...

"Are you watching Buffy?" My voice has a tinge of a squeal.

He rolls his eyes. "Deal with it."

"I'm just so..." My hand flutters to my chest. "Are you sure I'm not being punked?"

A snort escapes him. "You're not famous, so no. I, on the other hand, have my moments of doubt that you aren't here to punk me."

I'm so happy, I have to fight grinning like a loon as I kick off my shoes and crawl onto the end of the bed. "If I were to punk you, I'd change out all your suits for polyester."

At that, his eyes finally slide to mine, and his skin actually pales. "That's just cruel, Darling."

"Stop calling me that." I steal his spoon.

"It's your name."

"Are you sure that's what you're calling me by?" I ask suspiciously, as he moves his bowl out of reach.

"What else would I be doing?" There's a glint in his eye

that leads me to answer in a sing-song voice.

"A term of endearment? Declaring your undying *lurve* for me."

His nose wrinkles. "You're going to put me off my pudding."

"Pudding? Is that what you're eating?" I lunge for the bowl, but he's too quick, and I end up sprawled across his chest.

We both go still, me clutching the spoon in one hand, my other palm pressed against the firm swell of his pec, him with one arm still outstretched, his other one pinned beneath me.

His breathing goes deep and strong as he peers down at me. My attention drifts to his lips, beautifully sculpted and softly parted. How would he kiss? Would he start off slow, taking little nibbles, testing the waters? Or would he be the type to go all in, possess my mouth with his?

Heat floods my body, fluttering through my belly.

Gabriel's lids lower, and his breath catches.

In the background, someone is shouting Buffy's name. It's enough to snap me out of whatever fog that touching Gabriel has pulled me into.

"You smell like apple pie," I whisper inanely.

His gaze darts from my mouth to my eyes. "It's crumble. Apple crumble."

"Why did you call it pudding?"

"It's what we Brits call dessert." He's still staring at my mouth. Dessert indeed.

My lips part, sheer lust making them plump. "Give me a bite."

With an audible swallow, he slowly takes the spoon from my hand. I don't look away from his eyes as he scoops up a bit of the crumble.

The spoon shakes just a little. Cool metal slides over my lower lip, and hot crumble fills my mouth. I barely suppress a moan, my lips closing around the spoon as he slowly draws it back out. He grunts in response, a short, helpless sort of sound that he quickly smothers.

"Delicious," I say, licking the corner of my lips.

The wall comes down once more, and he's back to his implacable self. With gentle hands he moves me to the side. "Off you go," he says lightly. "You're making me miss Buffy."

It takes me a moment to settle myself. I push my hair away from my face and snuggle back into the nest of pillows propped against the headboard. "I cannot believe you're watching this. With pride, even."

His big shoulder lifts on a shrug as he goes back to eating his crumble. "You're living here now; it's not as though I can hide my viewing preferences. And I'm not about to forego the small pleasures I get to enjoy."

"Geeking out on sci-fi shows and eating desserts?" I make a sound of amusement. "Try to contain yourself, party man."

He cuts me a look. "For the first few years of Kill John's existence, I fucked, drank, and partied my way across the globe. I can safely say I'm worn out on that life and completely bored with it."

My brain stutters on the word *fuck* coming from his lips in that crisp accent. He's used the word before, but we were fighting at the time. Now I'm paying attention. It's so tempting to ask him to repeat himself that I have to bite my inner cheek.

"What is that look all about?" he asks, catching my struggle. "I've learned many of your looks. But not that one."

"You know my looks? I don't think so."

Gabriel nudges me with his elbow. "You're blushing."

"Like hell." My cheeks burn.

The low rumble of his amusement lifts the little hairs along my arms, and my nipples tighten. Damn it. He's not allowed to affect me like this.

"The guys were giving me shit," I blurt out, my common

sense weakened by his nearness. "About you. They implied that you were a cold fish where sex is involved. That you don't...er...do that anymore."

God, I can't look at him. I brace for his ire, but he laughs. Not long or very loud, but his chest shakes, and he wipes a hand over his face as he tries to get control of it.

"And you, what?" he asks, his eyes gleaming with mirth. "Thought I was a virgin?"

"No." I kick his foot lightly. "No. I just...Gah! You said *fuck*, and it got me thinking about it."

"Fucking?" he asks, grinning wide enough to flash his white teeth.

I look away so I can't be charmed any further. "I hate you."

"No, you don't," he teases in a tone so unlike him—so like *me*—that I meet his gaze.

"No, I don't," I agree quietly.

And it's his turn to squirm. He stabs at his crumble with his spoon but doesn't take a bite.

"Is it true?" I can't help asking. "Are you...abstaining?"

"Jesus," he says, letting the spoon clatter to the side of the bowl. "Please, for the sake of my appetite, refrain from trying to phrase things delicately, chatty girl. It is painful to witness."

He'd look pretty good wearing that dessert right about now. "Then answer the question, sunshine."

For a second, I think he'll refuse, but he sighs in defeat and rests against the headboard. "Sex for me has always been..." He frowns as if trying to think of an explanation, then shrugs. "A release, I suppose. Hard, fast, mutual but impersonal satisfaction."

That really shouldn't sound appealing, but it does—at least when I picture him doing it. He's strong enough that it would be brutal in the best kind of way. I sit back as well, crossing my legs before me.

Gabriel continues in a dispassionate tone. "Living this life, looking the way I do, it's easy to get off whenever, however I want. I won't lie. I took advantage often. But then Jax happened." He stares down at his hands as they close tight around his bowl. "Everything felt false, ugly. Like we were all tainted by a lie, and those around us were liars. The amount of supposed close friends who jumped ship, turned their backs on Jax was staggering."

He glances my way, and his eyes are red at the edges. "Don't misunderstand; I expected it. I simply didn't expect it to bother me."

"Of course it would. They're your family. Anyone can see that you love them."

He stills as if he's absorbing my words. "Most people believe I'm incapable of feeling anything."

Outrage punches through my chest like a burning fist. In that moment, I know I'd go to war for this man. Even if he hated every second of it. No one should have to face the world without someone at their back. Especially not someone as dedicated as Gabriel.

"Idiots," I snarl.

He slowly shakes his head. "No, love, it's what I want them to see."

"Doesn't that bother you?"

"It helps. I was never particularly affectionate. But after Jax, I couldn't stand to have anyone touch me. Especially strangers. It makes my skin crawl, smothers me."

With a groan, I flop into the pillows. "And there I was on the plane, wrapping myself around you like cling film."

His mouth quirks, and he looks at me from under the thick fringe of his lashes. "Yes, well, I'm all cured of you. Call it a trial by fire. Or aversion therapy."

"Lovely. I'm feeling all warm and fuzzy now. No." I hold up a hand. "Don't hold back how you really feel."

He snorts and grabs my hand, his long fingers wrapping

around my smaller ones. He gives me a squeeze before gently setting my hand down on my thigh and moving his away.

"Our situation aside, casual contact irritates me, which means casual sex no longer holds any interest. In truth, I find it repellant now."

It's probably wrong that I'm relieved. But if I had to watch him hook up with women during the tour, I don't know how I'd handle it. Jealousy is not fun and also hard to control. Yet it also bothers me, thinking about him consigning himself to being alone.

"What about having a relationship?" I ask.

"Most people bore me."

I laugh, but my heart hurts. "This you make very clear."

A frown knits his thick brows. "I've never been affectionate or normal, Sophie."

He says it like a warning, or maybe a badge of honor. And yet I hear the worry behind it all, as if he fears he might be defective. I know that particular fear very well.

"Hey, what's normal anyway? We're all a bit crazy."

"Some more than others," he can't seem to help but murmur with a small, teasing smile about his lips. "And I don't usually have dessert. Crumble is special."

That catches my attention. "How so?"

He pokes as his desert before answering with a secretive smile. "Mary made this for me."

"Mary." The name tastes of bitterness in my mouth.

He glances at me, his brows drawing together before his expression smoothes into amusement. "Glorious woman. Excellent baker. The best, really."

"I prefer apple pie."

The bastard gives his spoon a lazy lick. I ignore that tongue. And those firm lips that are just a bit glossy with apple-cinnamon filling. "How American of you. Don't fret, love. I'm certain Mary could bake a luscious pie too."

"Maybe you should ask *her* to sleep with you at night. Then you can have your pie and eat it too."

"Good suggestion, Marie Antoinette. Only I think she'd turn me down. She's constantly telling me I'm too young for her." He shrugs. "Eighty-year-old women are prickly that way."

I grab his spoon and take an irritated bite of his beloved crumble while he chuckles, his eyes crinkling at the corners. I can't believe I let him goad me.

"Ass," I tell him around my mouthful of food.

"You wear jealousy well, Ms. Darling. Makes you all flushed and breathy."

"Deluded ass," I amend. When he won't stop grinning, I poke his chest. "So why is crumble so special?"

All the happy smugness falls off his face, and regret pangs inside my chest. His gaze drifts off as he speaks. "My mum used to make it for me as a special treat. The only crumble I've found that tastes even close to my mum's is made by Mary, who owns a bake shop here. I always order a batch when I come to town."

I want to ask him about his family and why his mom doesn't make him crumble instead. But agitation has settled on him like a heavy blanket he's trying to shrug off. I can't bring myself to pick at that scab.

With an ease I don't feel, I take the bowl from his unresisting hand and help myself to another bite of crumble. It's rich and buttery, crisp and spicy.

Kind of like Gabriel himself.

"Now then," I tell him around the mouthful, "you've completely lost points for being Team Jacob."

He snorts.

"So you'll have to redeem yourself." I wave the spoon at him threateningly. "Who was better for Buffy? Angel or Spike?"

Gabriel takes the spoon and bowl back. "Angel is a teen girl's dream, all sad sighs and mental angst. Spike is for when she grows up and realizes satisfaction is hers for the taking."

My grin slowly unfurls. "You, sir, are a romantic."

He glances at me in affront. "I just said all that romantic babble was childish."

"Only a romantic would put so much thought into that answer."

"You annoy me," he grumbles without heat. "And for the record, I was lying about Jacob. I think they're both prats."

I laugh and laugh, loving the way he eventually nudges me with his elbow. I get myself a bowl of crumble and give him another serving, then settle down next to him to watch Buffy.

I feel like I'm sixteen again, in my parents' basement with the hottest guy in school. Only I'm on thousand-dollar sheets in a million-dollar bus, driving through Europe. And Gabriel is no teen boy.

His long, lean body sprawls across the bed in complete repose, and I have to ignore that fact or I'll do something rash like slide my hand down his firm abdomen and slip it into his loose sweats.

By the time he reaches for the remote and turns off the TV, I'm a freaking mess. My mouth is dry, and my heart is trying to pound its way out of my chest.

"You can wash up first," he offers, subdued and not fully meeting my eyes.

If it weren't for the fact that Gabriel is waiting his turn, I would dither in the bathroom for far longer. As it is, I scrub my face, brush my teeth, and put on the baggiest shirt and shorts I can find.

My face flames as I scurry under the covers, all awkward and bumbling, sending a pillow to the floor in my clumsy attempt to haul the sheet up to my nose.

I wait in total silence for him to take his turn in the

bathroom. And when he comes out, I can't bring myself to watch him make his way to the bed. It's too intimate, too real.

Gabriel is far more graceful in sliding into bed. I cringe, imagining that unlike me, he's probably unaffected. Why should he be? He has made it clear I'm nothing more than a snuggle buddy. I probably rate somewhere between stuffed animal and oversized pillow.

The room plunges into darkness. I can hear myself breathing—too loud and too fast. I can hear him breathing—too steady and too controlled.

Fuck. What was I thinking? I can't do this.

The silence is so thick between us now that I'm suffocating in it.

Gabriel turns my way, and I immediately roll to my other side, facing away from him. It's basic self-preservation. If we're face to face right now, I don't know what I'll do. But I'm pretty sure it would end with me being utterly embarrassed.

He doesn't seem to mind. No, he moves closer. Goosebumps break out over my skin as his body comes into contact with mine. A heavy, muscular arm settles around my waist. And I forget to breathe.

What the hell is wrong with me? I napped with him earlier, and I was fine. Well, not *fine*. I wanted to stay in his arms forever. But I wasn't all out of sorts.

I wasn't fighting a shiver the way I am now.

His warm breath caresses the top of my head. "Relax, Sophie."

I release a breath. "I'm trying."

His voice is a whisper in the dark. "Are you uncomfortable?"

Uncomfortable? His big hand gently presses my belly, taking in the soft swell, which really sucks, but the way he keeps his hold there makes me think he either doesn't notice or likes what he feels. Wishful thinking.

And then there's the fact that he's so close. All I have to do is turn and I'll be wrapped around him like paper on a present.

"No," I squeak out. "I'm good."

I can feel him nod. The bed creaks as he eases closer. And then I feel it.

Oh, fucking hell. Just no. He can't do this to me.

It's big, it's hard, and it's nudging my ass.

We both freeze. Well, Gabriel freezes. His dick? It nudges me again, that blunt head pushing into the small of my back as if to say hello.

"Involuntary reaction," Gabriel says in a strangled voice. "Ignore it."

His hard-on says otherwise.

I swallow with difficulty. "Your hard dick is poking me in the ass. I can no more ignore it than if you slapped me in the face with it."

He stills, a sound gurgling in his throat. I'm about to apologize for being so crude, when he bursts out laughing.

Oh, how he laughs. He laughs with his whole body, shaking the bed as he flops onto his back and just laughs. The unfettered, deep, rolling laughter is so unlike his usual reserved self that I find myself grinning.

In the dim light, his body is little more than a silhouette, his teeth a flash of white across his face. He wipes his eyes as he giggles and snorts and laughs like a giddy boy. And I love every second of it.

Gabriel should always be like this, uninhibited and free. And if I have to suffer through his cock prodding my ass every night to get him there, I'm more than willing to make the sacrifice.

GABRIEL

IT'S BEEN SO LONG since I've full-out laughed that my abs are sore. Apparently laugh muscles aren't the ones I work with my morning sit-ups. This ache feels different. Good and full, as if exhausting myself from laughing put something back in me that I'd lost. I rest my hand on my stomach and stare up at the ceiling, letting the sensation sink in.

At my side, Sophie flops her head back against the pillows, drawing my attention. She's beaming at me as if I've made her night, and she's so bloody gorgeous, my breath hitches.

This girl. I could lose myself over this girl. Who would have thought?

My smile fades as reality sets in, hard and uncomfortable. "Chatty girl, what are we doing?"

The light in her eyes dims. "What do you mean?"

"This." I gesture between us and sigh. "Me asking you to be my sleep partner. It was a mistake."

"What?" She comes up on her elbows, moving into the light slanting through the windows. "Why? What's going on, sunshine?"

I hate the hurt that's clouding her sweet face, but I'm doing us both a favor. I pinch the corners of my eyes to ward off an incoming headache. "Lack of sleep has addled my judgment. It was unfair to ask you sleep with me like a goddamn security blanket night after night."

"Gabriel—"

I can't stand the soft almost-pity I hear in her voice, and I cut her off. "We're adults, not children. Sleeping together every night will lead to expectations. Mistakes."

Silence looms. I don't want to see her expression.

"I'm attracted to you," I blurt out. Heat swamps my cheeks as frustration claws at my gut.

Sophie swallows hard, and I risk a glance. Her eyes are wide and darting over me, but a smile is pulling at her lips. I hate that smile. It holds too much hope.

"Sophie, I have no capacity for relationships. I've never had one, never wanted one."

Her nose wrinkles. "That sounds lonely, if you ask me."

I'm beginning to agree.

"I'm too busy to be lonely." Also true. Months can pass in a blink, and I will not have noticed.

The bed creaks as she eases closer. The lemon-sweet scent of her surrounds me. I know how smooth her skin is and how soft her body feels. I hold myself still, refusing to grab hold.

Her face hovers above me.

Don't do that. Don't dangle in front of me like some carrot. I'm holding back by a thread here.

I pinch my eyes closed. Her delicate fingers touch my shoulder.

"Truth, Gabriel? I'm attracted to you too. But I think you know that."

Of course I know. That only makes the temptation sharper. It would be so easy to use her. Sophie deserves more.

"This job is my life and the entirety of my focus," I say. "This tour is long and tight-knit. I cannot worry about hurt feelings or regrets. And I cannot do casual with you, Sophie. You deserve much better."

Her voice is gentle and thoughtful. "I get that. I don't want casual either. I'm through being someone's fun time. I want more."

I'm proud of her for demanding better. I still can't look at her. "Which is why I said it was stupid of me to ask you to do this."

She hums in agreement. And though I've cleared the air, I hate that sound. I don't want her to leave. Lonely, cold, and sleepless nights loom ahead. I might not survive it. I'm more relaxed than I've been in over a year, and I haven't yet had the pleasure of sleeping next to her.

"Thing is," she says. "I don't want to go back to the other bus."

I turn to look at her sharply, my insides clenching.

She faces me without flinching. "I like it here with you. And maybe... Well, maybe I need you too. Maybe we need each other for whatever it is we have between us." A flush suffuses her rounded cheeks. "So maybe we don't analyze it or expect things from each other. But let's just...I don't know... hang out."

"Hang out," I repeat like a stunned parrot.

"Yeah," she whispers with an encouraging smile. "Watch cheesy TV, eat desserts—"

"Dessert was really a one time thing—"

"It's on the roster, bud. These hips don't grow themselves."

"I wouldn't want to be responsible for their demise," I murmur. *No, don't flirt. Don't think of her spectacular arse.*

She waggles her brows. Which is adorable and ridiculous all in one. "And we cuddle."

I want those cuddles. I don't fucking care if it makes me weak or foolish. I want them enough to ignore how much I'd love to roll over and sink deep into her body. For now, I can stand it. I think I can stand almost anything if I can get some rest and have her company.

"All right." My voice is rough, unsteady. I clear my throat. "Then I suppose there's only one question left to ask."

The tension visibly flows out of her body with a breath, and she rests her head in her hand, looking me over with inquisitive eyes. "What's that?"

"Do you prefer the left or right side of the bed?"

GABRIEL 12

IT ISN'T difficult to track down Liberty Bell James. I simply go where Killian is, knowing she'll in the vicinity. At the moment, it's Charles Ehrmann Stadium in Nice, France--this week's venue--where Kill John is conducting a sound check.

Liberty is in the center of the hall, comfortably lounging in one of the seats at the end of a row, and apparently playing a game of Candy Crush on her phone.

I lean against the seat in front of her. "A cable network contacted me this morning. They want to use 'Reflecting Pool' for the start of one of their shows this season."

A soft flush runs over her cheeks. The woman isn't fully comfortable with success, but she's getting there. "That seems really...commercial."

No shite. "Actually, a car company wants to use 'Lemon Drop', too. I think we ought to say yes to both."

"Ugh. And have the threat of hearing myself every time I turn on the TV?" Her nose wrinkles.

I cross my arms over my chest, bracing my feet wide. I'll be here for a while. "We'll work in a clause to cover how long the commercial can run to avoid overexposure."

"Missing the point, Scottie."

"I believe you're the one missing the point, Mrs. James."

"For the last time, call me Libby or Liberty, Scottie."

"But you are Mrs. James now. I'm showing you the proper respect."

She gives me a light punch on the arm. "Your formality is killing me, Mr. Scott."

"Stick to the matter at hand, please. We need exposure at this point in your career. Car commercials have launched many an artist simply because people hear the song and want to buy it. Need I remind you of Sia?"

"Like I can stop you," she mutters.

"The program *Six Feet Under* played 'Breathe Me' for one bloody show, and it launched her in the US."

Liberty's chin lifts on a stubborn sniff, but I see the capitulation in her eyes.

"I understand you want to keep things low key," I say. "This is a good way to do it. No talk show appearances, media junkets, and the like. You simply let another massive media source do the work for you."

I don't add that I'll work toward setting up a mini-tour when the public starts clamoring for her. Baby steps are needed with Liberty. But despite her protests, she does love the stage. Killian knows as much, which is why they'll be performing a few songs together on this tour.

"Fine. Tell them yes."

"Enthusiasm, Mrs. James. It's what makes my day."

She laughs. "Yeah, I just bet it does." Liberty stands and gives me a long look. "And your nights? How are they doing now that you've got yourself a roommate?"

Sly little shit. I want to tell her to mind her business. But now I'm thinking of Sophie. How are things? I wake with my hands full of luscious, warm woman. I smell her on my clothes throughout the day. I barely have a moment's privacy once I'm on my coach or in a hotel room, and I look forward to that. I'm beginning to hate silence, because it means she's not there.

And I'm surrounded by all things Sophie. Her battered

little trainers. Camera equipment. Makeup, hairbrushes, lotions, and hair products.

My collar suddenly feels too tight.

"Tell me, Mrs. James," I find myself saying. "Is there a reason you women feel the need to wash your underthings in the sink and hang them over the shower like some sort of profane Christmas decorations?"

I was treated to this particular form of visual torture earlier, when I went to have my morning shower, only to find lacy bras and delicate little knickers strewn about the place. What was I supposed to do? Take them down? I'd have to touch them.

If I'm going to put my hands on Sophie's knickers, she's bloody well going to be in them when I do. My collar squeezes my throat yet again.

Liberty laughs. "It's not as though you can toss good bras and undies in the laundry. They're hand wash only."

"But must you leave them hanging out in the open?" Hell, now I know exactly what size Sophie's bras are. I'm only human. I looked. How could I not? Particularly when she left that pretty white lace one trimmed in scarlet ribbon, so well constructed, it seemed to hold her shape even though she wasn't in it.

"You've pulled your tie all out of whack," Liberty says, bringing me back to the present.

I blink down at her for a minute, trying to clear my mind of the fact that Sophie favors satin panties with lace panels that hug her peachy bum to perfection.

Liberty gives me a soft smile. "Here, I'll fix it. I know how you hate being rumpled."

She moves to straighten my tie, but I wave her off. "Leave it."

I hate being fussed over more. But I don't bother fixing my tie either. I want to pull the damn thing off and toss it in the nearest bin before it strangles me. Liberty looks at me as if I'm off my nut.

"Well," she says, clearly struggling not to tease. "You could always ask Sophie to send her things out to be dry cleaned."

And miss the post-wash show? "That would be rude," I mutter.

Liberty's expression is too neutral to be serious. "It's probably a good idea not to tick off your new roommate."

I shrug, tug at my tie again, then leave off—because fuck all, I will not fidget. "It's fine. I simply hadn't thought there would be quite so many...accessories. I've never roomed with a woman before."

It's too silent. I glance at Liberty to find her grinning. Her grin grows when I glare.

"It's cute to see you with a girlfriend," she says.

"What are we, sixteen?" I sneer. "She's not my girlfriend."

"Fine, your lover."

"Christ. We're friends. That is all."

"Right." She rolls her eyes.

"I told the lot of you to mind your business."

Liberty laughs. "Oh, come on, Scottie. You brought a woman into your Fortress of Solitude. Did you really think we wouldn't talk?"

"And what is your role here?" I ask. "Did you draw the short straw to come fact check?"

A grin spreads across her face. "I volunteered. Everyone else is too chicken to ask."

"Lovely. You can go back and tell the rest of the clucking hens that Sophie and I are just friends."

"Hey," Jax says, sauntering up. "That rhymes."

He gives Liberty a kiss on the cheek. "Killian's looking for you. You giving Scottie a hard time for us?"

"He's in a mood now."

"I'm not in a mood." I'm lying, and we all know it. Tension

locks my jaw and rides down my neck.

"His tie is askew," Jax says, frowning. "That's practically undressed."

Liberty nods, staring at my wrenched tie. "He won't let me fix it."

I give them both the finger, which they find hilarious, and walk away. The urge to fix my tie is strong now, but I leave it on principle.

I don't know where I'm headed. I should find Jules and ask her for a progress update. I'd call her, but I forgot my phone. It unnerves me that I actually left the coach without my phone—didn't even think about it. My head was filled with...other things.

As if called by my thoughts, Sophie appears at the top of the aisle, her smile wide and fresh, camera case slung over her shoulder, a takeout cup in her hand. "Hey! I've been looking for you."

I don't stop until I'm close enough for my body to block her from the others' sight. I don't want them to see her yet. "Have you?" I ask, peering down at her.

She's wearing bright red Chucks, worn jeans cuffed wide to her shins, and a white camisole that strains over her breasts. We couldn't be more incongruously attired if we tried. I drink her in, suddenly so thirsty my mouth dries up.

"Here," she says, lifting her cup toward me. "I brought you some tea. One sugar, light on the milk."

I blink in shock. She knows how I take my tea. She *brought* me tea. Even if it is in a paper cup, which will make it taste like shit.

As if reading my mind, she snorts, and her mouth quirks. "It's ceramic, designed to look like a takeout cup."

"Why on Earth would someone design a cup to look like something it's not—"

"Just take the tea, sunshine." She shoves the cup at me, and

I have no choice but to obey. While I inspect it, she sighs. "Before you start complaining again, the lid is rubber. You could drink through that little hole, but I know you won't. Take it off and drink."

Afraid to disappoint her, I do as directed. The tea is hot, and a bit weak, but it soothes the sudden lump in my throat. I take two more sips before clutching the cup in my hand and staring down at the murky tea. The steam rising from it makes my vision blur. "Thank you."

"Sure thing. Oh, hey, your tie is all pulled out."

She sets down her camera bag and reaches for my tie. I lean toward her so she doesn't have to stand on her toes, and hold still. Or I try to. I find myself listing closer until her lemon-sweet scent fills my lungs and the warmth of her body buffets my skin.

"How did you do this?" she mutters as she tugs at the tie and tucks the length farther down beneath my vest. "You're never mussed."

"I don't remember," I say, fighting the urge to rest my forehead on hers.

"Tough day?"

I think about where we are, and everything clenches cold. "I've had better."

"Well, drink your tea." She smoothes a hand over my chest and across my shoulders. "Let it work its magic on your British soul."

Stroke me more. Forever.

But she stops and gives me another happy look. "Oh, I found your phone on the dresser."

She pulls it out of her pocket and gives it to me.

I stand there, phone in one hand, tea in the other, unable to form words.

Sophie pats my shoulder. "Can't believe you left that behind."

I can't believe anything about myself anymore. I don't know whether to run or grab hold of her and never let go.

"Walk with me?" I ask, pocketing my phone.

"Where?"

Anywhere. "Outside. I need air."

Neither of us mentions that we're in an outdoor venue. She simply takes my free hand. "Lead on, sunshine."

SOPHIE

OUTSIDE THE STADIUM isn't exactly conducive to a nice walk, as it's in a fairly industrial area. Of course Gabriel, being Gabriel, texts his driver to pick us up and take take us to a nearby harbor.

It's gorgeous here: the Riviera sparkling in the sun, palm trees rustling overhead. Gabriel fits right in with his tailored light grey suit, sunglasses covering his eyes, his coal-dark hair swept back from his face. Images of Cary Grant dance in my head.

I'm no Grace Kelly in my jeans and Chucks. But he never makes me feel frumpy or underdressed. Even now, he walks at my side, his hand lightly touching my lower back as he guides me around an older couple strolling along hand in hand.

As soon as we pass them, Gabriel shoves his hands deep into his pockets and stares out over the sea. He's so pretty against this backdrop it almost hurts to look at him.

But he also appears distracted and unsettled.

"You okay, sunshine?"

He doesn't say anything for a moment. "We didn't have very much money growing up. My father was a mechanic. Originally from Wales, but he settled in Birmingham."

I have no idea why he's talking about his dad, but I'm not about to stop him. I know without a doubt that The Book of Gabriel doesn't open very often, if ever.

"Was? Did he retire?"

He snorts. "Retire would imply that he worked steadily. He never held down a job for very long. He preferred to live on the dole." Gabriel's jaw clenches. "I don't know if he's alive, actually, since he walked out of my life when I was sixteen."

"Oh." I don't say anything else, sensing that he needs to talk more than I need to question him.

He keeps walking, his pace slow and steady, his eyes to the sea. "My mother was French. Her parents emigrated to Birmingham after her father took a managing position at the Jaguar plant. For a time, she worked as an accountant. She met my when she did the books for one of the shops where he worked."

"Do you get your love of numbers from her?" I ask softly, because he's drifted off, his expression tight.

"I suppose I do." He glances at me. I can't see his eyes behind the shades. "My mum died when I was fifteen."

"Oh, Gabriel." I want to take his hand, but they're still tucked in his pockets. I wrap my fingers around his thick forearm instead, leaning slightly into him. "I'm sorry."

He shrugs. "Lung cancer." A deep breath rattles him. "Rather, she was diagnosed with stage four, non-small cell lung cancer. However…she, ah, decided to take her own way out."

I stop short, and he does too, since I'm still holding on to him. A lump rises in my throat. "You mean she—"

"Took her own life," he answers shortly. "Yes."

"Oh, hell."

"I don't…blame her," he grits out. "I simply… Ah, bollocks, I resented the hell out of her for taking what short time we had left away from me. Which is selfish, I know, but there it is." He spreads his hands as if to encompass his pain.

A thought occurs to me, and my skin prickles in horror. "And then Jax…"

"Yes." The word is a bullet, his face flushed and full of rage before going blank.

I move to hug him, but he turns and starts walking again, still controlled but his pace faster now.

"As I said, we did not have a lot of money. But Mum always wanted to go back to France. Her parents had died, and she felt a bit lost, I think, missing her country. This one time, Dad piled us into the car and we drove here, to Nice for holiday." He stops and stares at the sea. "I was ten. It was the last time we went anywhere as a family."

He lets me take his hand, and his cold fingers twine with mine.

I hold him more securely. "I'm sorry, Gabriel."

Nodding, he keeps his gaze averted. "I remember being happy here. But it brings back other memories I'd rather forget."

"Of course."

We don't say anything for a while, simply walk.

"I feel shitty now," I confess. When he glances at me with confusion, I bluster on. "I went on and on, complaining about my mom showing up, and what a pain my parents are—"

"And I loved hearing about it," he cuts in. "Don't you dare think otherwise. And don't you dare pity me. I won't stand for it."

"It's not pity," I say softly, squeezing his hand. "I just…" *Ache for you.* "Hell, I don't know. I feel like a shit just because, okay?"

He chuffs out a half-laugh. "Well, okay. And I do have a family."

"The guys and Brenna?"

"Yes." His hand slips from mine, and he clears his throat. "After Mum, well, Dad was around even less. But I'd always done well in school. I received scholarship for an independent school. You'd know it as a prep or boarding school, I suppose."

"I know Harry Potter," I offer.

He almost smiles. "I think we'd all have preferred Hogwarts."

"Was it bad?"

"It wasn't good," he says with a touch of asperity. "I don't know how much you know about Britain, but whether we admit it or not, classism is very much alive. All I had to do was open my mouth to speak and the other students knew I was working class."

"You?" I have to laugh. "You sound like Prince William to me."

His ghost of a smile is bitter. "Mimicry. You learn to adapt to survive. And there are days I hate the sound of it coming out of my mouth. Because I ought to have stayed true to myself. At the time, however, I just wanted to fit in. Didn't work, though."

"Did they give you shit?"

"Scholarship Scott with his dad on the dole? Of course. And I was a bit of a runt until I hit twenty. Stick thin and about six inches shorter."

I have to grin at that, imagining Gabriel in his puppy youth, all awkward angles and blooming male beauty.

"I was having the crap beat out of me when I met Jax." He says it almost fondly. "Jax jumped right in the middle of it, scrappy as a dog. Next thing, Killian, Rye, and Whip were there, pummeling the shite out of anyone left standing."

He looks up at me and laughs, the first truly amused sound I've heard from him since our walk began. "I was brassed off. Who were these tossers? They didn't know me. Why help?"

My throat constricts. "You'd never had anyone help you just because it was the right thing?"

Eyes the color of the sea meet mine. "No. At any rate, I told them to piss off."

"But they didn't."

"Of course not. Firstly, they'd heard I could secure dope —"

My steps halt. "You? Smoking up? No."

"How very scandalized you sound, Darling," he says, fighting a small smile. "I was a teenager stuck in boarding school with a bunch of elitist wankers. Passing through some of those long hours in a haze was part of survival."

"I'm now picturing you slouched on a couch, doing bong hits." I grin at the thought. "Did you get Scooby-snack cravings?"

He looks at me blandly. "Yes, but only after riding around in the Mystery Machine, searching for villains. Hard work, that."

Snickering, I start walking again. "So after you became the guys' supplier?"

"Hilarious," he mutters. "And it wasn't about drugs. Not really. They were outcasts in a way too. They came from money, but they were all either half-American or had lived there for a majority of their lives."

"I can see that. They all basically sound American. Especially Killian and Rye. I mean, sometimes I hear a faint English accent when Jax speaks," I say, thinking back on our conversations. "And Whip has a slight Irish lilt."

"Jax and Whip—or John and William, as they were known back then—spent more of their time in the UK than Killian and Rye, so that isn't surprising. At any rate, they decided I was worth adopting, and they wouldn't go away. I was doomed."

"Poor baby."

Gabriel stops and turns toward the breeze coming in from

the water. "It's…hard letting people in. My dad was a drunk, almost never home. Mum was gone. And here were these four rich boys trying to take me in like I was Oliver fucking Twist."

"And yet here we are," I say softly.

He nods, almost absently. "Some things are hard to resist, no matter how badly you try to maintain your distance." He begins walking again, back toward the waiting town car. "I spent summers at Jax's house, went on holiday with Killian or Rye or Whip's family. And I saw how life could be."

We near the car, and he glances my way. "And when they began their band, their talent was brilliant, even then. But their organization was shit. So I stepped in, promised their parents I would do my mates right. Always."

I stop short. "Gabriel."

He stops as well, his brow quirking. Framed against the French Rivera, the massive yachts and sleek sailboats resting in crystalline waters, his pale suit cut to perfection and highlighting his dusky skin, he looks every inch the international playboy. I can't even picture him poor and struggling. Until I meet his eyes.

Such beautiful eyes. But the fine lines around them, and the weariness that always seems to linger in those stark depths, tell me a new story now. All he knows is to fight and protect, both himself and those loyal to him.

"It wasn't your fault."

He blinks, a slow sweep of long lashes, and his expression goes blank.

"I mean it." I take a step closer. "None of it. Not your mom. Not Jax."

It's as if I've slapped him. His head jerks back, and his lips flatten. For a second, I think he might shout at me. But then he gives me a one of those fake-ass polite looks he saves for sponsors and record executives.

"This conversation has run away from me. I hadn't meant

to go on a poor-me walk down memory lane."

"Stop." I touch his cheek and find him so tense, I imagine he might shatter. "We don't have to talk about this any more. But I'm not backing down from what I said. We can't control the actions of others. It will never happen. We can only control our own. Kill John would not be what they are without you. And those guys wouldn't love you like they do if you weren't worthy."

His shoulders don't lose their starch. If anything, he seems to harden all over, his armor forming right in front of my eyes. But then the corner of his mouth lifts.

"Is this how it's going to be?" he asks in a slightly husky voice. "You championing me, whether I want it or not?"

"Someone has to do it, sunshine." I give his cheek a gentle pat then get my ass in the car before he can say another word.

GABRIEL 13

"WHY…the…fuck…did I agree…to go on this death run with you?" Jax's panting whine is pathetically weak as we make our way through El Retiro Park in Madrid.

"You asked to go," I say, not breaking stride. Perspiration trickles down my skin; my heart pumps steady and sure. "Said you needed the exercise." I glance at Jax stumbling along beside me, his chest shining with sweat. "You weren't wrong."

He gives me the finger, apparently past talking, and I take pity on him, slowing down.

"Enjoy the scenery." I nod toward the manmade pond that reflects the monument to Alfonso XII. Couples row around it, laughing, kissing, or lounging in the sun.

I wonder if Sophie has been here yet. She'd probably head straight for the boat, demanding that I row as she took pictures of it all.

I shake my head. I do not row women around in boats like some sort of cliché sap.

But you'd do it for her. Lie to yourself all you like. You'd do it and love every second.

I tell myself to shut it.

"I can't appreciate the scenery," Jax grumps, "when my legs are on fire and my lungs are waving the white flag. I mean, what the fuck? I perform every night on stage. For fucking hours."

Jax doesn't have an ounce of fat on him, but he's kept so much to himself this past year and a half that he's grown weaker than he once was.

"Different type of endurance, mate."

He grumbles, and we fall silent. Despite his complaining, I'm glad he chose to come out with me. Though he never ran with me before, we used to lift weights together, spotting each other because we were of a similar strength then. It was one of the few things we did as friends, without business taking centerstage.

I haven't thought of it until now, but I miss that time with him. I run a few more beats. "Perhaps it's best if you find an alternate form of exercise."

Though I'm not looking his way, I hear his scoff loud and clear. "Don't you dare go easy on me, Scottie boy. I count on you to kick my lazy ass."

It's a struggle to keep a straight face. "Very well then, move that lazy arse, and stop complaining."

We pick up our pace once more. Or I do. Jax groans and plods along with terrible form.

The hotel looms in front of us.

"I'm warning you now," I tell him as we pass slow, strolling people. "I'm taking the stairs to my room."

"Oh, fuck no," Jax says, looking horrified. "I'm stopping in the lobby." He flashes a rare, wide smile. "I'll pace around panting and guzzling water. Probably take me under a minute to find someone to rub me down."

Of course he will. I'd have to be willfully blind to miss the attention we both receive, even now, as we sweat under the hot Spanish sun. Wherever we go, eyes follow.

I could do the same as Jax. It'd be easy as snapping my fingers to find sexual release. These days, my body is aching for it, my balls sore from lack of fulfillment. And yet the thought of finding some willing woman in the hotel lobby makes my stomach lurch. Needing sex isn't precisely the problem; it's more an issue of being constantly tempted by one, certain woman.

As soon as we enter the hotel, I leave Jax to his hunting and take the stairs, pushing myself to go faster, harder. My thighs scream in protest, my lungs burning as I pound along. I don't stop. I want the pain. I want to be so exhausted that my body gives up asking for what it can't have, and I can go through the day with an ache in my muscles, not my cock.

By the time I get to the room, I'm so spent, I'm nearly stumbling. It's blissfully Sophie-free in the cool of the room. I grab a bottle of water from the mini fridge as I pace around, my chest heaving. My blood rushes through my ears, my vision a haze as I bumble my way into the bath, drinking as I go.

Shoving my shorts down and toeing off my trainers, I turn to reach for the taps and knock down a small laundry basket sitting on the sink.

I rub the sweat out of my eyes and find myself facing yet another batch of Sophie's knickers, now scattered all over the floor in a patchwork rainbow of silk.

Fucking fuck. A pair of little white panties patterned with tiny red cherries rests on my foot. My hand closes around cool silk, and my cock rises so swift and hard, I actually groan.

I'm not prepared; I'm too weak this time. Too fucking weak to stop myself from lifting the panties to my nose and breathing in deep. A wave of lust slaps through me so hard, my knees nearly give out.

Because these are Sophie's dirty knickers. And I'm the perverted bastard who's getting off on the musky scent of Sophie's pussy.

Another groan tears out of me as I fall against the cold tile wall. I close my eyes tight, fighting the urge to take another breath. *Don't do it, mate. Drop them and get the hell in the shower.*

But I can't. My cock is so hard it throbs in time with my frantic heartbeat. God, her scent…the tart-sweetness of her perfume lingers, calling the golden hue of her skin to mind. Only this time, I picture her on the bed, wearing noting but these cherry panties, her tits thrust in the air, her thighs spread wide. Just waiting for me to nuzzle between them.

Without my permission, my hand slides over my chest, rubbing those dirty little knickers on my skin, as if I can soak up that scent and make it part of me.

I'm shaking, my breath disjointed and deep as my hand descends. Smooth silk wraps around my cock. I fist it and squeeze my eyes tight as I give myself a hard tug.

Sweat trickles down my stomach, my pulse thrumming on my neck. I jerk at my needy cock, my sore muscles bunching with each pull. It feels so damn good, and not nearly good enough. I almost hate her in this moment. Hate her for making me this needy. Only, I don't. Not even a little bit.

I want. I want. I want.

It's a refrain in my mind as I fuck her panties like some naughty schoolboy. If she knew what I was doing… Heat licks down my spine, up my trembling thighs.

"Gabriel?" The sound on her voice, and the knock on the door, stops my heat.

For a hard second, every muscle freezes. My gaze snaps to the door in horror. I locked it. Didn't I?

"Are you in there?"

Fuck, don't try the door.

"Yes!" I shout in a gurgle of desperation. "Christ. Use the other toilet."

If she opens this door, I'm done for. I'll have her on her back and my cock balls-deep in her heat in seconds. I almost *want* that door to open.

Her muffled voice sounds slightly put out and slightly

amused. "Testy. I was just going to say I left my laundry in there…"

I look down at the white silk clutched in my fist and the swollen, angry head of my prick peeking out. I shiver and give it a slow stroke, my eyes fluttering in agonized pleasure as I do.

"Go away, Sophie."

"But…"

"I'm showering." My free hand fumbles for the taps and turns them on.

"You just turned the water on."

God, her voice. This is wrong. So wrong. Squeezing my eyes shut, I keep tormenting my knob, denying him the satisfaction of the real thing.

"Can I just step in and get it before you start?"

Already started, love. Why don't you come in and finish me off?

The image of her lips wrapping around my pulsing head is so vivid, a surge of pre-come leaks onto the panties in my hand. My come on Sophie's panties. I suck in a breath. "If you don't move away from this door, I'll watch my entire collection of Star Trek movies on the next leg of the trip. All thirteen of them."

I hear a gasp. "That's just cruel."

Cruel is fucking silk when I could be in the real thing. Hot, tight, slick. My teeth grind together.

"There will be a quiz at the end of it," I say in a strangled voice.

I'd pin Sophie down, question her on all the ways she likes to be pleasured, and then do them one by one. Unable to hold back, I beat myself off hard and fast, biting my lip so she can't hear me.

"Fine," she says, oblivious to the tremors wracking me as my balls draw tight and lust sucks me down. "I don't know why you have to be so snippy."

Her voice follows me into oblivion. I come in hard jets that splatter over my abs and chest, as I milk every last drop of profane, stolen pleasure I can. I swear I whimper.

Silence rings out on the other side of the door. I sag to my knees and try to catch my breath. Behind me, the shower roars and steam fills the room.

I crawl into the stall and let the hot water wash away my sins. It's only after I reach for the soap that I realize I'm still clutching her panties as if I'll never let them go. I swear this woman is going to kill me.

SOPHIE

THINGS TO LOVE ABOUT MADRID: The architecture. Gorgeous, ornate, timeless. The food. Savory, salty, rich, spicy. The *café con leche*. Don't get me started. So rich and creamy, it's like coffee-flavored hot chocolate. I drank three cups of it one day and reached for another until Gabriel dryly pointed out that I was hopping around like an overexcited bunny.

But the best thing about Spain? Siestas. God bless any country that has decided *yes, we shall shut down business and take a long nap in the middle of the day.* How can you not love them for that?

This means I have a government-sanctioned excuse to sleep cuddled up next to Gabriel for most of the afternoon. Yesterday, when I pointed this out, he grumbled about it once, and not very convincingly. Not when he was fast shedding his jacket and slipping into the bathroom to change into a T-shirt and sweats.

Pervy me wants to suggest he quit with the coy hiding himself away to change and just strip down in front of me. Hell, I want to help him out, unbutton his crisp shirts and slowly pull the zipper on his fine slacks. But it would upset the status quo, and I have no idea which way the scales would tip.

It's strange not knowing. Normally I'm excellent at reading men. They're fairly simple creatures, after all. Most of them are, anyway. They want you, they make it known.

Gabriel? He's not most men. True, a man as stunning as Gabriel never has to work at getting a woman. He can attract invitations just by standing still. I've seen it happen. Many times. Women take one look at him, and it's on.

Only he never bites. Never even bothers to fully look at whoever is hitting on him. His expression is always bland with a hint of boredom as he casually yet politely gives her the brush off. It's an art form, really, how effectively he rids himself of unwanted advances. I've taken notes.

And I'd be inclined to think he was asexual at this point, except he's not. Not even close. Not given the amount of times his gaze collides with mine and the heat in his expression takes my breath. God, it burns, the way he watches me. It's covetous and possessive.

He looks at me as if he's mentally stripping off my clothes. With his teeth. He looks at me, and the bottom falls out of my belly. My heart swoops down to my toes, and my nipples go so hard so fast it almost hurts. Almost, because it feels so freaking good—that tight throb, knowing that the only thing that will make it better is his mouth, wet and hot, pulling on them.

I think those dirty thoughts—of Gabriel on his knees, his cheeks hollowing out with the force of his sucks, his hands on my hips, holding me still so I can't move to alleviate the pressure between my legs—and I get a little lightheaded.

And Gabriel must know. He must see what he does to me. I'm a blonde. I blush like one, all pink and sweaty. Too many times, I've seen that hot blue gaze of his stray downward, lingering on my horny nipples. They aren't exactly shy about showing themselves, damn it all.

His nostrils always flare just a little bit, and then a sharp, deep breath, as if he's bracing himself. But it inevitably ends there and then. Because he's unwilling to go any further.

And yet that thick, hard cock of his pokes at my ass every time we crawl into bed. He never pulls away to hide his erection, nor does he grind himself against me to move things along. No, he just leaves it there, snug on my ass, his big, wide hand gently molding itself to my belly, his chin on the crown of my hair. He holds me like a lover might, tender yet lingering. But he treats me like a friend, respectful, kind, never taking advantage.

And I let him do it. I lie there, day after day, night after night, my body yielding to his, soaking up his heat, reveling in his possessive hold. It'd be so easy to turn in his arms, press my lips to his, slide my hands down his waist to slip under his lounge pants. I've imagined grasping his big dick—and I know it's big at this point— so many times that my palms tingle with phantom memories.

Today, however, there will be no napping. Gabriel has gone out on a run instead. Odd, since he already went on one this morning.

God, this morning... My cheeks burn at the memory. Okay, so I interrupted his "man time" by knocking on the bathroom door. I shouldn't have done that; Lord knows I'd be pissed if he had done the same. But I hadn't expected him back so soon and went to go get detergent. Imagine my horror when I returned and realized he was locked away with my dirty underwear.

And clearly he found them. He hasn't been able to look me in the eye since he finally got out of his shower, practically grunting out answers every time I bothered to talk to him.

So embarrassing. I don't even know why I thought cleaning them in the bathroom was a good idea. I didn't even bother washing my undies after Gabriel left the room, but stuffed them all in a bag and sent them down with housekeeping. Only, they lost my favorite pair—the cute boy shorts with cherries on them. And no one on staff can find them. So, joy all around today.

I'm so worked up now, when my phone rings, I almost jump out of my skin. Sad that I hope it's *him*. But it's my friend Kati from New York.

"Hey you," I answer with a smile. "Isn't a little early to be calling me?"

It's two in the afternoon here, which means it's eight in the morning in New York, and I know Kati is a late sleeper like me.

"It would be," she answers, "if I was in New York."

I flop back on the bed. The stupid empty bed which will not be used for napping. "Where are you?"

"I'm in London at the moment. There's a certain pop star who has broken up with her high-profile boyfriend, and everyone wants the scoop."

Kati is a reporter who covers the music industry. She was the one to get me into celebrity photography, and also the first to support me leaving the business when she saw how hollowed out I'd become.

"Tough life, isn't it?" I say.

"The worst," she agrees with a laugh. "And might I add, I'm shocked to hear you're back in it."

"In a much better capacity this time, thankfully." I roll onto my stomach, my head hanging over the bed. A tiny glint of red peeking out between the mattress and the box spring catches my eye. Frowning, I scoot closer. "And how did you know I was working with musicians again?" I ask, half distracted.

"It's a small world. People talk…"

Listening to her, I reach down and touch the scrap of red

fabric playing peek-a-boo with the mattress. It's silk, and it's not just red. It's red and white.

Kati's voice ebbs and flows in my ear. "...and not just any musicians. Kill John? How the hell did that happen? Do they know about...well, your pictures?"

"They know. We talked it out, and everything is cool." Biting my lip, I tug at the fabric. It resists for a second, and then yanks free. For a moment, I just stare at the panties dangling in my hand. White with little red cherries on them. *My* panties.

They're slightly damp and completely rumpled from being crammed beneath the mattress. On Gabriel's side of the bed. Unable to resist, I bring them to my nose and take a cautious sniff. They smell like his shower gel.

Gabriel washed my panties? Why?

A naughty thought runs through my head: Gabriel touching my dirty panties and what he might have done with them that would necessitate cleaning.

Oh, yes, please, and can I watch next time?

But, no, he couldn't have. Not cool, collected Gabriel Scott. Could he?

Maybe he found them on the floor of the bathroom and washed them for me.

But he kept them. Hid them away as if he might... What? Want to use them again?

Flushing hot, I press the cool, damp silk to my cheek. And promptly flush again.

"Sophie? Hello? Are you there?"

"Shit," I gasp, plunging back into reality. "Sorry. I...ah... dropped the phone down the front of my shirt. I hate when that happens, don't you?"

Kati laughs. "Goof."

"Sorry." I stare at my contraband panties in wonder. "What were you saying?"

"I said Martin has been talking about you being on the Kill John tour."

All thoughts of panties flee, and I sit up straight, my heart pounding. "What?"

"Yep. He came into my office the other day and started spouting off about how proud he was of you being able to get on the tour. That he didn't realize you still had it in you to be such an opportunist. His words." Her tone is dry and disgusted.

"That asshole. I'm not trying to take advantage of the band. I'm in charge of their social media, for fuck's sake." That I even have to say so burns. Can a person ever truly shake their past? Or will we always be judged by it?

"If he had a brain in his head, he'd know that," Kati says, clearly trying to reassure. "I only mentioned it because you know how he gets. He's interested now and smells a story. I don't know if he'll try to make contact. But I thought I'd warn you."

"Thanks, K."

I hang up with Kati as soon as I can, because I'm fairly certain I'm going to be sick. Martin and I have been history for a long time. He can't hurt me. I know this. But just the thought of him brings back the ugliness of who I used to be.

I'm a better person now, someone who takes responsibility for her actions. I'm no longer flitting through life like a modern-day Scarlett, vowing to think about repercussions tomorrow instead of today.

But am I truly different? I still don't have a set goal in life other than to enjoy it. My natural inclination is to laugh and tease first, be serious later.

Suddenly, I no longer care about pilfered panties or suppressed sexual needs; I want Gabriel to be home. I want to cuddle up and have him hold me. And yet part of me doesn't want to look him in the eye.

Gabriel isn't trusting by nature. In this business, he shouldn't be. And yet I'd been insulted and hurt when he didn't want me on the tour.

Looking at my past dead in the eye, I understand the full extent of what Gabriel has done by welcoming me into the band—into his life. He let me in, despite my mistakes, and never once has he tried to use me for anything other than comfort and companionship.

He *cares* about me. He *trusts* me.

The weight of that settles around my shoulders like a plush blanket. I'd teased him before about being his champion, wanting to lighten the moment and make him smile. But the truth is Gabriel Scott has become my top priority in life. Whatever we are, whatever we'll be, that will not change.

GABRIEL 14

"WHICH ONE IS BETTER?" Sophie asks, her voice soft in the stillness of the room. "Star Wars or Star Trek?"

We're lying face to face on the bed in our suite. Just outside the open terrace doors is Barcelona and the harbor. Sounds of laughter from late-night revelers and the occasional cry of gulls drift in with the briny scent of the sea.

In here, however, it is quiet, peaceful. The ambient light from the street below paints Sophie's curves in a palette of soft blues and grays. There is a gleam of relaxed happiness in her eyes that only I am privy to. Because this is our time, no one else's.

"Which one is better?" I scoff, even though I secretly love her line of questioning. "First off, Star Wars is a space opera. Star Trek is a space odyssey. They're completely different storytelling approaches."

It's going on three in the morning, and I've been up since five. The irony isn't lost on me that Sophie's here because I need her to sleep. But the best part of each day is when I am in bed with her, and I refuse to waste it by sleeping more than I have to. Especially now that she's in a chatty mood.

The last day and a half, Sophie has been subdued and a bit downcast. Since I've been avoiding direct eye contact after tossing off in her panties, guilt sits heavy in my gut. But perhaps her mood isn't about me at all. She seems happy now, content even. So I fight sleep and drink in the sight of my chatty girl basking in the plush comfort of our bed.

"You are such a dork," she says grinning. "They're both about space and laser guns."

"You're taking a piss," I tell her with a laugh. "I refuse to believe you can't tell the difference between the two."

"I'm not..." She puts a hand up and finger quotes, "'taking a piss.' I'm just don't see what the big deal is. Pick a favorite, already."

"No. It's like that old dilemma of trying to choose between The Beatles and The Stones. It can't be done."

Her blunt nose wrinkles, and I have the overwhelming urge to kiss it. "Of course it can be done," she says, oblivious to my thoughts. "The Beatles for joy or nostalgia. The Stones for drinking or sex."

At the word *sex* my cock jumps as if to remind me that I've been ignoring him and he is not amused. I tilt my hips toward the bed and press my irritable cock to the mattress. The randy bastard jerks in protest. I empathize with my needy willy. Truly. But some things are worth more.

Keep telling yourself that, mate.

"Why not The Beatles for sex?" I can't help asking. Mistake. Turning any conversation towards sex is playing with fire. But apparently I like the sweet pain of being slowly burned.

Sophie shrugs, sending the white sheet farther down the curve of her shoulder. "Name one Beatles song that's sexier than a Stones' song."

I stare at her shoulder. Her fucking shoulder has me enthralled. And it isn't even bare. Every night, she wears an over-sized t-shirt and little boy-short panties to bed. I'm fully aware she believes this to be as sexless an outfit as she can manage to sleep in—I've tried the same, usually wearing loose lounge pants and a t-shirt—but she is wrong.

Her breasts, unfettered by a bra, are soft and round. Trying not to notice them sway and bounce beneath thin cotton that lovingly clings to her shape is impossible. Every fucking night, I imagine rolling her onto her back and sliding the shirt up over her fantastic tits.

I've pictured it so many times, holding her hands over her head so her back arches and lifts those plump mounds high. I'd drink in my fill, just looking, making her squirm as she waits for first contact. I'd take it slow, pepper kisses over every inch, leaving the buds of her nipples for last when she's whimpering for me to suck them.

The notion of sucking on Sophie's tits has my tongue pressing to the roof of my mouth. Shit. I clear my throat, try to focus on her question. What was the question again?

"I can't think of an answer," I tell her truthfully.

She makes a sound of triumph. "See? I'm always right."

"Keep telling yourself that, chatty girl. Won't make it true."

Our hands are so close that our fingers nearly brush. I keep still. And it is an act of will, an exercise I endure every night. There are rules: I can hold her, but I cannot explore. No stroking of her skin, no drifting of my hands. I can tuck her up against my side or press her back to my stomach, but no letting my hard cock grind into her plump arse.

And when we lie together like this, talking deep into the night, I never, ever focus on her mouth. That mouth, plush and rosy, always moving—talking, pursing, smiling. I want to lick up her smile, suck in her words, her laugh.

And yet it is her smile and her laugh that holds me back from taking what I want. Because this isn't solely about sex; if it was, I'd have fucked her already. This is uncomfortably *more*.

I have never experienced intimacy. I did not know how good it felt to simply be with someone and let everything else melt away. The world can fuck off when I'm with Sophie Darling. There is only us. I don't have to be anyone else but Gabriel.

If I give into my base wants it will complicate things. I do not know how to be a boyfriend. Hell, I hate that sodding word. It sounds juvenile and inadequate. If I claimed Sophie, she'd be mine. I'd be hers. And I'd cock it up.

My life is Kill John. Where would that leave Sophie? With a cold, emotionally stunted bastard who's barely there?

"I love Spain," she whispers now, breaking me out of my brooding.

I watch her in the dark. "Why do you love Spain?"

"I don't know. It's something in the air. I want to go dancing, eat tapas, get drunk on Sangria."

"Small list," I murmur. "Dancing, eh?"

She glances my way, her eyes flashing in the dim light. "I know it sounds stereotypical as hell, but I think of Spain, and I imagine flamenco dancing while wearing some frothy skirt with a flower in my hair."

A low chuckle escapes me. "Do you know how to dance flamenco?"

"In my mind I do. And I'm fabulous."

"You always did have an elaborate imagination, chatty girl."

She gives me a happy, agreeing hum, and then spins her pillow to the other side; something she does when she's ready to sleep. It's a cool gel pillow she bought after falling victim to Libby and Killian's sales pitch about this "magical" pillow and how it would give her the best sleep of her life.

She bought me one too, because she wanted me to have the same comforts. Little did she realize that her small act of caring tore my heart from my chest and laid it on a platter for her to claim.

"You'd have to dance with me," she murmurs.

"In your dreams, love."

I get a pleased chuckle in response.

Oblivious to the fact that I'm slowly unraveling, she snuggles close, her head finding the crook of my shoulder. That's her place now, tucked up beside me, her hand lightly resting over my heart. When her finger idly traces little patterns on my chest, my eyes close tight.

I'm in pain now, actual physical pain—in my balls, my abs, my chest. Everything aches with a throbbing persistence, wrought from self-denial. I want this woman more than anything I've ever wanted in my life. But I want to keep her. I have no idea how to keep anyone close to me. Because I have no idea how to expose my heart.

Sophie keeps drawing on me, and my closed-off heart beats faster, harder. I need her to stop. I need her to go lower. I bite down hard on my lip and focus on the breath moving in and out of my lungs.

"What are your plans after the tour ends," I find myself asking, if only to distract myself.

Her voice is slightly husky with sleepiness. "Not sure. I'll still help out the band with social media. But I won't be around to take pictures, obviously." Her slim shoulder shrugs. "Brenna's been talking to Harley Andrews's publicist. Apparently he's looking for a social media expert."

My eyes snap open. "Harley Andrews, the movie star?" The sodding "sexiest man alive" according to People magazine? I'm going to kill Brenna. Throw her Louboutins in the harbor.

"That's the one. Can you believe it?" Sophie sounds so bloody happy, while I'm fighting being ill. "He's got a movie coming out in a few months. Set in the outback of Australia. So the idea is that he'd go on a press junket there first. I've always wanted go to Australia."

My back teeth meet at hearing her dreamy sigh.

Considering the average flight to Australia is over twenty hours, my chances of visiting there are nil. And Sophie wants to travel the country with Harley Sodding Andrews and his supposed irresistible charm.

I pull her a little closer under the guise of getting comfortable, and then clear my throat. "Sounds like a good opportunity. However, just so you have your options open, I know that Maliah is also looking for someone."

Ponce. You dirty, opportunistic ponce.

Sophie's head pops up. "Really? I love her music!"

"Oh?" I've only heard her listening to the woman a thousand times by now. "Well, I could put in a word."

"Ah, sunshine, you're the best."

Not hardly. Just a jealous prat.

She leans in to give me a quick, friendly kiss on the cheek. My body reacts before my mind can stop it. In a blink I have her, my hands tunneling through her hair, holding the sides of her head to prevent her from retreating. And she stills, shock widening her eyes, her lips hovering inches from mine.

I can't move: I just hold her imprisoned, staring at her in similar shock.

Let her go, you git.

I try to make my fingers release, but my body has locked up, protesting. The soft warmth of her panting breaths caress my skin. She's so close, I can almost feel her lips—those lush, pouty lips I want on me. Anywhere, I'm not particular. No, first I want to kiss them, lick and suck their plump curves. I want to feel the slickness of her tongue against mine.

My abdomen clenches, and I swallow down a groan, my chest heaving. A tremor starts deep in my gut, and my cock pulses. It wants in, deep and snug.

Let her go. Kiss her. Let her go. Kiss her.

Rage fills me that I am so cocked up, I can't act like a normal man.

I don't know what she reads in my eyes, but her lips part, a little gasp escaping that I can practically taste. Christ Almighty, give me strength to let her go, or let me do her right.

The choice is literally ripped from my hands when she moves back, slipping out of my frozen hold.

"I have to pee," she says baldly. The panic in her voice scrapes against my skin, and I flinch. But she's already up, fleeing to the bathroom.

When the door shuts, I flop onto my back and let out a pained breath. *What the sodding hell have I done?*

Outside the open windows, a woman's laughter echoes. I wince and rest a forearm over my eyes. I'd wanted to know how Sophie would react if I made a move. Running to the toilet appears to be the answer.

Nausea roils in my gut.

From the bathroom comes the sound of water, and I know she'll return soon. A part of me doesn't want her to. But I need to apologize.

She's quiet when she gets into bed, crawling tentatively under the covers.

Words clog in my throat.

For the first time since we've started sleeping together, she doesn't draw near. I feel the absence like a cold hand along my skin. I turn to say something, but she beats me to it.

"Good night, Gabriel."

The finality in her voice, and the clear warning that she doesn't want to talk, settles like a stone in my heart.

I swallow hard. "Good night, Sophie."

On the opposite sides, I stay silent, listening as the soft sounds of her breathing slowly change into the steady cadence of sleep, and dread fills me.

I can't do this any more. I cannot keep denying myself, and I clearly cannot keep my hands off her. Yet the idea of never sleeping next to her again fills me with inexplicable fear.

In her sleep, Sophie turns with a deep sigh, and her hand reaches out to me. I don't move a muscle, but the whole of my being concentrates on the brush of her fingertips against my forearm. Such a small thing, her touch, barely even true contact, and yet I cannot pull away for the life of me.

Be her friend. I can do that. It will torture me, but not having this will outright end me. So I will tuck my needs away, put them somewhere deep and dark, and turn my efforts toward making Sophie feel happy and safe.

SOPHIE
15

"YOU OKAY, hon?" Jules yells in my ear. She can't be heard any other way at the moment. Kill John is going full tilt, and music pulses around us.

I must look miserable if she has to ask right now. I give her a wide smile that feels pained. "Just a bit tired," I shout back.

She nods and says no more, but I catch her quick, worried glance.

I'm a terrible liar. But what do I say? *Hey, I think Gabriel almost made a move on me the other night.* Only, how lame am I? Because I'm not sure.

God, I must be losing it if I can't even tell if a man is making a move.

I am wreck. My mind is stuck on last night, going over every moment in detail.

I went to kiss Gabriel's cheek. And he grabbed me, holding me close as if he'd also been unable to help himself. At first my heart had jumped into my throat, a heated elation rushing through me. I wanted him to kiss me more than I wanted my next breath.

But he didn't. He stared at me as if I pained him, as if he was pissed. That look flipped everything on its head.

Had I gone too far by kissing his cheek? Was he telling me to cut it out? I panicked, so embarrassed I could have cried.

And call me a chicken shit, but I just couldn't ask him what that look had been all about. Not then.

I might have caved this morning, but by then Gabriel was back to his slightly ornery but always solicitous self.

Now I'm at a loss. He insists this isn't about sex. Maybe it truly isn't for him. And there is no way in hell I'm telling him I want more now. Not with Gabriel "Ice Man" Scott back in control.

Call it pride, self preservation, whatever you want, but I'm not caving. No matter how badly I want to.

So now, I'm focusing on work. Which isn't exactly a punishment.

Tonight's concert is hot, frantic, and energetic. The boys play with renewed enthusiasm and verve. I swear there's magic in the air. I crawl and scurry around their moving bodies, getting breathtaking shots: Killian midair, his guitar in one hand, his legs kicking out. Jax bent over his Gibson, his corded forearms flexing, his bare chest gleaming in the red glow of the lights. Rye standing on a massive amp, his hips thrusting, lower lip caught in his teeth. And Whip, arms flying, sweaty hair in his face as he beats the shit out of his drums.

I capture as much as I can, little slices of life held forever in an image. Pure, honest, and good moments that will never happen again. That I have saved them fills me with pride.

And when Killian sings *"Hombre Al Agua"* by Soda Stereo, a '90s-era Spanish-language rock band, the crowd goes absolutely ape.

Such power Kill John has in this moment, holding thousands of people utterly in thrall. It's a thing of beauty. I'm so caught up in it, I let my lens lower and just grin, dancing along to the music. I feel Gabriel's gaze, as I inevitably do, and look up.

His eyes meet mine, a one-two punch to the heart and gut.

He never smiles when he's working, never shows any emotion. But tonight I nearly lose my balance, because he does. He *so* does.

His teeth flash white in that tanned, perfect face, the little dimple breaking out one side. Holy hell, I can't breathe.

He stands in the shadows, so beautifully sculpted, he appears untouchable. A rock. But that smile is my undoing. It holds all the joy of the crowd. It reflects my awe and excitement. He knows what I'm feeling. He knows because, unbelievably, he feels it too.

I realize he loves this part of the life; he's just never shown it. He lets me see it now. This is the man behind the curtain.

They've had him all wrong. He isn't cold or unfeeling. He's just hiding. I want that unleashed—all that strength and simmering emotion he holds beneath the surface.

One day I'm going to get it. Screw pride, I'll push and I'll tease. It's the only way I know how to break down his walls. And if, at the end of the day, he doesn't want me, I'll find a way to live with the loss.

A stagehand steps between us as he hustles to get Jax's next guitar ready. By the time the stagehand passes, Gabriel has moved off, strolling along the edges of the backstage, his eagle gaze roving for potential problems. A record exec waylays him, and they stop to chat.

Killian plays a hard riff, and I snap out of my haze, turning my attention back to the concert. Time flies in a whirl of sound and colors. I capture as much as I can, little slices of life held forever in an image. Pure, honest, and good moments that will never happen again. That I have saved them fills me with pride.

By the time the concert is over, energy zings through me. I'm usually tired, but not tonight. The guys are talking about going clubbing, and I'm all for it. After a much-needed cool shower, I'm changed and raring to go. I put a coat of red on my lips and leave the bathroom, only to find Gabriel waiting for me.

I'll never grow accustomed to the sight of him. He's just too beautiful. He's leaning against the doorway to the bedroom, his hands tucked into the pockets of well-worn jeans. A white T-shirt stretches tight across his broad shoulders and strains against the swell of his biceps.

If there was any justice in the world, he'd look awkward out of his suit. But he wears all clothes well. The corner of his mouth quirks as he looks me over. "I thought I might find you in your nightie."

He almost sounds disappointed.

"You gonna put me on a curfew, sunshine?" I grab a little clutch from the closet and tuck my lipstick, phone, and room key into it.

"Would you stick to it?"

"What do you think?"

He laughs, low and brief. "I think I'd have to sleep with one eye open."

God, don't remind me that we sleep together. Not right now, when only I get the intimacy of seeing him like this in the privacy of *our* room. When he's watching me get ready as if it's his right.

I'm finding it harder and harder to refrain from throwing myself on him.

Instead of that, I give him a long look-over, not because I need to, but because the view is just so pretty. "I'd have never guessed you own jeans."

"Lived in them from the ages of ten to twenty-one," he answers easily.

"Before you became The Man in the Suit."

"The Man in the Suit is off duty now." His eyes track my movements. "Where are you going?"

"The boys are hitting the clubs."

"So I've heard.

"Thought I'd tag along. You going as well?"

"No. I've other plans." He pushes off from his perch by the door and stands tall. "Come out with me."

It's given as an order, but softly, with butter-smooth persuasion behind the demanding words.

"Where are you going?" It's a stall tactic, me asking, because who am I kidding? I'll go wherever he goes. But I don't want him knowing that.

He flashes another rare, full smile, further crumbling my resolve. "It's a secret. You'll have to come along to find out."

I place my hand over my heart in dramatic fashion. "Damn you, sunshine, you've used my one weakness against me."

"Curious as ten cats. Yes, I know. Which means you're helpless to resist." He inclines his head toward the door. "Come along, chatty girl. The night is young."

It's two in the morning. But Madrid is just getting warmed up. I move to do up the tiny buckles of my high-heeled sandals but pause. "These okay for where you're taking me, oh secretive one?"

His gaze slides over my bare legs to where my sky blue sundress flirts with my thighs, and his lids lower a fraction, his expression turning hooded. "You're good."

Oh, that voice, so growly and gruff, deep and rich like hot cocoa and buttered toast. He talks, and I want to eat him up. I both love and hate what his voice does to me. One man shouldn't have so much power. Two words shouldn't be able to make my thighs clench and my skin turn hypersensitive.

Maybe that's what makes me raise my foot, pointing my toe to show off my leg to its best advantage. "You're sure?" I run a hand along my thigh, lifting my skirt to show a bit more skin.

Gabriel's nostrils flare. The muscled breadth of his chest expands and slowly lowers as he exhales. That he's visibly calming himself sends a bolt of pure heat straight through me, and my knees almost buckle.

"Sophie," he says, low and tight.

"Yes?" Damn, that sounded too breathy.

"Cut the shit."

I grin wide. *Gotcha.* I give him a shrug and let my skirt settle back around my legs before walking toward the door with a little extra wiggle in my step.

He follows with a grunt, which could mean annoyance or humor—it's hard to say with Gabriel. But I know this: the man needs to be teased and challenged more than anyone I've ever met. Sometimes I wonder if he's been waiting for it, bored out of his mind.

Or maybe I'm the one who's been waiting. Everything feels strange now, and nothing is as it used to be. Before I was going through the motions of life. Now I'm aware of every step I take. I'm aware of his hand hovering just behind the small of my back as he walks with me, and of the steady cadence of his breathing as we take the elevator down.

Anticipation zings through me, and it's not because we're going out for the night; it's because I'm with him.

We don't speak as we make our way downstairs and out to the car he's hired. Doesn't matter. It's a comfortable silence, the kind you have with people you've known for ages. I suppose sleeping together all the time will do that for you.

He takes us to a club with a long line around it. Not surprisingly, we pull right up to the front door and someone whisks us inside, much to the interest of the people waiting in line.

Inside, it's packed. Beautiful women, dressed in next to nothing, undulate and sway to the beat. Their eyes track Gabriel's movements with blatant interest. A few hands reach out to caress, running over his arms and shoulders. One bold woman makes a grab for his ass.

I don't even realize I've hissed at her like a possessive cat until Gabriel gently grasps my elbow and steers me away. "Put away the claws, chatty girl. My honor is secure."

"I'm pretty sure referring to women as cats is sexist," I say, never mind I just thought of myself in the same way.

He doesn't spare me a glance. "I'll turn in my feminist card when we get home."

Home. No, I will not enjoy that word too much. It's temporary. It's all temporary. And if I remind myself of this enough, I'll eventually believe it.

Gabriel makes his way to the bar, and I check out the scene while he orders. He comes back with two icy cocktails. "Black mojitos," he says, handing me one. "House specialty, apparently."

It's so rare to see him drink that, when he does, I notice. "Do you not drink often because your dad…"

"Was an alcoholic?" he supplies dryly. "In part. And I don't like losing control."

"No, I don't suppose you would." But I'd like to see it. Not in an ugly way, but Gabriel unleashed in bed? All that icy power morphing into a powder keg of heat and want?

His blue gaze rakes over my face at that moment. "Why are you blushing?"

"Not blushing. I'm hot, is all." I take a big sip of my drink. God, that's good. And dangerous. I cannot get drunk around Gabriel. My mouth will spew all sorts of lewd suggestions.

He gives me a dubious look but says no more.

While we have our drinks, a few techs mess about on the stage, setting up for a concert. I lean closer to Gabriel to be heard above the noise of the house music. "You know who's playing?"

He gives me a slightly smug look. "Patience, chatty girl."

By the time we're finished with our drinks, the lights are dimming. Gabriel sets our glasses on the bar and grabs my hand. His grip is warm and solid as he leads me through the crowd, closer to the stage. It doesn't surprise me at this point that people step out of his way.

He doesn't stop right in front of the stage, but a little ways back, so we're buffeted on all sides by people. The lights go dark and then pop up again in flashes of red and yellow. The band comes onstage, and people cheer. The lead singer is a woman. Aside from her, there are three guitarists, a drummer, and a guy manning a mixing board.

Gabriel moves slightly behind me, as if bracing himself between me and others. I feel the warmth of his body along my skin.

And then the band starts playing. The music isn't what I expected. It isn't rock. It's flamenco with a modern twist— funk, hip-hop, even a bit of Bollywood, blending into a sound unlike anything I've ever heard. Happiness is a lightning strike through my system. I jolt and turn my head.

Gabriel's smiling eyes look down at me. He doesn't say a word, doesn't need to. But he *does* pull a little rosebud on a stem from his back jeans pocket. When he picked that up, I don't know. I'm too shocked, standing there gaping as he tucks it behind my ear.

"There you go, Darling," he says in my ear. "Now we dance."

He puts his hands on my hips and begins to move us to the rhythm of the song, picking up the pace as my body starts to respond. And I'm so shocked by the fact that he is willingly dancing, I can't even form a coherent thought. So I don't. I let the music take me, let Gabriel's capable hands and swaying body guide me.

And he can dance. I don't know why I'm surprised. His footwork is better than mine, and I follow his lead, laughing and going more on enthusiasm than finesse. He doesn't seem to mind. His eyes lock with mine, and the dancing people around me fall away. There's just him, his hips moving with mine, my heart pounding in my chest.

Warm hands glide up my sides, the barest of touches. I shiver, sway closer, my arms settling around his neck. His body is hot and tight. His palms skim along my arms and up to my hands. Fingers intertwining, he lifts my hands overhead, taking total control.

This isn't dirty dancing; he keeps a bit of distance between us, ever the polite and controlled Gabriel. Doesn't matter. He's dancing with me, and I'm alive with the joy of it.

With a flick of his wrist, he spins me outward, my skirt swirling around my thighs, and then he brings me back, dips me, and twirls me again.

I laugh and laugh. I've never danced like this, the moves traditional and a bit old fashioned. I love it. He took my dream and made it real. For me.

Our gazes clash and lock. There's a smile in his eyes, and a question. *Is this what you wanted?*

How do I tell him I'm looking at what I want? Boyfriends have always come easy to me. They were guys who complimented my body, told me I was a good time, easy to be around. What they really meant was I wasn't someone they'd get attached to. And if I'm truthful, I didn't get attached to them either.

This is different. I'm already attached.

Gabriel has seen all that I have to offer, and still he doesn't take what he has to know I'll willingly give him. Fully falling for him would be akin to tossing myself off a bottomless cliff. Down, down, down I'd go, nothing to hold on to and no way back to solid ground.

My smile is bright and painful, but I can't let him see what's bothering me. I don't want to answer those questions. He seems satisfied, his smile moving from his eyes to embrace his whole face.

We dance until dawn and tumble home laughing, me more than a little tipsy.

And never once does he try for more.

Which cements it. I have to pull back, learn from him and put up walls around my heart. And when this tour is over, I have to get as far away from Gabriel Scott as possible.

SOPHIE
16

IN AN ATTEMPT TO keep myself occupied with work and not with thoughts of a certain roommate, I head out early to the venue we have lined up for tonight's performance. It's a small space, and they're having a highly publicized meet-and-greet before the actual concert.

The air is humid and thick by the time I arrive. The crowd outside the doors is amped up, and not in a good way. The potential for things to get out of control is high. Even thought I spent only one year as a pap, I can spot the signs. There's a certain agitation rippling through the crowd, an edge of desperation I don't like.

I vetted out a good spot to catch the guys exiting their limos, and to take pictures of the onlookers as well. It tells a better story for this night, and it keeps me away from Gabriel. I'm trying not to regret my decision given the nasty tinge that's in the air right now.

Teenage girls vie for position, jostling each other, throwing elbows in a not so subtle manner. They haven't devolved into fights, but it's a close thing. Glares and shoves are increasing. Security looks annoyed, and they aren't exactly kind with their attempts to keep the fans back, resorting to shoves as well.

Around me are fellow photojournalists. Many of them I don't know, but some are familiar.

Even though I don't want to, I search the crowd for Martin's face, fearing that he'll decide to pay Kill John, and me, a visit. I'd rather see him coming than be sucker-punched by him suddenly showing. I've done this each and every night, all the while cursing him to hell. But, thankfully, he's nowhere to be found.

"How'd you get a job traveling with Kill John?" Thompson, one of my old colleagues, asks me as he sucks on a cigarette. He's got a bloated look about the face, his skin grayish in the harsh marquee lights. "You fucking them?"

"Yes, all of them." I don't bother looking at him. "It's kind of a train situation. I hear they've got an opening for a bottom, if you're interested."

"Cute." He tosses down his cigarette butt, not bothering to snub it. The glowing stub comes close to my open-toed sandal. "I should quote you, brat."

"Because your credibility is so reliable," I mutter.

The weasel stomps out his cigarette, barely missing my toe. I don't react, though I want to.

Never get emotional. A good mantra, but not one that's easy to follow. I'm regretting my plan more and more as bad memories of desperate days fill my head and make my stomach churn. I hated being a pap. Hated who I was and how I felt—as though I was covered in mud from the inside out.

My phone buzzes.

Brenna: We're coming around the block

Go time. I'm about to tuck my phone back into my pocket when another text chimes.

Sunshine: 30 seconds ETA

His text does for me what Brenna's can't: make me feel cared for, and make me care back.

Keeping my distance from him isn't going to work, not when we're in constant contact, anyway. But I can't bother worrying now. Kill John's motorcade is in sight.

The crowd erupts into pandemonium. Girls scream, shoving turns rough. All of us are so packed together that we seem to undulate like a raging sea.

I brace my feet and start snapping, capturing chaos.

The first large SUV pulls up to the curb. The guys are in there. Gabriel, Jules, and Brenna will be in the next one.

Jax is the first to exit, and it's like he's touched a live wire to the crowd. Everything amps up. My view behind the camera shakes as I'm jostled. But I get the shot of Jax's face— the flinch and then the smoothing of his features into some bland neutrality. He smiles, but he's not really there.

None of the guys are. Not this time. The crowd is just too wild for them to linger. They move toward me at a steady pace. At my back, people shove and push. I'm in a good spot and clearly that's not sitting well with more than a few girls.

"I can't see!"

"Get out of the way!"

"Move, I was here first."

"Fuck you."

Those last two were not aimed at me, but I'm in the middle of it. Suddenly arms are flailing, hands slapping. I duck a few blows and edge away. But that fuckface Thompson shoves me right back into it. I'm glaring at him when someone grabs my hair and pulls. Hard.

Tears prickle behind my lids, my scalp screaming. I lower my head and twist my body, my elbow connecting with the wrist of my hair puller. The girl lets go with a squawk.

Someone grabs for my camera, and I slap the hand away. Around me, other fights break out.

In my periphery, I see Jax. His gaze catches mine, and he frowns, slowing down.

No, no, no. Get out of here.

The other guys are pausing too, seeing me in the melee. Not good. The crowd surges again, crushing me into

Thompson and a security guard. A blow hits me right in the eye, and I see stars. It hurts so badly, I cry out. Another blow comes. Pain sparkles and tears.

It occurs to me that Thompson just elbowed me twice. He actually hit me.

I'm about to rip into him, when a body pushes between us with enough force to send Thompson sprawling on his ass. Gabriel stands before me with an expression of rage so fierce my skin prickles.

I can only blink up at him before he grabs me close and hauls me up in his arms.

I will not swoon.

But my head falls to his shoulder. And I cling. Because he is a wall against the world. My wall. He moves through the crowd without pause, and they get out of his way, instinctively knowing he will mow them down if they don't.

One snarling look at security has them hustling us to a door that leads to a quiet, dark hall. Compared to the bright heat of the lights and noise of chaos outside, it's like a balm to my tense body. I sag further into Gabriel's hold.

He doesn't stop but marches along, muttering under his breath. It's a stream of pissed off *motherfuckers* and *bloody stupid* and *son of a bitch* mixed with other choice words. I let his low growls flow over me like warm hands.

My heart is still racing, and I'm shivering. I don't want to. I want to be strong. But the adrenaline is wearing off, and I've no place to go but down.

The side of my face throbs like a heartbeat, pain punching out in all directions. I think about Thompson elbowing me and whimper despite my anger.

Gabriel's arms squeeze around me. "Hush, now. I've got you."

We enter Kill John's dressing room, and the guys are instantly up and surrounding us.

"What the fuck was that shit? What happened to Sophie?" Jax says, peering at me. "You all right, honey?"

"It is bloody apparent that she is not," Gabriel snaps at him as he pushes past and sets me down on a chair.

"Fuck. That was a disaster," Killian mutters. "Shit crowd control. We should have pulled you in with us, Sophie."

"No, you shouldn't have," I say weakly as Gabriel kneels before me, his gaze darting over my face. "You would have been mobbed."

"They wouldn't have hurt *us*." Rye looks sick, his golden complexion pasty as his gaze lingers on me.

"You don't know that."

Gabriel scowls and thumbs aside a lock of my hair. "Got you good, chatty girl." Anger radiates over his frame. "You're bleeding."

"Here." Whip hands him a first aid kit and gives me a smile. "Babe, you stick with us from now on, right?"

My lip wobbles. "Right."

"I want to go back there and kick some ass," Brenna mutters. She's lost her glasses, and her hair is mussed. I hadn't even noticed her in the scuffle. She hands me a cold compress. "Those fuckwads."

From behind her, Libby watches with wide eyes, as does Jules. They're all watching, sadly looking at my face. I duck my head.

"All right," Gabriel says in a firm tone. "Let's give Sophie some room. Go about your business."

No one argues, though Jax gives my shoulder a squeeze before leaving.

With Gabriel's body blocking everyone's view, it's almost as if we're alone. He opens a disinfectant wipe and, with a frown, gently dabs at the bottom of my eye socket. It burns, but I keep still.

His voice is soft when he finally speaks. "I could kill him."

"You going to jail over human garbage would be a travesty. And a wasted effort."

The cool cloth runs along my bruised face. "No, it wouldn't."

I clutch his wide wrist, feel the rapid thrum of his pulse just below the surface. And his eyes meet mine, all dark with rage. It softens my heart, even though I have to be the rational one here. "No retaliation, sunshine. Promise me."

When he doesn't answer, I stroke the skin of his wrist with my thumb. "Please, Gabriel. For me."

His lips flatten until they're edged in white, but he nods, his gaze sliding back to my eye. With careful touches, he cleans me up and then smears a layer of Vaseline over the cut. "Keep putting this on until that heals. It will help prevent scarring."

He hands me the tube of Vaseline and holds the ice pack to my face.

"You an expert on dealing with contusions?" I joke. I have to joke or I'll cry.

He stares back at me, his expression solemn. "Yes."

My hand settles over his, ready to take up the job of keeping the compress in place, but he doesn't let go. His thumb edges out, strokes my face, rasping over the corner of my lip. "Whip is correct. No more going out on your own."

"I'm a big girl. I can handle myself."

He looks pointedly at my face.

"A fucked-up fluke," I retort.

Again, the tip of his thumb caresses my cheek, touches my lips. His lids lower a fraction as he inhales sharply. "You asked a favor of me. This is mine. Don't make me worry about this happening again." He holds my gaze, and the emotion there is a punch to the system. "Please. I won't be able to function properly."

I swallow past the lump in my throat. Tears well in my

eyes. Stupid tears. I start to tremble, everything crashing all at once. "I was scared."

He sucks in a breath, and his forehead rests against mine. His free hand goes to the back of my neck, holding me there, steady, solid.

"So was I," he whispers, shocking me enough that I flinch.

Misinterpreting my surprise for pain, he hisses out a curse. His fingers give me a gentle squeeze. "You're safe, Sophie. This will never happen again."

"I know." I take a shaky breath as I close my eyes and breath in his scent. "You keep your people safe."

"I look out for my people." His lips ghost over my unmarred cheek, the touch so light I might have imagined it. Only I didn't. I feel it to my toes. It hums along my skin even as he pulls back slightly to look me in the eye. "I protect what's mine."

GABRIEL

IT TAKES me too bloody long to get away. Too long, holding in the rage, breathing like a normal man, talking like a calm one. By the time I head out into the back alley, my hands are shaking so badly, I can barely open the door.

Warm, muggy air slaps heavy against my skin. I draw in a breath, smell the sour stench of garbage and the musky fug of wet cobbles. Doesn't matter. I breathe in again, slow, long. Dizziness threatens, and I lean against the slimy back wall of the theater.

My suit will be ruined. People will notice.

I don't sodding care. Not anymore.

Staring up at the bleak, orange light flickering by the door, I wonder who the hell I am now. Scottie is crumbling. The cracks of his venerable armor are appearing over my weary body. And Gabriel? Only one person calls me that name anymore. Only one person makes me feel like a man of tender flesh and not a cold machine. And I let her down.

The image of Sophie's battered face fills my mind. The way that fucking cockwomble bashed her with his elbow. Twice. Before I could get to her.

My heart beats so hard, my shirt trembles. Again, I am short of breath, struggling to get enough in my tight lungs. The ground beneath me tilts and rolls. I'm going to be sick.

Two rapid steps have me hunched over a rubbish bin. I retch until there's nothing left. Until my throat burns.

Fuck, I hate that it takes me an eternity to stand straight, and that even when I do, my head throbs, feels both too heavy and too light. I hate that my hand still shakes as I take the silk handkerchief from my breast pocket to wipe my mouth.

Warm wetness rolls along my lip. The white silk handkerchief is stained crimson. Another nosebleed. My fingers go cold. I think of Mum when she faded—the dizziness, fainting spells, nose bleeds.

Another wave of cold washes through me.

The titter of feminine laughter rings through the night. Little snatches of conversation bleeds in and out—how hot Jax was during his solo, how this one prefers watching Whip beat his drums, the other wants to have Killian's love child. Concertgoers leaving the show, enjoying themselves. They're calling this the best night of their lives.

I helped bring it to them. These girls will never know that, or care. As it should be. But the pride I feel in knowing I brought them a bit of happiness is there all the same.

If I'm gone, someone else will do the job. But will they do it as well? Will they watch out for my boys and make certain everything runs like silk? Or will they think only of their own gain?

The fact that there are no guarantees chafes.

Laughter rings out again, husky, unfettered femininity. It reminds me of Sophie's laugh, though hers always has a tinge of self-deprecation to it, as though she's part of the joke, never ridiculing.

I've never been one to freely laugh and often found those who did rather annoying. Life isn't a joke—not for me. And yet I want to swim in the sound of Sophie's laughter, let it cleanse me and wash away all the heaviness in my life.

I don't know how to ask for that, or even how to *let* myself ask.

I called her mine. She'll want an explanation for that. I've none to give. It just *is*. Whether I fuck her or not, it doesn't matter; she has me now. Even if she doesn't want me.

A text buzzes on my phone.

Brenna: *Car is here. Where the hell are you?*

The idea of sitting in a car with Brenna, Jules, and Sophie while I stink of vomit and most likely have blood smears on my face, makes my mouth sour even more. I don't have the imagination to come up with a plausible excuse for my appearance, nor do I want to lie—or tell the truth.

But lie I do. My thumb types out a quick message.

GS: Already left. Have some business to attend to. Be safe.

That last message is for Sophie, and Brenna will know this.

Sophie. She'll be hurting and is probably unsettled. It was clear she isn't accustomed to being hit or treated with violence, and thank Christ for that small mercy. I should be with her, offering her comfort. Our bed—because it's ours and has been from the moment she laid down in it—will be cool and soft.

But if I get into it with her tonight, I don't know how I'll react. I've already shown too much of myself to her. Exposure has never been easy. I can't do more of it right now without losing the hold I've kept on myself for years.

Sophie. Regret pinches my chest.

I tap out one last message to Brenna.

GS: I'll be a while. Make certain Sophie is settled and icing her eye.

Little dots appear on my screen.

Brenna: You know it, boss man. Be safe yourself.

I suspect Brenna knows exactly what I plan to do, even though the urge has just registered in my own head. But I need it. I need the release.

Scrolling through my contacts list, I find the one I want.

GS: What do you have available for tonight?

Not five seconds later, the answer comes.

Carmen: It's been too long, S. Beginning to think you'd forgotten all about me. Have a slot. 2am.

And address follows.

I tuck the phone away, feeling dirty, depraved. I shouldn't. I've nothing to be ashamed of. But I am. I always am when I give in to weakness.

SOPHIE
17

IT FEELS wrong somehow to hang out alone in Gabriel's coach. Oh, he's made it perfectly clear that I should consider this my space as well. But I don't. Every inch of the place is all Gabriel—something I actually enjoy. Over the years, I've had enough of living by myself. I don't need to feel like I'm in *my* space. I like being in his domain.

Normally, stepping inside his bus is a little like being wrapped up in the man himself; everything is cool, calm, orderly. It smells of him, crisp and expensive. It feels safe.

Right now, however, I don't like it one bit. Because he isn't here, and I don't mind admitting that I want him here. I need him here. As much as I hate my weakness, my body hasn't yet let the incident go. I keep shaking, my fingers and toes ice cold. My face hurts, despite taking painkillers and icing it.

I need the distraction of Gabriel. And quite frankly, I was holding on to the promise of eventually sliding into bed with him as a reward for getting through this miserable night.

He didn't come home with us, telling Brenna he had business to attend to. The pinched expression on her face when she read his texts makes me think she knew more than she let on, and that whatever he was doing, she didn't approve.

I didn't text him. For once, pride wouldn't let me. He

abandoned me when I was scared and hurt. Maybe I shouldn't look at it that way, but shaking that feeling has proven impossible.

Worse? He never came home.

It's morning now, and my head hurts after a long, sleepless night of flopping around on the bed, trying to shut off my mind and let my body rest.

He made *me* promise every night. Every damn night.

Did that not imply the same for him? That he would be here Every. Fucking. Night?

I slam a coffee cup down on his glossy black counter and pour a full cup. Yeah, that's right, coffee. Not tea. Tea is *not* the answer to all of life's problems. Sometimes dark, bitter as fuck, American-style coffee is the answer.

I glare at the door as I take a defiant sip, then wince. I actually don't like black coffee. I'm more of cream and two sugars gal.

"Fucking tailored-suit-wearing Brit, making me drink black coffee," I mutter, grabbing the sugar and cream. A blob of cream lands on the counter. I ignore it. Ha. I can imagine his sneer upon seeing it.

Unfortunately, petty, pathetic victories aren't very satisfying.

I'm clutching my mug and curled up on one of the armchairs when he texts me. Apparently, I've lost all shame because I leap for the phone.

His message is a kick to the chest.

Sunshine: I'm away on business for a few days. Have already notified others. See you in Rome. Play nice with my boys.

A few days? He's already told everyone else?

It's embarrassing how disappointed I am. How...hurt.

This isn't good. He's doing his job, and I'm ready to stomp my foot like a disgruntled child.

Biting my lip, I answer him.

Me: I'm throwing a party in your coach with the band while you're gone.

So clearly, being petty is not out of the picture yet.

There isn't even a pause before he answers.

Sunshine: Good. You shouldn't be alone. Have Jules charge everything to me. Or find the black credit card I have tucked in my sock drawer.

That...that... My teeth snap together. I can't think of a bad word to call him. Paying for my party as if he's my dad or something. *Off you go, Sophie. Behave now while I'm away.* But he's being *nice*. Great gravy, he's actually agreeing to let people into his bus. Or is he calling my bluff?

Fine. I tap out. *But I'm not going in your sock drawer. I might get the colors out of order and then where would you be?*

The implacable jerk responds easily.

Sunshine: Reorganizing my socks. Have the party, chatty girl. It will be good for you. See you in a few days.

So that's that. He's left.

I need to nip this clingy feeling right in the bud. Setting my phone aside, I finish up my coffee and go to get dressed. I'm not going to mope around anymore. I've a party to plan.

GABRIEL

AN ELBOW CATCHES me on the cheekbone. The pain is white, exploding like a camera flash behind my lids. It crackles through me, rings in my ears. A kick to my side has me staggering back.

Jeers and shouts surround me, a blur of screaming faces. This I know. This joy of violence and greed, fed to me since childhood like milk and buttered toast.

Another punch flies. I dance away, and it misses me. I

block a kick with my knee. Pull it together. Focus.

My opponent is hardened, likely fighting nightly. In my youth, I was better than him, but I'm now softened by a comfortable life. Yet I know how much I can handle. I can wear him down, wait for him to tire. But I'll have to take a beating.

Bruises I can hide. Open cuts and split lips are another issue. This is my second night of fighting. I'm already battered. If I get cut up any worse, I'll have to stay away from Sophie for too long.

Sophie. Sophie elbowed in the face. Twice.

Rage pulses hot, pushes through me.

Hold it.

Another punch flies, grazing the edge of my jaw. Were this a professional fight, I'd already be knocked out. But we're amateur entertainment, fighting each other in a pristine, white living room—marble floors, wall-to-wall windows overlooking the harbor—as rich, bored people watch.

It is perverse. Stinks of privilege. Blood splatters stark against white leather walls.

I don't give a shit about them. All I need is the pain.

The man before me is a Spaniard, long and lean and fast. My mind morphs his appearance. He's a cameraman, stocky and bloated, and hitting Sophie.

I promised I wouldn't retaliate. She made me promise not to hurt him.

I won't. But this man here? He wants the fight.

All the rage, all the helpless fucking frustration builds, growing tighter, stronger. Anger goes cold and silent.

My fist connects with fleshy meat and bone. That's another kind of pain, a bright, clean release.

Again, again. Controlled hits. Punch to face, knee to kidneys, elbow to jaw.

Sweaty, hot skin, metallic blood. Solid flesh giving under

my knuckles. I revel in it.

There is a point in fighting at which you are no longer a man. You become a machine. No more thinking, just reacting, giving yourself up to muscle memory and technique.

We grapple, locking up and breaking away. He stumbles back before charging.

A roundhouse kick, taking him on the jaw, ends the fight.

My opponent falls back and hits the floor with a slap.

He remains down, chest heaving, head lolling.

Cheers erupt. They break me out of my haze and irritate my ears.

I stand, breath sawing in and out. My body throbs, burns. It is pure and real, as close as I can get to the release I truly want.

No one comes near me; they know better by now.

Someone helps my opponent up.

My gaze goes to the windows, where the night is black ink and gold stars. Sophie isn't here anymore. She's headed to Rome.

Already I feel her absence in my soul, a tear that won't mend. I'm battered and bleeding. I'll have to stay away for days. The tear within me grows bigger. I ignore the feeling. I need time anyway. To regroup and calm down.

"Scottie, *mi hombre hermoso*, another win for me, si?" Carmen smiles up at me, blood red lips, glossy raven hair. "Ah, but I have missed seeing you fight. I'd forgotten how coldly you play your game. Come." Gold-tipped nails glide up my arm. "I have a room ready. Shall we?"

Lust and anticipation lower her lids as she looks me over, her gaze lingering on my bare chest. Subtlety was never Carmen's style.

I move away from her touch. "A cab is all I require."

Pouting, she snaps her fingers, and a woman comes forth.

"Teresa will take you to a room where you can change

back into your suit." Now that she's been denied, Carmen is all business. I appreciate that about her. "And your winnings?"

"Make the usual donations."

A thin smile pulls at her lips. "To battered women's shelters. You, *mi amigo*, have a perverse sense of humor."

Sophie thinks I'm a goof. I miss her. I need her. I can't go back to looking like this. "So they tell me. *Buenas noches*, Carmen. I won't be returning tomorrow."

I head out into the darkness and back to my hotel. But I won't be sleeping.

SOPHIE  18

THROWING a party on Gabriel's coach is akin to being in high school and having your friends over when your parents are out of town. At least if feels that way.

The guys, Libby, Jules, and Brenna enter with caution, looking around as if Gabriel might pop out and scold them at any second.

"You are one ballsy chick," Killian tells me, bringing in a cooler full of beer. "I like it."

"I have Daddy's permission," I say with an eye roll.

"Keep telling yourself that." Jax takes a seat and grabs a handful of chips. "You don't even have coasters out. There will be hell to pay." His smile is wide, as if this pleases him greatly.

And then I realize, they want to get caught. Because they want Gabriel here too. Oh, they love teasing him, but they're happier when he's around. Why can't he see that?

Brenna hauls in a karaoke machine, and Rye helps her set it up. "I don't know why I agreed to bring this," she tells me. "It's a completely uneven playing field."

"We'll go easy on you, Bren," Rye promises with a wink.

"Going easy on us won't help," I tell him. But I'm happy they're here. The coach is filled with laughter, chatter, and the warmth of bodies—a far cry from the cold and silent place it had become when I was alone. Doesn't stop the pervasive ache in my chest, though. I miss him.

But I'm not even going to utter his name in my head any more. Out of sight, out of mind, out of heart. It has to work.

"I have this app," Brenna says as she curls up on the couch next to me. "It gives you a category, and you have to choose a song that fits."

"Okay." Rye takes a long pull of beer. "I'm ready. Hit it."

Brenna taps a button on her phone, and we all crane our necks to see. I'm too far away, but Brenna starts cackling as Jax and Killian groan. She holds up the phone and announces, *"Yo! MTV Raps."*

"How convenient," Killian drawls, giving Brenna a look I can't interpret. She avoids his gaze with a little sniff.

"Fuckin' A," Rye says with a chest thump. "I will slay ya'll motherfuckers."

Jax blows a raspberry while making a jerk-off motion with his hand. "Sure you will."

"You quake in terror, JJ."

"Aren't you the wannabe JJ?" he counters. And I bite back a laugh because Rye kind of does look like the linebacker, JJ Watt.

Rye gives him the finger before rubbing his hands together. "Okay, okay, this is gonna be good." He glances around the room. "I'm picking Whip as my musical backup, and Jax, since you've been so encouraging, you're with me on vocals."

Jax makes a pained expression. "Hell."

Rye nods. "We'll go against Killian and Libby."

Brenna settles down next to me. "He's up to something good."

"You know it, babe." Rye winks at her.

Brenna flinches as if he'd pinched her instead before she's back to her easy demeanor. "Well, get on with it."

"Run-D.M.C.'s version of 'Walk this Way'."

Everyone starts laughing.

Killian grabs his guitar. "I get it. Libby and I are singing Aerosmith's part, right? Because someone thinks he can rap."

"Knows, Killian. Not think, knows." Rye takes a mic and glances at Whip. "You good with the beat? Or are we using the karaoke machine?"

"You're seriously asking me that?" he scoffs. He's only got his small electric drum kit, but he's already messing with it. "Don't piss me off, Ryland."

"Instruments it is," Rye answers easily.

"This is going to be so good," Libby says, her eyes bright. She doesn't seem to be the type to get excited over trying to mimic Aerosmith, but she's clearly in her element.

She and Killian put their heads together to plan, and the guys do the same in their corner.

"You know we're next," Brenna says to me.

I laugh a little. "I was terrified when I thought I'd have to sing in front of these guys. Because screeching cats is an understatement."

Brenna grins. "So annoying, isn't it? When they make it look effortless?"

"Daunting as hell," I agree. "But rapping? Ha. I can rap."

She raises one perfectly plucked brow, and I feel a twinge of heartache. That look reminds me of Gabriel. His brows are thick and imposing, but he and Brenna both have that elegant way of expressing themselves with a simple look.

"Most people would be more afraid to rap," she says.

"Eh, it's all about owning it. Besides, I had a babysitter who loved hip-hop. This is literally the music of my childhood."

Brenna grins suddenly and leans in close. "I love hip-hop too. Which is why I totally rigged the game to choose that."

"You evil genius," I say with a gasp.

Her grin goes wider before she gets it under control. "I'm pretty sure Killian is on to me."

So that's what the look was about. I don't mention that Rye seems very pleased by Brenna's pick as well, as if she's done him a favor too.

"I thought you'd be freaking out," Brenna says, eyeing me.

"Now you know better." I give her a nudge on the shoulder with my own.

She nudges back. "If Scottie hadn't already claimed you, I just might."

I drop right out of my happy place, and clearly my expression shows it because Brenna winces. Thankfully I don't have to hear any awkward apology or deflated ego soothing. Whip starts up with a beat.

Killian begins to play the guitar, and they're on.

Brenna and I squeal with glee as Jax and Rye begin to rap RUN-D.M.C.'s lyrics. I expected Rye to own it, but not Jax. We can't stop laughing, but we lose it when Libby—not Killian— takes up Steven Tyler's part, making her voice screechy and throaty just like Aerosmith's legendary singer.

Killian is grinning so wide, I think he might strain he cheeks. But his playing is on point.

I've always wanted to live a life less ordinary, see the world in a way few others have. And I know I'm not alone in that desire. Who wouldn't want to escape the mundane? Yet, I've always known I was ordinary. Not in a bad way, but I was simply Sophie Darling: mostly happy, likes people, has a talent for taking snapshots of daily life. Nothing amazing. I tried to soak up the excitement of fame by being an entertainment journalist. But that only left me feeling tainted and foul.

I'm not certain where my future lies. But I'm here now, living this life. And it is extraordinary. I have one of the best rock bands on Earth singing karaoke for me. Even better? They're my friends, these funny, talented, generous people. They like me, past wrongs and all.

I soak in the moment, laughing and watching them dance around. And yet, there's a cold spot along my back, in the center of my chest, that won't go away. I yearn for the one man who isn't here, who left me behind.

It hurts, and I have to swallow down the pain, my smile too brittle.

The song finishes, and they're all giving happy high fives, while Brenna and I wolf whistle and cheer.

Whip plops down next to me, a sheen of sweat shining on his brow. He flicks a lock of inky hair back from his face and smiles. "That's gonna be hard to top."

"Show off," I tell him, nerves fluttering in my belly. I know the song Brenna and I chose by heart. Still, I have to perform it in front of these freaking music virtuosos.

"No stalling," Rye says, sitting on the other side of me. "It's your turn now."

Brenna stands up and smoothes her skirt, taking a mic from him. "We're doing 'Shoop'."

Everyone cheers, and I rise on unsteady legs. Libby hands me her mic.

Brenna is taking Pepa's lyrics, and I'm Salt. And because neither of us can play an instrument to save our lives, we're using the karaoke machine. We glance at each other. Brenna's eyes are gleaming, but her smile is nervous. "All in?"

"All in," I say, giving her a fist bump.

The song starts, and I can no longer worry. Brenna is true to her word, delivering her lyrics with sass, her hips gyrating. She slaps her butt, and Rye howls, laughing so hard tears stream down his face.

But they're all looking at Brenna with pride and encouragement.

And then it's my turn.

I don't think. The song takes me. I dance, gyrating, and Brenna joins me. It's so freeing; I understand why these guys sweat their asses off night after night.

"Kill it, Sophie," Jax yells, clapping.

So I do. I'm rapping about nice dreams and big jeans, my ass wiggling, when *he* walks in.

It's pretty impressive, actually, that the man can simply enter a room and everything stops.

I mean, the background music plays on, but all of us have halted as if he's pressed pause.

Gabriel freezes too, his brows knitting over that arrogant nose. Impeccably dressed in a blue suit, platinum cufflinks glinting in the low light, he's king of all he surveys. The guys in this room might be the biggest rock stars in the world, but they stand silent before him like recalcitrant kids caught stealing liquor from Dad's stock.

As if to punctuate that thought, Rye suddenly points at me. "She made us do it!"

"We didn't touch a thing," Killian wails dramatically while flailing his arms out. "The lock on the liquor cabinet was already busted!"

It breaks the tension, and everyone laughs. Well, everyone except for me and Gabriel.

Because his gaze has landed on mine. And I can't look away.

Why him? Why is it that one direct look from this man has the ability to paralyze my body, take my breath, make everything hot and sticky along my skin?

I didn't lie that day on the plane. He is the most devastatingly attractive man I've ever met. But what I feel when I look at him, when we silently assess each other, has nothing to do with how he looks.

His male beauty isn't what makes my heart ache like a tender bruise. It isn't what has my insides swooping to my toes and my lips suddenly turning sensitive. And it certainly isn't what makes me want to cross the small distance between us and wrap my arms around him, hold him close.

Because he looks so very battered. Thinner about the face, shadows beneath his aqua eyes. His gaze conveys pain, yearning, need. I see it, even if I'm fairly certain he doesn't want me to see. I've always seen the loneliness.

Maybe because it matches my own.

We're both experts at hiding our true selves behind a public mask. I make jokes and smile. He plays the robot.

The karaoke machine stops with a click. I still can't look away from Gabriel. I've missed him. Too much.

He hasn't acknowledged anyone, hasn't even budged from his stance just inside the door.

"Time to go," Jax murmurs, and everyone shuffles, grabbing instruments, their stuff—Killian takes the tequila.

They leave without another word.

Gabriel's voice is rusty when he finally uses it. "You've been well?" His gaze flicks to the mic still in my hand and a flash of humor lights his eyes before neutrality settles back into place.

I'm sweaty and flushed, my heartbeat still rapid from abruptly stopping my dance.

"Don't I look well?" It's a cheap tactic, but the insecure part of me needs some sort of sign. And he still hasn't moved from the doorway.

He glances at my breasts, the swell of my hips, making all those places perk up, become tender with the need to be touched. He meets my eyes again.

"Very well indeed."

Damn, that shouldn't fill me with heat. I set down the mic, take a swig of my beer. It's warm and flat now. "You should have let them stay."

"I didn't ask them to go." He says it softly, his expression a bit perplexed and a bit pissed off.

"You didn't have to. You show up and everyone scatters

like cockroaches to the light."

His nostrils flare in clear irritation. I ignore it.

"Why is that? Why don't you let anyone in here?" I take a step closer. "Why don't you let anyone in?"

"You're in here," he retorts hotly, his gaze cutting away, as if the sight of me pains him. "You're in."

"Am I?" My heart pounds now, pushing the blood through my veins with too much force. It makes me jumpy, in need of comfort.

Gabriel frowns at me. "You have to ask?"

I take another step, aware that he stiffens when I do. "Were you really off doing business?"

"What else would I be doing?"

Another step. Close enough to catch his scent. Heat radiates off him despite his cool outward appearance. He stares down his nose at me. Arrogant bastard.

"You look like shit," I tell him.

He scoffs at that. "Well, thank you, Darling. I can always count on your candor."

"Yes, you can." I look up at him. "You've lost weight. Your color is off—"

"Sophie," he cuts in with a sigh, "I've traveled all day. On a bloody plane. I'm tired, and I want to sleep." He inclines his head, his chin set in defiance. "Shall we?"

For a second, I can only blink. "You honestly expect me to sleep with you now?"

That stubborn, blunt chin rises. "You promised me every night if I wanted it. Well, I do."

"Not until you tell me where you've been."

"What?"

I lean in, my nose nearly brushing the lapel of his perfect suit, and breathe deep. I straighten with a glare. "You may have had a shower, but your suit stinks of cigarettes and perfume."

His eyes narrow to laser-bright slits. "What are you implying?"

"Were you off fucking someone?"

There. I said it. And I'm sick with the idea.

"That is none of your business."

I don't care if he says it without inflection, it still feels like a slap to the face.

"It is if I'm sleeping with you," I snap.

He takes a step into my space. "I told you at the beginning, this isn't about sex."

The tips of my breasts brush his chest with each agitated breath I take. "You're right. It's more than that. *We* are more. And you fucking know it." I poke his hard shoulder. "So stop being such a coward and admit it."

With an actual growl, he backs me against the wall, his arms caging me in. Our noses bump as he bends down.

"Here is what I will admit: I was not 'fucking someone' and it pisses me off that your first suspicion went directly to that."

He's so close, his angry heat feels like my own. I can't move or avoid his eyes. I don't try to. "Why shouldn't I think that when you smell of other women?"

"Because there is only you!"

His shout rings out, broken and desperate. But it's the rage in it, as if he hates the truth, that has me flinching.

Even so, his confession sits between us. And I can't help but put a hand to his waist. Tension vibrates through his frame. But he doesn't pull away, just stares down at me, breathing hard.

"Gabriel, you think it's any different for me?"

He pulls back at that, his expression going blank.

I don't let it stop me. My voice stays soft. "Why do you think I push?"

"Because you can't help yourself, stubborn, chatty girl."

His gaze darts over my face. "Even when you should."

"Why should I, Gabriel?" I use his name to keep him from retreating. I know how much he craves hearing it. Even now, when he's angry, his lids flutter each time I utter it. "I'm tired of pretending I don't want you. I do. We dance around it night after night. And it's a fucking lie. I'm tired of the lie. Tell me why you resist."

His lips pinch. "I have already told you. I will fail you, Sophie. Christ, look at me. I left when you were in need."

"Did you do it to prove that to me?" I press, tears threatening. "Is that why?"

That clearly doesn't sit well with him. "No. I needed a break, time for myself."

Oh, that hurts. And yet he's been a solitary man for so long, can I blame him for wanting his space?

Exhaustion lines his face as he watches me with cautious eyes. "I can't be the man you expect me to be, Sophie."

The faint yellow of a bruise on his cheek catches my attention. I lift my hand to touch it, and he takes a step back, evading my hand. "Can't or won't?"

"Does it matter?" he counters. "In the end, the result is the same."

I should walk away, save what's left of my pride. But I've never been able to hold back from engaging with this man. "Are you going to tell me where you were?"

"No."

Jesus, I want to stamp my foot. On his. "Why not?"

He's fully away from me now, retreating to the kitchen to grab the kettle and fill it with water. "Because I don't want to."

"Asshole."

"Admitted that already, love."

My back teeth click, as he fusses with his tea leaves.

"Teatime, is it?" I grind out. "Having a problem that needs soothing?"

"Yes," he says without turning. "You."

A gasp of pain leaves me before I can hold it in.

He turns at the sound, and his brows lift in apparent surprise. "Chatty girl?"

I blink rapidly. "You *are* an asshole. And it isn't something to be proud of."

I grab my shoes and head for the door.

"Sophie." He makes a grab for my arm, but I evade his reach.

"Don't," I say, wrenching the door open. "I need to be away from you for a while."

He runs a hand through his thick hair and grips the ends as if he needs to hold something. "At least tell me where you're going so I don't have to worry."

A bitter laugh leaves my lips. "Oh, the irony." I glare at him. "Guess what, *Scottie*? I'm not telling. Because I don't fucking want to!"

I slam the door behind me and head out into the night.

GABRIEL
19

"YOU TUG at those cuffs any harder and they're going to fall off."

I don't bother turning to acknowledge Killian at my side. It will only encourage him. And I don't have it in me to pretend I'm impenetrable right now. I hurt Sophie last night. I ruined her fun and then made her think she was a problem to be solved.

I didn't realize how badly I was mucking things up until she stormed out. I'd only thought to protect my private life as I've always done, by putting up a wall and sniping at anyone who tried to look over it.

The method still works; she left. Cut me off at the fucking knees. I'm stuck walking on stumps and trying to pretend it isn't agony.

Around us, stagehands, lighting engineers, and sound techs scurry to and fro, getting ready for the concert. On the other side of the massive screen we're standing behind, the crowd fills up the stadium. Their murmurs and laughs create a constant hum.

"Shouldn't you be in the dressing room getting your hair artfully disheveled?" I ask him.

"Libby does that for me in her own special way," he answers easily.

Of course she does. Every damn person on the tour has been treated to the sounds Killian and Libby preparing for concerts. And celebrating the conclusion of each show. I don't know how they ever thought they were being secretive.

"Then go find your wife," I say. "I'm fairly certain she's waiting for you in the lavatory."

"Man, don't let on that you know about the bathroom hookups or she'll never give it to me there again."

"It would do well for you not to provide me with ammunition at this moment."

He falls silent, standing at my side and watching the well-choreographed art of the stagehands' work. I know what he's doing. Babysitting. Killian knows me too well. Just as I am able to tell if he's hurting with one look, so is he. Granted, it's been over ten years since he's seen me hurting. Thinking about that time adds another stone to the gravel pit that's formed in my gut.

Sophie didn't come home last night. Home. I have not thought of any place as home for so long I'm surprised I even remember the concept. My houses are dwellings in which I rest when not working. Given that I'm always working, I rarely spend time in any of them. Yet from the first night Sophie settled her things alongside mine and filled those quiet, orderly spaces with her effusive nature, wherever she is feels like home.

Last night, alone in my bed, it was more like hell. I wasn't able to lower my pride enough to ask any of my crew if they knew where she was. But it was a close thing. I'd been tempted to beg. That chafes too.

Eventually the tour will end. Sophie will move on to other projects, and my life will return to normal. Why that thought makes my gut clench isn't something I want to dwell on.

Knowing Killian as I do, it isn't a surprise that he can't keep quiet for long.

He huffs out an impatient sound. "Seriously, dude, what's got your dick in a knot?" From the corner of my eye, I can see him grinning, wide and smug. "I thought for sure your coach would be rocking for a few hours."

"Don't be disgusting," I snap, leaving my damn cuffs alone.

"Hot lovin' is never disgusting." He nudges me.

"I might be emotionally scarred for life after hearing you say *hot lovin'*. And mind your business."

"Oh, please. It's not like you're hiding anything."

I finally glare at him, and he keeps that smug grin in place.

"You are so gone on Sophie," he says happily. "You have been since you got off that plane."

Sophie had been so happy, dancing like an erotic weapon and rapping—the lyrics falling from her lips in syncopated rhythm without falter or embarrassment. It was unexpected and lovely. I'd wanted to laugh just for the joy of it. I'd wanted to haul her over my shoulder, take her to my bed, and have her sway and thrust those hips of hers right over my mouth. My cock stirs at the thought, and I remember Killian is standing there, looking at me as if he's never seen me before.

"Why are you grinning like a fool? You don't even like her."

"Eh," he shrugs. "I was pissed about old shit. She's cool. Just took me a bit to let myself see it."

Despite the fact that I want to tear my skin off and throw myself into traffic for putting that hurt on her pretty face, I'm mollified by Killian's acceptance. The fact that it means so much to me also irks.

"Everyone likes her," he adds as if he's trying to reassure me.

"It's impossible not to," I mutter. A mistake. It gives Killian an opening.

"So..." he prompts with a wave of his hand. "Why aren't

you knocking boots with Sophie right now? You two are clearly dying to fuck like horny bunnies—"

"One well-placed punch, Killian. That's all it would take to have you silenced for the rest of the night."

"Touchy. Touchy."

He's loving this. Throwing myself into traffic sounds more appealing by the second.

"I'm just saying," he goes on, "I've never seen anyone more in need of a good, hard fuck than—"

"Shut your fucking gob."

"You," he finishes broadly, dancing out of striking range. "But it's good to know you're protective of Sophie's rep. Means you care."

My hand curls into a fist. Killian dances back a few feet more, flashing me a cheeky smile. "I'm done. No more poking the bear. I'm going now."

"Your timing has been off during 'Distractify' lately. You're late on the opening riff by two seconds."

Killian laughs. "Low blow, man. But correct. Don't know why I'm off, but I'll work on it." He pauses, his heel poised to turn. "Whatever you did to make Sophie storm into Brenna's coach, just tell her you're sorry."

Regret is a fist through my heart. It's a struggle to get in a breath. But at least I know where she is now. Safe with Brenna.

"Women need us to acknowledge their hurts," Killian says, digging the knife in farther.

"You think I don't know as much?"

His dark eyes are suddenly solemn, and I know he's about to gut me. "She missed you when you weren't here. As much as you hide, Sophie sees right through it and still cares. Don't fuck that up, man. Trust me on this."

I don't nod. I don't have anything to say. I've already fucked it all up.

SOPHIE

"YOU'RE TAKING the night off." Brenna's tone brooks no argument.

Doesn't mean I'm not going to try. "That's ridiculous," I say, dabbing a bit of her concealer beneath my eyes. No way in hell am I allowing Gabriel to see me with puffy, bruised eyes.

I haven't cried over him, but I did spend a good chunk of last night drinking vodka tonics and cursing his name while a sympathetic Brenna and Jules agreed that the man can suck it. "I'm fine."

Brenna slicks on a deep plum lipstick before handing me a tube of rosy red. "I know. Doesn't mean you can't enjoy a night off."

We stare at each other's reflection in the mirror of Brenna's bathroom, both of us wearing stubborn expressions.

Jules pops her head in. "Yeah, read a book, watch cheesy movies."

Cheesy movies just makes me think of Gabriel and his threat to force a Star Trek marathon on me. Less than twenty-four hours, and I miss him like a lost limb.

"If I stay here," I tell them, "I'll go batty."

Brenna smoothes her hair into her trademark high ponytail. "So go to the concert and enjoy it as a fan."

The idea doesn't sit well with me; I've been hired to do a job, not wuss out because my feelings have been hurt.

Unfortunately, if I want to work, I have to go back to the bus and get my equipment. That's not happening. Maybe I am a wuss, because I need to lick my wounds a little longer.

"I don't have anything to wear."

Brenna is at least three sizes smaller than I am, and Jules is four inches shorter.

"Excuses, excuses," Jules says. "I'll find you something.

Hold up."

Her bright head disappears, and then she comes back with a flowing green, stretchy jersey skirt and white tank top. "The skirt is mid-calf on me so it will probably be at your knees, but it's better than chocolate ice cream-stained clothes." She grins wide, showing her dimples.

"Don't remind me." Last night ended with a raid on their emergency ice cream stash. I'm still feeling a little queasy.

I put on the skirt and top and frown down at myself. "I look like I'm headed to the beach."

"You look hot," Jules says, giving my butt a slap. "I'm off. A certain man who shall not be named just texted that he's at the stadium, and he gets pissy if his employees aren't on time."

She shakes her head, but there's no real irritation in her expression. If I'm not mistaken, she looks eager to start her night as she hurries off. I envy her.

With a suppressed sigh, I run a hand through my hair. Still rose gold, it falls in waves to the tops of my shoulders. A small line of darker blond roots shows. I'll have to pick another color soon, but at the moment, I'm just tired.

"Fine, I'll go," I tell Brenna. "But I'm doing so under protest."

She smiles. "So noted. And look, about Scottie…"

"Don't worry," I cut in, not liking the pity in her eyes. "I'm over it."

"No, you aren't." She shakes her head, smiling softly. "But that's okay. He's…well, yes, he can be an ass, but he's one of the best people I know. Behind all that starch is a marshmallow who any one of us would kill for."

I slump against the counter. "I know that. Too well, unfortunately. It's just the asshole part is getting in the way at present. How do you let yourself care for someone who won't let you in?"

Brenna's pretty face closes up, and she makes a production of quickly putting her makeup back in her travel case. "I think we'd all be happier if we knew the answer to that question."

"Hell. Let's just go back to 'men can suck it' and leave it at that for now."

Brenna laughs. "Yeah, except part of the problem is that we love it when men suck it."

"True."

Laughing together, we head out for the venue. And I pretend the whole way that I'm not both dreading and anticipating seeing Gabriel again.

Having worked multiple concerts at this point, I know the places he haunts backstage and how to avoid him. That doesn't stop me from catching glimpses of his sharp, stern profile now and then. And each time I do, my stomach cramps, and my heart gives an unruly thump.

I want to look longer, but I know he'll notice me if I do. I swear the man has a sixth sense that way. Even skulking in the shadows, I can tell he's scanning the area, a dark scowl on his face. Looking for me? Or just in his usual work mode? It's hard to tell without studying him for too long.

And I hate that my awareness is constantly on him. I barely notice the concert as I tuck myself behind a stack of crates on the far to the side of the stage. Leaning against a concrete wall, I close my eyes and let the music pour over me, the pulsing throb of it vibrating my bones.

I don't think I can stand it if Gabriel seeks me out, only to apologize and expect everything will go back to normal. I cannot go back to what we were.

Maybe it's because my eyes are closed and my other senses are more alert, or maybe it's because I'm just that attuned to him, but I feel it the second Gabriel comes to stand next to me.

I don't have to look to know it's him; even in the dank humidity of backstage, I catch his scent. And no one else but him makes my skin tighten and my heartbeat go into overdrive just by being near.

He stands so close, my shoulder blade brushes against the sleeve of his jacket.

Keeping my eyes closed, I swallow hard and try to remain passive. My body betrays me, sending happy little zings of pleasure through my chest and along my skin.

I'm pissed at him, yet it doesn't stop me from thinking, *Finally, you're here. What took you so long?*

We stand there, listening to "Apathy," neither of us moving, even though the crowd is going wild. The song ends, and Jax and Killian begin to talk about a new song they're going to play.

Backstage, it's quiet enough that I hear Gabriel when he speaks, his words stilted as if he's forcing each one out.

"I am a cold man. Any happiness or warmth I've felt died when Jax tried to take his life. Until you." His ragged breath gusts over my cheek. "You are my warmth."

My heart stops, my breath hitching painfully.

His voice gains strength. "The second you are out of my sight, I want you back where I can see you."

I want to turn and tell him I miss him too. All the time.

But then he moves. The tips of his fingers skim the curve of my shoulder, and I stiffen in shock. We have held each other night after night, without hesitation or fear. But outside of bed, Gabriel rarely makes prolonged physical contact.

And this touch isn't friendly or fleeting. It's an exploration, tender but possessive. My knees go weak, my head falling forward as he caresses my neck, a slow sweep over my skin as if savoring the moment.

His voice is low but powerful at my ear. "If I can see you, know that you're all right, I can breathe a little easier, feel a little human."

I lean into his touch and he cups my nape, holding me

steady. Holding me. I need his touch so much it hurts.

"Then why did you leave me?" My voice isn't strong; I can't seem to find my breath.

His fingers tighten a fraction. Before he can answer, another song starts up. Music crashes over us, and there is no more talking. I can only stand there in the dark with Gabriel.

He does not move for a few beats, and then his fingers slide slowly up into my hair to cradle me. I don't resist when he eases me closer, turning me into him.

With a sigh, I lean against his side, my head on his shoulder as he massages me with steady strokes.

Unable to help myself, I rest my hand on his firm stomach. A sigh rumbles through him, and though he does not move, it feels as if his whole body is melding with mine.

In the dark, we are hidden. Music pulses around us—loud, rhythmic sounds of angst and rage and defiance—but here there is stillness. I close my eyes, breathe him in. Fine wool, spicy cologne, the indefinable scent of Gabriel's body. He is my drug of choice.

When he touches my cheek, all the nerves along my skin prickle with awareness. He is a man of business and should have smooth hands, but his skin is slightly rough and very warm.

The tips of his fingers press into my jaw as he tilts my head back. I catch the the pained look on his face, as though he's hurting, and the regret, as if he'd do anything to make us right again. His expression subtly shifts to one of intent.

I can't breathe. Because that look wants to own me. It reaches into my heart and takes hold of it.

And then he bends down. His lips ghost over my cheek, pressing light kisses along my temple. I clutch the edge of his jacket and hold on. I'll sink to the floor if I don't. Because Gabriel is touching me as if he's been aching to all along.

He nips my earlobe, and my body jerks in response,

pushing against his. Warm breath tickles my skin.

"I can't leave you, Darling. You're always in here." Gently, he takes my hand and touches it to his head.

With a shiver, I thread my fingers through his hair. It's thick and silky, and he makes a sound of appreciation, nuzzling my neck with his nose as he continues to kiss his way around my jaw.

"And you're in here," he tells me, moving my other hand to his chest where his heart pounds against the solid wall of muscle.

"Sunshine," I whisper, turning to kiss his cheek.

A tremor runs through his frame, and his arm wraps tight around my waist. I kiss him again, finding his jaw. His crisp scent and the slightly salty taste of his skin make me want more and more. But he's holding me too close, shaking as he takes increasingly deeper breaths.

The pad of his thumb finds my bottom lip, and my breath stutters as well. For a long moment, he simply runs his thumb lightly over my lip, tracing its curve, opening my mouth a bit more. And with every sweep, I grow hotter, the sound of my blood rushing through my ears.

My lips feel swollen and dry. Without thinking, I lick them and catch the blunt tip of his thumb.

Gabriel grunts, his hand clenching. But he leaves his thumb there, pressing against my lip, pushing just slightly into my mouth as if asking for another lick. I taste his skin, suck the tip.

He groans low and deep, his body clenching. His eyes find mine, and the heat in his sears my skin.

We stare at each other, both panting, and then his gaze lowers to my mouth.

"Sophie—"

Someone bashes into us. Gabriel braces, but the spell is broken. He turns to glare over his shoulder.

"Sorry!" a guy in an ill-fitting white suit shouts.

Gabriel straightens, his hand sliding down to cup my elbow. I feel the loss of his body heat acutely.

The guy does a double take and moves closer. "Scottie! Just the guy I've been looking for."

I'm beginning to suspect dude knew exactly who he was bumping into, and by the grim expression on Gabriel's face, I'm guessing he thinks so as well.

"Andrew," he says, his voice clear over the music.

Stage lights flicker over Andrew's face, and I realize he's one of the record executives. I take a step back, knowing the moment is over and Gabriel needs to talk business. But his clasp tightens, and he turns toward me with a frown.

"Go work," I tell him.

His frown grows. He shakes his head in refusal.

I squeeze his hand. "I don't want it to be here." Because if he kisses me now, I won't be able to stop—I won't want *him* to stop.

For a second, I don't think he'll let me go. But then the mask falls in place, and he gives me a tight nod. I start to move away, but he suddenly pulls me back, bending down to growl in my ear.

"One hour. Come home, or I'll find you and bring you back myself."

SOPHIE
20

WE ARE IN A HOTEL TONIGHT. My hands are shaking as I let myself into the suite. He's waiting for me; I feel it in my bones.

The living room is empty, only a side lamp on, illuminating the buttery, cream leather chairs, glossy wood tables, and soft gray sofa. French doors flank one wall, a pair of them open, and the gauzy white curtains flutter in the warm night breeze.

The sound of a door opening comes from the bedroom.

"Chatty girl?" A second later, Gabriel walks out.

And my mouth falls open, a faint squeak escaping. "Holy fucking hell."

He stops short, halfway into the room. "What's wrong?"

Wrong? Nothing. Not a single thing. I swallow hard for fear my tongue is hanging out.

He's taken off his shoes, socks, belt. The button of his fine slacks is undone, showing the black band of his briefs—I don't know if they're boxer briefs or regular. I *want* to know. As in, my fingers actually twitch with the urge tug his zipper down and explore.

But that's not what has me dumbstruck, heat flaring along the backs of my thighs. No. His jacket and tie are gone, and his shirt is unbuttoned and open.

In all this time, I had yet to see Gabriel without a shirt. He hides his body like a pious Victorian, never letting me see anything other than him fully dressed and polished. Now I know why. Had he let me get a glimpse, I might never have been able to form a coherent thought around him.

This man's chest is a work of art. It's every fantasy I've had about a man's body made real. I don't even know how that's possible, but I'm not about to complain. God, he looks touchable. Olive skin, tight little brownish nipples, a smattering of dark chest hair over the most incredibly honed—

"You're staring." His tone is dry.

"Yes, I am." I drag my eyes up and find his expression bemused.

A thick brow lifts. I try to mimic the look and fail when both of my brows lift as one. His lips twitch in amusement.

He shifts his weight, causing his abs to clench. Good Lord. He's not some overdeveloped gym worshiper, just solid and strong, that perfect balance between defined musculature and healthy male—

"You're still staring, Sophie."

"You think it's easy looking away from all this splendor?" I ask his belly button, licking my lips when he huffs out a laugh and just a little bit more of his lower abs are revealed, slanting toward the thick bulge of his cock, which is lamentably hidden behind his slacks.

"You're impossible," he mutters, though there is humor in his voice. He strolls farther into the room and then practically kills me when he sits in one of the low-slung armchairs. That body, sprawled out on display, those thick, long thighs braced as if to take me in his lap—it's too much.

I want to straddle him and lick my way from the hollow of his throat to the tip of his cock.

He eyes me as if he knows what I'm thinking, and the air thickens. So many things we left unsaid. I'm remembering his lips now, surprisingly soft, but strong with purpose.

From the way his lids lower, I wonder if he's remembering things as well. But he doesn't move. Tension glides over his body and snakes around the room. I feel it in my throat and down my spine. We're closing up again, retreating.

Slowly, I toe off my shoes and set my gear down, never breaking eye contact. "I was being completely honest," I tell him. "I see you like this and I want to stare forever."

He snorts, shaking his head even as he rests his temple on his knuckles. "What do you mean 'like this'?"

"Undone."

He tenses. It does lovely things to that chest. I focus on his face, mainly to maintain some semblance of decorum.

"You think this is me undone?" he asks quietly.

"It's a start." I reach for my camera bag. "Will you let me photograph you?"

There is safety to be found with the camera between us. A way for both of us to hide until we're comfortable around each other again.

"You're serious?"

"You sound surprised." Holding my camera, I sit in the sofa opposite him. "Don't tell me no one has asked to take your picture before."

"They've asked. I never saw the point." He shrugs. "I'm not the story."

You're my story. You always were.

"This is just for me," I say instead. "No one else."

His shrewd gaze pins me. "Why do you want this?"

So I can have a bit of you forever. "Pictures capture moments in time. I want this one—when you finally let me see a sliver of the man behind the clothes."

His nostrils flare on an indrawn breath, and he slowly lets it out. When he speaks, his voice is a rasp. "Take the pictures."

So I do, testing angles. The warm glow of the lamplight highlights the planes and hollows of his body. He sits still, a king lounging on his throne, granting me this small whim.

He doesn't love this; his muscles tic with each click of the shutter. But he doesn't stop me either, just watches as I work.

It's too easy, taking shots of him. The camera loves him. But more than that, I have a valid excuse to look at him to my heart's content.

"I feel like a bellend," he grumps.

"A what?"

High color paints his cheeks. "A prick head. An idiot. A poseur. Take your pick."

I have to laugh. "So sensitive."

"You try being on the other end of that thing." He gestures toward the camera with his chin.

"I won't apologize," I tell him. "You are beautiful, Gabriel."

His expression shutters. "It is only a veneer. Nothing of what I am on the inside."

My fingers tighten around the smooth edges of the camera. "You think I don't see you?"

He simply stares, blue eyes startling and intense beneath the dark sweep of his brows. I've never seen so much power in a man's face; sheer grit and determination forge the lines and curves of his features.

I raise my camera, capture the image as I talk. "Your nose is big and hawkish."

He visibly flinches, and I know I've hit a rare sore spot with him. I don't stop, though.

"There's a bump on the bridge, and it lists slightly to the side. I've often wondered if you broke it at some point." I take another picture, noting the way his brows lift in surprise.

"I was fifteen," he says. "Three boys jumped me on the way back to my room."

My heart gives a great thump. "Stubborn nose. You take hit after hit, but never back down. I'd bet good money you never let those boys break you."

"I would not kneel," he whispers. "That's when they broke my nose."

I take another picture, my focus narrowing on his eyes. Those glorious eyes that can appear like glacial ice or the Caribbean Sea, depending on his mood. They burn like blue flames now.

"Did they also give you the faint scar bisecting your left eyebrow?"

"No. That was my dad." He glares, as if daring me to pity him.

I don't do that. But I do hurt for him.

"You have two permanent lines between your brows," I tell him, moving on. "You frown when you read your phone, watch TV, or listen to others talk. It makes you appear stern and vaguely pissed off, but it's really that you put the whole of your concentration into every task."

His breath becomes agitated, the wide, muscled expanse of his chest lifting and falling.

"Your body." A lump rises in my throat, my mouth going dry.

Silence falls.

"My body?" he prompts, low and forceful. He's reclined in his seat, spread out like a damn feast, but tension rides through his muscles, making them bunch.

"It is perfect. A work of art." *Lickable.* I take a shuddering breath, lift my camera back up, and take a shot of his torso—defined abs, tight pecs, little nipples. *Utterly lickable.* "You work hard to maintain that body, which I'm sure some would think is due to vanity."

"It's not?" His voice has gone rough, agitated and thick.

"No. You use your body like a weapon, a perfect shell so no one bothers to look too closely at the real you."

He shifts in his chair as if he's fighting the urge to flee. I push on.

"And you do it to be strong. Because you hate weakness."

With a rush, his breath leaves him, and he sags in his chair. "Yes," he rasps. "Only I believe you are my greatest weakness now, chatty girl."

My camera lowers, and I stare at him, unwilling to hide my hurt. "You hate me?"

He blinks as if trying to break out of a fog. Color tints his cheeks, and his breath kicks up once more. "I think," he says, "adore would be the better word."

Oh. Hell.

Those intense eyes fixate on me, baring his soul. It is filled with pain and need. "You are my greatest weakness because I have no defense when it comes to you."

Warmth rushes through me. I blink rapidly, my lips quivering, caught between wanting to smile wide and feeling the strange urge to cry. He's split me wide open. And I know exactly how he feels, because suddenly I want to hide from this too.

Sex is one thing; what is before us is something more. I thought of him as my friend, a man I wanted to bed. But, if I let myself, I will completely lose my heart to him, a man who refuses to let himself commit to anyone.

I force myself to lift the camera, focus it on him, make my voice light. I probably fail, my hands are shaking, my voice is too breathy. "And yet you don't want to fuck me."

It's supposed to be a tease. We both know it's not. And I'm cursing myself for speaking because I know he'll volley right back. I feel it in the air, and my heart starts to pound.

Gabriel smiles then. It's the smile of a predator: a slow curl of the lips, his eyes narrowing on me. A deep rumble sounds in his chest. "You believe that, do you? Shall I tell you all the ways I want to fuck you, chatty girl?"

I make an incoherent sound, my insides swooping wildly.

"Tell me."

"You talk of scars," he says. "You have one too. On the right side of your upper lip."

"An Indiana Jones moment gone wrong when I was six."

His eyes crinkle, but he doesn't smile. His expression borders on pain. "I've wanted to suckle that little bump from the moment I noticed it on the plane. Every time you talk I want to tongue that lip, taste your soft mouth."

I breathe harder, setting the camera aside.

"It drives me to distraction," he says, "wanting to hunt you down at all hours of the day. Just to hear your voice, see those lips move."

I can't talk now, and my lips are parted, flush and wanting.

He doesn't seem to mind my silence. His gaze moves over me like a hot hand. "The nights are the hardest. But I suspect you know that."

"Yes." It's a strangled whimper.

"I lie there holding you, telling myself I will not roll you onto your back. I cannot push up those thin shirts that taunt me with the shape of you to finally find out if your nipples are pale pink or blush brown."

He takes a deep breath, and his abs clench, drawing my eyes to the thick rise of his cock, growing visibly harder as he speaks.

"There are times I torture myself by thinking of those fantastic tits. Of how I'd lick them like ice cream, tasting every luscious curve. Slow, long licks." His lids lower as he stares at my breasts, and my nipples stiffen painfully. "How would they taste? Would you like it best if I sucked those nipples hard? Or mouthed them so softly you barely feel it and have to beg for more?"

God. I'm squirming now, everything going deliciously tight.

He makes a low hum in the back of his throat, seeming to

enjoy the show. "Some nights, it's so bad I don't want to bother with foreplay. I want to lift your leg, make room for myself between your thighs, and rut like a selfish, greedy bastard. I want to fuck the wetness into your sweet box, feel you grow slick around me."

His rough voice is so disgruntled, I let out a breathless laugh—because my head is spinning, my skin so hot, I feel faint. "You think I'd object?"

His eyes snap with heat. "You want me to use your body for my pleasure?"

Fuck yes. "As hard as you can."

A shudder wracks his frame, and he digs his fingers into the chair arms as if holding himself back.

I can't have that. I slouch further on the couch, spreading my legs just at bit. The air feels cool against my heated skin.

His gaze goes immediately to the shadowy space beneath my skirt, and my thighs clench in response.

"But you wouldn't have to fuck me wet," I whisper, heart pounding. "Anytime I'm in bed with you, I'm wet."

A low, strangled grunt leaves him.

"So fucking wet, Gabriel. Every night. All night."

As his head lolls against the back of his chair, his gaze going somnolent, I give him a weak smile. "Why do you think I'm washing so many panties?"

It's almost sleepy, the look he gives me, but I see the calculated gleam in his eyes. "Are they wet now?"

"They've been wet since you walked through that door."

His nostrils flare as if he can draw in my scent from all the way over there. "Show me."

My clit swells, pressing tight against the gusset of my panties. I'm so turned on, my stomach quakes. I spread my legs for him, the soft fabric of the skirt slithering up my skin. With shaking hands, I pull the skirt higher, present myself fully to his gaze.

Color floods his sharp cheeks, his lips parting. I picture myself, white panties darkened by a flood of need, outlining the rude shape of my swollen sex, and I whimper, canting my hips.

"More," he rasps. "Give me a peek of that honey I've been craving."

Oh, shit. I can't breathe. My hand shakes as I hook a finger in my panties and almost shyly pull them aside. I feel so naughty, a dirty girl giving an illicit glimpse, that my skin flares white hot.

He groans, low and pained, his body tensing in the chair. His gaze stays locked on my exposed flesh as his hand slides over his hard abs and closes over the immense erection straining against his pants. He gives himself an impatient squeeze.

"Gorgeous," he says, gripping himself tighter.

"Take it out," I tell him, trembling. "I want to see you too."

He doesn't hesitate, just unzips and pushes his trousers and underwear down low on his thighs. His cock bobs free, rising to kiss the hollow of his navel.

Gabriel's cock. For a second I can't believe I'm actually looking at it. My gaze slides over the tender curve of his weighty balls, up to the meaty jut of his dick, so engorged it visibly pulses. As if it pains him, he strokes its long length. Just once.

I swallow hard. "I want to do that."

He strokes again, a lazy glide. A tease. "If you get anywhere near this cock, it's going to be fucking you."

I want that so badly. I can almost feel him between my legs, pushing in hot and thick and strong. Somehow I find my voice.

"You should know, I can't be a fling. Not with you. If you want me, you have to be all in."

A frown knots his brows, and when he speaks, his voice is

a rasp. "I've lived my whole life denying myself what I truly want. And yet I cannot turn from you. Haven't you realized it yet? I am yours. I will always be yours, whether I touch you or not."

Something inside of me snaps. I'm through waiting. In a daze, I rise from my seat. My skirt flutters around my legs, my skin so sensitive now, the fabric tickles.

Gabriel watches me come to him. With each slow step I take, his breathing gets deeper, as if he's struggling to draw in enough air.

I straddle his lap, and that first point of contact—my bare thighs sliding over his—has me whimpering. God, he feels good. His skin is hot, a sheen of sweat covering his chest, his body thrumming with tension. The length of his cock lies heavy and thick between us, pressing into my fluttering belly.

A grunt escapes him, and his big hand comes down on my butt, kneading it—as if he can't help himself—before he hauls me closer. My breasts cushion on his hard chest. His other hand grips of my hair, holding me right where he wants me.

Our breath mingles as we stare at each other. Gabriel studies my mouth, a tremor running through him. When his eyes meet mine again, they're filled with heat.

"I wasn't prepared to need you this much. I don't know who I am anymore if you aren't with me."

He trembles again, holding himself so stiffly.

"I need you too," I whisper, stroking his shoulder. "So much it hurts. Take the hurt away, Gabriel."

"Sophie." His grip in my hair tightens. But when his lips touch mine, they're soft, a gentle brush. I've been waiting so long for this touch, it does something to me, sends my pulse skittering. My belly clenches sweetly, breath leaving me in a rush.

And he sighs, as if he too has been waiting for this. My eyes close, and I let myself just feel him, the way he slowly explores me—a nuzzle of my lower lip, a slow, delicate suck of my upper lip.

We're locked tight, his cock pulsing between us, our hearts thudding so hard I can feel the answering beat of his against my chest. And yet he kisses me as if he's memorizing this moment, our lips melding, then drifting away.

My head spins, my body becoming heavy. I kiss him with more intensity, needing, just needing. He feels so good; every time I touch him, my insides ease with relief and then tighten with greedy want.

The chair beneath us creaks. Gabriel's other hand slides up my back to tangle in my hair. His kiss grows hungry, going deeper, wetter. He groans, and then he's not so gentle or polite.

Whatever tether he's had on himself snaps. He lurches up to devour me with a hot intensity that has my head spinning.

The sounds he makes, as if he's so hungry, dying for it. There is no end, no beginning, only our mouths meeting, messy and uncoordinated.

More and more, I'm whimpering and impatient, needy and lustful. His mouth moves to my jaw and down my neck, where he finds a spot that curls my toes. Rough hands grab my ass, haul me closer.

The thick, round tip of his cock notches against my sex and pushes in, stopped by my panties. But he's in me, that wide head pulsing and stretching my opening. I'm balanced there, unable to get more, unwilling to move off.

His teeth graze my bare shoulder, hands delving beneath my shirt to stroke my sides. "Off."

He yanks my shirt over my head and sends it sailing across the room. He doesn't bother removing my bra, but with a grunt, simply tugs down the cup. My breast pops free, and his hot mouth is on my nipple, sucking with greedy pulls.

"Oh, shit." I clutch his hair and rock my hips on his cock. It pushes just a bit farther, straining against my panties. I need them off. I need him in me.

Squeezing my ass, he gives a hard thrust as if he, too, is impatient. And then the world tilts as he stands, carrying me. My back meets the cool wall, and his mouth is on my neck.

I'm pinned there, held by his hips against mine. With an impatient sound, he grabs the side of my panties. The elastic stretches tight and then snaps. Another breath and he's ripping the torn fabric out of his way.

He doesn't wait, doesn't ask. I'm so wet, the tip of him glides right in. But he's a big man, thick and meaty. The delicious girth of him stretches me wide, owning every inch he takes. And he has to work for it, shoving and thrusting, using the wall as leverage. Breathless, I spread my thighs wider to make room for him.

And each time he thrusts, he grunts deep in his chest, his hips meeting mine with a hard slap. He's fucking the hell out of me, and I love it, I love it.

I'm orgasming before I can even think, and it's like nothing I've ever felt, this insane crescendo that keeps rising and rising. It's so strong, it almost hurts, this pleasure. I can only slam back down on him, fuck myself against his cock, crying out with helpless need.

And the more I do, the harder he goes, as if he's feeding off my desperation. The walls rattle with the force of our movements. A picture falls with a crash.

Gabriel strains against me, his cock so deep I feel it in my throat, down to my toes. He groans long and pained as he comes. Heat fills me, and I topple, sagging against the wall, my breath coming in disjointed pants.

Huffing out a breath, he leans into me, his mouth open and trembling on my shoulder. I look up at the ceiling and push a shaking hand through my damp hair. My heart beats like a snare drum.

Sweaty and shaking, we remain as we are. When he stirs, the movement sends a twinge through my aching sex.

"No condom," he rasps. "I didn't think."

I feel the evidence trickling along my ass. A strangled laugh escapes me. "I guess it's a good thing we're both in the clear and I'm on birth control."

His fingers flex, pushing into my upper thighs as if he can't help himself. "You aren't upset?"

"Can't worry about barn doors when the horse has already bolted," I say, still dazed. "Or however it goes."

He lifts his head, and our eyes meet. A strange shyness flutters over me. Holy hell, I've never had sex like this, as if my life depended on riding cock. Sex that has me so mindless with lust I forget the basics of protection. Shit, I forgot my name, if I'm being honest. The heat building in his gaze tells me he knows this.

I feel him there, deep within me, still pulsing. I give a little wiggle, and he twitches, that long dick of his getting harder.

"No one else," he says, his voice a thick rasp.

He doesn't say if he means for me or for him. It doesn't matter. It's clear there is only us now.

Still, I lick my swollen lips and respond. "Only you."

GABRIEL
21

DESTROYED. My polished armor. My stubborn resistance. My hardened heart. She's smashed through the first two and laid total claim on the third. And I don't feel like running.

In truth, I can barely move. Hours of coming together, resting, catching each other's eye, then coming together again like greedy fiends who fuck as though the world is about to end, has taken its toll.

I'm replete and sweating in a tangle of Sophie's curvy little body and the sheets that have long since pulled from the bed. She lays her head in the crook of my shoulder where she belongs, and I play with the rose-gold strands of her damp hair.

I could have lost her tonight, missed this perfection by being a prat. Gratitude swells in my chest and clogs my throat. Sophie Darling didn't walk out on me. She gave me a chance.

"Thank you for coming home," I tell her, unable to hold back the words.

Home. Does she realize how many times I've referred to wherever we rest our heads as my home? I hadn't meant to betray myself that way, but I can't seem to stop. I want her to know what she means to me, and yet the sensation of exposing my heart is so foreign, I find it hard to breathe as she stares at me.

But her expression goes soft, her brown eyes shinning. Relief is liquid cool along my tight muscles as she reaches up to tuck my hair back from my brow.

"You came home first."

I didn't have a home until she came into my life. She gave me one without hesitation, as if she's been waiting for me all this time, knowing I was meant to be hers. I touch her cheek just to remind myself she's real.

Her voice is a thread in the dark. "You have fading bruises on your side and all over your face."

I don't move. I knew I wasn't fully healed, but I'd stayed away as long as I could stand.

"They're faint," she says slowly as if she's measuring her words. "But I saw them when we were in the shower."

Where it was too bright to hide anything.

Her hand smoothes along my side. I'm no longer tender, but the touch raises little bumps on my skin.

"Are you going to tell me where you were?" She doesn't demand, which makes it worse.

My voice sounds like rust when I finally speak. "Fighting."

"Fighting?" She rises up on one elbow. "Who? Where? And what the fuck?... Why?"

The horror in her eyes makes me feel small. "I grew up fighting. When I was younger, I did it for money, and because it released something in me that needed freeing."

Her gaze darts over my face. "And you needed that release again?"

"Yes."

"Because of me."

I cannot lie to her. Never again. "Yes."

She sucks in a breath, and I grab her nape, afraid she'll go. "Because I was an idiot, Sophie, who couldn't go back to that hotel room that night without breaking. I couldn't let myself tell you the truth then."

She doesn't pull back, but instead gentles her voice. "What truth?"

The words pour out. "That I wanted you to the point of pain. That I needed you more than anything."

A sigh escapes her, and she rests her forehead to mine. "Gabriel, I needed you too. It isn't weakness to admit that."

Silently, I nod.

Sophie strokes my side where the bruises are fading. "Please don't do it again. I can't stand the thought of you being hurt."

"Does it help to know I won?" I'm only half-joking, but I hate the sadness I put in her eyes and want it gone.

"No." Her smile is tremulous and brief. "Yes, a little." The edge of her thumb runs along my cheekbone where I was hit. "Promise, sunshine? That you'll come to me instead when you're needy."

"Darling, coming with you far surpasses any brief release I'd find fighting." It's a horrible quip. But this is what she's done to me; I've become a blathering, bestowed idiot.

Doesn't seem to matter; her expression goes soft, pleased. "Okay then."

"Okay," I whisper in agreement, set free by her simple acceptance.

She pulls me closer and kisses me—little presses of her lips, sweet darts that shoot straight to my heart and make it flutter.

If I looked at myself from the outside, I wouldn't recognize this man who acknowledges his heart is all a-flutter, who smiles against Sophie's mouth as she keeps kissing. But I like it. I love it.

"More," she demands, suckling my lower lip. "Kiss me more."

I chuckle, a breath of sound she captures. "You're kissing me," I point out.

"Because you're delicious." She dips her tongue between

my lips, a slow glide, a lazy taste. "I love your mouth."

I angle my head, taste her back. "I love yours more."

"Mmm." She melts into me, takes my breath and gives it back to me. "Give me another."

I lick deeper, my mind going hazy, my mouth sensitive to every touch.

"Again," she says, smiling, kissing.

My hand cups her sweaty cheek. "My greedy, chatty girl."

With an adorable little grunt, she pushes me onto my back, going at my mouth as if I'm her first taste of chocolate. And I laugh, a low breath against her lips, my heart still fucking fluttering. I wouldn't be surprised if there are cartoon hearts in my eyes, and I don't bloody care.

We drift, content to simply kiss and touch each other as if we're reassuring ourselves this is real. Pleasure makes my body heavy and warm, my movements slow.

"You do apologies pretty well," she says after a time.

We're nose to nose, our limbs so entwined she feels like a part of me.

"Pretty well?" My thumb glides along the elegant line of her collarbone. "I do many things *very* well."

"Excellent, even," she agrees, kissing the bridge of my nose. "Now do me well."

With an evil grin, I slide my hand down the curve of her thigh and grasp the crook of her knee, bringing it up to my hip. Exposed, she's glistening wet, pretty pink. My cock pulses in approval.

"As you wish," I say, guiding myself to her warm, wet well of addiction and pushing in deep.

She gasps and groans, the sound so erotic, I thrust harder than planned. But she merely grins. "Quotes *The Princess Bride* and has a big, hard cock. I've hit the jackpot."

I know I'm the true winner, but that doesn't stop me from taking her hands in mine and raising them over her head so her pretty tits lift high.

"Hush now and spread those lovely thighs wider like a good, chatty girl. I've work to do here."

———

SOPHIE DRIFTS away from my side as we take the elevator down to the lobby in the morning. I tug her right back where she belongs, and wrap an arm around her waist to keep her there.

A soft blush colors her cheeks as she smiles up at me. "I wouldn't have taken you for a handsy guy."

I've had my hands on every inch of her at this point—an experience I want to repeat. Often. I rub the delectable curve of her hip, because I can.

"I'm not. This is a Sophie only condition. Does it bother you?"

I don't know what I'll do if she doesn't like it. Probably live with my hands permanently tucked into my pockets to keep from reaching for her. But she simply grins wide and rests her head on my shoulder, her hand smoothing down my chest. It feels so good, I find myself leaning into her touch.

"I think last night made it clear that I love you touching me," she says.

Last night. Heat licks over my skin and settles in my cock. We fucked until we were shaking and breathless. I kissed her until I couldn't feel my own lips. And still I kissed her some more.

I want more now. But I'm not sure I can handle it. The battering my body took fighting, the lack of sleep when I feared I'd lost my chance with Sophie, and the lack of sleep when I finally had Sophie is catching up on me.

I'm lightheaded, slightly dizzy—euphoric and just plain exhausted. I wouldn't change a thing, however. Not when the end result is Sophie being well and truly mine.

The elevator arrives at the lobby, and we exit. Across the way, the guys have congregated, drinking coffee in the lounge. They've drawn a fair bit of attention, but they don't seem to care.

At my side, Sophie's steps slow.

I slow too. "What is it?"

She nibbles on the corner of her lip. "How do you want to play this?"

"This?" I ask blankly.

She glances toward the guys. "I'm thinking you're not big on public displays of affection. If you'd rather we kept things to ourselves—"

I step into her space, cup her cheeks, and kiss her. Do I care for public displays? No. Can I keep my hands, my mouth off Sophie? Hell no.

When her lips yield to mine, the world falls away. I groan, tilt my head, and go deeper, luxuriating in the feel of her mouth and the taste of her tongue on mine.

I kiss her until I run out of air. And even then it is a struggle to stop.

She utters a happy sigh, her lips returning to mine again and again.

Behind us, someone gives a wolf whistle. I'm guessing it's Rye by the sound of it. He can sod off.

I end the kiss with one last nibble on her lower lip. "Consider yourself outed," I whisper against her mouth.

She smiles, her brown eyes dazed. "Wow, you really go all in."

"For you? Yes."

She grins. "As long as you're okay, I'm okay."

I'm dizzy again, sweating a bit. I need a strong pot of tea and a good breakfast. But Sophie's needs come first. I give her a reassuring peck on her nose. "Don't worry, chatty girl. All is well now."

I take two steps. The world goes black.

SOPHIE  22

"I DO NOT NEED to be here," Gabriel announces. "Get this IV out of my arm."

Gabriel Scott: worst patient ever. I should have expected as much.

Brenna apparently thinks the same. "Shut up and take your medicine, Colossus."

He narrows his eyes in warning. "Colossus?"

Brenna gives him a cheeky look. "You know, the Colossus of Rhodes? One of the Seven Wonders of the Ancient World. They say when it fell, it was quite the spectacle."

"Hilarious," he deadpans.

But I laugh, grateful for the emotion. I was terrified when he fainted. Gabriel is eternal in my eyes. Superman in a tailored suit. He cannot topple. To see him take a step and suddenly crumple to the ground as if the strings of life had been cut is a sight I never want to witness again.

Now, he sits stiff and pissed off on our bed, because, according to Brenna, Kill John and company have a strict, no-alerting-the-press-by-going-to-the-hospital-unless-you're-truly-dying rule. One that pissed me off when my man was lying prone on the floor, but in hindsight, I can appreciate it. I know for a fact that Gabriel would have gone ballistic if he'd woken in a hospital room.

He's so pissy now that he's scared away the guys. Only Brenna and I remain. I'm guessing this is because Gabriel never yells at women.

There's a light knock on the bedroom door, and Dr. Stern lets herself in. She is the band's on-call physician. Apparently she's been going on tour with Kill John for years. I met her once—she keeps to herself and flies to all the cities instead of using a coach.

Elegant yet down to earth, she reminds me of the Upper West Side moms who work full time but still take their kids to the Museum of Natural History on Sundays.

"How is my patient doing?"

"Annoyed." Gabriel lifts his arm. "Would you please remove this?"

The doctor is immune to his evil glare. "When it's finished. You mind telling me how you felt before you fainted?"

"As though I were about to faint but hoped very much it wouldn't happen."

"Stubborn," I mutter under my breath.

Dr. Stern nods. "And have you felt this way before?"

A mulish expression mars Gabriel's face. When he doesn't speak, Brenna stands. "I'm gonna head out."

As soon as she leaves, Dr. Stern asks him the question again.

With a sigh, he answers. "Yes."

"How many times, Scottie?" she persists. "And for how long?"

Seconds tick by.

"Since the beginning of the tour. On and off, perhaps ten times. I didn't count."

"Jesus," I blurt out, getting up from my seat and pacing to the window before rounding on him. "What the hell, Gabriel?"

He won't meet my eyes.

Dr. Stern sighs. "I'd say you're extremely stressed and

overworked. Have you been sleeping well?"

A faint flush hits his cheeks. "Not lately."

God, it's my turn to blush.

"You need more than a good night's sleep, Scottie. In fact, I'd prescribe a long vacation."

"I'll go on holiday when the tour is over."

The promise does not sound very convincing.

Dr. Stern apparently feels the same. "You're ignoring your health, which is never a good thing."

"I have not ignored the situation," he snaps. "Christ, I was willing to turn my life upside down to get a proper night's sleep—"

He abruptly shuts up and pinches the bridge of his nose. "Shit."

"By asking me to room with you," I finish for him.

His gaze slides to mine, and I see him wince. "Are you upset?" he asks.

"Why should I be? You told me from the beginning me why you wanted me there."

He can't hide the flinch of surprise. But he doesn't say a word, just eyes me as if waiting for me to explode.

I laugh. "How could I be mad about that? I'm the one you needed. If I'm honest, it kind of melts me."

He begins to smile.

"But I am pissed at you."

"Oh, for pity's sake," he bursts out, lifting his hands in exasperation, as he turns to the doctor. "You see? *Lei è completamente pazza.*"

Whatever he said makes Dr. Stern chuckle.

I glare at both of them, stalking over to his bedside. "Don't you go yammering off in Italian. I don't care if it sounds like hot, buttered sex; I'm still pissed."

Gabriel shakes his head. "Why are you angry? I don't understand."

"You never told me how badly you were suffering, you stubborn ass. You let it get to this point." I lean in until we're nose to nose. "I *care* about you. I don't want to see you faint like that ever again."

"Trust me, Darling, I'm not planning on fainting like that ever again."

"Is that supposed to reassure me, when you refuse to see a doctor when you're feeling ill? You can't control everything, you know."

My answer is his stubborn chin lifting and his lush mouth flattening. But I see the flash of fear in his eyes before he conceals it. I've been so worried, I missed the signs. He's terrified right now. I glance at Dr. Stern.

"May we have a moment?"

"Certainly."

As soon as she leaves, I sit by Gabriel's side and take his hand. It's cold and clammy. "Talk to me."

His thumb runs along my knuckles. "There's nothing to talk about."

"Do I need to do some cuddle therapy here?"

His eyes meet mine, and I see the weariness in them. He clearly thought he'd hidden his feelings well and good. It makes me smile, sadly.

"I know you, sunshine. We might as well be on a plane right now." I squeeze his fingers. "You are not all right."

With a sigh, he rests against the headboard. His throat moves on a swallow. "I hate doctors."

"Dr. Stern is very nice."

"No," he shakes his head. "Not in that way. Bugger...I didn't get myself checked out because I hate seeing a doctor." Blue eyes filled with pain meet mine. "My mum... She was fatigued, always sleeping. Fainting spells."

I go ice cold. "You think you might..."

I don't say the words. I can't. I will not give them credence.

But I crawl into bed and wrap myself around him.

He leans into my touch. "I fear it. I always have."

I see the effort it takes for him to admit that, and I snuggle in closer. He wraps an arm around my shoulders and squeezes back, his lips pressing to the top of my head.

"Do the tests, Gabriel." When he tenses, I push on. "It worries you, and that makes everything worse. Do them and get that fear out of the way."

He doesn't say a word, just breathes against my hair, his hand clutching my shoulder.

I raise my head. "If it were me, what would you say?"

"To take the bloody tests," he grumbles.

I kiss his lips. "I will not leave you. Ever."

He must see the determination in my eyes, because he gives a short nod.

When we call in Dr. Stern and tell her his concerns, she calls the nearby hospital and sets up a few tests.

IT TAKES two days for the results to come back. Two days of Gabriel stomping around like a snarling bear to hide the fact that he's terrified. Two days of me distracting him with sex and holding him tight when he sleeps to hide that I'm terrified.

Nothing gets done, despite Gabriel's insistence that everyone go about their business. At the moment, he is the top priority, whether he likes it or not.

On the day the doctor is supposed to call, I outright give up trying to pretend I'm okay. I don't bother getting out of my PJs but sit in a chair and flip through a magazine, seeing absolutely nothing.

Somehow Brenna, Rye, Jax, Killian, and Libby find ways to be near him too. They've all ended up in our suite sitting around as well. It's as if we're all waiting, circling our wagons.

And oddly, Gabriel doesn't send anyone away. He might not admit it, but he needs his friends.

Silence settles over us so thickly it's choking.

When Gabriel's cell finally rings, I think we all jump out of our skin a little. I stop breathing all together for a moment. I can't move. Gabriel answers, his voice low. And when I can't hear what's being said, I go to him, take his cold hand in mine. My heart pounds so loudly, I hear it reverberating in my ears.

A tremor goes through him, and his hand jerks. My breath hitches.

When he hangs up, everyone stares at him. The silence grows, and then he finally speaks. "All clear."

I sob and throw myself into his arms. Around us, the guys and Brenna are talking, laughing—I'm not even sure. There's only Gabriel for me at the moment, the sound of his pounding heart, the faint dampness of his shirt, and the scent of his cologne mixed with the sweat of his body.

He holds me so tightly, my ribs ache. But the hug is over soon, and he sets me away and stalks over to the window. He doesn't fool me. I see the sheen of sweat on his brow and the way his hand trembles before he tucks it into his pocket.

Jax speaks up first. "That settles it, then. You're taking a vacation."

Gabriel doesn't bother looking our way. "No."

"Ah, yeah you are," Killian snaps. "And if you say *no* again, I swear I'll clock you one. I don't care if you can kick my ass or not."

Gabriel snorts and turns to face us, his cold mask firmly back in place. "I do not need—"

"Stern literally said you need a vacation, Scottie," Whip cuts in, looking pissed. "So stop messing around."

All the signs of an imminent blow up are rising in Gabriel: eyes going icy, cheeks flushing, nostrils flaring. But his voice remains calm. "There's too much to do."

"Jules can handle it." Brenna gives a firm nod. "You told me yourself she's getting on well. And everything is set, so all she needs to do is steer the boat, so to speak."

His eyes narrow. "Yes, thank you for that observation, Brenna."

"You're welcome."

With a huff, he tugs at his cuffs. "Go on holiday. It's absurd. Where would I even go?"

Rye laughs without humor. "You're in Italy, for fuck's sake. Laze around, eat good food, drink wine, fuck—"

"Do not finish that statement, Ryland." Gabriel's stare is suppressive.

Rye shrugs. "You get my point."

"I think it's a great idea." I pipe up.

Oh, but Gabriel looks at me as though I'm the worst traitor. I move closer and put my hand on his forearm. It's like rock beneath his jacket. "Come on, sunshine. You've got the all clear. Let's celebrate life, laze around like Rye suggests, and…" I grin wide. "Eat. We'll hole up in the room, just you and me."

"Nah." Jax shakes his head. "He'll find a way to slink off and work."

Whip nods. "Truth."

"See?" Gabriel gestures toward them. "It is agreed."

"Go to your villa," Killian says, firmly.

"You have a villa?" I picture wineries and rolling Tuscan hills.

Gabriel's jaw bunches. "On the coast. In Positano." He glares at Killian. "But it's all closed up."

"You can have it aired out with a call. Come on, man, try a little harder with your protests."

"Arse."

"It must be beautiful," I say. With Gabriel's sense of style, it's probably perfect.

"We wouldn't know," Rye says with a dramatic sigh. "He never invites us anywhere."

"Because I work, you git."

Rye waggles his brows. "I bet you'd take Sophie."

If looks could kill. "Sophie has to work too."

Hurt makes my voice small. "You don't want me to see your villa?"

Gabriel's brows lift. "What? No. My home is your home, Sophie. I thought you knew that much."

I smile at the tender reproach in his voice.

"Or take her to one of your other houses," Jax puts in.

"How many houses do you have," I ask, because, really?

Gabriel glances away. "Five."

Every time I feel I've finally got to know all there is about this man, he surprises me with more. "Where?"

With a long-suffering sigh, he answers. "The flat in New York. The townhouse in London. A flat in Paris."

"The lodge in St. Moritz," Brenna adds.

"The villa in Positano," Rye reminds us.

Gabriel's gaze darts around, glaring, as if he can't figure out how to stop them all from speaking but is dearly wishing he could.

"And didn't you buy a place in Ireland last year?" Jax asks.

"Right," Killian snaps his fingers. "That little cottage in County Clare."

"Near my place," Whip says with a grin. "By the Cliffs of Insanity."

"They are the Cliffs of Moher," Gabriel says with a grimace. "Christ, you're half Irish. Know your country."

"Dude, whatever, the Cliffs of Insanity sounds way cooler."

"So that's six homes," says Libby, who has been quiet this whole time.

"Great gravy," I mutter. I rent my place, and it is literally the size of a walk-in closet.

The difference between our stations is staggering, and yet I can't see him as anything other than mine.

Gabriel ducks his head and shrugs. "Property makes for a good investment."

Jax saunters over and puts an arm around my shoulders. "Sophie girl, you don't know the half of it. Scottie is a genius with money. Our boy here is solely responsible for all of us being obscenely rich, as opposed to mostly rich. Seriously, stick with him."

I roll my eyes. "I'd stick with him if he was a pauper."

Gabriel looks up and a quiet smile softens the hard edges of his expression. I return it, my heart beating a little faster. Relief that he isn't terminally ill weakens my knees, and the lump has returned to my throat.

I will stay by his side in sickness, in health, the whole deal. Yet I'm so very glad that he's safe, my voice comes out thick and husky. "Given that Positano is the only place we wouldn't have to fly to, I vote we go there."

His eyes search mine for a long moment. "Do you truly want to go?"

I could give him a hard time about trying to pawn this off as doing me a favor, but there's something to be said for picking your battles. So I nod and give him the puppy eyes.

"Do this for me? Please, sunshine?"

He sighs, and his shoulders lower from their defensive stance. "All right, chatty girl. You win."

"Awesome," Jax says, lifting his hand for a high five.

Gabriel doesn't move.

"Always leaving me hanging." Jax shakes his head.

"Just one thing." Killian rises from his seat to face Gabriel. "You're leaving your phone with Brenna."

"What?" Gabriel snaps. "Absolutely not."

Killian holds out his hand. "Give it up, Scott, and nobody

gets hurt."

"Over my beaten and bloody body."

The guys all stand, and Rye rolls his head, setting off a dozen cracks in his neck. "Fellas," he says, flexing his hands, "let's do this."

And they do. They actually jump him.

The scuffle is a loud, curse-filled tangle of flailing limbs and grappling men.

It ends with a bloody lip for Rye, a poked eye for Jax, Killian without a shirt, Whip without a shoe, and Gabriel on the floor, suit rumpled and his precious phone spirited away by Brenna, who can run surprisingly fast in her heels.

"Bastards," he mutters as they file out the door.

"It's for your own good," Killian says.

"We love you too, Scottie boy," Jax calls.

I kneel and kiss a scuff mark on Gabriel's forehead. "Poor baby. I'll make it better. I promise."

He does not look appeased, but his lip quirks. "I'll hold you to that."

SOPHIE
23

GABRIEL HAS something to pick up for our trip, and he's gone when I wake. He's left me a note that says I should be ready to go by nine. Mother hen that he is, he also set my phone alarm for seven, something I bitch about for a good ten minutes as I bumble my way into a hot shower.

As it nears eight, room service arrives with cappuccino and a little bowl of extra creamy, ridiculously thick yogurt, topped with roasted hazelnuts and drizzled in golden honey. It's not something I'd have thought to try, but I scrape up every little bit clinging to the glass bowl.

Determination steels my spine. I'm supposed to be taking care of Gabriel, helping him relax, and here he is pampering me, arranging every step of my morning without even being present. I cannot let myself forget that I'm contending with a professional manager of people's lives. I need to step up my game.

I'm not remotely surprised when a bellhop arrives at eight forty-five to take my bags and escort me down to the lobby. Mr. Scott, he tells me, is waiting.

Wry amusement puts a bounce in my step as I walk through the lobby. Were I someone into high fashion, my heels would be clicking on the marble. But I'm in white flip-flops and a red, cotton eyelet sundress. Gabriel has warned that it will take about four hours to get to Positano, and I intend on being comfortable.

The bellhop leads me out to the front drive, and my steps slow as I catch sight of Gabriel waiting for me.

"Oh, fuck me," I blurt out.

At my side, the bellhop makes a gurgled sound of shock. I'm too busy staring at my man to care.

Dressed in a crisp white polo shirt, which shows off the deep gold of his skin and stretches around the bulge of his biceps, and slouchy, gray slacks that highlight the narrowness of his hips and drape over his thick thighs, he leans against a red Ferrari, his hands tucked into his pockets.

Move over Jake Ryan.

When Gabriel smiles—a full one, complete with that cute dimple on his left cheek, the corners of his eyes crinkling in joy —I'm tempted to look around before mouthing, *"Who me?"*

But I don't do that. I run to him like a loon. He catches me with a soft *oof* and wraps me up in his arms as I kiss his cheeks, the corner of his eye, the edge of his jaw. Chuckling, he captures my mouth and gives me a proper kiss.

He tastes faintly of tea. His body is warm and solid, and he is mine.

I give his lip one last nibble before pulling back. "Sexy beast, you're going to melt me on the spot one day, you know."

He gives the tip of my nose a quick kiss. "If you're taking requests, I prefer that you melt on my mouth."

"Sweet talker." I glance at the car, truly taking it in now that I've had my Gabriel fix. "Holy shit, that's a Ferrari 488GTB Spider."

He blinks, swaying a little. "You've just given me a hard-on."

He's not lying; I can feel it rise against my belly. I grin, pressing into him just a little.

"Will you be able to drive? Or should we take care of it now?"

His lips purse, but there's a glint in his eye that promises retribution. With a subtle shift of his hips, he prods my belly with that hard dick, then moves me away from him.

"Get in the car, chatty girl, before I call this trip off and take you to bed instead."

"As good as that sounds, the car is calling my name." And Gabriel needs this vacation. I have plans for him. Most of them dirty, all of them fun.

Gabriel opens the door for me. "Thrown over for a car, lovely."

I grin. "Not just any car."

And oh what a car it is. The bucket seats are dark grey leather, buttery soft. They're designed to hold your ass in place as the car zooms down the road, but I'm not complaining. I touch the gray and red dash as Gabriel closes my door.

He tips the bellhop after the luggage is placed in the front trunk, and a moment later, he's sliding into his seat. With a push of a button, the car purrs to life.

"Is this what you were picking up?" I ask, stroking the seat leather.

"Yes." For a second, his expression is so pleased he looks almost boyish, but it soon morphs into the cool loftiness he uses when giving a lecture. "If we're going to drive along the Almalfi coast, we're going to do it in style."

So very Gabriel.

"How did you get your hands on one of these babies? Aren't they, like, impossible to buy?"

"Not if you're on a list," he says as he pulls into traffic.

Good Lord, there is something sexy about a man who knows how to handle a car. If Ferrari execs saw Gabriel driving this, I'm certain they'd try to hire him as a spokesmodel.

"Of course you're on a list. Why am I not surprised?"

He glances my way. "How do you know about this car, anyway? From what I've heard, you don't even know how to drive."

"Hey, a lot of New Yorkers don't."

"This sad state of affairs must be rectified as soon as I buy a proper car to teach you in. Now, answer the question."

"I read your car magazines when I got bored one day." I turn a little in my seat to face him. "You realize they're the male equivalent of *Vogue*."

He gives me a sly grin. "But far sexier."

The drive goes quickly, in part because the car is speedy and luxurious, in part because the scenery is so blindingly beautiful, but mostly because I'm with Gabriel.

We never run out of things to talk about, whether it be music or movies or speculating on history as we drive by through the area where they've excavated parts of Pompeii and Herculaneum—both sites he promises to take me on day trips to explore. And I realize that no one else sees him this way, as the man who has tons of tidbits of knowledge stored up, the man who smiles frequently and with ease, and who teases me with jokes as lame as my own.

It's afternoon when we arrive in Positano, a town so picturesque it brings a lump to my throat. Colorful stucco buildings that look almost Moorish in architecture cling to the steep green mountains that plunge toward the turquoise sea. The air is fresh, tinged with hints of sweet lemon and salty ocean.

Gabriel's house is a little way out, nestled between the crags of two mountain outcrops and guarded by a tall gate. You can't tell much about it from the drive, but inside it's all crisp white stucco walls, airy spaces that face the blue sea, with endless French doors open to the breeze.

A small, elderly lady greets us. Gabriel kisses her cheeks and talks to her in Italian. I've never had a fetish for foreign languages until I heard him speak in one. He introduces her to me. Martina, who is both cook and housekeeper, doesn't speak English, but she doesn't need to. Her welcoming smile says enough. She leaves us, bustling off toward the back of the house.

"How many languages do you know?" I ask him. I've heard him speak French and Spanish on the tour.

"English, of course. Italian, French, Spanish, a little German, and a bit of Portuguese. A few phrases in Japanese."

"You're killing me."

"Languages always came naturally to me." A smug smile unfurls. "Your expression, Darling... You like that?"

"I'm going to demand that you speak to me in Italian in bed."

His expression goes thoughtful and he leans down and whispers in my ear, his voice hot cream. *"Sei tutto per me. Baciami."*

I swear my knees go weak. "Jesus, give a little warning. What did you say?"

His smile grows secretive. "I said 'kiss me'."

It sounded like more than that, but I lift to my toes and place a soft, lingering kiss on his lips. He kisses me back, keeping it light and gentle.

"Come on," he says. "Let's get you fed before you become hangry."

"You know me so well."

Hand to the small of my back, he guides me out to the terrace. It's enormous, surrounding the property and carved out of the hill. It's part garden with lemon trees and rustling palms, part slate-lined terrace with an infinity pool hovering along one cliffside, and a dining area shaded by a trellis covered in bougainvillea. Sunlight filtering through the fuchsia blooms tints the air pink.

Gabriel watches me take it all in, then comes to stand by my side, shoving his hands into his pockets.

"You own a slice of paradise," I tell him, staring out at the sea.

His shoulder brushes against mine. "Paradise is a state of mind, not a location."

"Fair enough. You own the perfect place to evoke paradise."

Behind us, Martina sets the table. She waves off my offer to help, and we're soon sipping icy limoncello.

"This tastes like summer in a glass," I tell Gabriel.

He lounges in his chair, stretching his long legs out before him. "Wait until you taste Martina's food."

When she plunks down two bowls of pasta, I can see why. Clams and mussels tangle with linguine, all glossy with olive oil and fragrant with little bits of garlic, parsley, and lemon zest. It's the best thing I've eaten in my life, and I sop up the juices with crusty white bread.

For a while, we are silent, simply enjoying the food and the sea breeze that cools our skin. When we're done eating, Martina comes and takes the plates away, and Gabriel says something to her again.

It's fairly ridiculous how much I swoon when he speaks; he's probably saying something banal like, *hey, thanks for the meal.* But it sounds like pure sex coming from his mouth.

I sit back with a sigh. He seems equally content, his hands folded over his flat belly, his expression calm as he stares at the sea.

"I don't understand it," I find myself saying.

He looks my way. "Don't understand what?"

"This." I wave my hand around. "You have this stunning house that you rarely visit, and other houses that are presumably equally gorgeous, and yet none of the guys has been to any of them. Why bother?"

A frown wrinkles the space between his brows. "Killian's dad once told me the best thing a man can invest in is property. It is tangible, true, eternal. I agree."

"I get that, but why have these properties if you're never going to enjoy them, never bring your friends here?" I lean forward. "Why don't you let them in, Gabriel? They love you, and you keep them at arm's length."

A flush tints his cheeks, and he lurches up from his chair to pace. "I'm not a social man, Sophie. You know that about me."

I watch him walk. "I'm not talking about hosting wild parties. I'm asking about you systematically building a wall between you and the people who mean the most." He glares at me over his shoulder, and I soften my tone. "And I think you know that."

Our gazes clash, but I don't blink. He curses under his breath and squeezes the back of his neck.

"Gabriel, you are a charming, witty, kind man—don't roll your eyes at me, you *are*." I stand and walk over to him. Not too close, because he's cagey right now. "You are kind. The guys, Brenna—they're your family, and you treat them so well, care for them better than anyone I've ever met. Why won't you let them care for you too?"

A breath bursts from him, and he whirls to face me. "I don't know how," he snaps.

"What do you mean?"

"Sodding…" He rakes a hand through his hair and grips it hard. "My mum, my dad…They…They fucking left me, yeah? The two people who were supposed to love me the most. Left. And I know the guys and Brenna love me. But if I let them in then…"

He paces away before coming back, his eyes wide and pained. "If they're fully in then *I'm* fully in. It will hurt more, Sophie. Do you understand? It will hurt more if…"

He looks off, scowling so hard his lips pinch.

"Gabriel, they won't leave—"

"I can barely handle letting you in. Opening up is so foreign to me; I don't know what the bloody hell I'm doing. But I'm trying for you because you're…" He struggles for the words, looking panicked.

I wrap my arms around him and hug him close. I expect resistance, but he yields, burrowing his nose in my hair and breathing deep, hugging me as if I might disappear.

"It's all right." I stroke his tense neck. "I'm sorry. I shouldn't have pushed."

"No, you should. Protecting myself is hurting them. I see it. But I don't know how to change."

My fingertips trace the narrow groove of his spine down his strong back. "Just do what you did with me."

The shift of tension in his body is subtle but significant. I can almost feel him smiling, and I definitely feel the heat building between us.

His voice grows deeper, intent. "I don't think they'd appreciate that approach, Darling."

A hand slides down to cup my butt.

I smile. "Probably best you keep this particular treatment just for me."

"Only ever for you," he promises, his other hand moving down. He grasps my ass, kneading it with a growl of approval.

I jump into his arms, wrapping my legs around his waist. "Take me to bed, sunshine."

He begins walking, but doesn't go into the house; he lays me down on the double-wide lounger beneath the shade of the bougainvillea before prowling over me, his lips finding my neck. One good tug at the bodice of my sundress, and my breast pops free.

"Gabriel—" I groan as he sucks my nipple into his hot, wet

mouth. "Not here."

"Yes, here," he says around the stiff tip, flicking it with his tongue.

I squirm, but my fingers find their way into his hair, holding him tight as he continues to lick and suck me. Another tug at my top and my other breast is exposed.

I glance at the open doorway that leads to the kitchen. "I won't be able to look Martina in the eye if she catches us out here."

He kisses his way over to my neglected breast, and catches the stiffened nipple with his teeth, pulling just enough that I lose my mind a little. I arch up, silently begging for more.

A dark chuckle rumbles in his chest. Peppering my nipple with suckling kisses, he slides his hand under my dress and cups between my legs, where I am damp and achy. "I told her to take the rest of day off."

I rock into his touch with a moan, craning my head down to kiss his temple. "Fuck... I say we give her the week off."

He hums in his throat, slips his fingers beneath my panties. "Good plan."

We don't talk for a long time after that.

"WHERE ARE YOU GOING? I'm not done with you yet." His voice is a love song, soft and tender, deep with possessiveness and the promise of luscious sin. It dances over me like a caress, and I shiver in its wake.

"I want to touch you," I complain, though it's not really a complaint. How can it be when he's reduced me to this quivering, boneless mass of warm lethargy?

His dark chuckle is knowing. "Later. It's my turn now."

Big, hot hands slide up my legs, cup my ass. I close my eyes and hug the rumpled bed covers as those talented hands delve between my thighs and spread them wide.

Exposed. Swollen and wet. He's taken me twice now. Once on the terrace, and then on the bed, where he was slower, more thorough, taking his time, making me beg for it. And beg, I did, pleading and panting, losing my ever-loving mind.

He rewarded me for it, making me come until I wept, stroking my skin, telling me I was his good girl in that low, stern voice I'll forevermore equate with sex and pleasure.

He uses it now, a weapon in its own right. "So pretty," he says, from his spot between my thighs. "I knew you'd be so pretty."

The need to please him rises up within me. I tilt my hips, lifting my ass higher, showing him more of me. He hums in approval, his hands caressing my lower back, behind my knee. His breath tickles my inner thigh, and then he blows on my clit.

I groan, fighting the urge to push down and catch his mouth.

He knows. The dirty bastard *knows* what he's doing to me. I feel the smile on his lips as he presses a kiss to my butt. And, really, I should make him pay for that, but his hand slides up my thigh, and my breath stalls as the tip of his finger slowly circles my opening.

"Mmm," he says, swirling his fingers around, gently teasing. "So pretty."

He dips his finger into me, barely enough to feel, then slides back out, gathering my wetness only to sink back in, deeper this time.

A soft kiss to the sensitive swell of my clit makes me jolt. Gently, so gently. Barely there at all, and yet it holds all of my attention. The lazy flick of his tongue, a lingering suckle, little kisses, and all the while slowly fucking me with his finger.

I close my eyes, concentrate on his touch and the way he keeps teasing, collecting the slick wet pooling at my opening, then plunging deep.

My eyes snap open, a gurgle of shock leaving my lips. He's pushing his come back into me.

It's so fucking dirty, so illicit, that heat and lust take my breath. A shuddering moan leaves me. I undulate against his touch, begging. Slower. Deeper. Harder. Faster. I don't care, as long as there is more.

A soft huff of breath against my skin, almost a laugh but lower, as if he too needs more. Slow kisses map their way up my back, as he presses me into the bed with the heat of his body. He doesn't give me all his weight, just enough to make me feel him.

He kisses my neck, his breath coming faster as he sinks another finger in. He goes so deep this time, straining against me, it almost hurts. But it's not enough.

"Gabriel," I choke out, spreading my thighs wider.

"Shhh," he whispers, kissing my cheek, sliding his hips between my thighs. His cock lays heavy and hot on my ass. His fingers work me, a slow plunge, a teasing drag.

"Now," I rasp. "Now."

"Darling," he whispers. My name, an endearment. They're one and the same now.

I lay beneath him panting and shaking, so hot I can barely breathe. But he's right there with me, his breath a rasp, tremors running through him and into me. He lifts his hips, and his cock sinks into me, the fit tighter now because he hasn't removed his fingers.

The stretch burns, and I'm coming before the first thrust. It washes over me in a slow, rolling wave. I cry out, sobbing.

Gabriel pulls his fingers out and grasps my hands in his. "Sophie," he says as he begins to thrust, slow yet intense, as if he never wants to stop.

"Don't," I say, unable to form proper thoughts. "Don't ever stop."

He shudders and groans, his lips against my damp cheek.

His answer is one word. "Mine."

And it is everything.

GABRIEL

"LOOK, this isn't rocket science. Simply lift your leg and straddle it—"

"I'd rather attempt rocket science."

"You're kicking up too big a fuss over this."

"It's a death trap on two wheels. *Tiny* wheels."

"It's a Vespa, Darling. We're going to tour the town on it. Very *Roman Holiday*."

"We aren't in Rome."

"Stop nitpicking. Come along, get into the spirit. You love that movie."

"True. You'd make a great Gregory Peck, but sadly I'm no Audrey Hepburn."

"You're definitely more a Marilyn."

"I'm not seeing that as a compliment, mister."

"Believe me, it is. Now onto the scooter with you, chatty girl. I want to feel those fantastic tits pressed against my back."

"I'm beginning to think you have a preoccupation with my boobs."

"I have a preoccupation with your everything. Stop stalling. The day is wasting, love."

"You're not going to let this drop, are you?"

"We're supposed to be relaxing—"

"Careening down mountain roads on this toy is not relaxing."

"It will be fun, and that is relaxing to me. You want me to relax, don't you?"

"Gah. Don't give me that sad puppy look."

"I wasn't aware I was giving you any look."

"Dial it back, sunshine. You're burning my retinas."

"I will if you get on the scooter."

"Fine. Just don't go driving off a cliff and getting us killed."

"I plan on dying when I'm very old and fucking you while hopped up on Viagra."

"You really do say the sweetest things."

"*Sono pazzo di te.*"

"Okay, what did that mean? It sounded sexy as hell."

"I'll tell you if we survive the ride to town."

"Gabriel Scott—ahheee!"

"NOW, listen up, I rode on that speed demon from hell here—"

"It's a scooter. Its speed is limited."

"It has a top seed of sixty miles per hour. I checked. That's fast."

"That's hardly what I'd call fast."

"Coming from someone who drives Ferraris, I guess you would think that."

"Precisely."

"Bully for you. You won that argument, but you're not winning another. We're eating here."

"Darling, this place is a hole in the wall. There are literally holes in the wall."

"Maybe they're bullet holes from the war."

"Which one?"

"Ha. But you see my point."

"That it's run down?"

"That it's been here long enough to have a history. Look, it's filled with old Italians eating."

"I hadn't noticed. I was too distracted by the rat skittering by."

"That wasn't a rat. It was a cat."

"A rat as big as a cat."

"Stop being such a snob. Jesus, didn't you grow up in poverty?"

"Which means I know enough to stay away from dives."

"Argh. Look, you want great food, you go where the grandmas cook. See? There's a little nonna in that kitchen."

"Well, I suppose that's—"

"We're eating here."

"Did you just tweak my nipple?"

"Is that rhetorical?"

"Beware, chatty girl. I can retaliate."

"Promise? Ooh, I like that smolder, it's very Flynn Ryder."

"You're comparing me to cartoon characters now?"

"Animated characters. Huge difference. And it's cute that you know who he is. Come on, sunshine."

"Wait—"

———

"SEE? Didn't I tell you? Delicious food."

"Yes, you're very smart. Shut up."

"Another Princess Bride quote. You, Gabriel Scott, are my perfect man."

"*You* say the sweetest things, chatty girl."

"Now, tell me what you said in Italian on the death scooter."

"*Sono pazzo di te.* I am crazy about you."

"Gabriel…"

"Eat your food, Darling."

GABRIEL 24

I THOUGHT I'd find it difficult to let work drop and simply be. I'd never done it before, and honestly, I wasn't sure I'd know who I was if I wasn't working at all hours.

Sophie makes it remarkably easy to enjoy the simple things in life.

Days pass, and we fall into a sort of lazy rhythm. We sleep in until one of us wakes, make love, then drift off to sleep again. We eat when we're hungry. And when we're horny, we fuck again, which is all the time and all over the house—my favorite spot being on the terrace where the sun gilds Sophie's fine skin and her cries echo off the cliffs.

If we are feeling particularly motivated, we take the Ferrari or the Vespa—which, despite Sophie's initial panic, she now loves—into town and explore. And we argue. Over everything: where to eat, where to shop, how fast I should go on the Vespa. The Italians approve because they know it's foreplay.

And, truly, there is nothing more alluring to me than Sophie's eyes snapping with intelligence and building desire, her cheeks flushed, and her breasts rising and falling with each verbal exchange. I swear, I hobble around half or full-on hard most of the time. Completely worth it.

At some point during each day, by some silent agreement,

we do our own thing.

Though Sophie is social where I am reticent, we both need time alone to recharge. Even when we were touring and stuck on a bus together, we found ways to give each other space. This has its perks now since our reunions are that much sweeter, a few hours apart feeling more like weeks.

And so I'm alone now, waiting. Sophie has gone to town with Martina's daughter Elisa. Since my phone has been confiscated, Sophie cannot text me, but I know she'll be back soon. I don't know how I know, I simply do.

Minutes later, I hear Elisa's car in the drive.

It's easy to track Sophie's movements; the woman sounds like a marauding yeti whenever she invades a space. The front door opens and slams shut, shoes clatter onto the floor. She's singing "Ruby Tuesday" off key and getting the lyrics wrong.

I bite back a laugh.

"Sunshine?" Her happy voice echoes. "Where you at?"

There is something entirely gratifying in knowing that, whenever Sophie comes home, the first thing she does is seek me out.

"Your grammar is appalling," I call back, fighting a smile; there's something anticipatory about withholding the full scale of my happiness. I let it build as she tromps up the steps.

"You don't want me for my grammar," she says near the top of the stairs.

"Your tits and arse definitely rate higher."

"Feel free to show them some appreciation." She stands in the doorway to our room, blue sundress rumpled, the rosy light of sunset slanting through the wide widows and illuminating the gold of her hair.

I'm struck speechless, my breath cutting short.

I am not a poetic man, but I want to be one now. I want to do justice to her beauty and the way she fills me with a strange mixture of utter peace and demanding need.

It's always this way with Sophie. I look at her and want to simultaneously hold her close, cherishing her as though this is our last day alive, and tumble her onto the bed and fuck her until my cock chafes. Which is rather perverse, I suppose.

Doesn't matter. Not when she's looking at me as if she wants the same. But then her sweet face pulls in a frown.

"You're working."

Hard to deny when I'm holding a contract in my hand. "Just a bit of light reading."

While Sophie was in town, I went for a run. The second I returned, I downed a protein shake and took a shower before lounging in the bed in my boxer briefs and reading over a contract. I don't classify this as work per se since I'm only skimming.

Sophie appears to disagree.

Her hands go to her hips. "I should have searched your bags for contraband. You're supposed to be relaxing."

"Forced relaxation is an oxymoron." I go back to reading said contract because I know it will stir her up. I fucking love Sophie stirred up. The results are always naked, sweaty, and in my favor. "Besides, this is a standard contract, nothing too involved or detailed."

A sigh rings out. "What am I going to do with you?"

Fuck me. I have needs. "Come to bed and read something alongside me?"

She takes a step in my direction but halts. "You're wearing glasses."

There's a strangled note of lust in her voice that kicks my own into overdrive. I don't look up from the contract. "As one does when one needs reading glasses."

"Smart ass. I've seen you read plenty of times, and you've never worn glasses."

"I have contacts. But my eyes are irritable today."

I suspect this has something to do with going down on

Sophie in the pool this morning. It had been an experiment of sorts, figuring out just how long I could hold my breath. We laughed and applied ourselves to the task with much enthusiasm.

"You should always wear your glasses while reading," she says, heading my way. "And I mean always."

Did I know Sophie would react favorably to my reading glasses? No. But by the wide-eyed, slightly dreamy look in her eyes, I'm fairly confident she appreciates them. I'm man enough to admit I want to entice her.

She sits on the bed, and her warm thigh rests next to mine. My body goes on alert, but I don't let it show. Not yet. That's not how our game is played.

God help me if I no longer had Sophie to play with. It is one of the best parts of my day.

"You know," she says, trailing a finger along my kneecap, "there's this Tumblr. Hot guys with glasses..."

"Don't even think about taking a picture." I pretend to ignore the way her touch sends a ripple of lust straight to my cock. A lost cause. And I know she sees my growing interest. Her path heads upward.

"What about hot guys reading? They even made a book. You're definitely cover material."

I glare at her over my glasses. She's giving me that saucy look, her head tilted just so, those ripe lips pursed. A band of hot greed tightens low around my gut and gives a swift tug. My cock rises hard and fast.

Sophie licks her lower lip, never breaking eye contact with me. "You're not playing fair, sunshine." Her voice goes husky. "I can't take that silent reprimand, combined with those glasses. You'll have me combusting over here."

"Hmmm." I turn my gaze back to the contract, as if I'm not tight as a fucking drum. The reward will be much greater if I make her work for it. "I fail to see how this is my problem."

"Oh, no?" The bed creaks as she crawls closer.

My cock throbs in time to my heartbeat and pushes uncomfortably against my pants.

"You're the one affected," I tell her. "Best you do something about it."

Her low chuckle ripples over my skin. The silk of her hair tickles my chest as she eases under the papers I'm holding. *Yes, love, step into my parlor.*

"And this massive hard-on is over what..." She glances at the contract in my hand. "Licensing percentages?"

"I have a thing for details," I murmur, my breath catching as she places a light kiss on the center of my chest.

"Well..." She kisses me again. "Don't let me keep you."

I pretend to read while she slowly, thoroughly kisses her way across my chest. Each lingering press of her lips upon my skin undoes me a little more. The tenderness mixed with heat, as though she's both worshiping and reveling in me, makes my heart clench and my cock throb.

Her tongue flicks over my nipple, and my hand shakes, my breath stuttering.

"God, you're so hot this way," she says. Her teeth catch the tip of my nipple and tugs.

I grunt, liquid heat licking up my thighs. The contract falls to the bed, my head hits the wall with a dull thud.

Farther down she goes, following the valley between my abs. "So. Fucking. Sexy." Each word punctuated with a kiss. "I want you to fuck me while wearing those glasses, Gabriel."

This woman will kill me.

I swallow hard, search for my voice. "If you're a good girl, perhaps I shall."

I don't miss the way her peachy arse clenches. Something primitive and base flows through me. My voice roughens.

"Take my cock out. You're going to suck it."

A little sound rises in her throat, and I know I'm getting to her, which gets to me. My skin is so hot, I can barely breathe.

Sophie's hands trace the edge of my boxer briefs, a sly tease. My cock pushes rudely against the fabric, and she lifts the elastic away from my waist. The throbbing tip catches on the band of my pants. She frees me, and I'm so hard, my prick slaps against my abdomen.

"Love that sound," she whispers.

Good. It's only for you. "Take me in hand."

Her warm fingers wrap around me and squeeze. My eyes nearly roll back in my head. I swallow a groan, my hips lifting up to meet her.

"Softer," I pant.

"Softer?" She kisses my chest again as her grip eases.

I nearly weep it's so good. "Make me beg for it."

Her lashes flutter, a breath leaving her parted lips. The tips of her fingers glide down my length, teasing.

I struggle to hold still, but she gently cups my balls and gives them a little tug. A groan rumbles in my throat. It turns to an outright whimper as she bends down and mouths the head of my cock.

Not enough.

"Sophie..."

"Mmmm?" The sound vibrates against my skin, and a throb of pained pleasure pushes through me .

I nudge upward, but she evades. A teasing lick flickers on my tip. "Fuck... Suck it, Darling. Suck it well."

Brown eyes smile up at me, and she does, for one glorious pull, sucking me deep and tight. I arch off the bed, groaning. But she stops there and plays with me again, her pouty lips barely wrapped around my flesh.

Heat flushes my skin, and I give her what she wants. "Please. Please..."

And she does please me, lavishing me with attention, drawing out my pleasure as if her pleasure is connected to seeing mine. I lose myself in her, until my throat tightens with emotion and my balls clench with impending release.

I don't want to spend in her mouth. Not this time. I pull her up, trying to be gentle, but my hands shake. She makes a noise of protest that I swallow down with a kiss as I tumble her onto her back, fumbling to hike up her skirt.

"I wasn't finished," she pants between kisses.

My hand slides beneath her little pink panties. Sweet slickness greets my fingers.

"I need to be in here." I pet her soft, swollen sex before plunging in deep. And she cries out—a lovely plea that makes me greedy to hear more of them.

I kiss her mouth as my fingers work her within the tight fit of her panties. She moves with me, her hips thrusting and grinding on my hands. Our breath mingles, growing disjointed.

No more waiting. I wrench her knickers off, roll between her thighs spread wide for me. The first push into her is agony and heaven, because nothing will ever feel as good as fitting myself inside Sophie. We're both frantic now, panting. I know she expects me to plough her hard and fast.

I slow down, cup her cheeks and softly kiss her as I slowly work her slick clasp.

"Gabriel," she whimpers into my mouth. "More."

I know she means faster. I plunge as deep as I can and hold it until she quivers before easing back out.

"I'll give you everything," I whisper.

She eats at my mouth, her body wriggling beneath me as she tries to change the tempo. But I have her where I want her. I move in her, let her feel each inch. She huffs out a half-laugh, half-disgruntled complaint.

"Sophie." My voice is clear and firm, demanding her attention.

Her eyes meet mine, and I let her see everything—what she

is to me, what she does to me.

Her breath hitches, her eyes wide and shining. I feel her body yield, becoming softer.

"Gabriel." Her trembling fingers touch my cheek.

And suddenly I'm terrified. Because she does see me, every dark corner and imperfect edge. It sparks something between us. I can't look away or stop myself from rocking into her, saying with my body what I'm too afraid to utter.

Take me, have me, love me.

But I don't need to say those things, because I know in that instant that she already does. On rumpled, linen sheets, she claims me, body and soul, and then offers herself right back. In that moment, I am no longer Scottie or Gabriel, I am something more. I am home. Finally. At last. Forever.

SOPHIE

ALL GOOD THINGS must come to an end. I knew my time with Gabriel to myself had a limit; he's too much of a workaholic to stay on vacation for very long. But though we had two glorious weeks to ourselves, it doesn't feel like enough. Still, I cannot deny that it's done him well.

Days of sleeping until midday, spending lazy hours in bed making love, or lounging by the pool soaking up the sun, have given him a healthy glow and an easy smile in his eyes.

Days of drinking rich red wine and sopping up olive oil with crusty bread, devouring ripe tomatoes and creamy cheese, have filled out the hollows in his cheeks.

I thought Gabriel was gorgeous when I met him. Now I realize I hadn't gotten the full story. He's robust, deeply tanned, and so attractive in his tailored linen suit that I get a little lightheaded whenever I look at him.

He flashes me a quick, happy grin as he navigates the Ferrari over the switchbacks along the Italian coast, and I'm thankful I'm sitting.

"I can almost hear you thinking," he says, downshifting with authority. Good Lord, the way his thighs strain against his pants...

I cross my legs. "All dirty thoughts, I promise you."

His grin grows but he keeps his eyes on the road. "Behave yourself, chatty girl. I need to concentrate."

"It's like I've fallen into the cover of *Suit and Car Porn*."

A low chuckle rumbles in his chest. "There's no such magazine, Darling."

"There should be."

Laughing, he shifts again and accelerates. I'm thrust against the seat as the car leaps forward. Squealing, I throw my hands up and let the wind catch my hair as we race down the coast.

We arrive at our hotel in Naples all too soon. Kill John is doing a show tonight, and then we're headed up to Milan, and finally Bern in Switzerland.

Gabriel takes my hand as we walk into the lobby. I wouldn't have expected it, but he loves holding hands. Whenever we're in close proximity, he finds a way to thread his fingers with mine, his thumb caressing my knuckles or the back of my hand as if touching me soothes him.

One evening during our vacation, I sat with him on the terrace, me drinking wine and him playing with my hand, looking down at it as if he wasn't sure how he'd arrived at the place were he could freely touch me.

I'd smiled at him then, and he'd tugged me onto his lap. He put his hands to better use after that. And I'd licked wine from his skin until he shivered and growled and demanded dirty things of me in that bossy, manly way of his.

A wistful sigh escapes me, and Gabriel gives me a squeeze.

"What's that all about, chatty girl?"

"I don't want to say."

"Which only makes me want to know more. Talk to me, Darling."

We reach the elevators, and he hits the up button. I shake my head, but give in.

"I'm just being ridiculous and greedy. I already miss it being just the two of us."

His brows draw together, and he takes a step closer, wrapping me up in his scent and the strength of his arms. Warm fingers slide to my nape.

"Where we are is simply a matter of geography." Soft lips brush my cheek, and his voice rumbles in my ear. "Remember, chatty girl? I'll never truly be apart from you because you're always in here." He takes my hand and puts it against his temple as he did that night backstage.

I smile and rest my cheek against his chest where his heart beats strong and sure. "And in here."

"Precisely."

I love him. I love him so much it doesn't feel real. I love him so much it terrifies me a little. I've never been in love before. I don't have any experience with processing the emotion. How can it make a person so happy and yet so afraid? I can't lose him. I can't. My heart won't survive.

But he's here, holding me as if he'll stay right here, giving me comfort for as long as I need it.

The elevator dings, and I step back. That's when I see him. He's looking a little worse for the wear, with a sunburn on his face, but I'd recognize him anywhere.

The bottom falls out of my stomach, and I swallow hard, feeling dangerously close to throwing up.

He's looking right at me from his spot across the lobby. The calculating glint in his eyes tells me he knows exactly who Gabriel is, and he's figuring out how to use the knowledge that we're obviously together.

A cold sweat breaks out along my skin as Gabriel puts his hand on the small of my back and guides me into the elevator. The last thing I see before the doors close is Martin's smug grin and ugly wink, as if to say, "I'll be in touch soon."

SOPHIE
25

WE NEED TO TALK.

I stare at the text on my phone, and my rage grows to a black haze that blurs the edges of my vision. My gut churns. That motherfucker still has my number. I'm sorry I didn't change it long ago. But it wouldn't have mattered; Martin always finds a way to get what he wants.

My stomach lurches, and I press a hand to it.

I should tell Gabriel that Martin is skulking around the lobby. But I don't want to. Speaking his name is like calling forth the devil. I don't want to remind Gabriel of what I did. Of course he knows, but seeing Martin, visually linking him with me, will make it more real. More pungent. Because that's what Martin is: a foul odor hanging around, stinking up the place. The bastard wants to talk. It takes little imagination to discern about what.

A breeze blows in from the harbor. I huddle down in the lounge chair on the balcony, drawing my knees to my chest. It's not cold out here, but I'm freezing inside, while my skin burns hot.

"Sophie." Gabriel's face hovers in front of me, a frown marring his brow.

Startled, I blink and look around, taking in the dark sea and the lights along the shore. "Yes?"

He sits on the foot of the lounger. "I called your name three times."

"Sorry. I..." I don't know what to say, so I shrug.

He assesses my face, worrying. "What's going on in that head, chatty girl?"

"I don't feel well." It's true. I want to climb under the covers and cry. "Too much driving on mountain roads, I guess."

The cool press of his fingers to my brow almost has me weeping, and I have to blink several times to keep from losing it.

His frown deepens. "You feel warm."

"And you feel nice and cool." I force a smile. "Kiss me and make it all better."

He leans in and kisses my forehead. But he's on a mission. "I'm serious. I want you to stay in tonight. I'll text Dr. Stern and have her come look you over."

"No, don't," I say to Gabriel. "I'm fine. I'll be better off working."

"Bollocks to that." Without an apparent effort, he scoops me up and carries me inside. Despite myself, a little thrill runs through me. I've never been carried around, or handled as if I were precious. And though I'm not really sick, his care makes me want to cling to him and cry my troubles away.

He sets me on the couch. "Stay."

"Yes, sir." I salute him, but he's already going into the bedroom.

He returns with a blanket, which he promptly tucks around my body. "There."

"You're acting like a mother hen." Which I love.

"Cluck, cluck," he deadpans as he picks up the house phone with one hand and grabs the TV remote with the other. I'm impressed by his multitasking; he scrolls through the movie selections and selects a rom-com, while simultaneously ordering a soup and bread basket through room service.

"And a pot of tea," he adds, finishing up the call.

My poor, battered heart turns to mush there and then. He's getting me tea. My voice is too thick when I speak. "Italians aren't known for their tea."

"It'll likely be rubbish," he agrees. "But it will have to do."

And though I'm all tucked up like a package, he moves me once more, lifting me onto his lap and snuggling us both under the blanket. It's so much better being held. I burrow against his chest, and his arms wrap around me.

"I don't want to leave you," he murmurs in my hair.

"I'm fine. Really. I can go with you—"

"No." His voice is gentle but firm. "Even if you aren't ill, you need rest. Now, shut up and do as directed for once."

"Bossy."

"You're only sorry it's my turn to do the bossing."

Unable to help myself, I stroke his chest. Touching him is a luxury I don't think I'll ever get used to. "What was you said about forced relaxation being an oxymoron?"

"I don't recall that at all. You've grown delusional in your exhaustion."

I snort, and he kisses me on the forehead, chuckling.

The movie starts playing, and we fall silent.

"How did you know I love *When Harry Met Sally*?" I ask softly.

He shifts a little beneath me, propping one foot on the table. "You told me."

"What? When?"

"The third night on the coach. You were taking a piss at my love of all things Star Trek, and I asked what your favorite movies were. And I still take umbrage that you think *Spaceballs* is on par with *Star Wars*."

I grin at the disgust in his voice, but a small jolt runs through me as I think back on that night. "You remember all of that?"

His hand sifts through my hair, spreading lovely little shivers down my spine. "I remember everything you say, Darling. You talk, I listen."

I almost tell him I love him then. The words bubble up and dance on my tongue. But my mouth refuses to open. Fear holds me back, as if by saying it I'll somehow start the beginning of the end. It makes no sense, but I can't shake the feeling.

I kiss the underside of his jaw, where the scent of his cologne blends with the warmth of his skin, and hug him close.

He holds me until room service arrives. Given the speed at which they show up, I'm guessing we get preferential treatment. A perk, I suppose, of Kill John renting the entire floor.

Gabriel pulls on his suit jacket and tugs his cuffs into place as I pretend to find interest in my meal. But my appetite is gone.

"Don't poke at your soup," he says. "Eat it."

"I'm waiting for it to cool down."

Apparently I'm terrible at lying because he hovers at the end of the couch, peering at me as if he can pull the thoughts from my head by sheer will.

"I should stay," he says finally.

When he pulls his phone from his pocket as if to start texting, I touch his hand. "No, go. I swear I'm all right. I'm just having an off night. It happens."

I need him to go so I can hunt down that fuckwit Martin and tell him to eat shit and die—or something to that effect. I can't do that with Gabriel around. I'm fairly certain his version of telling Martin to eat shit would probably lean more toward actually kicking the shit out of him.

That would be kind of satisfying to watch, but the idea of

Gabriel getting into trouble with the law or having his reputation tarnished horrifies me.

He must see my urgency, because he sighs and leans down to kiss me. This kiss isn't quick, it's soft and languid, as if he's luxuriating in my taste. And I melt under his touch, kissing him back, my hands threading into his thick hair.

High color stains his cheeks when we finally break apart, both of us breathing faster. His forehead rests against mine as he cups my nape. "Sophie," he says. "My darling girl."

Tears threaten. He's too tender. Too wonderful. I close my eyes, run my thumbs in circles along his temples. "I'll be here when you get back."

Making a sound of agreement, he kisses me once. Then once more. Gentle, kisses. Kisses that feel like love.

"Sophie, I…" He takes a breath, shaking his head. When he steps back, I feel the loss of him like a cold hand to my skin.

He tugs his cuffs in place once more and searches my face. I don't know what he sees, but his voice is soft when he finally speaks. "Be well."

"I will." But my promise is empty; because this sickness won't go until I make a stand against Martin.

GABRIEL

I HATE MEET AND GREETS—the inane parties both before and after each concert, where press, fans, fan club runners, other people of fame, and record industry heavy hitters all congregate into one, boring, who's-looking-at-who cluster. They're the bane of my professional existence.

Over the years, I've perfected a remote look that keeps people at arm's length during these torturous hours. Only the very brave or the very stupid approach me. The very brave have my respect and are usually intelligent enough to converse with briefly. The very stupid are easily dealt with.

It is inevitable, however, that I must talk with people throughout the night. And this night is extremely long. I've forced myself not to text Sophie more than once, lest I "mother hen" her. But I want to.

I don't like the wan, yet agitated expression she had earlier, or the way she trembled in my arms, even though she clearly wanted to hide her upset. Something is wrong. Something more than the carsickness she claims.

Whatever the problem is, I want to make it better. It is imperative that I do. My entire life has been dedicated to looking after people I care for, and she sits at the top of the list now.

I should have stayed with her. I'm feeling...possessive— yet another emotion I don't any familiarity with.

Men can't go around introducing their woman as, "Mine; Touch her and lose a finger." Can they? I doubt Sophie would appreciate being labeled as such. Or perhaps she would if I told her to label me in the same manner?

"Scottie, dude, you're drifting."

"Pardon?" I find Killian standing next to me.

"Completely spaced out." His grin is annoying. "I guess the vacation did the trick."

"I'm cured of the compulsion to check my phone every two minutes," I tell him grimly.

"Uh-huh, that's exactly what I was referring to."

I ignore his smug look. "It was..." *The best time of my life.* "...I enjoyed it very much."

Killian makes a noise of amusement. "Good to hear."

He doesn't say anything further, but he doesn't move away either.

Sophie believes I should try harder with them. I clear my throat. "I'm thinking of taking Sophie to the chalet for the New

Year. Would you and Liberty like to join us?"

I grimace. That probably sounded as stilted coming out of my mouth as it did in my head. By the way Killian's lip twitches, I am correct. Bugger.

But he answers before I can say another word. "Liberty and I would love that."

"Shouldn't you ask her before committing?" I know that much about women.

"No need. We have mind-melded." He leans in. "Besides, she's behind you."

Startled, I step back and find Liberty grinning so wide, her cheeks bunch. "Hey, Scottie." She gives me a punch on the arm. "Can we go skiing, and eat fondue, and do other James Bond-type things?"

"Such as jumping off cliffs and deploying parachutes with the Union Jack on them?" I drawl.

"Yes. But I need stars and stripes on mine. It's my patriotic duty."

"I'll put it on my to-do list."

"Hee!" She hugs me before I can get away. "This will be the best New Years ever!"

Killian laughs, but then looks around. "Anyone seen Jax?"

I disentangle myself from Liberty and nudge her in Killian's direction. "Not since the concert ended. He was a little off tonight."

Killian scans the room. "He looked like shit. And now he's gone."

When Jax disappears, we all worry. It is an automatic reaction now, no matter how trustworthy he seems. Instantly, I'm alert, my lower back clenching.

"When did you last see him?"

"Walking off stage."

"That was..." I glance at my watch. "Forty-two minutes ago."

Killian waves over Whip and Rye. "You guys seen Jax?"

Our worry is contagious. Rye frowns. "No, man."

"I saw him go into the bathroom when we got off," Whip says.

Rye jogs away to search the bathroom, while Killian heads for Kip, our head of security.

I move that way as well, and reach them just as Kip tells Killian he saw Jax go upstairs, hanging on to a groupie.

"And some guy," Kip adds.

"A guy?" Killian repeats, confused.

"Yeah, kind of sleazy looking. He had Jax by the other arm. But Jax waved me off." Kip shrugs. "So what could I do?"

Do your bloody job and tell me what was happening, I think with a silent snarl.

Killian's gaze darts to mine. "Jax is not into dudes."

"I know that," I snap, then take a breath. "Look, we don't know what's going on; we're simply being cautious. And I do not want to call attention to us, so let's calm down."

Killian's jaw tenses, but he nods.

"Keep on with your duties," I tell Kip. "Come with me, Killian."

Rye finds us as we walk across the room, his expression is grim. "Not in the bathroom."

"Apparently he went upstairs," I say. "Stay here and be you."

He knows exactly what I mean, but he doesn't appear happy.

"Some days it sucks being the class clown. Text me when you find him, or I'm gonna be pissed." He salutes us and runs off, jumping on the couch between two women. "Ladies, who wants to do shots?"

Liberty is with us, and I touch her elbow to slow her down. "Go tell Whip to stay down here. If we all go, people will notice."

Killian and I fall silent as we wait for the elevator.

"We have no real reason to worry," I tell him.

"He's probably fucking some girl."

"Right."

A row of numbered lights track the elevator's descent to our fifth floor level. Killian and I both watch it.

"Why do I feel like it's something more?" Killian whispers, staring at the lights.

My heart gives a pained thump. "I don't know." But I feel the same.

SOPHIE
26

TURNS out I don't have to hunt Martin down. He finds me. Of course the bastard does it his way, texting me to say he's off to the concert—where I can't follow without being seen by Gabriel—and then smugly adds that he'll text again when he's free.

Fucker. Fuck-faced fucker.

I have no choice but to sit tight, bide my time, and grow more anxious.

I've doodled devil faces on half the models in my magazine when I hear the elevator ding in the hall. A woman's obnoxious laughter rings out, followed by the lower tones of Jax's voice. The concert is over, and he's clearly in the mood to entertain.

Their voices drift off, and I try to lose myself in TV. Unfortunately, nothing's on, and I find myself watching *Alvin and the Chipmunks* in Italian. I have no idea why a kid's show is playing in the middle of the night, but high-pitched chatter in rapid Italian is definitely a distraction.

I don't know how much time passes, but a terrified, ear-piercing screech coming from the hall has me jumping up and running for the door.

A young woman runs toward the elevator in hysterics. Her brown hair is wild, her makeup smudged. Vomit splatters cover one side of her chest. That doesn't stop me from hooking her by the arm and yanking her to a stop. She's running from Jax's room.

"What happened?" I snap, my heart pounding. She tries to jerk free, but I hold her tight. "Answer me."

"I don't care if he's famous. He barfed on me. Eww…" She flails her hand. "So fucking gross."

She's an American, and probably no older than nineteen. I tug her along, hurrying down the corridor. "Show me where he is."

"Let me go."

"No. You don't get that luxury right now." And I'm stronger. Worry and fear for Jax has that effect.

"He's with that other dude," she whines. "He'll take care of him."

I don't stop, but my steps stutter. "What dude?"

"I don't know. Some guy. Marty."

I can feel the blood draining from my face. I find myself rushing forward, the girl in tow. "Shit, shit."

The girl wrenches free. I don't try to catch her but run to Jax's room and bang on the door.

My worst fear is realized when Martian opens it with a shit-eating grin.

"Well, this was easier than expected. Hello, pretty Sophie."

I shove him back with all my strength. "What the fuck did you do!"

He stumbles a step but then steadies, laughing. "I didn't do shit. Just followed the trainwreck that is Jax Blackwood."

From the bathroom comes a pitiful moan and the sound of retching. I give Martin a death glare as I hurry off. He follows as if he can't wait to witness this.

The smell hits me first. It's so foul, I stagger. Jax is on the floor by the toilet, his skin sickly gray and covered in sweat, among other things.

"Jax," I fall to his side, heedless of the mess. "Honey, what'd you take?"

His head lolls but he blinks, trying to focus on me. "Nothing, babe. Swear. Don't feel so good."

He shudders, then blindly reaches for the toilet, knocking me back in the scramble. I hear the distinctive click of a photo being taken. Martin has his cell out and is clicking away with glee.

"Put that fucking phone down or I will cram it up your ass, I swear to God!" I lunge for it, but Jax collapses on the floor.

"Jax! Shit. Give me that phone," I snarl at Martin. "I need to call a doctor."

Martin dances back, holding the phone high. "Baby, I knew it would be worth it to follow you, but I didn't realize you'd make me this lucky. Thanks, Soph. Again."

The words are barely out of his mouth when Gabriel and Killian appear in the doorway. Relief washes over me. Gabriel will know how to best help Jax. But a few things happen in rapid succession that prevent me from getting a word in.

Killian shouts in fear and rushes over to Jax.

Gabriel's gaze darts between me and Martin. Before anyone can move, he grabs Martin by the throat with one hand, smashing him into the wall, and plucks the cell away from Martin with the other hand and pockets it.

"Stay," he snaps at Martin, slamming his head against the wall one more time.

"Get the fuck off me," Martin says, trying to break free. "I'll fucking sue."

Gabriel simply pins him to the wall with the strength of one arm. Already he's on his phone. "Stern, I need you now. Bring your bag." He calls another a second after that. "Kip. Up here now."

Never once does he look at me.

Killian has Jax in his arms. "No fucking way are you doing

this again," he rasps looking panicked.

Jax moans and stirs.

"What did he take?" The harsh question from Gabriel is directed at me.

"I don't know. He said he didn't. Just that he feels sick."

Gabriel's attention cuts to Martin's phone as he scrolls through the pictures. Every inch of him seems to vibrate with suppressed rage. His lips are white around the corners, his grip on Martin so tight that the man starts to claw at Gabriel's fingers.

"You're choking him." Personally, I want to beat the shit out Martin, but Gabriel has too much to lose by seriously hurting a photographer.

Gabriel's eyes meet mine. Rage flares so hot in his expression that I viscerally react, recoiling into myself.

"Good," he snaps, returning his attention to Martin's phone. His nostrils flare as he looks over what has to be dozens of pictures, the last one being me hunched over Jax.

With a few moves of his thumb, he deletes them all.

"Hey," Martin tries to protest and earns another slam of his head.

Dr. Stern and Kip rush in a second later, and everything becomes a blur of helping Jax. I find myself pushed out of the bathroom, and I slump into a chair to shake and sweat. There's vomit on my knees, which I'm trying very hard not to look at, and I'm afraid for Jax. I'm also worried about Gabriel's behavior.

I know he's in emergency mode, but I don't like the way he refuses to look at me.

Kip marches Martin out of the suite, with the little rat bastard protesting the whole way, and I'm alone.

Gabriel is still with the others in the bathroom. I can hear them talking.

"It isn't an overdose," Dr. Stern says. "I believe he has food poisoning. I've already had calls from a few of the roadies who are suffering as well."

Killian's voice is subdued. "He went out to dinner with Ted and Mike earlier."

"Those would be the two who I've seen," Dr. Stern says. "I'll keep him hydrated until it passes through his system."

Jax moans. "Can everyone get the fuck out? I've got more to pass through my fucking system…"

Killian and Gabriel exit the bathroom and close the door behind them. Gabriel is on the phone, giving someone an update. He keeps himself turned from me.

Killian takes one last look at the door and lets out a shuddering breath. Weariness lines his face as he rubs a hand over it. With a pat to Gabriel's shoulder, he walks out, never once acknowledging me.

The sick, jumpy feeling in my belly intensifies when Gabriel finally heads my way.

"Sunshine—"

"Not here," he snaps, in a low, tight voice. He turns and heads for the door.

I have no choice but to follow.

＊

HE WAITS until we're in our room to round on me. "All right, what the hell is going on?"

"Don't snap at me like I'm one of your lackeys."

"Answer the goddamn question," he roars.

My ears ring with his fury. It's so sudden and intense, I flinch. I've never seen him like this, white about the lips, his eyes burning into mine. My lip wobbles. I want to cry. But I've never been the type to cower. I won't now, and I find myself shouting back at him.

"I don't know! I only got there a few minutes before you."

He snorts, the sound loud and obnoxious. "He sent you the

first text when we checked into our room."

Shit. "That had nothing to do with Jax."

Gabriel grinds his teeth. "You weren't sick at all, were you? You lied to me."

My stomach lurches. "I was sick. With worry and shame. The mere thought of that worm being around and wanting to talk made me ill."

If anything, he looks more upset, hot color rising up his neck. "That's all you had to tell me, if that was the case. Instead, you made me worry and regret leaving you behind. And all the while you were planning on meeting up with that little fuck."

He's right, and there's nothing I can do to change my mistakes. "I'm sorry. I just wanted to handle it myself, get rid of him and get on with my life. I didn't mean to hurt you, though."

Gabriel waves his hand as if swatting a fly. "Fine."

"You don't sound fine."

His gaze cuts to me. "Because I am. Not. Fine. I am bloody-well pissed."

I finch again at the hardness of his voice and the way he uses it as a whip. Having never been on the receiving end of his anger, I hadn't realized the power of it. I'm ashamed that I've earned it. And I'm hurt that he won't let it go.

He paces over to me, but halts as if he suddenly doesn't want to be too close. "It's bad enough that I have to walk into what appeared to be a replay of one of the worst moments in my life, but I get the distinct privilege of witnessing your supposed ex-boyfriend thanking you for helping him film the whole fucking thing!"

Guilt and shame hit me anew, but my mind skids to a halt. "What do you mean supposed? He *is* my ex. How can you even think that—"

His lip curls in disgust. "You're not stupid or blind. You

damn well know how this looks."

"And how exactly does this look to you?" I ask, my heart thudding loudly in my ears. "Tell me, Gabriel, what do think went on here?"

For a second, I don't think he'll answer. But then something defiant flashes in his eyes, and he stiffens, those icy, business-like walls slamming down around him. It's so swift and effective, I can almost hear their phantom clang.

"It looks like you fucked us over."

He might as well have punched me in the gut. For a second I can't breathe.

"Right. All of this, all of what we had together, was just some elaborate ruse to get a story. Sure, why not? I can play a whore, can't I?"

I will not cry. I will not cry.

"Do not twist this, Sophie."

"I'm not twisting anything. You flat-out said it. I'm only clarifying your theory."

"I wouldn't have to theorize if you would simply tell me what the fuck happened!" He punches the air, as the words tear from him.

"I shouldn't have to explain that I'm not some gutter slut," I shout back. "You should trust me enough not to leap to that disgusting conclusion."

"And if it had been me? Had you walked in on me with someone who had already hurt your family, someone you knew I'd been in a relationship with *while* hurting your family? You'd honestly just assume it was all fine because you trust me?"

He looks at me with wide, pained eyes, and my heart squeezes. "Well…"

"No, you wouldn't," he cuts in, going hard once more. "At the very least, you'd expect an explanation without having to ask for it. And I would bloody well be giving it to you," he shouts. "Because you'd deserve that courtesy. Anyone would. And most certainly from the person you—"

His mouth snaps shut, and he turns away, running a hand through his hair. Hunched and trembling, he looks so defeated that I move to go to him. Because if he's hurting, I need to stop it.

But he doesn't give me a chance. He straightens once more and turns to me. "I am trying my best to give you a chance here. Because what Killian and I walked in on tonight did not look good." He spreads his hands in a helpless gesture. "Christ, Sophie, give me something to work with, a bloody breadcrumb of an explanation to take back to Killian."

My face burns so hotly it throbs. "Killian? You think I give a shit what Killian believes right now?"

"You should be extremely worried about what the bloody hell Killian thinks of you. The band's welfare should be your top priority, damn it."

"It's obviously yours," I snap.

"Of course it is." He slashes the air with his hand. "I'm their goddamn manager! What did you think?"

"I thought," I answer with a shaking voice, "I meant enough to you that you wouldn't make ugly assumptions. That you wouldn't worry about soothing Killian's feelings at the expense of mine."

All emotion wipes from his face, and he straightens to his full height, rolling his shoulders back as if to brace himself. "This is real life, Sophie. Not some movie. You don't get to use this as some test to see how much I'll blindly accept, as if that somehow will make me worthy of you."

I stand there, mouth open, unable to form a word. A test? He thinks this is some stupid test? But a small, dark part of me wonders, *am I testing him?*

I would explain all of it if he gave me half a chance to get a word in.

And yet I *am* hurt that he immediately thought the worst of me. How could I not be? We're better than this. I gave him my heart; I would never intentionally hurt him or anyone he loves. If he doesn't know that now, I'm not sure he ever will.

His voice is cold and methodical as he keeps picking, his fucking logic stomping on my heart with every word. "You think I don't understand what you're doing? Give me a little credit. I know you as well as you know me. Did it become too much fun, believing you could manage me?"

This pain is dull and hollow, and somehow worse because of it. I close my eyes against him. "First I'm a sleazy schemer, and now I'm some jerk who enjoys leading you around by the balls for fun? Is that it?"

"Goddamn it, you don't get to be the injured party here. Not this time."

My eyes snap open. He looks so genuinely put out and hurt that I don't know what to say. But I won't apologize now, that's for damn sure.

"Well, too bad, because I am injured. And you don't get to tell me how to feel." I take a step closer, my fists balling at my sides. "And right now, you're making it really fucking hard not to hate you."

He rocks back on his heels. Silence wells up between us like a living, dark thing. When he finally speaks, his voice is low and unsteady.

"You have always pushed me to express myself. This is me expressing myself. I can concede that I need to let myself live more in the moment and enjoy life. But you, Sophie Darling, need to grow the hell up and take responsibility when things go into the shitter. And if you cannot do that, you don't belong on this tour."

I hear him. I know he's right about this. But his ugly conclusions and the way he jumped to them loom large as well.

Licking my dry lips, I make my voice as calm as I can manage. "Right now, the tour and whether I should be on it are the least of my worries."

He frowns, tilting his head as if he can't understand me. Part of me wants to laugh, only I know I'll end up crying. Maybe we are too different, our priorities too far apart.

A knock on the suite door has us both flinching. Gabriel turns toward it, his mouth pinched, weariness lining his face. In this light, he's almost haggard. He runs a hand over his eyes.

"That's Jules. She's here to give me an update—"

"I'll leave you to it." On wooden limbs, I head to the bedroom.

He doesn't try to stop me.

And I don't cry once I close the door behind me. I pack.

GABRIEL 27

"REPORT?" I ask from one of suite's dining room chairs. My head is too heavy to hold itself up, so I rest it in the cradle of my hands.

"The girl you caught on the elevator is Jennifer Miller. She's a roadie, working in lighting." Jules's voice is hesitant and soft.

Regrettable, but apparently I'm quite good at cowing women. A lance of pain drives through my heart. I clear my throat, having trouble finding my voice.

"Go on."

Jules takes a breath that sounds more like a sigh. "According to her statement, she'd been wanting to hook up with Jax. When she saw him having trouble getting to the elevator, she offered to help."

Well, give the girl points for being an opportunist. I shouldn't care, but I'm so bloody bitter at the moment, it's all I can do not to sneer.

"And that cockwank? How did he get in?"

From between my fingers, I see Jules's lip quirk in a smile before she presses down on them. "He, ah, approached them at the elevator. Told Jennifer he was an old friend of..." Jules coughs, her eyes darting away.

"Of Sophie's?" I offer. Goddamn it, it hurts to say her

name. I don't know how I manage to utter it without inflection.

Sophie. She retreated to our bedroom after I ripped into her worse than anyone I've ever had a go at. She went with quiet dignity, and I felt small and full of regret. I don't even remember the last person I cared about with whom I've truly lost my temper. There's a reason for that. I cut people open with my words, as surely as a surgeon with a scalpel.

That fucktrumpet Martin, however... My hands curl into fists. It's all I can do not to hunt the tit down and bash his fucking gob in. A shudder works through me. I'm regressing back to my feral youth, when I was a few steps away from becoming a chavvy thug.

Jules watches me with weary eyes.

I force what I hope is a bland expression. "Well?"

"Yes, that's what he said. And he offered to give them a hand. Jax let them both up."

My hand is cold and clammy as I rub it over my face. "What happened in the room?"

"Ah, Jennifer says she started...ah, making out with Jax. He didn't appear to mind."

Which means he was so out of it, he let the twit do what she wanted. I wave a hand, encouraging Jules to speed things up. I can hardly stomach sitting here, listening to this. I want to pace. I want to hunt down Sophie and crawl into bed with her, beg her to forgive me for shouting.

No, I cannot be a complete doormat. She was in the wrong too. She lied, refused to explain, and held my exacting nature over my head. We'll never go forward on equal ground if I'm the only one to admit my failings.

It's not like you gave her much of a chance to explain, mate.

It's not as though she tried to explain.

Sod it all, I'm arguing with myself now.

Jules is talking, and I force myself to focus.

"...Martin started taking pictures of them. Said he thought they looked cute together and Jennifer would like a..." Jules winces. "A souvenir."

"Fucking hell."

"Yeah," she agrees quietly. "Anyway, Jax suddenly threw up. On Jennifer."

She pauses, and our eyes meet. I can't help but smile a little. Jules does too.

"Go on," I say, fighting that smile.

"She runs, gets caught by Sophie, who apparently detained her, demanding to know what was going on, and tried to drag her back to the scene."

My Sophie. She'd acted as I would have. Guilt settles in my throat like shards of glass.

"Jennifer broke free, and presumably that's when you found her in the elevator."

"Yes." It had been an unwelcome surprise to discover a hysterical, vomit-covered woman in the elevator when the doors opened. Killian and I had stared at her in shock before snapping out of it and delivering her directly to a security guard manning the area.

With a sigh, I sit back in my chair. I ache. All over. And I know it is from sorrow. "Relay all of this to Killian and the rest of the guys." Since I know full-well Killian will have told them everything by now. "I don't want them thinking badly of Sophie."

It hurts to say. It hurts to even think. Sophie hadn't understood that the mere idea of them disliking her would be a wound in my heart. She's too important to me for there to be discord.

Jules nods. "And Jennifer?"

"She's out. Give her two weeks severance and a ticket home."

"I'm guessing not in first class?" Jules's joke falls flat. And her smile dies. "Too soon?"

Not bothering to answer, I stand and squeeze the back of my stiff neck. "And go over the NDA she signed. Make certain she understands the repercussions if she talks."

We both turn at a noise from the living area. Sophie stands at the threshold to the dining room. Her hair hangs damp and limp around her shoulders. She appears smaller somehow, diminished. The light has gone out of her pretty eyes.

I did that to her. My heart thumps in my chest, pushing against my ribs, which squeeze tight at the sight of her.

"Sophie. We were finishing up here."

"Yeah, I see that." She sounds like a ghost of herself.

Dimly, I'm aware of Jules leaving. I only have eyes for Sophie, however.

Silence ticks by. I take a step in her direction, but her voice stops me.

"You were right. I don't belong on this tour. It's no longer fun for me."

"Fun?" The word is like a slap to the face.

"Yeah, fun. You know that concept you have a hard time embracing?"

I wince.

And she winces too. "I'm sorry. That was shitty. I didn't mean it."

"You wouldn't have said it if you didn't mean it," I say quietly.

Her eyes narrow. "So you meant every word you said to me then?"

There's a trap here. I can see it laid out, waiting for me to fall into. Only I have no idea how to circumvent the damn thing.

"I shouldn't have shouted at you," I say. "I regret being so..." *Vicious.* "Aggressive."

"But you don't regret what you said." A flat statement.

Irritation flares. "What do you want me to say, Sophie? We had words. All couples fight." *And then they make up. Why can't we get to the make up part of the program?*

Apparently, we aren't anywhere near that segment.

Her expression goes colder. "Couples trust each other."

"This again? You lied to me," I bite out. *And that hurt me.* Somehow that is harder to admit.

"And I apologized," she snaps.

I should let it go. I know this. "You lied to me about someone who...fuck all, Sophie. He's been *inside* you."

I don't even know what I'm saying, only that the thought of him being with Sophie turns my stomach and makes me want to pummel something.

Her mouth falls open. "You're jealous? Of Martin?"

Her voice saying his name sets me off. "More like disgusted by your life choices."

Shit.

She gasps. I can't take the words back.

"Sophie...I didn't—"

"First I'm immature, now I'm disgusting?"

"You are *not* disgusting." I take another step toward her. "I spoke out of turn. I am a jealous prat. I didn't expect to be, but I am."

I move closer. If I can just get to her, simply hold her, things will be all right. They have to be.

But she holds up a hand, warning me off. "Look, I'm going to stay with Brenna tonight."

This is wrong. She shouldn't go. "You should stay."

A bitter smile pulls at her lips. "But I don't want to."

I swallow so hard it hurts. "Oh."

Brilliant rejoinder. Bloody brilliant.

She makes a noise in her throat as if she's thinking the same thing. "Like I said, I don't want to stay on the tour either."

My body strains toward hers. "Why?" It sounds more like a plea than a question.

She huffs out a toneless laugh. "Jesus, you can't be this thick. You gave me an ultimatum. Either grow up or get off the tour. And by what I've heard from you tonight, all this is moot anyway. And you know what? I don't want to grow up. Not if it means being coldly clinical like you, so I guess I'm out."

She grabs the bag I'm only now seeing and heads for the door. My feet are rooted to the ground. I have to force them to move, to follow her. I feel hollowed out and numb. My head pounds with her angry words.

"Wait," I say.

She doesn't turn. "You know," she says. "I like you just as you are, faults and all. But you clearly don't accept me for who I am."

"That's not true!" I'm walking faster now. But she's already at the door, opening it. "Sophie."

She pauses, but still doesn't look my way. "Leave me alone, Gabriel. I've reached my limit tonight. I can't talk to you any more."

Give her space. That's what men are supposed to do when a woman requests it, aren't they? I don't know. I've never had a woman I wanted to call my own before. It feels wrong, but I've done everything wrong at this point. So I shove my protests aside.

"All right. Good night, Sophie."

"Goodbye."

The door shuts with a soft click, and I am alone.

SOPHIE

JUST GET TO THE DOOR. *Just get out of the room and then you can lose it.*

He lets me go with a softly offered, "Good night." As if he hasn't just torn me apart all over again.

As if he hadn't just told Jules I was out. No first class this time? Well, fuck you and your first-class tickets.

A sob tries to break free, and I hold it in by sheer will. My feet propel me down the hotel corridor, but my body is throbbing with this horrible, dull pain. He fired me? And then acted like it was all on me?

I should have thrown it in his face. But I'm so hurt, so shocked. I don't know what to say. I can't think properly. I thought he loved me. True, he never said the words, but every look, every action… That was love. It had to be.

And yet here I am again, coming in second to a man's business needs. It wasn't as if I didn't have warnings this time. I knew Gabriel put the band above all things. But I had hoped there was equal room for me.

I make it to Brenna's room. My knuckles feel brittle as I knock on her door.

The second she opens it, I start to cry.

"Honey," she says, pulling me in. "Honey."

Everything that happened comes out of me like word vomit. And she holds me, letting it all flow.

"He did what?" she shrieks when I tell her about Gabriel ordering Jules to fire me.

"He told her to remind me of the fucking NDA I signed," I say bitterly.

"No." Brenna shakes her head. "No way. That is not the man I've seen with you. He's crazy about you, Sophie."

I wouldn't have thought so either. A sigh shakes me. "I heard him." I walked in just in time to hear those orders loud and clear.

"You have to talk to him. Because I cannot believe it."

She guides me to a chair as I shake my head. "I just talked to him. I said I was leaving the tour, and he let me go."

Why didn't he come after me? Tell me that he loves me? Is that what I want? I'm so battered and tired of the whole thing, I can't think straight. I only know that I hurt, and I miss him. Even when I want to hit his stubborn, thick head, I miss him. Life is an empty road if he isn't on it beside me.

I hate this weakness. Being in love is akin to losing my mind and having my heart flayed open all at once. It sucks.

"Look," Brenna says gently, "you two have had a bad night. Let it settle and discuss it in the morning." She grows quiet and then bends her head to peer at me. "You really want to leave the tour?"

It occurs to me then that she's not just a friend. She's my boss.

"I'm sorry," I say, twisting my fingers. "It isn't just Gabriel. Killian wouldn't look at me tonight. Logically, I don't blame them. But it was as if all that we've been through means nothing." I shake my head. "And call me a wuss, but I just want to go away and lick my wounds in privacy for a while."

Brenna appears to think that is a terrible idea, but she's kind enough to let it go. "Let's get you to bed. It will be better in the morning."

I'm fairly certain that means Brenna is going to try to talk me out of things, or into things. Either way, I can't face being asked to review the stinking NDA I signed. The humiliation would level me.

Maybe Gabriel has it right; maybe it's better to take a step back and protect yourself. I've always been a walking ball of emotion. Maybe if I take some time for myself, get away from the heady experience of being wrapped up in Gabriel, I'll see things clearly.

Brenna stands, cutting into my thoughts. "I'll leave you to get ready." She takes a few steps, then turns back. "If things turn out for the worst, Harley Andrews is very interested in working with you."

"That's flattering." I feel absolutely nothing. I don't care anymore if I'd be working with a huge movie star. And yet Australia sounds like an adventure right about now. I could go there, take in the country, get some perspective.

A little voice whispers that I'm running away like a chicken. I ignore it.

GABRIEL 28

THE GUYS FIND me the next morning in a pathetic heap on the couch, a pillow over my face. I would say it is my lowest point, but that's already happened. The second Sophie walked out the door and out of my life will always be my lowest point. No, the second I doubted her and tore apart her trust in me was my lowest point.

"Jesus," Jax says, somewhere above my head. "He's wearing sweats. Dirty ones."

And rather foul-smelling ones at that. I don't bloody care.

"Is he drunk?" Whip asks with some concern.

"Naw," Killian drawls. "All I see are empty water bottles."

"Drowning his sorrows in bottled water. At least he's not cliché," Rye murmurs before sitting next to me. His hand comes down on my shoulder and he gives me a shake. "Scottie, man, what's up?"

It takes true effort to make my mouth move. But I know if I don't answer, they'll never leave.

"I'm fairly certain Sophie wants to leave me."

They're all silent, which grates even more.

Then Jax sighs. "Fuck, man. That sucks."

The pillow lifts from my face, sending blinding light into my eyes. I squint as Killian frowns down at me.

"What did you do?" he asks.

I don't answer. My body is so leaden, I can't find the energy to talk. I just want them to go away.

"Was it the sex?" Whip asks tentatively.

I give him a glare that, in a perfect world, would cause instant annihilation.

Unfortunately it does little more than make Whip wince. "Sorry, sorry. Just thought I'd ask."

I stare up at the ceiling. Behind me, Jax rummages through the suite's kitchenette and finds some beers.

"Should you be drinking those?" I feel compelled to ask. He looks about as good as I feel.

Jax limps his way to the other couch and falls down on it. "It settles my stomach."

Doubtful.

"Are you all right?" I ask, partially afraid he'll be sick all over my suite.

He gives me a knowing look. "I feel like shit warmed over and left out to dry, but I'll live."

Rye passes beers to the others, but I wave off the offer. I don't remember when I last ate, and in my current mood, I'm likely to punch someone if I get drunk.

"Once found a book of Brenna's," Rye says, making a face. "Dude in it had some 'monster cock' that was ten inches long."

"Yeah, right," Jax scoffs. "Was it a fantasy? The likelihood of a dude with a tenner is slim."

"Speak for yourself," Killian says with a smug grin.

"I am, anaconda. Just simmer down and keep it holstered."

They both snicker. But Rye shakes his head. "How are dudes in real life supposed to compete when women are reading about python dicks and pussy whisperers?"

Whip snorts and spins one of his drumsticks. "The average length of a woman's vagina is three to four inches. A ten-inch dick doesn't mean shit when it's all said and done."

"Are you trying to justify having a three-inch dick?" Rye

asks with a growing smirk.

"Nice try, but you're not getting a look at this magnificent specimen, no matter how badly you want to." Whip grabs his crotch and hefts it in Rye's direction before rolling his eyes. "I'm trying to say, asshole, that men shouldn't be worrying about how big their dicks are, but how to use them. I've had women weep with gratitude because they're used to lazy cock."

Jax laughs at that. "Lazy cock. So fucking true. You get a woman to come on your dick, and she's fucking hooked."

"Someone make it stop," I mutter, putting the pillow back over my face.

"Look, man," Whip says somewhere around the vicinity of my head. "We're just trying to give you some advice."

"Fuck all..." I tilt the pillow to the side to glare at him. "Sophie has been well satisfied. Repeatedly."

Hell, now I'm thinking of that look she has when she comes, the way her little nose wrinkles and her eyes squeeze tight as she arches her neck and moans... I put the pillow on my lap and snarl.

"Are you sure?" Rye waggles his brow. "I mean she's obviously not happy about something—"

"She's upset because I tore into her like a jealous, untrusting asshole, you git. Not because I couldn't get her off. Fucking hell."

"Ah."

Yes, *ah*. As if that does me any good.

Rye turns on the TV and settles down in a chair. "Oh, *Supernatural* is on."

"No," I cut in, pained. "Not that one. Sophie has a thing for Dean. I can't watch it without hearing her sigh and coo." God, I miss her.

Rye quickly changes the channel to a car show.

Unfortunately, all I can think about is Sophie lusting over

my Ferrari. Shit. The woman is threaded through every fiber of my existence. I'm unraveling.

"I love her." The words come out stilted, foreign on my tongue. But they are the truest part of me.

"Of course you do," Jax says with the patience of a father talking to an irritable toddler.

Killian snorts. "We've all known since you threatened to kill Jax over her."

"I don't recall such threats." I only thought them. I was so blind back then, trying to convince myself Sophie was a passing fancy when I'd been falling for her from the moment she opened her mouth. My clever, chatty girl. She's turned me on my head, made me a better man, made me live for the moment.

I glance around. The guys are giving me my privacy by watching the TV. But they are here. For me. They'll never leave me behind. My mates. My family.

"I love you too," I blurt out.

And instantly regret it. My face burns as they all turn my way with varying degrees of shock in their expressions.

Rye gurgles on a laugh.

"Fuck," I mutter. "That's not... You know what I mean. You're my mates."

"'In Whoville they say that the Grinch's small heart grew three sizes that day,'" Killian drawls.

They all laugh.

"Sod off," I growl, fighting a smile. But I won't retreat anymore. Sophie was right; it hurts both me and them when I do that. I look each of them in the eye. "I mean it."

Whip tosses himself on me, which bloody hurts, and musses my hair. "We love you too, Scottie boy."

I shove him to the floor. "Animals, the lot of you." But I feel better. Except I don't. Not at all. "I am fucked, aren't I?"

"Pretty much," Killian says with a nod.

"I'm not falling in love," Jax declares. "I have enough fucked emotions to work through."

"Famous last words, dude," Whips says from the floor.

"So, did you apologize to Sophie?" Jax asks.

"Of course. But I cocked it up, and she asked for space."

"You didn't give her space, did you?" Killian sounds horrified.

It gives me pause, and I peer up at him. "Wasn't I supposed to?"

"No, you don't give them space," he wails. "That's only some shit they say to see if you'll fight for them."

Outrage punches through me. "Why the bloody hell would they do that to us?"

"To see if we're paying attention?" Jax offers.

"To torture us?" Rye counters.

"It's simply biology," Whip says as if he's suddenly an expert. "Men are wired to love the hunt, and women are wired to love being hunted."

"That sounds like something women would call sexist," I counter.

"They might protest," Whip agrees. "But deep down they know it's true."

"Women should come with instructions." Rye takes a sip of his beer and stares down at the bottle. "Or a warning label."

Killian laughs. "They do, man. You just have to learn how to read them. Problem is, most of us don't learn how until a woman has knocked us on our asses. Trial by fire, my friends. And you will burn."

"Killian James, prophet of doom," I say, knowing he's right. And hating it.

"Look," he kicks my foot. "You fucked up. Now you gotta go make a gesture that shows her she's the most important person in your life."

"Should I go sing a song that calls her an easy lay?" I ask.

Which is low, because that was Killian's mistake with Libby.

The guys snicker, and Killian kicks me again. "I married the girl, jackass, so I won."

Marriage isn't something I've ever wanted, or even considered. But I could marry Sophie. I picture it: my ring on her finger, all my assets guaranteed to go to her. She'd be financially safe for life. She'd be *mine* for life. And instead of the future being a blank wall I never examine, it would be sunshine and light. It would be her happy laughter and soft warmth. Perfection.

Yearning adds to the ache in my heart.

I haul myself up, wincing at the pain in my chest and stomach. "Everyone out. I have gestures to plan."

"Thatta boy, Scottie." Rye slaps my shoulder. "Just, whatever you do, don't make it a Star Trek theme."

Because I know it will please them, I flip the finger as I head toward the shower.

My progress stops when Brenna bursts into the room.

"You complete asshole," she says by way of greeting.

"I see you've been talking to Sophie." I refrain from demanding where she is and how she's doing. But only just.

Brenna sneers. "Did you really tell Jules to send Sophie home? Like she's some fucking lackey you can fob off when things get difficult?"

My blood runs cold. "What?"

"Sophie heard you telling Jules to put her on a plane. Not first class this time? Ring a fucking bell?"

"Oh, shit," Rye says somewhere behind me.

I ignore him, horror prickling my skin and making my ears ring. Sophie thinks I want her gone? No wonder she appeared so hurt, lashing out at me like the walking wounded. And I gave her space with *that* to brood on all night.

"I was talking about Jennifer, the sodding roadie who let that fuckwit Martin into Jax's room! Sophie is my life, for fuck's sake."

"Oh," Brenna says, looking pleased. "Well, that's good." But then her happy face falls. "Actually, it's bad."

"Why?" It's all I can do not to grab Brenna and shake her.

Brenna's nose wrinkles. "She, ah, left a note saying she was going 'on walkabout'."

"What the fuck is a walkabout?" I roar.

"*Crocodile Dundee*," Killian calls out behind me. "You know, when he went roaming around the outback?"

Sweet hell, my girl is a nut. An adorable little nut.

"Where is she walking about?" I grit out.

Brenna grimaces. "Australia. Her flight leaves at five."

My girl is an adorable, misguided, evil nut who I'm going spank as soon as I get my hands on her. I need to get to her. Oh, God help me, I need to make that gesture Killian was going on about.

I might truly be ill when it's all said and done. But I can do this. For her, I'll do anything.

I let out a breath and shove my hands into my hair to hold my pounding head.

"All right," I say. "All right, I need help, and I need it now."

And my mates, God love them all, rise to the occasion.

"What do you need, Scottie?"

"I need my lawyer, and I need to get on that plane." I'll make the rest up as I go along.

SOPHIE

THEY SAY you never really know what you have until you lose it. I'm not sure how accurate that is. I know what I have with Gabriel is something special, a connection few people are lucky enough to find. And yet here I sit on a plane that's getting ready to take me away from him.

Of all the rash, impulsive things I've done in my life, this one really takes the cake.

I'm so angry with myself that my nails are digging into the meat of my palms. I should have stayed and apologized for not explaining things straightaway, for saying hurtful words in an attempt to protect myself. Gabriel deserves that. He deserves the world. A few asshole comments aside, he is the best man I have ever known. And I want to continue to know him, to care for him.

A passenger headed down the aisle bumps my shoulder with her butt and mutters a quick apology as she angles her way down the narrow passage. First class, this is not.

With my salary, I could have paid for a premium-fare ticket. But I couldn't fly that way. Not without him by my side. Luxury has lost its luster without Gabriel to share the experience.

"Shit." I grab my purse and yank it from beneath the seat in front of me.

The man sitting next to me sends a curious glance my way.

"I have to go," I tell him, as if he needs to know.

Dude gives me a salute as I scramble from my seat.

It isn't easy, navigating up the aisle while everyone else is boarding. I'm a salmon fighting my way upstream. Frustration prickles at my lids. I need off this plane. I need Gabriel.

A flight attendant sees the struggle and meets me at the first emergency exit. "Is there a problem, miss?"

"No problem." I haul my purse strap higher up my shoulder. "I just need to get off."

She slowly looks me over.

Great, I'm probably broadcasting crazy. Not something you ever want to do on an airplane.

"Are you Ms. Sophie Darling?"

"Ah…yes?"

She smiles, going from weary to strangely affectionate. *"Bene.* I was on my way to find you."

"You were?" *Shit, what did I do?*

She links her arm with mine. "Come with me."

I follow, because what else can I do? People give me looks, and I look right back. *Hey there, tell my story if I'm Tasered, okay?*

But she doesn't take me off the plane. She leads me into first class. My steps slow, a protest rising. I don't know what the hell this is about, but I'm not accepting any charity…

Then I see him. Crisp, gray three-piece suit, ice blue silk tie, coal black hair perfectly combed: the man of my heart. He sits in a cabin made for two, his eyes narrowed and tracking my movements as if he's waiting for me to turn tail and run.

Relief has me swaying. Joy has me embarrassingly close to tears.

I'm so surprised, I've lost the ability to function, and the flight attendant all but pushes me into my seat.

"Gabriel? What are you doing here?"

His brow quirks. "Coming after you, obviously."

God, his voice, all low and rich and rumbly. And irritable. I've missed it so.

"But you hate flying. This flight is twenty hours long!"

He grimaces, going green at the edges. "Yes, I know. You're more important."

My heart goes all fluttery, and I want to jump in his lap and kiss the hell out of him. But the flight crew is clearly getting ready to close the doors.

"You can't suffer for that long. I won't allow it. We have to get off." I grab his hand and tug, but he pulls me back down.

"I have things I need to say." His expression is set, and I know he won't be swayed.

"Okay…"

As if facing a firing squad, he sets his shoulders and lifts his chin. But the look in his eyes is vulnerable, exposed.

"First and most importantly, I love you. I have never said that to a woman, and I will never say that to any other but you. I've lived long enough to know that you are completely it for me. This is a done deal—signed, notarized, what have you."

Happiness bubbles through my veins like warm champagne. "Gabriel…"

"I'm not finished."

He looks so adorably committed to having his say that I bite back a smile. "Okay."

He nods, takes a breath. "I will say the wrong words from time to time. And I will cock things up. That's a given, unfortunately. But there will never, ever be a time when I do not love you or want you in my life."

I blink rapidly, stunned to tears.

He scowls as if annoyed at himself and bends down to pull a slim file out of his case. He hands it to me. "This is for you."

My hands are shaking too hard to open the damn thing. "What is this?"

"My will. I almost didn't get it done on time," he muses. "I've left everything to you."

My words come out in a high squeak. "What? Why? What?"

He looks at me, perfectly calm, as if he hasn't just leveled me. "I want to give you tangible proof that—whether you marry me or not—my life is literally linked with yours until the day I die. Actually, long after I die, too, if you want to be technical."

"Marry you?" My cheeks are tingling.

His brows lift in confusion. "I hand you everything I own, and that's what you focus on?"

Because the rest doesn't matter; I can never conceive of a life he isn't in. "Answer the question, sunshine."

"Yes, I'm going to want to do that. As soon as possible, if I have my way." Uncertainty fills his eyes. "That is if you'll have me, of course."

I gape at him, words stuck in my throat.

Gabriel tugs at his cuffs. "If you do not, I should warn you now, you'll have a hard time getting rid of me. I can be persistent when I want something."

I press my hand to my hot cheek. "Holy shit. I'm dizzy. Did you...was that a proposal? I can't tell."

"Sod all," he mutters, flushing. "I told you I'd cock things up—"

I launch myself at him, wrapping my arms around his neck and kissing his mouth to shut him up. He freezes for a second, as if too surprised to react, and then kisses me back, taking control. His hands hold my nape, and he goes at my mouth as if I'm the only one who can give him air.

It feels so good, and I've missed him so desperately, that I do cry—soft tears that he kisses away, whispering words of reassurance, stroking my cheeks with the rough pads of his thumbs.

I give him a watery smile when we break apart.

"You didn't mess anything up," I tell him, smoothing my hand over his hair. "You're perfect. I love you, sunshine. Exactly how you are."

He lets out a lengthy sigh and rests his forehead against mine. "Thank Christ for that." His strong fingers grip my hips. "Tell me again."

"I love you, Gabriel Scott."

His smile is so sweetly pleased, I have to kiss it, taste it.

"Once more," he demands. "I'm not certain I heard you correctly."

"I love you, Gabriel Sunshine Scott!" My shout earns a couple of stares and a few chuckles.

Gabriel grins like it's Christmas morning. "I love you too,

Sophie Chatty Girl Darling. More than you'll every know."

I pepper him with kisses because he's here, and he's mine. "I'm sorry I ran off. I'm sorry I didn't explain myself right away. It hurt you, and I never want you to hurt."

"Thank you," he says between my attacks on his mouth. But then he holds me still by cupping my cheeks. "I am rather annoyed about one thing, however. How could you have thought I'd send you away?" His gaze warms, but his expression is solemn. "You're my life, chatty girl. It has no joy without you in it."

Sweet man. I'm keeping him forever.

"I was afraid," I admit with a cringe. "Afraid that you meant more to me than I meant to you. I wasn't thinking very clearly."

"Neither of us was."

With a sigh, I kiss his brow, his cheek, wherever I can. "Why is it that we're so very good at talking and so very shitty at fighting?"

Because there's a difference between our bickering and when we're really mad. I don't have to explain this to Gabriel. I know by the amusement in his eyes that he understands me perfectly.

He nips at my earlobe. "Maybe it's because we hate fighting and fall to pieces when we try. Truthfully, I'd rather wear polyester suits for the rest of my life than have another row with you."

I gasp. "Don't even joke about polyester!"

He chuckles against my skin, the sound sending little shivers of pleasure dancing down my body.

But then he grumps again. "And of all the places you have to go. Australia?"

Guilt twinges in my belly. I was so stupid leaving. "I needed to clear my head."

"Clearing one's head means taking a walk. Not going to

the opposite side of the planet." He eyes me with suspicion, but his expression is too happy and content for him to pull it off properly. "I'm beginning to think you wanted to torture me."

"I was about to get off the plane to find you, Sunshine. Because being away from you is torture." Which is the absolute truth. "So reassess that comment."

As he hums dubiously, I snake my hand down his body to cup him. A choked gasp has me grinning. "Besides," I say, giving him a light squeeze. "I have better ways to torture you."

His hand settles over mine. "Behave yourself, Darling." But he doesn't move my hand away.

I feel him grow thicker against my palm. "I still can't believe you got on a plane to Australia," I say, subtly kneading him beneath our joined hands.

He shifts a bit, nudging up into my touch. "It's my grand gesture, as Killian says. If you don't understand how much I love you after this, there's nothing for it."

Smiling, I press my lips against his arm. "My grand gesture is going to be giving you head at some point during this flight."

His cock twitches as I stroke it, and his voice comes out a tad rough. "Sexual acts on a plane are illegal, Darling."

"Then you'll have to be very quiet while I suck you."

I love the strangled sound in his throat and the way his dick goes rock hard against my palm, despite his weak protests.

"Sophie," he says, returning to the stern tone I love. "You never actually gave me an answer."

"Mmm?" I stop my exploration and meet his gaze. He waits, one brow raised, a muscle ticking on his jaw. "Oh, you mean the 'cocked up' proposal?"

"Darling…"

"I'm going to want babies," I tell him with a smile. "And to dress them up as Princess Leia or Han Solo on Halloween."

His answering smile is so pleased, the look in his eyes so anticipatory, that it makes me a little dizzy. "I look forward to giving you babies. And I vote for a Spock costume."

"Okay. Then you can dress up as Han Solo and I'll be captured Princess Leia in that little gold bikini."

"I love you," he declares in a rush. "So very much. The luckiest day of my life was when I sat next to you on that plane."

With a happy sigh, I snuggle closer. "I'm going to marry you, Gabriel Scott."

He releases a breath and presses his lips to the top of my head. "And I'm going to love you until the day I die, Sophie Darling."

"You know," I say. "If I take your name, I won't be Darling anymore."

Gabriel swoops down and captures my mouth. The kiss is slow and just a little bit dirty, his tongue plunging deep. I'm lightheaded and needy when he pulls back. The hot, knowing glint in his eyes doesn't help.

"You will always be my darling," he says against my lips. "My Sophie darling."

GABRIEL
Epilogue

"I THINK I'm going to refer to this house as The Shoebox," Sophie calls from the terrace.

She has a point. The bulk of the house is one long, clean rectangle jutting out toward the harbor with glossy wood floors, soaring ceilings, and retractable glass walls that let in the breeze. Compared to being stuffed in a plane, this airiness is paradise, as far as I'm concerned.

Following the sound of her voice, I find her leaning against the reinforced glass rail that runs around the terrace. Behind her, Sydney Harbor glitters in the fading evening light, its iconic bridge and—if you squint—the white sails of the opera house visible just to the right.

But I only have eyes for Sophie, her curvy body golden and tanned, the breeze picking up the ends of her hair and sending them dancing about her smiling face.

Sophie's hair is pink now. She tells me it's the color of true love and pure passion. It looks more like cotton candy to me, but I'll never tell her. I've learned at least that much about women along the way. And besides, I'll always equate Sophie with delicious treats, so her hair color is fitting in that regard.

I move behind her and wrap my arms around her shoulders. Her skin is cool, and she nestles back against my chest with a sigh.

"I still can't believe you bought a house here."

"Twenty fucking hours in a plane to get to Australia. You'd better believe I'm taking my time about going back to London. We might as well be comfortable for the interim."

"Hey, a good many of those hours were spent fucking, so it couldn't have been that bad."

This is true. Struggling to be quiet, and the fear of being caught, made for some truly spectacular make-up sex. I'm such a fan now, I plan on bickering with Sophie tonight in some public place so we can find a way to do it again.

"You know, I might be cured of my fear of plane travel," I tell her, bending to kiss the curve of her neck. "However, we'll have to conduct experiments on our return trip to make certain."

Sophie nudges her sweet arse back against my waking cock. He stirs, wanting to say hello.

"I hear there's a first-class flight that now has a full shower on board." Her hands reach back and slide up my hips. "That could be interesting."

"Sod it, let's shower now," I demand, inching up the hem of her skirt.

Rye's voice breaks through my happy bubble. "Oh, God, my eyes. They burn."

I sigh against Sophie's skin. "Why did I invite them here again?"

"Because you love them," she whispers against my cheek.

"I love you. I tolerate them."

"I want the old Scottie back," Whip whines.

Sophie laughs at that.

"Jesus," I grumble. "They're all behind us, aren't they?"

She cranes her head to look around me. "Yep. All of them."

"Scottie has left the building," Jax tells them. "You now have Gabriel to contend with, and he appears to be a randy bastard."

At that, I smile, because he isn't wrong. "It'll happen to you too, *John*."

"Don't count on it."

Poor sod, he doesn't know what he's missing.

Finally, I turn and tuck Sophie against my side. Jax, Rye, Killian, Liberty, Brenna, and Whip have all managed to leave their appointed rooms and congregate in the massive living room.

Killian and Libby are tucked up on the sofa as Brenna hands out some sort of fruity-looking cocktail. They've taken over my house. And it isn't uncomfortable or strange to see. It feels right. It feels good.

Rye and Whip appear to be bringing out a small drum kit and portable keyboard. Only then do I notice that Jax and Killian have their guitars.

"Planning to sing for your supper?" I ask.

Jax plucks at his guitar's strings. "For Sophie." He gives her a wink. "Because she's the best hostess."

She blows him a kiss.

"Any requests?" Jax asks.

"Yes." I lean in to tell him the song I have in mind, adding, "'From me to you."

He shakes his head, grinning wide. "No, man, that one is definitely from me to you."

I pull Sophie onto my lap, and we make ourselves comfortable in a low-slung chair as the guys fiddle with their instruments. Though I rarely let it show, hearing my mates play, seeing their progression from bumbling lads who could barely coordinate a sound to seasoned musicians who create transcendent music, fills me with pride.

Sophie lights up as they begin to play "With a Little Help From My Friends."

"Beatles for joy," I tell her softly.

Her head rests on my shoulder, and she places a hand over

my heart. "And for love."

I close my eyes and let the music wash over me. "Always for love."

THANK YOU!

Thank you for reading *MANAGED*

Reviews help other readers find books. If you enjoyed MANAGED, please consider leaving a review.

I like to hang out in these places: Callihan's VIP Lounge, The Locker Room, Kristen Callihan FB author page, and Twitter

Would you like to receive sneak peaks before anyone else?Or know when my next book is available? Sign up at www.kristencallihan.com for my newsletter and receive exclusive excerpts, news, and release information.

ACKNOWLEDGMENTS

To Kati Brown, Sahara Hoshi, and Tessa Bailey for early reads and encouragement. Sarah Hansen for always making me kickass covers. Jennifer Royer Ocken for copy edits and being the Good Kramer. Jennifer Miller for proofing. Elisa Gioia for help with the Italian bits. For the readers who are always so awesome, and the bloggers who are always so supportive.

CPSIA information can be obtained
at www.ICGtesting.com
Printed in the USA
LVOW12s1519061216
516056LV00002B/202/P